SAVAGE
ARENA

⊱⊱⊱⊱⊱⊱⊱⊱⊱⊱

A cry from the stands alerted the peasant to the entry of two hunters into the arena. They were dressed in the pelts of the *hanis*, indigenous to the savannahs of Lysis. Each carried a net in his left hand, a spear in the right. In their belts were poisoned darts, like tiny, finned javelins. They spread out, one to each side of the peasant.

He turned suddenly, charged the man to his right. One blow of the *barang* snapped the spear, the second took the hunter's arm off at the shoulder. The peasant spun, cut the second hunter's flung net in twain, grabbed the thrust spear and jerked the hunter toward him, unto the point of the *barang*.

The peasant went to stand by the carcass of the vi-cat. He looked up to the now silent stands.

There was a blast of trumpets, and from the gate of the fighters strode forth two gladiators. These men were matched, trained fighters. It was not likely that one would die . . .

THE TELNARIAN HISTORIES

THE CHIEFTAIN

JOHN NORMAN

WARNER BOOKS

A Time Warner Company

WARNER BOOKS EDITION

Copyright © 1991 by John Norman
All rights reserved.

Questar® is a registered trademark of Warner Books, Inc.

Cover design by Don Puckey
Cover illustration by Dorian Vallejo

Warner Books, Inc.
666 Fifth Avenue
New York, NY 10103

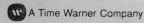 A Time Warner Company

Printed in the United States of America

First Printing: September, 1991

10 9 8 7 6 5 4 3 2 1

This book is dedicated
to all who disapprove of blacklisting.

··· **PROLOGUE** ···

"In this year war was carried on with the Aatii."—The Annals.

The above entry is not untypical of the dark and troubled times to which I should like, in what follows, to devote my attention.

I suppose one might distinguish between history and chronicle, though the distinction must surely be one of grades, or shades, rather than of kinds, for there is seldom a history which does not clearly contain chronicle, nor a chronicle which does not, at least implicitly, recount a history.

We do not know, incidentally, who kept the Annals. Quite possibly they were set down by a succession of individuals, men who occupied remote, fortified places, places within which the most precious of the treasures of Telnaria might be kept safe, the ability to read and write.

"In this year war was carried on with the Aatii."

This entry, with which I have begun, surely approximates to pure chronicle. There is doubtless an explanation for this. The men of the remote, fortified places had, for most practical purposes, turned their backs on history and the world. Such matters

· 1 ·

had little left in them to interest them. They had little to do with their studies, and the pursuit of their personal salvation, to assure which they may have withdrawn from the world. Also, they probably knew very little about the world they had left, perhaps some gossip, some remarks, picked up from merchants or traders. Yet they did keep the chronicles. Indeed, were it not for such sources we would know much less than we do about the dark and troubled times.

"In this year war was carried on with the Aatii."

If one listens carefully, perhaps one can hear, beneath this laconic sentence, the ships, the roar of the engines, the bursting of the shells, the blare of trumpets, the hiss of weaponry, the running feet, the screams, even the clash of steel. Not all entries in the Annals, of course, are so terse. I have chosen this one because, you see, my story begins in the year referred to in this particular entry, the year, one of several, actually, in which war was carried on with the Aatii.

I have wondered sometimes why men tell stories. I suspect they have always done so. In the beginning perhaps they danced them, or drew them. A man is, after all, a story-telling animal. One needs no reason to tell a story, or to sing. Those are nice things about stories, and about singing. Perhaps the story, the song, like seeing, and thinking and breathing, if you like, is its own justification, its own reason.

I shall, in what follows, speak in simple, familiar terms, for these are the terms in the light of which we live and understand ourselves, and the worlds, both those without and those within. I shall ignore then the terrors of distance, the puzzles and paradoxes of time, her crevices, the clashing and grinding of her walls, the opening and closing, like the coming and going of tides, of her gates. Though these figure in our story they have little to do with it.

It is raining outside. Water runs down the casement. It gathers on the sill.

I think the vastness of it is what is most frightening. Perhaps, in the corner of some droplet of water, perhaps even one at hand, one lingering on the sill of the casement, some tiny, in-

finitesimal creature, one in which has just arisen the first glim-
mering of consciousness, trembles at the awesomeness of his
universe. And perhaps we, ourselves, and all our time and space,
and our history, and all the vastness of our own universe, those
plenitudes before which we tremble, lie only upon another sill,
inhabiting merely another droplet, somewhere. But the magnitude of man is not measured in the quantity of his being, that
he lingers for such and such a time in such and such a place, a
small time, in a small place, or that his frame contains so many
cubits or less, but in his heart and soul, as tiny, as foul and
dark as they may be. He, in his tiny place and time, may do
deeds, and in these deeds he stands among the loftiest, farthest
of stars. A smile, a gesture, an upraised fist, a laugh, a song,
with these things, seemingly so small in themselves, he exceeds
dimensions, he challenges all time and space.

Greatness, you see, is not measured in size. The magnitude
of man is not measured in cubits.

We must understand that, in the dark and troubled times, the
billions of worlds met, in the course of their turnings, their
billions of mornings and evenings, and seasons came and went,
as usual, and vegetations waxed and waned, as was their wont,
and so, too, men, and other creatures, some like men and some
not so like them, came to be, and suffered and died. Those times,
you see, were not so different from our own.

I have not written this history to edify or instruct. I have not
written it to praise or blame. I have not even written it, really,
to explain, or understand, for who can, truly, understand such
things. My purpose, rather, is a simple one, merely to tell what
happened.

Early in the dark and troubled times the wings of the Telnarian
empire still spread over galaxies. My story begins on the provincial world of Terennia, in an arena.

Notes pertaining to manuscript 122B Valens:

1. The Chronicler:

We do not know, at this time, at any rate, the identity of
the chronicler, or historian, responsible for this particular

version of the Telnarian histories. This, however, is common
with the various manuscripts. It is interesting to speculate
on this. Perhaps, when they sang, or wrote, they knew well
who they were, and it did not occur to them that their names
might be lost, blown away in the winds of time. Perhaps they
thought their names would stand forever. Indeed, how many
founders of cities and nations, occupants of thrones, com-
manders of armies, wielders of scepters, discoverers and clai-
mers of worlds, have not subscribed to a similar delusion.
In most cases, we do not even know who named the planets
in our own system. How many immortals have died, how
many imperishable gods, and peoples, have perished! But
one suspects that the reasons lay elsewhere, that the invest-
ment of the time, and toil, the pain and love, was not to
procure the glory of their own names, but to make a thing
of meaning, of beauty and significance. These are not the
men to whom ''I made this'' is all-important; rather they
are the men to whom ''This has been made'' is all that
matters. It is not even clear whether the chronicler, or historian, here is a single person, or more than one person,
nor whether the manuscript was written rather at the same
time, or has been added to, and glossed, at different times.
Clearly the chronicler, or chroniclers, had at their disposal
various manuscripts, and documents, which, as far as we
know, are no longer extant. Some scholars, and commen-
tators, from various details, have speculated that the nar-
rator's relationship to the story may be more intimate than
appears upon the surface. This seems to me unlikely, but
much is obscure.

2. The manuscripts:

We have known of the existence of the Telnarian histories
for several hundred years, but, initially, only in virtue of
some references, which seemed quite clear, and several seeming allusions, less clear, more disputable, in certain classical
authors, notably Asclepiodorus, Singer of Olrion; Chi Tung,
to whom is attributed the founding of the imperial academy
at Hinan; Umake, counselor of Kreon, lord of Corathon;

Philip, count of the Taurine Marches, who apparently composed his works in exile; Regius, tutor of Urik, tyrant, and third elector, of Kash; Leland, courtier of Lemanthine; and Heiband, the Benellian, who once served as secretary to Loren, prince of the Rosterdam Gates.

The first actual Telnarian histories, or fragments thereof, came to light four hundred years ago, when a cache containing them was accidentally opened by workmen engaged in the construction of the Andirian Canal. As sometimes happens, once the existence of such things is indisputably established, and authenticated, a serious search was undertaken in numerous archives, libraries and treasuries. To the embarrassment of scholarship more than forty versions of the histories, or fragments thereof, were found cataloged, and apparently forgotten, in almost as many locations. The manuscripts, of course, were derivative, being copies of copies, and so on. One of the puzzles concerning many of these manuscripts is why their existence was not more clearly established, and understood, earlier. The various versions are clearly of different ages, and different hands. It is not as though they were written at the same time, or copied at the same time, or even cataloged, at the same time. Perhaps original documents, suggested by the classical references, were forged, but, if so, why were these "forgeries" not brought to light, that their perpetrators might then attempt to reap what profits they might? Some of these fragments tend to reciprocally authenticate one another, and yet others seem utterly independent. It is almost as if these various manuscripts were placed, in one century or another, in one location or another. Their origins remain obscure. Perhaps, somewhere, in some dim archive, other such manuscripts exist, remaining to be found. It is difficult to say.

The current manuscript is that known as the Valens manuscript, because it was found in the ducal library of the district of Valens, one of the minor duchies of the Talois Confederation. It is known as 122B, following the system devised by the *collegium* of Harcourt, to which institution the original trove, consisting of more than one hundred manuscripts, primarily fragments, was referred.

This particular manuscript, portions of which I have prepared for the press, is unusual among the manuscripts, as it deals on a personal level with affairs of states, movements of men, the destinies of nations and worlds, such matters as seen by individuals involved in them. In such a sense the vast pageants involved, the sweeping biographies of empires and peoples, are only dimly hinted at. What a tiny particle of space and time falls within the brief purview of any individual! We are but specks on a cosmic sea. In this manuscript one discerns, and this seems precious to me, not so much the vast tides of time and space, the configuration of those awesome seas, understood in terms of charts of currents and winds, but what it was, at a given time, to be embarked upon them.

The manuscript may have been glossed. I have, in certain places, set certain materials in italics. These italicized portions of the manuscript almost invariably provide background information without which certain actions and events in the story would be obscure. Some regard the glosses as interpolations by an independent hand, to supply later readers with political, historical and religious background. My hypothesis with respect to such passages is that they are by one, and the original, author, and constitute glosses, if they are even to be understood as such, which seems to me unlikely, on his own work. Certain statistical studies of a linguistic nature support this theory, that of the single author, both in the more narrative and in the more expository or explanatory remarks, without which the narrative passages might seem less intelligible.

3. Telnaria:

There seems no reason to doubt the existence, at one time, of Telnaria, and her empire. Too many records, too many allusions, too many stories and legends, too many ancient place names, too much linguistic evidence, embedded in current languages, too much archaeological evidence, now-silent beacons, debris, claiming stones, coins struck by barbarous kings bearing the devices of an empire perhaps even then little but a memory and a legend, support the hypothesis.

In the legends Telnaria seems mythic to us, but, indubitably, at the bottom of such myths there once lay a far-flung, bright, formidable, perhaps even terrible reality. The location of the empire in time and space remains obscure, as do those modalities of being themselves. It is usually assumed that Telnaria has fallen, and long ago. But this is not actually clear, even in the manuscripts. Perhaps the empire has only drawn back a border, that it will later fling forth again, with a hand of iron. Some think that the Telnarian world lies before us, that it is our own world, others think that it was once our world, others that it recurs, coming again and again, perhaps as our own might, in the cycles of nature, in years so large and meaningless as to baffle our comprehension. Some speculate, interestingly, as suggested above, that the empire never fell, but survives, that it exists even today, and that we are but a lonely, isolated world, forgotten, or neglected, for a time, and that one day the ships will return, demanding their claiming stones, their taxes, their tribute. Who knows. Perhaps Telnaria lies at our elbow, and at that of other worlds, as well, our sleeves perhaps brushing, now and again, a column, unnoticed, in a temple not antique but one fresh and golden, consecrated but a moment ago. Can you not see the processions of robed priests, detect the bells, hear the chanting of the choirs, smell the incense? Universes, you see, might not be parallel, or fully so. Perhaps, now and then, they touch one another, and a corridor, as sudden as the snapping of an electric spark, forms a crossroads between realities, perhaps intersecting for a moment, or perhaps longer, perhaps forever, at certain points. Are there such portals, such gates? Let us believe that Telnaria is past, for I would not care to glimpse the pennons of her fleets upon the horizon, nor hear the tread of her legions in the night.

In our own small galaxy there are more than a billion stars, and for each of these stars, another galaxy can be glimpsed beyond.

Sometimes one is afraid.

Which of us, at one time or another, has not heard the cry of a distant voice? Which of us has never heard a footfall behind him?

Once, long ago, you see, when I was very young, for the briefest instant, my sleeve did brush such a column.

· · · CHAPTER 1 · · ·

It is odd, sometimes, how one notices little things, the way a step is splintered, the eleventh, rather at the corner, on the climb to the platform, how a cloud, over the rooftops, seen from the height of the platform, moves in the wind, like a flag, how a board is stained near a block, how the patterns of dryness and dampness, and, here and there, a bead of dew, appear on the fiber of the rope, and exactly how it hangs from the hook, slack, bent a little, not yet straight, not yet taut. One supposes such things are there to be noticed always, the lie of a pebble, the way a blade of grass bends, such things, but often one does not notice them, nor, I suppose, generally, should one. There is not much economy in doing so. Often other things are more important, much more so, the shadows cast by the great stones, the scent of a cat in the wind, the hum of an engine, far off, in the darkness. But when one has nothing much else to do, and one must choose how to spend a last handful of perceptions, one, or at least some, grow curious about little things, a splinter, a stain on a board, a drop of dew on a rope. It is surprising to realize just how meaningful, and beautiful, such things are. Too,

· 9 ·

at such a time, one sees with great vividness. At such times, life gleams.

It had been some thousands of years since the skies had come alive.

Oh, there had doubtless been sightings even before that, long before that, the detections of the scout ships, not known for what they were, and such, but records of those sightings, if, indeed, they had been made, were now lost. Some things will not be seen for what they are. One refuses to understand them. One looks upon them but refuses to see them. The defense mechanism is a familiar one, common to the rational species. And so the day the sky came alive came as a surprise to the old world, one far from this one, as it had to hundreds of other worlds before. Evidence, later clear, had been understood in terms of misleading categories of interpretation, old categories, comfortable categories, categories more acceptable. The hints had been neglected, save by some fanatics. Sometimes, of course, only the insane can see a certain form of truth, one which is beyond sanity, as it is then understood. But even so, one does not listen to the insane, and one always hopes that a truth, like some of the cats, not looked in the eye, will go away. The deep archives, later ransacked by historians, unwilling to accept the abruptness of the advent of the ships, were silent. But all that took place long ago, and much in it, even today, remains obscure.

He knelt in the deep, warm white sand.

It was late afternoon.

The sun was warm on his back and shoulders, as in the fields.

He was a large man, unusually so, particularly for one who had been raised in a *festung* village, one of the villages in the vicinity of a high, fortified place.

He noticed the sand, as one might on such an occasion. Light sparkled here and there among the grains, flashing from some tiny crystalline surfaces, suitably oriented to the sun. An ant, as we shall call the tiny social insect, came within his view, going about its business, trekking its awesome hills and valleys. He watched it, with interest. He had never really considered such creatures before, except to remove them from his tunic or blankets. To the ant, he supposed, this day was no different from a thousand others. He could also detect, what he had never noticed before, the shadow of the ant, moving with it, hurrying a little before it.

Many worlds, of course, had, long ago, offered resistance to the ships. The ships had not won their worlds, or many of them, with ease. In many cases steel had met steel. Had it not been the case the ships might have come centuries earlier. Sometimes the issue had been genuinely in doubt. Long ago, you see, the ships had not their reputation of invincibility, casting centuries before them their image of power and terror. There was a time when standards stood against standards. There had been the wars with the Valeii and the Torinichi, that with the system of Aurelian, those with the Genteii, and their systems, and, later, with the federation of the thousand suns, and, even later, entire galaxies became battlefields of unimaginable scope. Ships, in vistas of spinning, clashing millions, thousands of navies, wrought out the destinies of universes in silence. Armies, bred on millions of worlds, over thousands of years, beached on millions of worlds. Planets swam in blood. Boundaries extended now, it was said, beyond the territories of the former Hermidorian and Vincenzian alliances, beyond the 712th, the 808th, and the 1161st galaxies. The claiming stones of the ships, some vestige of a primitive rite, the origins of which were lost in time, had been set on innumerable worlds, the claiming beacons within a thousand galaxies. This had not taken place, of course, in a short while, not in a rotation of gigantic Cyline 7, nor even within an orbit of the Comet of Hilbreth, but it had taken place. For more than a million years the ships had left their orbits, burning forth in the quiet night of space. In the beginning, it was said, there had been only one world, a primitive world, and only a few ships, ships which could not, at that time, even traverse galactic space. Then there had been seven worlds, and then others, and others. There seemed no obvious reason why that particular world, a seemingly insignificant world, not particularly endowed with resources, not much different from millions of others, rather than any other, or any world, should have accomplished what it did. Many were the historians who sought, lengthily, unconvincingly, to penetrate the secret of its success.

To be sure, ruthless conquest had been followed by surprising consideration, bewildering the prostrate and subdued, by lenient levies and tributes, by invitations to alliances, in dozens of forms and, in some cases, eventually, and more later than before, in the extension of the citizenship itself. Much was the iron gauntlet of war feared, in all its merciless, bloody weightiness, and rightly so, but when that heavy fist opened, it held, more often than not, to the amazement, gratitude and consternation of the defeated, the branch of tolerance, of friendship. For the most part the ships left behind them not enemies but friends, grateful, loyal allies. To be sure, it was not always so. Some planets were riven to the core, even their tiniest stones atomized; others were ruined, thousands of square latimeasures burned black and desolate; in some entire planetary populations were placed in chains and transported to processing worlds, for shipment to the markets of ten thousand worlds, their world itself then itself reduced to no more than an orbiting cinder, a monitory instruction to passing ships. Such object lessons, dark and obdurate, in their subtle, unspoken delicacy, were not easily ignored. It was speculated that they had their role to play in the programs, the policies, of intergalactic power.

Kneeling in the sand, he watched the ant, the tiny, nine-legged insect, blind, the odd leg like a walking stick poking quickly about before it.

In the myths it was said the claiming stones flowed in meteor rivers as far away as the sunless worlds of Sheol, that they reached even to the lofty halls of Kragon, the long-forgotten god of war.

He watched the insect.

It was having difficulty climbing a small hill, no more than an inch in height. It slipped back, again and again.

Certain it was that they had, only a century ago, extended to the molten deserts of Saritan, first born of the yellow star, Nobius, to the plains of Gurthan, to the seas of Hysporus, to the Odonian forests, even to the remote ice mountains of tiny Durniak 11.

He was, at this point, kneeling docilely in the sand. His limbs were not encircled with bonds.

The ant, or its people, doubtless claimed all the sand within their purview. But there was a great deal of sand on this world, and even in this small provincial arena. How many grains of sand were there in this arena, or on this world? Less than there were galaxies, demonstratively. He had learned that from the teaching of the brothers. They were wise, the brothers. And the shadows of the ships fell upon worlds, and upon galaxies, more than a thousand of them. But there were other worlds, and other galaxies, surely. How vast was the domain of the ant. And how fixed, and eternal, was the Imperium, the Empire, the power of Telnaria! It was the world, or all the worlds which counted, the others not mattering. Oh, there must be other worlds, other galaxies, but they were far away, beyond comprehension, beyond belief, beyond the stones. They did not count. They could not matter. Telnaria was the world, the Empire was fixed, it was of steel, it was eternal, it was civilization. Within it was peace, outside it was nothing.

Not bound, he reached out and, with one finger, furrowed the sand, bemusedly smoothing the way for the small creature. It hurried down the track. It was not thought necessary, generally, incidentally, to bind those who had been raised in the shadow of the *festungen*, even those from the schizmatic *festungen*. That was why he was not bound at this time. To be sure, several events might have turned out differently had they not bound him later, had they left him free, as he was now, only within his own bonds, the worst and most terrible bonds, the invisible bonds which had been put on him long ago, bonds he was not even certain he wore. Then, you see, he might have held himself, for it is quite possible he was weak enough, or strong enough, at that time, to do so. Of course, he might not have held himself. It is hard to know what would have happened. Perhaps it was wise to have had him bound, as was soon done. It is hard to say about such things. It is always difficult to know the future. Even the readers of the mystic tables, the counters of the stars, the casters of the bones knew that. It was hinted that the tables guarded their secrets jealously. Certainly they were hard to read. Few could do so. And surely they spoke darkly, in riddles and paradoxes. And it was whispered by some that the living stars, for all their fiery, savage immensity, knew no more than men, that they, too, for all their size, their ferocity and beauty, were ignorant, or indifferent. And others admitted, in their cups, that at times the bones themselves could do no more than guess. He supposed that the ant, or its people, claimed the square yard of sand about his knees. But did not every wind, every passing foot, expose them to stirrings of a nature beyond their comprehension?

He watched the ant scurry away, its path smoothed. It was the sort of thing the brothers would have wanted. He had wanted to please the brothers. The brothers were kind, and wise. He wanted to please them now, by submitting to death, if not joyfully, for his blood, a foreign blood, found that hard to understand, at least resignedly, as an intellectual matter, in deference to their teaching.

"I should not have made the way smooth for the ant," he thought. "I should have let it go its own way. I should have let it succeed, or fail, by itself. I should not have interfered. I should not have adjusted its world. It may come to depend on such things. But they cannot be counted on."

That was a strange thought, for one from a village in the vicinity of a *festung*.

But such thoughts may come to one sometimes, ancient thoughts, thoughts from lost lakes and caverns, from forgotten fields and forests, from a time when a world was new, strange thoughts, strange understandings, that cruelty can be kindness, that kindness can be cruelty.

It was at this time that he lifted his head, that he heard the blare of the trumpets.

He has had many names, and in order that we may follow these matters rather as they developed, without anticipating, and understand them rather as men then understood them, we will call him, for the time being, by the name he bore in one of the high places, as a child, 'Dog,' to which he had been taken as an infant, by a warrior, or soldier, of the tents of the Heruls. The name of the warrior was Hunlaki.

· · · CHAPTER 2 · · ·

The column was a long one.

It was in the bitter winter of 1103, dated from the setting of the claiming stone, when time began in the galactic records for this world. To be sure, it remained a primitive world, a border world, left much to its own devices, the imperial administration located in the provincial capital, in the southern latitudes, at Venitzia, in one of the native tongues called Scharnhorst, in another Ifeng. The forces of the Imperium, after the time of the Tetrarchy, and the Barrack Emperors, when the empire had been torn for centuries by civil war, had been divided into the outpost, or garrison troops, and the mobile forces. The pay of the mobile forces, and the quality of the men, though it was forbidden to say this, was superior to those, generally, of the border troops, the outpost troops, the garrison forces, as they were variously known.

The column made its way across what was then known as the plain of Barrionuevo, but which is now, in these later days, known as the flats of Tung. The mountains, bordering the plain on the east, however, as the river of Lothar does on the west, are still known as the heights of Barrionuevo. The name lingers. Too, the mountains were held. In the heights, or mountains, of Barrionuevo is found the *festung*, or fortress, or holding, of Sim Giadini, or, as we might sometimes say, thinking the translation, all things considered, to be justified, Saint Giadini. To be sure, Giadini is not to be found today in the calendar of saints, but things were more fluid in those times. The outcome of certain political and doctrinal struggles was not at that time determined, and it was not, at that time, yet decided who the victors would be, to whom the prerogative of pronouncing the defeated to be schizmatics would fall.

Returning to our story, it was in the winter, that of 1103, in the chronology of the stone, in the coldest and most bitter of months, that of the god, Igon.

The sky was dark, and gloomy, and laced with falling snow. The track of the column was a long, narrow, twisting, tortuous churning of thickened mud, more than a dozen miles in length, frought with crystals of ice, melted for the moment here and there by the warmth of passing feet, many wrapped in rags, some bare, those of captives, cut by the wheels of the carts and wagons, pressed down, and churned, by the tread of the soldiers, those of the foot, and by the claws of the mounts, of those of the saddle, or riders. We shall call these mounts 'horses,' as that term seems suitable.

There had been some four or five thousand in the raiding party. It was a large one. Usually the Heruls came only in their hundreds. One supposes that their crossing of the Lothar had not been expected, and certainly not in the month of Igon. Their raids usually took place east of the Lothar, against the villages and fields near the river, and in the spring and summer. This was when they brought their herds into the plain for pasturage. Many tents had been summoned. It is said, too, that the Heruls had been joined by their allies, the tents of the Hageen. This matter is not clear in the annals.

The column continued to cross the plain.

It did not do so in silence.

Overhead, birds circled and screamed in the dark, cold sky, impatient.

Sometimes, eagerly, they would alight.

In places one could see only the birds, in jostling heaps near the columns, black, like living dung, beating their wings, climbing over one another, squawking. Sometimes a soldier, in passing, for the soldiers knew no love for these things, might rush out, and thrust at them with his spear, or whirl at them the stone, the spiked ball on its long chain, and they would squawk, and flutter, and then return, some with broken wings, flopping awkwardly, protesting, doomed, not knowing it, to their business.

There was the sound of the wheels creaking, turning in the half frozen mud, the sound of the feet, the growls of the horses, the snarls of the dogs, half-starved, crested beasts of war, which ran with the Heruls. They served in battle, simple, merciless, fearless, eager to be set on enemies. They herded animals, and slaves. They guarded camps. Their howls gave warning. Too, as was common with primitive folks, they could be eaten in time of need. Sometimes the dogs left the column. The birds would not challenge them. They would alight yards away, in the frozen grass, hunched up, their heads buried in their shoulders, watching, waiting until the dogs were finished.

There were other sounds, too, with the column, the clanking of chains, the groans of men, captives, struggling under the burdens of their victors' loot, often their own household belongings, or treasures, on their backs, and the lamentations of women, laden with plunder, serving, too, as beasts of burden, roped by the neck to the backs of wagons, some half-naked, barefoot, even in the month of Igon. Some of these women, too, were heavy with child. More than one, screaming, trying still to follow the wagon, had gone into labor, and then, the cart or wagon drawn to the side, her rope freed from the back of the cart or wagon, had been thrown to the ground, and there, screaming, weeping, thrashing, her neck rope still in the hand of a captor, had delivered herself of a child, in the mud to the side of the column. These children were dragged forth, hot and bloody, tangled with their afterbirth, and discarded, thrown to the side, left for the birds and dogs. The screaming woman was then dragged to her feet and fastened again to the vehicle. Weeping, screaming, her legs covered with blood, reaching out futilely for the child, she was turned about by blows, those of spear butts and whips, and, once again, as the wagon rejoined the column, returned to the march. Many died. Of those who died, they, too, were left beside the column, for the birds, for the dogs. The Heruls did not care for the cubs, the litter, of their captive women. It was not as though they were the female offspring of prize slaves, who might bring a good price in Venitzia. Too, if we may offer a partial extenuation for the behavior of the Heruls, and of what might otherwise appear to be an unusual harshness, it might be remarked that it was their custom to put to death the old and the weak, even those of their own tents.

Those times, you see, were not the same as now. You may judge them as you wish, for that is the prerogative of each age. Be advised, of course, that you, too, in future ages, may be judged, as well. Will you be convinced that you were wrong? But it is not my role to judge, but merely to relate. As I have indicated, my task is an unambitious one, a simple one, merely to tell what happened.

Hunlaki, a horseman, a warrior of the tents of the Heruls, was at this time a member of the rear guard. It had not been so three weeks before. At that time he had been one of the first who, at night, testing the ice on the Lothar, had taken his horse across, in a place hidden by trees, and a bend in the river. The raid itself had taken several days. The many clusters of cabins, the small wooden huts of the villagers, had been encircled, one by one, that none might escape to warn others. The territory had been scouted earlier by Hageen merchants, welcomed by the men and women of the villages. To be sure, as is always the case, some had eluded the nets of the horsemen, doubtless men returning to the villages, finding them burned, the occupants slain, or missing. The claw prints of the horses of the Heruls, the marks of blades on timbers, an occasional arrow in the soil, the marks on the bodies, the unmistakable print of the stones, the parts of bodies, the impaled bodies, made things clear enough. Indeed, perhaps the Heruls, in their roving patrols, dark against the snow, had been noted, the conical helmets, the furred cloaks.

Most of the villages near the edges of the forests, west of the Lothar, had been found deserted. The villagers had vanished into the forests. Neither the Heruls, nor the Hageen, would follow them into the forests. On the other hand, some of the villages near the edges of the forests, west of the Lothar, had been defended, or, perhaps one should say, certain high grounds, certain dirt hills, held as keeps, surrounded by a palisade, had been defended. One digs a deep ditch about a small hill and adds to the hill the dirt from the excavation. One surmounts the hill with a palisade. In such a way a tiny fort is constructed. The hill makes it difficult for the horses, and the foot, to gain a footing. At such times and places the Heruls would content themselves with burning the village. Heruls did not engage when it was not to their advantage.

Hunlaki had looked back at the Lothar. His leggings and boots were wet. He had, with the others, swum his horse back to the east bank. The ice, you see, had broken in the recrossing some days ago. Hunlaki's beast itself had had the ice break beneath it, and it had howled in fear, clawing and scratching at the gigantic, suddenly sloping plate of ice, unable to gain purchase. Then it had slipped backwards, and, twisting, had fallen to its side in the icy water. Hunlaki had almost lost his seat. Then, rolling with the beast, rising dripping from the water, he had struck it savagely about the snout. Thusly, by inflicting sharp pain upon it, by recalling it to itself, did he calm its panic, did he reassert his control of the mount. Then, blood from the beast's nostrils trailing in the water as it swam, he gained the opposite bank. That had been a terrible crossing for the captives. Many had crossed on the ice, it breaking under them. Many of them had been drowned. Others had been swum at the stirrups of captors, ropes on their necks. Others drew themselves across on a rope stretched from bank to bank. Horsemen moved about in the water downstream to slay any who might lose their grip on the rope. The foot of the Heruls formed for themselves, and for certain forms of loot, rafts, from the charred timbers of the riverside villages. Some prisoners, too, were permitted to cling to these rafts in passage. Some of the younger and more attractive women were put on these rafts bound, for the Heruls, recognizing their value, did not wish to risk them in the current.

The column had its vanguard, of course, and its rear guard, in which Hunlaki now had his place. It also had its flankers, as would be expected. A moment may be spent in mentioning the practices of the Heruls in such matters. These remarks serve, in effect, for the arrangements for the defense of the column. Long ago the Heruls, a nomadic people, had noted the seemingly uncanny ability of certain large, broad-winged scavengers to locate weakened, isolated animals on the plains, a lost flock animal, a lame herd animal, a wounded man, such things. Within minutes there would be one such unwelcome visitant in the sky, and then, a little later, three or four, and then, yet later, eight or ten, and then, in a few minutes, several. It was gradually understood that the birds, with their keen eyesight, which could detect the scurrying of the *dab* from a distance of more than a mile, patrolled given territories, patrolled them from a great height, one which brought more than a quarter of a latimeasure within view. These birds also were spaced in such a way that a given bird could just detect the position of the adjacent birds in their own, respective territories. When one bird left its position other birds, noting this, and perhaps curious, moved toward its position, and other birds, shortly thereafter, toward the newly vacated positions, and so on. In this way a large number of birds, from diverse positions, from diverse directions, could come together quickly, assembling in the vicinity of a find. The aspect of this practice which much impressed the Heruls was the principle of regularized, predictable contact, and the absence of this contact constituting the signal for the initiation of the assemblage behavior. Elements of the Herul vanguard, flankers and rear guard then maintained regular contact with the column, riding long loops between the outriders, the point riders, and the column. The absence of a predictable contact then triggered a twofold response, one of the contact riders investigating, the other returning to the column, or to his next contact rider, to report the failure of the contact. In this way, in a short amount of time, the column was apprised of possible difficulties with the outriders. In this way, the elimination of, say, a point rider, of a small squadron, to take a simple case, was not likely to expose the main force to the danger of a surprise attack. This is most effective, of course, in open country, of the sort favored by the Heruls. This practice is not unknown among certain other tent peoples as well, for example, their allies, the Hageen. We shall refer to the broad-winged scavengers, mentioned above, whose behaviors suggested these practices to the Heruls, as "vultures," as the word will be a familiar one.

After the crossing of the Lothar, Hunlaki had turned his horse about, it shuddering and shaking the cold water from its fur. Such mounts did not care for water. The east bank was a sea of mud now. There were cries of misery, grunts, the sounds of blows, as the prisoners were herded together. There were children among them, some clinging to mothers. Two men were slain at the edge of the water, one who had lifted his hand to fend a blow. Hunlaki considered one of the women on one of the rafts. She was half-naked. Her hands were tied behind her. Her ankles, too, were tied, a mere thong more than sufficient for the purpose. She looked away, not meeting his eyes. She was slender and well curved. Her skin was very white. Such looked well where they belonged, at the feet of warriors.

Then Hunlaki looked away from her, back across the river, where were the remains of one of the villages. The fallen timbers, those of sheds and cabins, charred, blackened from the flames, were now partly covered with snow. The remains of the village seemed very still, and very cold. They reminded Hunlaki of a woods in winter, where trees have fallen, of the edge of the great forest, where the Heruls had stopped. Snow, too, had drifted about the remains. Snow was falling even now, settling on the far bank, disappearing in the river.

Hunlaki again considered the female. Her ankles had been unthonged. She had been conducted from the raft, the aft portion of which was still in the water. She was conducted up the bank. She fell once, her naked flank muddied. She was kicked. She cried out in pain. She was on her knees, in the mud. She seemed bewildered. Perhaps she was trying to understand what had become of her. She was dragged to her feet and conducted to the back of a wagon. A rope was now being put on her neck. She looked back at Hunlaki. The rope was tied to the back of a wagon. Her feet were ankle deep in the mud. Hunlaki looked away from her.

A large floe of ice, from upriver, moved slowly past, turning in the current. Some yards away, half in the water, caught in the frozen, matted rushes, was the body of a man, that of the prisoner who had dared to fend a blow. The trunk of a tree was turning, too, in the water. A rider circled it, thrusting about, under it, with his spear. Hunlaki heard a cry of pain nearby, a woman's cry, but he did not think it was the girl. It was another female. She had presumably felt the knout. It is useful in the control of horses and dogs, and women. Hunlaki wondered how many of the women could survive the march, the weeks of the return to the tents. His thoughts strayed to other women, women of which he had barely heard, the soft women of the civilized worlds. He did not think such would fare well on the march. What were they good for, he wondered. He thought of them hurrying about, barefoot, bangled, on the deep, soft rugs in the tents, in their silks, warming the golden vessels with their bodies. Yes, they, too, in their collars, or locked wristlets, or anklets, with their delicate flesh, imprinted with the slave mark, had their uses.

Hunlaki was saddened, in a way, on the bank, as he looked across the river. The fighting was ended. It was over now. Hunlaki, you see, lived for the fighting, in which one became so alive, the terrible game, that with the highest of all stakes, and for the spoils of the fighting. There are such creatures, such beasts, if you like, such as Hunlaki, and also such races, and the Heruls, you see, were among them.

But Hunlaki was not now pleased. It is one thing to meet the shock lancers in battle. It is another to ride down farmers, and burn villages.

The earlier parts of the column had begun the march an hour ago. He could now hear, behind him, the beginnings of movement, that of the rearward portions of the column, the sound of arms, of chains, of wagons. It takes a long time for a column to move, particularly when it is large, when there is no cadence, when it is encumbered with baggage, and prisoners.

Hunlaki, and the riders with him, waited at the river for better than an hour.

There were dark clouds in the sky. There would be more snow. He listened to the sound of the river. He watched the ice, pale in the dark water. His horse growled and clawed at the earth. Breath from its nostrils hung about its snout like moist, cold smoke. Hunlaki noted an occasional branch, dark and leafless, flowing slowly past, an occasional piece of debris. He noted that the body which had been caught in the frozen, matted rushes, that of the prisoner who had dared to fend a blow, had been loosened, and washed free. He saw it, half-submerged, moving downstream with the ice.

Hunlaki then heard the sounds of horses, the rhythm of the heavy paws striking in the cold turf, audible in the winter air. He turned about. He could see, from the left and right, the approaching riders, like small dark clouds, the breath of the mounts trailing behind them. The side riders had now returned. The east bank of the Lothar was now clear, for better than five miles on either side of the crossing point of the column.

Hunlaki then, with the newcomers, turned about, and began to follow the column.

Hunlaki was not now pleased.

He did not joke with Mujiin, who, riding beside him, later left him to his own thoughts.

Hunlaki, you see, was not at all sure that his weapons had been worthily bloodied.

One need not be a warrior of the tents of the Heruls to have done what he had done.

· · · CHAPTER 3 · · ·

"Women wish to belong to men," she had said, leaning on one elbow, in the tangled covers. "You held me, as a master."

"You did not make me pay," he said.

"I had thought I would," she mused, "but in your arms I found myself a slave. Slaves cannot charge. They own nothing. They have nothing. It is they who are nothing, it is they who are owned."

"I do not understand," he had said.

"You are not a woman," she said.

"All are the same," he said, for he had heard this from the brothers.

"No," she said, "we are different."

"That is heresy, is it not?" he asked.

She turned white, and was silent.

After a time, she turned to the wall, and said, "I hate you."

"Why?" he asked, puzzled. She had seemed to be pleased but moments before, weeping, crying out for more, begging, subdued, ravished.

"Because you do not put a collar on me, and make me walk behind you," she said.

"I do not understand," he said.

"But this is not such a world," she said.

He did not respond.

"Too," she said, "you do not know who you are."

He looked up from his boots.

"That is why you hate me?"

"Yes," she said.

"Who am I?" he asked.

"A man," she said.

He shrugged.

"It was so from the first joining of the gametes," she said.

"What are gametes?" he asked.

"You are not educated, are you?" she asked.

"No," he said.

"Can you read?" she asked.

"No," he said.

"From the beginning," she said, "you were a man, or a male, from the beginning. It was so in the chromosomes."

"And you, in such things, whatever they may be, were female, or woman?"

"Yes," she said, "from the beginning, totally that, not other than that, never to be other than that."

"Interesting," he said, for he, though not educated, had an inquisitive mind, a lively mind. That there should be two forms of being, and in his own species, was surely worthy of note. This was not, of course, the first female he had held in his arms. There had been others, Tessa, and Lia, and Sut, or Pig, who had put themselves in his way, who had surprised him in the fields, at troughs, in the hay sheds, who had lain on the wooden floors of the varda coops, their smocks thrown off, the slatted shadows of the lath bars falling across their vital, waiting, beautifully curved bodies, an interesting symmetry. His favorite had been Pig. But there had been trouble.

"What is your class?" she asked.

"I am of the *humiliori*," he said, "but I am not a serf, nor a *colonus*." The *coloni* were tenants, under the protection of wealthy landowners. "What is your class?" he asked.

"I, too, am of the *humiliori*," she said. "Do you think I would be here, as I am, a pay woman, in this small room, with the single, tiny window, on this bed, over a wretched tavern, were I not of the *humiliori*?"

"I am of the peasants," he said.

She turned back, quickly, to face him.

"You do not have the body of a peasant," she said. "It is not deformed for the hoe, the plow."

He stood, belting his tunic. "And what sort of body have I?" he asked.

She slipped from the bed, and came to where he stood, and then she knelt before him, holding to his legs, looking up at him. "Linger," she said.

He looked down at her, regarding her.

"There are masters and there are slaves," she said. "Each must learn which he is."

Oh, he had intended, even before the trouble over Pig, to leave the *festung* village. Having come of age, and having refused the garb, the habit and hood, he might leave. Too, this was practical, for on the world in which stood the heights of Barrionuevo, and the *festung* of Sim Giadini, now far away, the villagers had not yet been bound, or the guilds, or the *coloni*.

"You speak well," he said. "You are highly intelligent. Can you read?"

"Yes," she said.

"You were not always of the *humiliori*," he speculated.

"I was once the daughter of a senator of a local municipality, on another world, one far away," she said.

"You were then of the *honestori*," he said, impressed.

"Yes," she said."

"But now you kneel naked," he said.

"It is said that women such as I make the best slaves," she said.

He supposed that much would depend upon the woman, whatever her class or background, on her capacities for love, her unbridled sexual needs, on her uncontrollable passions, which put her so helplessly at the mercy of masters, on her capacity for loyalty, for diligence, for service, such things. The more intelligent the woman, it was said, the less the need for taming and training. Such, it was said, arrived the most quickly at the deepest understanding of themselves, and were the first to yield themselves up wholly, helplessly, to the fitting raptures of their bondage.

"Beat me," she said, "Master."

"You are not a slave," he said. "Do not say such things."

It was a saying of slaves. It was not that they wished to be beaten, or seldom was it so. It was rather a way of professing to the master their slavery, that they understood their situation, that they were owned, that they acknowledged his punishment rights over them. The saying is useful, too, in reminding a slave of her bondage. The usual response of the master is the issuance of some innocent command, but the slave knows what might have been done. To be sure, it is a rare slave who does not long, at times, to be reminded of her bondage, that she is truly a slave.

"Where is your father?" he asked.

"He is dead," she said. "He was ruined, the taxes. He died of drink."

"And you fled?"

"Yes," she said.

"And so became of the *humiliori*?"

"Yes," she said.

On many worlds, many of the humiliori *class had been bound, the soil workers to the soil, to given fields, the members of guilds, and their offspring, to their crafts. Even the captains of ships, of merchant ships, and the bakers, and carpenters, the masons, the armorers, and those of many other crafts and occupations, even the members of actors' guilds, had been bound. This stabilized the population, holding it in place, that given taxations might be efficiently exacted. Many of the landlords, particularly the less wealthy landlords, those who could not afford the bribes to governors and prefects, and who did not have groups of armed retainers, feared by the tax farmers, at their disposal, and even the senators, of local municipalities, had been made responsible for the collection of taxes, due on their lands, or in their districts. Shortages in the collection were expected to be supplied by these unwilling deputies. Many were ruined. The father of the pay woman, we may surmise, was one. The population, you see, fleeing judicial and economic oppression, as presumably the pay woman had done, had tended to be fluid, too easily slipping away. The binding, to craft and locality, too, of course, made things easier for the tax farmers. These individuals, usually rented in gangs from certain wealthy entrepreneurs, licensed by the governors and prefects, were the usual instruments of tax collection. The tax farmers were to collect the due taxes plus a percentage thereof, as their commission. It was well known, however, that they normally collected far more than the due taxes and the commissions, the gang bosses, and entrepreneurs, pocketing the rest. Also, one might note, in passing, in speaking of taxes, the existence of various forms of* munera, *taxes paid in service, for example, manual labor on local roads and bridges, supplying free bread to local troops,* gratis *transport of goods on behalf of governmental commissaries, such things. A common form of* munera *was that of the peasant, required to donate military service some weeks in the year, expected to work in his lord's fields and vinyards at various times, such things. The* humiliori*, it must be understood, however, were free men. They were not slaves. A distinction was drawn between them and slaves. Indeed, on many worlds, slavery, or, at least, open slavery, was illegal. It was not that many of the* humiliori *were slaves; quite otherwise; it is only that they were bound. It had been too easy before, you see, on thousands of worlds, for, say, an extorted, despairing, overtaxed peasant to load his wagon and abandon his fields, disappearing into the wilderness, there to sow new fields, harvesting there his own crops, and not those of others. But the binding, for most practical purposes, stopped this sort of thing. Its value was obvious. It was instrumental in stabilizing the population, and the occupational groups. The*

Imperium had presumably not adopted such measures without thought. Indeed, perhaps they were necessary. Certainly the empire, for all its seeming eternality, its solidity, and such, was wracked by fiscal crisis, exacerbated by centuries of civil war. Worlds had been devastated; there had been frequent famines, these often consequent not upon natural causes, such as shifting patterns of precipitation, or soil exhaustion, but upon the literal, forcible disruption of agriculture, reduced or suspended in the dislocations of the wars, and sometimes from climatic changes consequent upon literal alterations in the rotations and axes of worlds, the effects of the impact of weaponry; and there had been plagues, in particular those of the second, the fifth and ninth dynasties; some blamed them for much; some worlds had been isolated, quarantined; others had been disposed of; bounties had been placed on the heads of individuals from such worlds; where found they were exterminated; mines had been exhausted; deficits in trade had drained bullion to the outer worlds; too, there was little doubt but what there must be some truth to the rumors of grievous mismanagement, of speculation, of broadcast corruption in high places; were there not stories of the pleasure worlds of emperors, entire planets devoted to their delight; it did not seem that frugality and nobility, so conspicuously absent on so many minor worlds, in the local halls of government, in the municipal offices, in the courts of the bishops, in the headquarters of the civil and military governors, would be likely to reign in the high palaces of power themselves. The bindings also introduced, in their way, a new social order. In any event, the taxes, those in coin, and those in munera, *were now easier to collect. One might also note, in passing, that with the binding, and the shortage of free currency, resulting in part from the taxes, that an economy of barter, and kinds, was becoming more widely spread. Even before the binding, many peasants had lost their lands to taxes, and become* coloni, *tenants on the lands of others. The landlord, often with his troops, provided protection to the peasants. This was particularly true of the large, powerful landlords, the sort who managed to acquire the lands of others, the sort who throve in such times. This matter of protection was not a negligible consideration. Bri-*

gandage was prevalent in many places, it itself in part doubtless a result of the ruin of many small farmers, and the flight from the land. When the bindings took place the lives of the coloni, the tenants, did not much change. Most remained where they were, though now legally bound, by imperial edict, recorded in the pandects, to the soil, and, in a sense, to the lord, who owned it. In this way, on many worlds there came to be what we may speak of as a manorialized economy, a largely agriculturally based economy, relatively self-sufficient peasant communities clustering about a given holding, a given stronghold, or manor. This thing, on many worlds, became increasingly widely spread with the collapse of the cities, the desertion of urbanized areas, the ruin and decay of thousands of small, once thriving munic-ipalities, the breakdown in order and policing, the general falling into disrepair of roads and waterways, the disruption of com-merce and communication, the gradual isolation and ruralization of the vast majority of the population. To be sure, such things take a long time. On some worlds they were more advanced than on others. There was, to be sure, one statistically minor coun-tertrend, minor at least, on the whole, to these rather general developments. That was the tendency for large numbers of the ruined, the destitute, and impoverished, as well as the curious and ambitious, the eager and adventurous, as always, rather than placing themselves under the protection of local lords, bosses, captains, and such, to seek out certain major cities, there to seek their fortunes. It was said that many embarked, in the holds of cattle ships, even for the worlds of Telnaria itself. There was some security in this, of course, provided the journey could be successfully accomplished, for in certain of the larger cities, and in the capitals, and in the worlds of Telnaria, too, one supposes, the state provided a dole of grain, and games. The situation thus, in some respects, was paradoxical. While thousands of towns and smaller cities fell into ruin, and the great majority of thousands of populations became increasingly iso-lated and ruralized, certain other cities, particularly metropo-lises, and the seats of governors, prefects, bishops, and such, places already overcrowded, experienced additional, unwelcome influxes of population. These frustrated, seething masses, idle

*and unproductive, demanding food and amusement, constituted
a force to be reckoned with, an expensive, explosive, difficult-
to-control, dangerous urban proletariat. Most were citizens and,
accordingly, the dole was their right. It was the duty of others,
the responsibility of others, those of other places, of other
worlds, you see, to feed and care for them, to entertain them,
and such. The support of these unproductive megapopulations
in certain large urban areas, it was speculated, further drained
the resources of the empire. Worlds were set aside to feed and
clothe them. Worlds were combed to find oddities, exhibits, animals, performers, and such, to entertain them. This influx to
the major cities, incidentally, was considerably slowed by the
stabilization edicts, the binding laws, and it is not hard to suppose that that might have been one of the elements of their
rationale. But, of course, the cities were already overcrowded,
even before the bindings, and their populations were continuing,
in one way or another, to increase. On Terennia, incidentally,
the world on which we now are, the bindings had not yet taken
place, but it was rumored they were imminent. To be sure, in
the cities there was not so much to fear from the bindings,
particularly if one did not have a trade or craft. Too, one could
always have a riot, and kill and steal, and stone the palaces and
houses of the rich, and destroy public buildings, and such, and
thus doubtless, in time, win for oneself an exemption from stric-
tures more generally applied elsewhere. It might be noted that
the peasant could not well be bound here for here he had no
land and here he was no tenant. The pay woman might have
been bound, perhaps, but then she was, in a sense, in virtue of
her loss of status, her new class, her profession, and such,
already bound.*

"I must go," said the peasant.

The warm, moist lips of the pay woman pressed against his
thigh. It was a kiss, such as might have been that of a slave to
her master.

The peasant stepped back from her.

"Return to the bed," he told her.

She obeyed, and knelt there, her knees half lost in the bed
covers, watching him.

"You do not seem like the other women of this world," he said.

"How so?" she said.

"They seem vain, cold, sluggish, petulent, inert," he said. He found them not of much interest. He did not know who could.

"They are equals," she said.

He did not contest this. He did not even, really, understand it. What did it mean to be equal, really? He thought them superior in some ways to men. Certainly they were more beautiful.

"Legally," she explained, "by law."

"How can law make what is so exquisitely different the same?" he asked.

"It cannot," she said.

"You are not like the other women here," he said.

"No," she said. "I am not like them."

"I wonder if they are really women."

"They are women," she said. "It is only that they are sleeping."

" 'Sleeping'?" he asked.

"It is only that they have not yet met their master," she said.

He regarded her, not speaking.

"Every slave needs her master," she said. "She is incomplete without him."

The peasant, not understanding these things, drew shut his cloak, and picked up his sack, that with the long straps, by means of which he could carry it on his back. When he had taken ship at Venitzia, it had carried several loaves of bread. Only part of a loaf was now left.

"You are not from this world," said the pay woman.

"How do you know?" he asked.

"From the way you handled me," she said.

"I have a coin," he said. "Are you certain that you will not accept it?"

"Keep it," she said.

His staff was by the door.

"If you are questioned," she said, "tell Boon Thap that you have paid."

"But I have not," he said.

"Tell him so, anyway," she said.

"I do not lie," he said.

"He will have gone by now, anyway," she said. "I am sure of it."

In time, of course, the peasant would have left the vicinity of the village, one of those within the tithing fields of the *festung* of Sim Giadini. He was strong, and ambitious, and curious, and wondered about the world, and worlds, beyond his village, and the ships that came and went each month at Venitzia, accomplishing their periodic rendezvous with what, to him, seemed no more than a star moving in the sky. It was said to be a vessel, a vessel which could fly like a bird between worlds. Often Brother Benjamin had pointed it out to him. Brother Benjamin, it seemed, had never really expected him to stay. In any event, the peasant would not have taken the hood, and habit. That had never interested him. Too, his decision to leave the village had been hastened by the trouble over Pig. Gathron had struck him with a post. The post had then been broken in two over Gathron's back. It had taken Gathron no more than two minutes to die. He had died squirming, gasping, eyes bulging, staring, at the peasant's feet. The peasant had watched this intently, for he had never seen a man die before. But he had seen animals die, of course, and had killed many of them, and then butchered them. So, too, had other young men of the village. He, and the others, were familiar with blood, and killing. It was part of their way of life. They thought little of it. Perhaps it is well to make that clear. It may then be easier to understand part of what follows, if that is not forgotten. We are not speaking of present times. We are speaking of other times, and other places. He had watched Gathron. It was not much different, Gathron's dying, from that of the garn pigs, some seven or eight hundred pounds in weight, whose head he and he alone of all the men of the village could snap to the side with his bare hands. The blow was delivered with the flat of the hand, the animal's neck held in place by the left arm. Still, this was, perhaps, one of the most dangerous, and fearful, things about the peasant, his temper. It would come, in time, to be feared by armies.

"Have you money?" called the pay woman. She had now

belted about herself a short smock, not too much unlike, save for its length, that of the peasant women of the village.

"Of course," said the peasant.

She smiled. "How much?" she asked.

"Five pennies," said he. *We shall use the term 'penny' for the coin of lowest denomination on Terennia, and certain other worlds, which seems practical. Too, this suggests what was the case, that the peasant had very little in the way of funds.* He had left the *festung* village with some seven pennies given to him by Brother Benjamin, who had been his mentor from childhood, those and a sack of bread on his back. He had walked to Venitzia, staff in hand, bread on his back. For the most part, he lived off the country. In this way he conserved the bread as long as possible. It is not hard for a given person, or a small group, to live off the country, at least for a time, if one can distinguish between what is edible and what is not edible, and is not squeamish. To be sure, he did stop at two villages, where he cut wood for his supper. At Venitzia, some days later, he, and some others, arranged to work their passage to Terennia, caring for cattle on the transport. The crew of the transport did not care for this work which was time-consuming and foul. The peasant, however, and some five like him, did not object. The smells, and the sights and sounds, were not, on the whole, unlike those of their villages.

"Wait," said the pay woman, and, going to a covered bowl, one on a nearby shelf, and removing the lid, she drew forth a silver *darin*, which would be the equivalent of twenty pennies. She thrust the *darin* into his sack, which he had slung on his back. She looked into his eyes, and then, suddenly, stripped from her wrist a silver bracelet, doubtless worth considerably more than the *darin*. This, too, now not looking at him, she thrust into the sack.

"You will need money," she said. "You can sell the bracelet."

He protested, but she would hear nothing of it. Indeed, she turned away from him. "Go," she said.

He had then turned and left.

· · · CHAPTER 4 · · ·

"Ho," said Mujiin, turning his horse. "There," said he, "one follows." At the same time he removed his lance, black, long, slender and resilient, from his back.

"It is a boy," said Hunlaki, too, turning his mount.

"You are sure?" inquired Mujiin.

"Yes," said Hunlaki. Hunlaki had seen him before. He had rather hoped that Mujiin would not. But Mujiin, too, was sharp-eyed. It was not just any whom the Heruls used as their outriders, their flankers. And one looks often to the rear. And there was not much cover here, on the plains of Barrionuevo, here, away from the river.

"He is mad," said Mujiin.

"Perhaps," said Hunlaki. He did not free his own lance.

Hunlaki had hoped the pursuer, a ragged, blond-haired lad, perhaps no more than fourteen or fifteen years of age, one who moved unsteadily, who was perhaps lamed, or ill, who carried a staff, would drop back, would fall back, would think the better of his pursuit, before Mujiin saw him.

"I will guess birds with you, or clouds," said Mujiin.

"One thrust?" asked Hunlaki.

"Let the birds, or the clouds, decide," said Mujiin.

On the plains, in the long hours on horseback, the Heruls found many ways to pass the time, to while it away while keeping the herds together. There were the poetries, the songs, the games. Some of them had marvelous memories, and could call songs which took more than two days to recount. They were fond, too, of stories, as well as women, and war. Also, they were fond of gamblings of diverse sorts, horse races, the fights to the death of matched war dogs, such things. In the guessings of birds and

· 34 ·

clouds it was not fair to look behind one, not until the time was called.

"Birds," said Hunlaki.

Mujiin looked at him, expectantly.

"Even," said Hunlaki.

"Done!" said Mujiin, and they both turned their mounts. The tip of Mujiin's silver-tipped lance traced the arc of the gambling field, earth and sky.

Hunlaki sat back in the saddle.

Within the circuit traced by the tip of Mujiin's lance, as though looking through a window, one could detect three birds.

They then turned their mounts, again, to watch the figure stumbling toward them.

"One thrust?" asked Hunlaki.

"Ten," said Mujiin.

In such a way, usually with prisoners, loosed in an open field, the Heruls honed their skills with the lance, skills which could mean life or death in battle.

"He is only a boy," said Hunlaki.

"Ten," said Mujiin, "and the tenth to the heart or throat?"

"To the heart," said Hunlaki. The thrust to the throat was a difficult one. It required often to be followed by at least one or two further thrusts. Death came usually more quickly, more mercifully, with the thrust to the heart.

"To the throat!" insisted Mujiin.

"To the heart," said Hunlaki.

"There is less sport then," said Mujiin.

"It is only a boy," said Hunlaki.

The lad had stopped now, in the tracks left by the column, an hour or more in advance of them.

The two riders, Mujiin and Hunlaki, began to ride slowly toward the boy. Mujiin did not wish to frighten him.

Perhaps two matters should now be made clear, one having to do with the raid across the Lothar, and the other with Hunlaki's lack of ease.

The object of the raid, or invasion, if you like, and the crossing of the Lothar, was the extirpation of a people, the extermination, the uprooting, of an entire folk. The strategic point of this action was perhaps to secure the plain of Barrionuevo, east of the Lothar, for the flocks, and the herds, of the Heruls. The Heruls, you see, as I have mentioned, were a nomadic people. To be sure, as has been made clear earlier, many of the Heruls' intended victims had eluded them. Some had successfully resisted them in the homely forts within the villages, and many others had managed to slip away, into the forests, into which the Heruls, and the Hageen, if they were truly with them in this action, did not care to follow them. It is very difficult to obtain numbers, or percentages, in matters of this sort, but it has been conjectured variously that some seventy to ninety percent of those attacked by the Heruls in this action, both west and east of the Lothar, but more to the west, were killed or taken prisoner.

Mujiin and Hunlaki now stopped, some fifty yards from the boy, who had also stopped. He backed a bit away from the black track of the column, onto the snowy grass. There was better footing there.

Fifty yards is a good charging distance. It gives the horse time to obtain a high speed, if that is desired, and it is long enough, if one proceeds more cautiously, to assess the likely movements of the target, to provide an opportunity for adjustments in the advance.

The people who had been attacked were a forest people, and related by blood to another people, who had once been a forest people. *A historical note is in order, for without it much of what follows will be more difficult to follow. Long ago, on a world far distant from this one, that on which Mujiin, Hunlaki and the lad are now, there was a given people, let us call them, for the time, the tribes of the forest, the forest being one such on that far world. These people were barbarians, surely, that must not be denied, merciless primitives with rude ways and savage customs. They lived in small villages, established in clearings within the forest. They were hunters and farmers. These people, these tribes on that far world, had, it was claimed, once resisted even the might of Telnaria, and, within the darkness of those vast, leafy forests, with smuggled arms, supplied by outer worlds, had more than once trapped and massacred expeditionary forces, the loss of which the empire at the time, pressed on many sides, could not well afford. Eventually, as the forces of the empire conquered many enemy worlds, of the sort so often sniffing and prowling at its frontiers, so often intruding across them, it had time to return its attention to the tribes of the forest. Various wars, over generations, took place. These tended to be bloody and merciless. There were diverse alliances and such, but, in the end, the tribes of the forest, as we have called them, and there were several such, were overwhelmed. Various treacheries and betrayals, and such, figured in these matters but, clearly, such tribes, isolated, deprived of support, sometimes divided against themselves, with their inadequate resources and armaments, were no match for the empire. In some cases, habitats were literally destroyed. The piteous remnants of the tribes, largely disarmed, were scattered about various worlds, in some cases to render various services to the empire, in particular, to supply selected forms of produce.*

These remnants, it should be noted, did not have the status of federates, *barbarian peoples permitted to remain within the domain of the empire, for which privilege they were expected to supply the empire with given quotas of recruits for the* auxilia, *the auxiliary forces on which the empire, eventually, would come so much to rely, this tending to compensate for the gradually increasing disinclination of citizens to concern themselves with military responsibilities. Some of these barbarians would come even to high offices in the regular forces. The military of the empire, it might be noted, once raised largely from its own militias, a universal military service once being a requirement for citizens, was now much separated from the common citizenry. It was now, on the whole, for most practical purposes, a professional mercenary force. It was now largely independent of the senate and state. Its political power was considerable. Its favor had to be courted. It was capable of making and unmaking emperors.*

The boy stood now in the snowy grass, grasping the staff. He seemed half-starved. He could not stand straight. His clothing, tattered, mostly in rags, blew about him, whipped in the wind.

Some remnants of two of the tribes of the forest had been

brought to this world, and the boy was of one of these. The Heruls had, only months ago, in the spring, and early summer, met the other of the two tribes in lengthy, and terrible, battle, in a series of engagements which had taken more than five weeks. That had been war. For that other tribe, you see, had had horses, and had changed their way of life to resemble that of the Heruls, changing to riders, to herdsmen. It was inevitable that they should clash, and they had, first, far to the east, even beyond the heights of Barrionuevo, where the plains of Barrionuevo began, and then later in the north, on those plains themselves. Hunlaki admired the riders, though the Heruls, in their vaster numbers, with their better mounts, bred for centuries for the chase and war, their superb skills, of horsemanship and war, honed by centuries of revered tradition, their swiftness, their forced marches, their encirclements, had defeated them. The king of that tribe had been slain in battle. His queen, heavy with child, with certain others, had eluded capture. It was not known where she had gone. No drinking cup had been made from the skull of the defeated king. Rather he had been burned on a pyre, worthy of a Herul chieftain. Hunlaki, and others, on horseback, had lifted their lances in salute as the smoke had wafted upward in the then summer sky.

"To the right forearm," said Mujiin, kicking his heels back into the flank of his mount.

In a moment Hunlaki heard the boy's sharp cry of pain.

There is some controversy concerning the name of the tribes of the forest, several of which had been placed on various worlds, two on this very world. 'Vandals' may be the original name. That is not known for certain. It is conjectured by some that, considering the current connotations of the name, they may have received it only later, in the writings of their enemies. It may, however, be the original name. In the beginning, it may have been simply a name, perhaps associated with 'Vanland,' which is "forest land." But, as I said, it is not really known. Another derivation is from 'Vanganz,' a word for a ritualized form of vengeance. We know them in history, of course, as Vandals, and I shall so refer to them, trusting that the reader will not allow himself to be misled by any inessential accretions which might now adhere to the name. Their like, you see, may not be unique to our own reality. Too, I do not presume to judge, leaving that for those who feel entitled to do so. My office, in this matter, as I have indicated, is a simple one, merely to tell what happened.

"The left forearm!" called Mujiin back to Hunlaki.

There was another cry of pain from the boy. Mujiin was skilled, almost as much as Hunlaki. Hunlaki wondered if Mujiin was showing off. Then Hunlaki surveyed the snowy plains about them. It would not do, of course, if the lad were a sacrifice, to distract the guard, while pursuit slipped past them, or might even be prepared to fall upon them. Later Mujiin would learn to be thoughtful about such matters, but Mujiin was young. He was easily distracted by blood, and the sport.

There was another cry of pain from the lad.

Hunlaki unslung his own lance.

It was not that he wanted to participate in the sport. It was only that the lad seemed too much weakened by the thrusts he had received. Surely he had not lost so much blood.

The boy cried again. This time he was struck in the left upper arm. That was the fourth strike. One begins on the right, assuming the target to be right-handed. To be sure, one can be mistaken about such things.

Hunlaki moved his mount a little closer, crossing the narrow track of the column, where the ground had been cut, like a wound in the grass.

Mujiin then struck the shoulders, the right, then the left.

The right thigh, and then the left, would be next. In that way the target can still stand, either for the final blow to the throat or the heart. It would be to the heart, as Hunlaki had had his say in that. Sometimes, if one wants to bring the target to its knees, the seventh and eighth blows are to the back of the leg, behind the knee. As Mujiin had called "ten" the ninth blow would be to the right side of the chest, just enough to draw blood, not enough to throw the target from its feet, then the tenth would be the driving of the lance tip through the ribs, to the heart. The blade of the Herul lance is smooth to the shaft, to facilitate its withdrawal. Else it would be too easy to lose it in combat. If Mujiin had called a "nine," the last blow would simply be to the heart. Or, if he had called "nine" and "the neck," the ninth blow would be to the back of the neck, attempting to sever the vertebrae there.

The boy reeled back, again. That had been the ninth thrust, that to the right side of the chest, little more intended than to turn and bleed the target.

Mujiin wheeled his mount.

The lad wavered. Surely he would fall. Surely Mujiin must hurry!

"Beware!" cried Hunlaki.

The boy suddenly, raising his staff, as the lance sped toward him, struck it to the side and slipped to the side of the horse, and then thrust up with the staff, brutally into the ribs of the horse, which howled with pain, and the lad then struck the mount twice more, with terrible jabs, and it squealed, moving suddenly, awkwardly, trying to avoid the stick, the pain, to the side, and it lost its footing, and Mujiin, his foot caught in the stirrup, went down with the horse, his leg pinned under it, and looked up to see the boy, wild-eyed, bleeding, over him, raising the staff, but the blow did not fall for Hunlaki rode him down, his lance piercing the boy's back, under the left shoulder blade.

Mujiin, cursing, rose to this feet, his horse having scrambled up.

Hunlaki drew his lance from the boy's back.

Mujiin was furious. He kicked the inert form of the boy.

His horse stood some yards off, its eyes wide with pain.

It shook the snow from its fur.

"Are you all right?" asked Hunlaki.

"Dog! Dog!" cried Mujiin, kicking the boy.

Hunlaki fetched Mujiin's mount.

Mujiin checked the girth strap on the horse. Then he ascended to the saddle.

Hunlaki surveyed the prairie about them. It was still. Then he looked again at the form of the boy.

"He was brave," said Hunlaki, "to follow us."

"He is a dog!" said Mujiin.

"But he is a brave dog," said Hunlaki.

"Yes," said Mujiin, "he was a brave dog."

"They are all brave dogs," said Hunlaki.

"Yes," said Mujiin, "they are all brave dogs."

"Worthy enemies," said Hunlaki.

"Yes," said Mujiin.

Then, looking behind them from time to time, they returned to the track of the column. In a few moments they saw their contact riders approaching.

· · · CHAPTER 5 · · ·

The peasant descended the narrow stairs, leading down to the main floor of the tavern.

It was late in the afternoon.

"Hold," said Boon Thap, from behind the counter, to the left, past which one must move to reach the door.

The peasant stopped.

Two others, nearby, looked up. They sat at a stained table to the right of the door, one of several. These were the only others on the main floor of the tavern. They had drinks before them, on the circled tabletop. They had been playing cards, Tanleel. The flat, revolving counterboard, with its pegs, was between them.

Boon Thap, who was the proprietor of this establishment, drew forth from under the counter a shallow, copper dish. He placed it on the counter. In this dish were four or five coins, pennies.

"Pay," said Boon Thap.

The peasant recalled the dish upstairs. It was in that dish that coins for the pay woman would be placed.

He was from far away, from another world, indeed, but it was within the empire. He knew that much.

"Why?" asked the peasant.

"Pay," said Boon Thap.

"I have not eaten here. I have not drunk here," said the peasant, slowly.

Boon Thap gestured toward the stairs with his head. "Was she any good?"

"Yes," said the peasant.

That was certainly true. She had juiced well. Too, in the beginning, she had shown him things he had not known, things he had not dreamed of in the village. But in the end, after an hour, she had been merely his, helpless, uncontrollable, begging, crying out, as had been Tessa, or Lia, or Sut. In the end she had been not an instructress, only a mastered slave.

"Did you like her?" asked Boon Thap.

"Yes," said the peasant.

"Pay," said Boon Thap.

"I have not eaten here. I have not drunk here," said the peasant.

"You pay here," said Boon Thap, pointing to the copper bowl.

The two fellows at the table slid their chairs back and came toward the counter. Then they were standing a little behind the peasant, one on each side.

"You must not make trouble," said Boon Thap.

"I am not making trouble," said the peasant.

He did not want to make trouble. He did not know this place, or these people. He was a stranger here. Too, he did not want to disappoint Brother Benjamin. Brother Benjamin, in his recent admonitions, had been very explicit on such points. Brother Benjamin had come down all the way from the *festung*, down to the road, by the village, to bid him farewell. The peasant had knelt in the road, his head bowed, to receive Brother Benjamin's blessing, administered in old Telnarian, given with the sign of the device. Brother Benjamin had never really expected him to stay in the village, for some reason, it seemed. In his journey the peasant realized that he had sensed this before, that he had known it, somehow, for years. Others had been there, too, to bid him farewell, others with diverse feelings. Doubtless some would miss him. Others were perhaps relieved that such as he was leaving. He had towered among them. He had not seemed to be like them. Too, he was dangerous. His temper was unpredictable, and violent. And he could break the neck of a garn pig in his bare hands.

"Who am I?" the peasant had asked Brother Benjamin, once again, before he left the village.

"You are 'Dog,' " had said Brother Benjamin, "of the *festung* village of Saint Giadini."

Then the peasant had left.

The peasant felt his sack taken from his back by one of the men behind him. He did not interfere, or resist. He was a stranger here. He did not wish to disappoint Brother Benjamin. It was put on the counter. His staff was removed from his hand by the other man, and leant against the counter.

"I will tell you what you owe," said Boon Thap. "How much did you pay upstairs?"

The peasant was silent.

"What did you give her?" asked Boon Thap.

"Nothing," said the peasant.

"Nothing?" said Boon Thap.

"She would not take anything," said the peasant.

"Liar!" said Boon Thap.

The peasant noted the resemblance of Boon Thap to a garn pig.

"Do you think she is a contract woman, kept in a brothel, chained by the neck to her bed, with a slotted coin box bolted to the bed?"

"No," said the peasant. He had heard of such things, and many more, he and the others who had worked their passage to Terrenia, from the sailors, when they were not on watch. The coin was put near the box, which was locked, in order to prove that the customer possessed the means wherewith to pay for his pleasure. Afterwards the coin would be placed in the box or not, according to whether or not the customer had found the services of the contract woman satisfactory. As a record was kept of the customers and the rooms to which they went, it was a simple matter, after undoing the locks on the boxes, after business hours, to count the coins and see if the amount of money in the box was correct, if it matched the number of customers. Sanctions, of course, were imposed on the contract women if the funds were short. Sometimes they were beaten, as though they might have been slaves. In such ways are the women encouraged to please the proprietor's customers, or clients.

"You are a thief," said one of the men behind the peasant.

"I am not a thief," said the peasant.

"If you did not pay her, then you will pay me, double," said Boon Thap.

"No," said the peasant.

"She is my employee," said the proprietor.

"No," said the peasant. "She pays you rent."

"I will beat her," said Boon Thap.

"But she is a free woman," said the peasant. He was not sure of these matters. Were free women in cities to be beaten? He did know that the fathers in the village would sometimes beat their wives, and their daughters. Certainly Tessa, and Lia and Sut, had been beaten, sometimes for having been seen with him, but this had not stopped them from coming back, from arranging to meet him secretly, behind the hay sheds, in the varda coops. But he had heard that on Terennia women were not to be beaten, whether they deserved it or not. That was perhaps why the women of Terennia seemed so spoiled. But there seemed no reason to beat the pay woman. She had done nothing to be beaten for. She had been kind, and loving. Too, she was not, as far as the peasant knew, the proprietor's woman. Too, this was Terennia, and she was free. It was not like she was a slave, who must expect to be punished if she is the least bit disobedient, or has not been in some way fully pleasing.

"We will see what you have here," said Boon Thap. He jerked loose the fastenings of the sack and turned it over, depositing its contents on the counter.

"He has money!" said one of the men behind the peasant.

"Look, a *darin*!" said the other.

"Ahh," said Boon Thap. "Look!" He lifted up the silver bracelet.

"He is a thief," said the man to the peasant's right.

"Yes!" said Boon Thap.

"No," said the peasant.

He gripped the counter.

He must not yield to the rage, not, at least, to that sudden, blinding, scarlet rage. There were rages among rages, of course. There was the scarlet rage, so sudden, so uncontrollable, like the breaking open of the bowl of the sky, as you could see, from the shattering, the lines of splitting and cracking. One could do little about that. One scarcely knew, until afterward, what one had done. You learned that, only later. It was this rage which the villagers had most feared. Then there were the rages you sensed coming, the rages which so sharpened the senses, which transfused one with such power, how eagerly you sensed them, like knowing a cat was about, then waiting tensely for it to spring up, somewhere, from the grass. And you were he who sensed, he who waited, and you were the cat, too, eager to spring up, that for which you waited. And then there were the cold, merciless rages, the most terrible of all, rages which the peasant had not yet learned, the rages as implacable as winter, which taught one patience, a patience colder and more cruel than ice.

"You must fight these things, my son," Brother Benjamin had told him.

"The bracelet is stolen," said Boon Thap. "I will keep it."

"And the *darin*," said the man to the peasant's left.

"We will keep this sack, these things," said Boon Thap. "Now, get out."

"They are mine," said the peasant.

"Get out," said Boon Thap.

The man to the peasant's right suddenly seized the peasant's staff. He lifted it.

"Get out," said Boon Thap.

The staff suddenly descended, smiting the peasant on the shoulder. It then struck him on the side of the head. The peasant felt blood at the side of his head.

The man with the staff seemed surprised that the peasant was still on his feet.

"You must learn to control your temper," had said Brother Benjamin.

Again the staff whirled toward the peasant, but the peasant

reached up and caught it, in flight. He then wrenched it away from the man.

The man backed away.

"If one strikes you," had said Brother Benjamin, "give him your staff, that he may strike you again."

The peasant handed the staff back to the assailant.

The man looked at him, in wonder. Then he laughed, and so, too, did the other, who had backed away, and Boon Thap.

"Go," said Boon Thap, smiling.

The peasant, his staff and sack left behind, left the tavern. Hot tears burned down his cheeks. He went to the curb, outside the tavern. There he sat down, and put his head down, in his hands. Then he raised his head, and howled in misery, to the sky between the buildings. He then reentered the tavern. Boon Thap and the others were seated at the table, that at which the two men had earlier been playing Tanleel. The counterboard was still on the table. Drinks were before them. The peasant took his staff and drove it through the diaphragm of the man who had struck him. This was done with considerable force. It tore through the body, and the backbone. It punched even into the wall behind the man. The peasant then seized Boon Thap, breaking his neck, as if he had been a garn pig. The other man fled, screaming. His exit was not contested. Then the peasant, after retrieving his staff and gathering together what he could of his belongings, once more left the tavern.

· · · CHAPTER 6 · · ·

And so the wagons rolled and creaked, and the men cursed, and there was the sound of chains, and, sometimes, the weeping, the lamentations, of the captive women, tied by the neck to the back of wagons.

Two days after the encounter with the youth on the snowy plains Hunlaki and Mujiin had returned to the column, their duties completed pending further assignments. Hunlaki did volunteer for further service at that time, but his request, quite sensibly, was declined. It was understood that he had been, for most practical purposes, in the saddle for days. Accordingly he was doing little now but riding with the column.

Mujiin had not found Hunlaki much in the way of good company of late. He had, accordingly, for the last few days, left him much alone. Hunlaki seemed too often lost in his own thoughts. Indeed, he had been acting a bit strangely ever since the recrossing of the Lothar. But Mujiin, who was very fond of Hunlaki, was patient. Heruls tend to be a patient folk. Hunlaki would doubtless come back to himself, as he always had before, after some of the simpler, more routine actions. Mujiin had no fear, incidentally, that Hunlaki would tell others about his embarrassment, that little *contretemps*, with the boy on the prairie, how he had been tricked, as though he might have been on his first raid, of how he might have been injured, or worse, if Hunlaki had not ridden to his succor. Mujiin did not fear this, for Hunlaki was not only of the tents of the Heruls, but one with whom he rode. Indeed, some years later, Mujiin would tell the story himself, as a joke on himself, and as a warning to young riders, about how Hunlaki had saved him, when he was new to the ways of war.

They had been on the march for several days.

Hunlaki, in this time, rode usually on the right side of the column. Sometimes he patrolled it, riding its length, back and forth.

The wagons, and the foot, moved slowly, and the prisoners, far too slowly for the taste of Hunlaki.

Hunlaki looked up.

The birds still followed, and their patience, as the days wore on, was less and less often disappointed. Many were now so swollen with food that they could not fly. Sometimes the dogs caught them. Bones littered the track of the column. Many of the more attractive women had been given rags to wrap about their feet, that they might not, in the cold and snow, lose their toes. Such a loss, as trivial as it might seem, would considerably reduce their value.

To one side dogs fought over a body.

Hunlaki was himself well aware that things were not as usual with him.

He had for two nights chewed on the fermented curds, and in the morning had had to tie himself in the saddle.

He had, several times, at night, when the column had stopped, and the fires were lit, made use of captive women, chained under certain of the wagons, put aside for the purpose. To be sure, as a rider, he could have his picks marked, a disk with his mark on it, tied about her neck, under the rope, reserved for him in the evening. The foot would make do with what was provided for them, not that some excellent women were not picked out for them. Sometimes Hunlaki used the women under the wagons as Herul women, but often, because they were women of an enemy, he put them in the pig position, even some very attractive women whom he had picked out earlier, whom he had put his disk on, reserving them for the evening, that they might understand that they belonged to the Heruls, and what was in store for them, the long days of tending flocks and, in the evenings, the contenting of masters in the furs. To be sure, some of these women might be sold in Venitzia, some to the soldiers there, others to be put on the ships, to be sent far away, to distant markets. The soldiers at Venitzia had flame spears, which could burn a rider from a thousand yards. The Heruls did not attempt to penetrate the strange fences about the towns. They had seen animals lying dead across the wires.

Hunlaki recalled the riders he had fought against in the spring and early summer. That had been war. The folk they had just raided, those in the vicinity of the Lothar, mostly west of it, near the forests, were said to be related to them. Hunlaki supposed it was possible. But the two peoples seemed very different.

Hunlaki looked up.

The birds were about.

They had been about, too, on the plains of war, far to the east, even beyond the heights of Barrionuevo, and then in the north, on the plains of Barrionuevo, when those of the tents of the Heruls had met the riders, those related to the folk near the Lothar, in the spring, in the early summer.

Too, here and there, the birds were on the ground, sometimes almost at the edges of the column, feeding.

Hunlaki did not care for the birds.

Hunlaki turned his mount suddenly to the right, uttered an angry cry, kicked back into the flanks of the beast, and charged at a heap of birds, clambering about food. They squawked, and fluttered wildly to the left and right, and Hunlaki, angrily, wheeled his mount back, to the left, to rejoin the column. When he looked back he saw that one or two of the bolder birds had already returned to their feeding.

Hunlaki, like most warriors, hated the birds, the patient ones.

The dogs had been at it first.

The column was now in the vicinity of the heights of Barrionuevo.

Hunlaki saw a woman to his right, several yards from the column. It would have to be a woman of the people near the Lothar, for no Herul women were with the raiders. One would take the women, the children, in the wagons, when one made the long journeys. But one would not take them on raids. Sometimes one had had to fight, on the long journeys, even before they had found the sweet, grass-fresh plains of Barrionuevo. One tried to keep between the enemy and the wagons. Before battles, and at night, one put the wagons together, forming closures, sometimes rings of defense, the cattle, the animals, the women, the wealth, inside. No, of course, it was not a Herul woman. Hunlaki moved his horse toward her, circling her rather, that he might have her between himself and the column. In a moment or two, the horse moving slowly, he saw that she had, indeed, wrapped several times about her neck, a rope. She had been gathering hineen, presumably for the cooking pots of the wagon driver, that behind which she would normally be marched prisoner. Hineen is somewhat rare but there were patches of it in this area. It is a pretty plant, coming in several colors. It is a spore bearer and blossoms, or, perhaps better, colors, in the cold. It sustains certain ungulates throughout the winter, which paw for it when the snow is heavy. Some of these animals come from dozens of miles away to find it. The spores of the hineen are carried about, partly by the hoofs of the ungulates. Heruls and the folk of the Lothar could also eat it. She was holding up the front of her skirt, which she had used as a basket, into which she had placed the hineen. It was very pretty, all the colors in the skirt. It seemed to be full now. Why was she dallying? And she was too far from the column. Did she think to run? Her calves were not without interest. She turned white, seeing Hunlaki approaching her. He had already freed his knout from the saddle ring.

Swiftly she knelt in the cold grass.

She put her head down and unlooped the free end of the rope, which she had wound about her neck, the end tucked in, that by means of which she would normally be tied to the back of a wagon. She then, her head kept down, lifted the free end of the rope toward Hunlaki, the other end remaining, of course, knotted about her neck. It was a placatory gesture, offering him, in effect, her leash. Hunlaki, from the saddle, looked down upon her. The wind moved her hair a little. The hineen had been spilled before her, before her knees, the skirt emptied.

"Look up," said Hunlaki.

She looked up. She was trembling. She did not lower the leash.

"You are far from the column," said Hunlaki. She was perhaps some fifty yards from it.

"I was gathering hineen," she said.

Hunlaki's hand tightened on the knout, held across the saddle.

"You are far from the column," Hunlaki repeated.

"Yes, Master," she said.

"Do you wish to be brought back on your rope?" he asked.

"No, Master," she said.

"You have learned already to call Heruls 'Master,' " Hunlaki said.

"All free men, Master," she said.

"You may lower your hand," said Hunlaki.

She did so.

"Rewind the rope about your neck, as it was," said Hunlaki.

She complied.

"Gather up, again, the hineen," he said.

She bent to the task and, in moments, had replaced the spilled hineen within the basket of her skirt. She still knelt. One could now see her knees.

"Rise up," said Hunlaki. "Return to the wagon."

"Yes, Master," she said.

She turned away from Hunlaki, and began to proceed toward the column. Hunlaki followed her. He was a little behind her, on her left. Doubtless she was much aware of him there.

"You were thinking of escape," said Hunlaki.

"Forgive me, Master," she said.

"There is no escape," said Hunlaki.

"I do not want to be marked," she said. "I do not want to wear a device."

"In the lands of the Heruls," said Hunlaki, "such things are not necessary. Do you think we do not know who is slave, and who is not?"

She sobbed.

"There is no escape for you," said Hunlaki, "no more than for the branded, collared girls of the civilized worlds."

She was then near the column, and she stopped. She looked back at Hunlaki.

"There would have been no escape," said Hunlaki. "The dogs would have come for you."

"I am afraid!" she said.

"That is fully appropriate, as you are a slave," said Hunlaki.

She looked up at him.

"Do you know what you must fear most?" asked Hunlaki.

"No, Master," she said.

"That you might not be found fully pleasing," he said.

"Yes, Master," she said.

"Turn about," said Hunlaki.

She did so.

She shuddered, not looking at him, as he, leaning down from the saddle, put the knout gently to the left side of her neck.

"Do not think again of escape," said Hunlaki.

"No, Master," she said.

"Hurry now to your wagon," said Hunlaki. "Hope that you will not be beaten."

"Yes, Master," she said.

Hunlaki, his knout restored to the saddle ring, followed her, slowly, some yards back, until he saw her at her wagon. The hineen was placed in a hamper. He then saw her tied to the back of the wagon, where, already, there were two others. She looked back once, but Hunlaki turned his mount, and retraced his steps.

A light snow had begun to fall.

Somewhere, ahead, he heard the cries of a woman in labor.

Birds screamed overhead, circling.

"Ho," said Mujiin, riding up. "I saw you with a woman. You are feeling better?"

"I am all right," Hunlaki assured him.

"I saw you had her away from the column," said Mujiin. "Did you knout her suitably? Did you make her kick well for you?"

"I did not knout her," said Hunlaki. "I did not make her kick."

"Did you put your disk on her, for this evening?" asked Mujiin.

"No," said Hunlaki.

"She had good calves," said Mujiin. "I saw. I will know her when I see her. I will put my disk on her for the night."

Hunlaki shrugged.

"You do not mind?" asked Mujiin.

"No," said Hunlaki.

"How shall I use her?" inquired Mujiin.

"As you wish," said Hunlaki. "She is a slave."

They were, as I have mentioned, at that time, near the heights of Barrionuevo. Indeed, in the late afternoon of the morrow's march, one might be able, from the track of the column, if the weather were fitting, to see the *festung* of Saint Giadini.

It was shortly thereafter that the column halted for the night.

During the night some children were born, and cast to the side of the march.

They were dead shortly thereafter, and the dogs, and then the birds, had them.

Hunlaki that night dreamed of the actions of the spring and early summer.

In the morning the fires were quenched with snow and the beasts harnessed. That day began like most days on the march, not muchly different.

Hunlaki remembered the boy he had killed on the snowy plains, days ago, only days from the Lothar.

And he remembered the riders. He had admired them. He admired the riders, and the boy. It was too bad, he thought, that such a people must perish.

It was such thoughts that were in his mind when he rode past a newly born infant. It lay to one side, in the snowy grass.

He had ridden well past it, when he suddenly wheeled his mount and rode back.

"Away!" he called to one of the dogs, smelling at the tiny, living thing.

Hunlaki looked down at it, from the saddle.

It was tiny, and reddish, lying to one side, on bloody, pressed-down grass. It was a few feet to the left of the wagon ruts, if one were looking toward the rear of the column, to the right, if one were looking toward the front of the column. It was bloody. Mud, too, had spattered upon it, from the wheels of the passing wagons. It had been born, Hunlaki surmised, but minutes before. The dogs had not yet had it. The cord which had bound it to its mother was still with it, and a mass of bloody tissue, to which it was attached.

Hunlaki saw one of the large birds alight nearby.

Hunlaki dismounted and examined the infant. It seemed sturdy. It was crying. Hunlaki did not really know why he had turned back or why he had dismounted. It felt very warm, which seemed strange to Hunlaki, as it was lying in the pressed-down, cold grass. Its small limbs flailed about. Hunlaki did not care for the crying. "Be quiet," said Hunlaki. Another warrior, mounted, stopped nearby. "Stand aside," said the warrior, "and I will trample it." Hunlaki did not respond. "Let us play the game of lances," suggested the other warrior. Sometimes the infants of the enemy were used in the game of lances, instead of the cloth ball or melon. Hunlaki waved the warrior on. Two other warriors rode by, looking at Hunlaki strangely. Then Hunlaki, embarrassed, remounted, to continue on his way. He saw the dog move a little closer. Its mouth was open. Its tongue was out, and moved about its teeth. The crest was back flat on its neck. Even the bird, which we shall call a vulture, moved forward a little, awkwardly, as such things move on the land. Hunlaki looked down, again, at the infant. Then he looked at the dog, and then at the bird. Then a second bird alit. Hunlaki had seen living infants drawn about by afterbirth, across the prairie, being fought for by the dogs. He had seen them torn to pieces, too, by the birds. Hunlaki again dismounted. He crouched down beside the small body. Curious, he put his hand to the afterbirth. It still retained warmth. The blood, the fluid, on the matted grass was still sticky. To be sure, it was cold, and that would slow its drying. But clearly the child had been born but shortly before, perhaps only minutes before. Hunlaki wiped his hand on his cloak. He then looked about, at the dog, and the two birds. He drew his knife. He put one hand on the infant's head to hold it steady. He put the blade to its throat. He withdrew the blade. He cut the afterbirth away, leaving enough of the cord to knot, which he did. He then resheathed his knife and lifted the small life in his hands, looking down at it. He stood up, holding the child. One could see the mountains quite clearly from where he stood. Looking down he was surprised to see something he had not noticed before. Near where the child had lain, almost under where it had lain, thrust under the matted grass, as though it might have been concealed there, bloody, was a medallion and chain. They seemed of rich stuff. Hunlaki took this chain, with its medallion, and slung it about his neck. In a little while he had rejoined the march. The infant, within his cloak, warm against his body, was asleep. Later in the day Hunlaki found a wagon in which rode a bitch with her pups. At the teat of the bitch, with her pups, the infant eagerly suckled.

Late that afternoon, from the track of the column, in the distance, looking like part of the mountain itself, partly lost in the clouds, could be seen the *festung* of Saint Giadini.

"What have you there?" had asked Mujiin, curious, riding up to Hunlaki earlier in the day.

Hunlaki showed him.

"That is not a Herul," said Mujiin.

"No," said Hunlaki.

"Kill it," said Mujiin.

"No," said Hunlaki.

"It may grow up to kill you," said Mujiin.

"That is true," granted Hunlaki.

Toward evening he rode alone up the high, narrow, treacherous path to the *festung*.

"If we do not accept this," said Brother Benjamin, "what will you do with it?"

"I will leave it on the plains, for the dogs," said Hunlaki.

"We will accept it," said Brother Benjamin.

"It has suckled on the teat of a dog," said Hunlaki. "If you have dogs, a nursing dog, it can feed."

"There will be nursing women in the village," said Brother Benjamin. "What is its name?"

"I do not know," said Hunlaki.

"It has suckled on the teat of a dog?" asked Brother Benjamin.

"Yes," said Hunlaki.

"Then it must be a little dog," said Brother Benjamin. "We will call it 'Dog.' "

Hunlaki touched the infant with an exploratory tentacle, and then placed it gently into the webbed fingers of Brother Benjamin.

"Oh," said Hunlaki, "this was with it." He removed the medallion and chain from about his neck and put it with the child, in the arms of Brother Benjamin.

"Do you know the meaning of that thing?" asked Brother Benjamin.

"No," said Hunlaki.

"I will keep it for him," said Brother Benjamin.

Hunlaki then remounted and rode down the long trail to the plain, leagues beneath. By the next morning he had caught up, once more, with the column.

· · · CHAPTER 7 · · ·

He lay in the white sand, on his side, his senses reeling. For a moment he had blacked out. His body felt numb, shocked, paralyzed. He had seen them approaching, the two guards, and the petty, officious officer of the court. He had remembered her from the hearing. He had watched them approaching across the sand, between the kneeling, waiting men. She wore now not the somber blue of the court, but a belted clingabout of white *corton*, a garb suitable for a holiday, for the games. He was surprised that she was dressed so, for, on this world, as he had noted, men and women, save in the lower classes, in the squalid, impoverished areas, dressed much alike, that seemingly to show their sameness, and their superiority to sex. That garment, lengthy and opaque as it was, would doubtless precipitate some scandal in the stands. He did not doubt but what many women there, hidden in their mannish garb, would find it daring, and offensive. How resentful they might be, how envious, how jealous! Who did she think she was! Was she not familiar with the proprieties? Surely she must know such attire would attract attention in the stands. Indeed, was she not publicly coming across the sand, even now. Who then could not but notice her? He could hear the ripples of outrage in the stands. But what had she to fear? She could claim that she was acting to rectify an oversight, that she had come forth onto the sand in the line of her duties. Too, what need she care for the opinions of others? She could be indifferent to them, for she was of the *honestori*. Too, he sensed she might relish being the object of such attention, even of scandal. What had she to fear? She was of high family. Indeed, her mother, who was the judge who had sentenced him, was in the mayor's box. She was high judge in the city. He saw the mother turn to the mayor, and speak with her. The guards coming across the sand with the officer of the court, the daughter, were in uniform. One of the guards held some loops of rope. They both carried stun sticks. He was now familiar with such things. It was by means of them that he had been taken into custody. Such weapons, and others, others still more dangerous, were scarce on this world. They were almost entirely in the hands of authorities, but, of course, not altogether. The population then was largely at the mercy of two groups, not always unallied, authorities and criminals. This was common on many worlds within the empire. Indeed, the manufacture of weaponry, at least legal weaponry, was on many worlds a monopoly of the state. Weapon makers, on many worlds, those who had possessed such skills, had been among the first bound. He had watched the three of them approaching. The sand was deep. It came well over the ankles of their boots. She, too, wore boots. This suggested to him that she had planned to cross the sand, before dressing for the day. Her presence here then was not an unplanned one, resulting merely from detecting some unexpected oversight. She had wanted to appear on the sand, before the assembled crowds, doubtless. He could see the prints behind them, where they had disturbed the sand, raked after the prisoners had been knelt. The attendants might not be pleased with that. They took their work seriously. The sand would be disturbed soon enough, though, given the beginning of the first amusements. Then the guards, and the officer of the court, the daughter of the judge, had stopped before him. He had looked up at them, from his knees. She pointed at him, grandly, rather for the crowd, he supposed. "He cannot be trusted," she said. "Rope him, rope him well." He did not doubt but what the men would obey her. Indeed, what power had she, if the men did not obey her? They would obey her, of course. They had been trained to adhere to the rules, not question how the rules had come about, or the utility of the rules, their ultimate consequences. Her face wore a haughty expression. She was fairly complexioned. Her body seemed cold, and tight. Her dark hair was tied back, behind her head, severely. Yet for all the neurotic coldness, and tightness, about her, he did not think she was utterly unattractive. He had even looked upon her, and watched her, and considered her, when he was sitting in the prisoner's dock, guarded by men with stun sticks, in her court garb. He now again considered her, in the white clingabout. To be sure, it muchly covered her. He wondered what she looked like, naked. One of the guards laughed. "Be silent!" she chided the guard. Doubtless the pupils of his eyes had dilated, as he had looked upon her. They had performed such a test on him before the hearing, when he was being held. A female prisoner had been brought in. His reactions had been noted. They had also been referred to, explicitly, in the hearing. "Rope him!" she said. The guards looked at one another. Then one lifted his stun stuck and pulled the trigger once, and then, as he had not fallen, twice more.

As he lay in the sand, his body ringing with shock, muchly paralyzed, he felt the ropes being put about him, tying his arms to his sides, his hands behind him.

"Make them tight!" she said.

The ropes were drawn tight. They were knotted.

He was then put again to his knees.

She slapped him twice, angrily. She could not hurt him. She did not have the strength. But the blows stung, and they were humiliating. He did not care to be struck, particularly by a woman. One could kill a man. It did not seem right to kill a woman. If he struck her he might have broken her neck. She glared down at him. There was laughter in the stands. She was furious. She stepped back from him. In the stands there must have been many who realized that she, an officer of the court, the daughter of the high judge herself, had been viewed with dilated pupils. But what did she expect, going down on the sand, clad as she was, standing before one who had chosen death to "true manhood," as it was defined on this world, to the improvement, the smoothing? He had struck a woman only once before, Tessa, who had first slapped him. He had slapped her back. Must she not expect that? But it seems she had not. She had looked up at him with awe, from where she had been flung by the force of the blow, on the floor of the varda coop, to his left. She had then crawled to his feet, begging his forgiveness. He had used her on the floor of the varda coop. After that she would meet him when and where he told her.

With what fury the daughter of the judge regarded him!

He looked away from her. His body was still numb.

The stands were almost full now.

The ropes about his upper body were tight. He could tell that. Still, oddly, it was hard to feel them, at least as one would normally have expected to feel them. It was almost as though they had been put on someone else. He wondered if Brother Benjamin were right, if he were not his body, as he seemed to be, but something else, hidden inside it. If that were so, it might explain why the ropes felt strange, because he was far within his body, far from the ropes. The body, in spite of appearances, its seeming to contain organs, and such, was really a shell, something within which he lived. Indeed, Brother Benjamin had told him that he was really invisible, the real him, that is, the one that lived inside the body, or somewhere. The real person was called the *koos*, an old word which had originally meant "breath." It was Floon, a rational salamander, or salamander-type creature, of the predominantly reptilian world of Zirus, who had first taught, to the surprise of many, as the idea was then new, that the *koos* was eternal, neither coming into nor going out of existence, but staying right there, wherever it was. A consequence of this idea was that rational creatures could not die, an idea with considerable appeal to rational creatures. The fact that Floon died, and rather miserably, in an electric chair, did little to diminish the persuasiveness of his doctrine. It was discovered that he had not really died but had later appeared simultaneously on several different worlds, reiterating his teachings. His teachings, a generation or two after his apparent death, had been gathered together by followers. The teachings seemed in places to be inconsistent with one another, but inconsistencies may always be reconciled, by drawing suitable distinctions. Too, certain of the teachings, for one reason or another, were rejected as inauthentic. This was done by individuals who had never known Floon, and several generations after his apparent death. Dogs and horses, Brother Benjamin had taught, did not have a *koos*. He had found this hard to believe, as it seemed they felt pain, and pleasure, and such. Their insides, their organs, and such, were relevant to their life. It was only that this was not the case with the rational creatures, or at least certain of the rational creatures. Rational aquatic mammals were a disputed point. Brother Benjamin believed that Floon was an emanation of Karch, but there was a great deal of controversy on this sort of thing in the worlds. I will briefly sketch the major positions. There was the illusionist position of Fingal, who taught that since Karch, who is perfect, and pain is imperfect, cannot know pain, Floon must have been an illusion, because Floon had apparently felt pain when he had been put in the electric chair. Some folks, of course, thought that Floon was merely a rational salamander, or salamandertype creature, no more, but a gifted, or inspired, prophet. That did not turn the trick, however, for many folks. One then became involved in whether Floon was truly Karch, or only a part of Karch, whether or not they were of the same substance, whatever a substance was, or different substances, or similar substances, or two substances united into one substance in one union, and such, the latter position, perhaps because of its inconsistency, or mystery, tending to become the most popular. In spite of the obvious verbalisms involved, the inability to provide empirical proof for any of these positions, and, indeed, the inability, even apart from questions of mere provability, to empirically discriminate among these various hypotheses, which was doubtless something of an advantage, many people took these notions very seriously. Indeed, many people were killed because of them, usually Floonians by Floonians. This was not unintelligible because it was natural that there would be serious competition for control of various dioceses, and the revenues, power and such, associated with them.

Her eyes met his. "You need not have been here," she said. "The choice was yours."

He did not look at her. What she said was true.

The Floonians had been a joke for some generations in the empire, among the honestori, *most of whom kept to the old ways, seemingly such a transparently infantile wish fulfillment, but then it had been noted that they, in their numerous sects, were becoming more and more powerful. That had given the empire pause. Even more alarming was the tendency among most of the Floonian sects to draw apart from the observances and customs,*

*the traditions, of the empire. Knowing themselves in all their
humility and self-effacingness to be superior to others, not that
that was to their credit, as it was due only to the blessings of
Floon, they consorted much with themselves, separating themselves from their fellow citizens. They declined military service.
This hastened to some extent the barbarization of the military.
They formed their own charitable societies, their own burial
clubs. They were reluctant even to place laurel on the altar of
the genius of the empire, which was understood by most as no
more than a token of allegiance. The priority in their life tended
to become not the welfare of their communities, or the empire,
but of their own koos. To many it now seemed that the Floonian
phenomenon, which by outsiders was commonly understood to
be more uniform than in fact it was, was not only an arbitrary,
ridiculous, egomaniacal aberration but a persuasion which was
both dangerous and unpatriotic. To be sure, at this time, the
empire had not realized the possibilities of turning the Floonian
phenomenon to its own purposes. That would come later. The
hierarchy of the Floonians, of course, would see in the alliance
with the empire, as opposed to an opposition to it, a route to
power not only within their own sects, but within the state as a
whole, indeed, as a way to turn the empire to its own advantage.
Later, you see, the Floonian phenomenon would become well
aware of the advantages of a controlled secularism. Soon, as
revelation was reinterpreted, or continued to unfold, or was
better understood, it would be discovered that the faithful, for
example, had not only a right, but a duty, to serve the empire,
to take up arms on her behalf, and such things.*

*But now, at the time of our story, the Floonians were outsiders.
They were still regarded, by most, even of the lower classes,
amongst whom they commonly made their greatest inroads, as
no more than contemptible deviants.*

*I am sorry to have taken time for these diverse doctrinal and
historical allusions, but it seemed desirable to do so, as without
them certain later developments, even in our simple story, would
be very difficult to understand. I beg the reader to put aside his
own prejudices, and to grant, minimally, that matters such as I
have been discussing, as bizarre as they may seem, as remote*

from common sense and rationality as they may be, can be, at least at certain times and places, taken seriously by rational creatures. We will concern ourselves very little with them, except insofar as they may impinge upon our narrative. Certain last remarks, however, are in order. First, although many points here may seem eccentric and airy, even amusing, there is nothing eccentric or airy, or amusing, about imprisonment, persecution and torture. There is nothing eccentric, or airy, or abstract, or amusing, about the hideous deaths to which millions of rational creatures were subjected on account of them. It must clearly be understood, further, that powerful, unscrupulous men, in the prosecution of a savage Realpolitik, can seize upon such things for their own purposes, indeed, as they might have seized upon many things, perhaps even more likely, or promising, things, more visible things, such as differentiations among species. Secondly, in accord with the first point, and more pertinent to our story, the Floonian phenomenon was soon to be appropriated by individuals who saw in it, on one level or on another, on one level of consciousness or another, a route to attention, wealth, prestige and power. Indeed, had Floon chosen to return yet again to the civilized worlds it seems likely that that sweet, timid, gentle creature so fearful of death would have been one of the first seized and condemned, for the institution would have found him a dangerous embarrassment. Certainly the ritual, the practices, the organization, the bureaucracy, the hierarchies would have puzzled him. Would he not have gone his own way, puzzled, shaking his head, turning away from such things, content rather with his own simple beliefs and ways? Thirdly, although the empire occasionally saw fit to persecute Floonians, it never did so consistently or systematically. Such would have been uncharacteristic. It would have been in contradiction to, and a violation of, the general, accepted and long-sanctioned practices and policies of the imperium. Indeed, the policy of the empire was almost invariably one of tolerance, tolerance for the millions of faiths of the millions of worlds. It was only later that this changed, when the Floonian phenomenon, which had for the most part been allowed to flourish within the empire, in accordance with the general policies of imperial toleration, became allied with the imperium. Things then changed. The Floonian hierarchy, having been permitted to rise to power in virtue of its own having been tolerated, now, once it was in a position to do so, repudiated toleration, no longer needing it, and instituted practices of consistent, systematic persecution that would have amazed and horrified even the emperors of the civil wars, famous for their proscription lists. Again, I do not wish to anticipate, but I will remark that the Floonian phenomenon may not have quite the same future in this reality as it might have had in others. Not all realities, you see, are identical. Indeed, our protagonist, and others like him, may have had something to do with that.

"Do not dare to look upon me," she chided.

"It is hard to feel the ropes," he said, puzzled.

"That is because of the shock of the stun stick, you barbarous dolt," she laughed.

She then turned about and, followed by the guards, recrossed the sand. She would ascend to the mayor's box by the throne gate, that which led to the privileged seating. It was called that because the seats of honor were reached through it, including the high seat, or throne, in this town occupied by the mayor.

"So," he thought, "it may not be then that Brother Benjamin, dear Brother Benjamin, was right. I may only seem to be somewhere inside my body because I cannot feel as I normally would. It is because of what they did, something which has to do with the sticks." He found it hard to understand how a stick could strike him without touching him. But he had heard of such things from the sailors on the cattle vessel. Indeed, he had pressed them relentlessly, for hours at a time, for stories, and facts, and customs. He wanted to understand the world, and worlds. He may have been illiterate, and a soil worker, and from only a *festung* village, but he was not stupid. He had an active mind, a very active mind. The sailors had enjoyed telling him things, relishing his eagerness, his wonder, his astonishment, and most of what they told him, interestingly, was even true. One of the things they did not think to tell him much about was the ship. They took it so much for granted. To him, of course, it was the greatest wonder of all.

He saw the throne gate opened, and watched her ascend to the high seats. The guards, within, parted from her. They took up positions at opposite ends of the closed box. Sometimes citizens took the opportunity of the games to press petitions into the hands of the civic authorities. Too, more than one governor, and emperor, even, it was said, had been assassinated at the games, though usually in the court outside the wall, or in the tunnel leading between the box and the street.

He looked at her taking her seat beside her mother, the high judge, who herself sat on the right hand of the mayor. He did not think he was a dolt. Too, he was no barbarian, surely. He was a peasant, from a *festung* village, from one of the Imperial worlds. It even had a provincial capital, Venitzia.

He had watched her cross the sand. Women did not move the same way as men. There was a difference in their walk. Too, it seemed that, for this world, the movement of that woman, despite the severity of her demeanor, and such, was unusually female. Many of the other females on this world, as far as he had been able to determine, attempted to conceal their natural gait. But she had not seemed as concerned to conceal it. There had been a murmur of female protest from the stands, but she had thrown her head back and continued to the throne gate. She was of the *honestore* class. It was supposed by him that she had mixed feelings toward her sexuality. He wondered if there were worlds in which women did not have such feelings, worlds on which they accepted their sexuality and rejoiced in it. He had heard that there were worlds on which some women were slaves. They were dressed for the pleasure of men. Their gait, and their garmentures, left them, and others, in no doubt as to their womanhood.

The trumpets blared again, and he saw side gates open, and the dwarfs, better than a score of them, some with high, flat measuring boards, taller than themselves, others with hooks and baskets, rushing out. There was music then, and cheering. Following the dwarfs, from under the stands, came several large, bulky, rather soft fellows, naked, save for an apron. Each carried a *barang*, thick, wide, single-bladed, some three feet in length, with a handle about a foot in length, so that it might be gripped with both hands. It would probably weigh about twelve pounds.

The peasant moved a little inside the ropes. They were tight. The wiry strands dug deeply into his arms. He could feel them now. His sensibility had much returned, long before it might have have been expected to have done so. He supposed that he might have remained kneeling, if only for Brother Benjamin, or as a matter of honor, or, say, of disdain for those of the town. But he did not care to be bound. Did they not trust him to remain there quietly, waiting for his *koos* to take flight, innocent, and unharmed? After all, they could not hurt a *koos*. That was part of the teaching. But perhaps he had no *koos*. What if he did not have a *koos*? What then? What if he were himself, and not a *koos*, really, which he had never seen, nor had anyone else, as far as he knew? Perhaps they were right not to trust him. But what could he do, run about, now, bound, while the dwarfs pursued him, with their hooks, to pull him down, while the crowd laughed, while the large, soft creatures waited the signal to rush up, wielding the weighty *barangs*? He moved inside the ropes. They were heavy, they were tight. The guards, and the officer of the court, it seemed, had decided to take no chances with him. Such ropes would contain a garn pig, even if it were agitated, doubtless even a sacrificial bull, snowy white, with gilded horns, hung with beads, the sort still said to be slain by *honestore* officiants on the Telnarian worlds.

The attendants had now entered through the dead gate, with their rakes. They stood about the edges of the arena.

There were several spectacles slated for the afternoon. The current portion of the entertainments was intended to be little more than preliminary. Indeed, there were still some empty seats in the stands, though the arena was a small one, suitable for a small provincial town. Not everyone came on time. Some did not mind missing the first events.

Some of the men kneeling about him, unbound, began to pray aloud, usually to Floon and Karch, but sometimes to the intercessors, as well. He detected no prayers to Saint Giadini, but that was doubtless because Giadini had been an emanationist, a schizmatic. Who would dare to pray to such a one, at such a time?

Various events were scheduled for the balance of the afternoon, songs and dances, footraces and competitions, beast fights, hunter-and-beast fights, gladiatorial combats, acrobats, rope dancers, brief dramas, mythological enactments, and such, and the program was calculated to last until twilight. The arena was lit only by the sun. Had something been scheduled for the evening, it would have been localized in a relatively small area, and illuminated by torches. On this world, certain forms of energy were now quite scarce, and tended to be reserved for the use of the empire, and its licensees. On the other hand, there was the light of the local star, or sun, and the winds, and the tides, such things, and certain reliable, renewable resources, precious things, such as wood and grass. Worlds made what adjustments they could, and, beyond the sky, reassuring them, in all its solidity and eternal strength, lay the empire.

He pressed against the ropes.

They could hold a garn pig, a sacrificial bull.

He saw the mayor rise up, before her chair.

She, like the judge beside her, was dressed in the concealing, sacklike, mannish garb affected by so many of the women he had seen in the town. Such garmenture was quite dissimilar to the white *corton* clingabout of the judge's daughter. To be sure, the judge's daughter was not the only woman so clad in the stands. Too, he could see some colored garments, here and there, in particular, yellow and red. Some of the women even wore necklaces, or bracelets. The female prisoner who had been used in the testing of him, when it had been determined that he was not a "true man," had been put in a necklace, and then, forced to stand straight before him, her shoulders back, weeping, had had her garments pulled down about her hips. The optical device had clearly registered his response. The evidence had been incontrovertible.

The mayor lifted her hands to the crowd.

There was another blare of trumpets.

Many of the men about him began to sing a hymn to Floon.

He did not sing the hymn, as he was not of the adherents of Floon.

Behind her chair and to the left, as he was facing it, was a small altar. Doubtless a tiny fire had been kindled there. The mayor took a packet from an attendant and shook the contents of this packet onto the flame, which spurted up, and then a long wreath of yellow smoke rose upward toward the sky. He smelled incense. It was an old custom, a Telnarian custom, much like the libations, an offering to the old gods, though few, he thought, now believed in them.

The strains of the hymn to Floon, though they seemed small, and weak, were clearly audible in the arena.

He watched the smoke drift away.

The mayor now stood again before her chair.

She lifted up, in her right hand, a scarf, or handkerchief. "Let the games begin," she called, using a formula whose origins were lost in antiquity.

She released the scarf, or handkerchief, the cloth she held, that used for the signal, and it fluttered to her feet.

There was then another blast on the trumpets, but their sound, renewed, was almost drowned in the anticipatory cry of the crowd.

It leaned forward, eagerly.

The large, soft men then whipped their aprons away from their loins and turned before the crowd, their arms uplifted, the *barangs* brandished. The crowd applauded. They were "true men," as understood on this world. When they turned about, again, to those on the sand, he, the peasant, could scarcely believe his eyes, though his vision was extraordinarily keen. He blinked. He shook his head. Could it be some trick of the glare, from the white sand? No, there was no mistake. It was as his senses had told him, and his mind, for an instant, had refused to believe. Then he turned his head to the side, sick, he who had lived with blood and butchery in the village, and threw up in the sand. They had been improved, smoothed. Doubtless many had requested this smoothing, that, emasculated, in this way most effectively devirilized, the mental techniques not always sufficient, they might prove more pleasing, more acceptable, to the women of this world. Many had doubtless requested this improvement, not only as a route to moral excellence, but perhaps, too, in their own best interests, economic and political.

"You need not have been here," the officer of the court, the daughter of the judge, had told him, rather angrily, he had thought, but moments before, on the sand. Surely it had been true. The judge had made that clear to him. She had been prepared to be merciful. Too, there were quotas of soil workers to be obtained, somehow, given the flight from the land in the vicinity of the town, largely a consequence of the newly imposed imperial taxations on provinicial worlds. Binding, too, was imminent, as the judge, the mayor and other officials knew. But he was dangerous. He was masculine. He was the sort of man women feared. He might have been simply executed. Certainly the guards had him within their power. There were the stun sticks, and other weapons, more dangerous, which could burn through bodies like a gas torch through paper. On the other hand, the judge was subject herself to various pressures, in particular, from the township, it, itself, reacting to imperial prescriptions. Soil workers were needed desperately. Too, the binding was imminent. Accordingly, she was inclined to be merciful, sparing him. Let him be remanded to one of the town farms, that as his sentence, and before the sentence had expired the binding would be safely in effect. He would then be bound there, for his life, to the soil. But the judge could see only too clearly that he was large and strong, unusually so. Too, she knew that he was dangerous. Too, she could sense, a part of his dangerousness, to her uneasiness, a powerful masculinity in him, a masculinity like that of an animal, a masculinity as rude, as simple, as primitive, as natural as rain and sunlight. This masculinity was not unique with him, of course, though we may conjecture, from certain events which followed, that it was unusually powerful with him. It was, on the whole, a masculinity of the sort which was not uncommon among the males of the illiterate peasantry. It had not been diminished by devirilizing teachings, by an emasculative education, by a thousand subtle negative reinforcements. The isolation of the peasantry, and their grueling labors in the field, gave them little opportunity or time for subjection to certain devices of pathological civilizations. Too, it was not obvious that the devirilization of the peasantry was in the best interests of the educated, urbanized communities. The peasants were needed, and, educated, subjected to programs of emasculative conditioning, devirilized, they would not breed as well. In a sense, however, we might note, as it is relevant to our narrative, his masculinity transcended that of the simple peasantry. It had within it certain other elements, as well, the intellect, authoritativeness and uncompromising aggressiveness of a different, more complex form of life. This form of life would be that of the warrior. The occurrence of these elements in one who was obviously a mere peasant was surely surprising, and seemingly inexplicable.

"I have here the results of the pupil-dilation test," had said the judge, lifting papers from before her. He could not see what was on the desk before her, because of the construction of the desk, also its height. "In the test situation your pupils clearly dilated."

The peasant had not said anything. He was not sure what the judge even meant.

"Do you understand what I am saying?" she asked.

"No," he said.

"You looked upon a woman, and saw her as a female," explained the judge.

"She was a female," said the peasant, puzzled.

"You are not on some barbarous world," she said. "You are in a civilized community, with civilized laws. Here men and women are the same, persons. But you looked upon the woman as though she were different from a man."

"Yes," admitted the peasant.

"These are dangerously antisocial tendencies," she said.

The peasant was silent.

"It is a violation of moral and civil law."

"Not on the world from which I come," he said. He could remember that he, and some of the other young men of the village, Gathron, and others, had often gone to watch the girls wading in the small lake, netting fish. Sometimes he regretted having had to kill Gathron, but he had had no choice. Gathron had first struck him. At such times they would have their skirts hitched up. They knew the boys were watching, and were very vivacious, very pretty. Later he had caught Lia in her own net and drawn her back among the rushes, half on the grass, half in the mud. She was the first woman he had had. How she had kicked and laughed, and kissed at him, helpless in the strands. He had then, amazed at the incomparable pleasures he had experienced, turned her over to Gathron, who was his friend. She had not much cared for this, but then she was helpless in the net and could not resist. Gathron, too, was muchly pleased. They had released her later. Then he and Gathron, arm in arm, had returned to the village. He had that day first truly understood how incomparably valuable women were and how natural and understandable it was that on certain worlds, as he had heard, they could be bought and sold. Surely they would look lovely chained at one's feet, owned, yours to do with as you pleased. He had wondered what Lia would have brought on a slave block, and certain others, whom he now, as of this afternoon, saw in an entirely new way, such as Tessa and Pig. Gathron had been a good friend, for years. They had often worked together, and hunted together. Then one day Gathron had struck him. He had then killed Gathron. This incident, doubtless, had its effect on him later. He was unwilling, it seems, to let anyone close to him again, not truly close. Gathron had been close. It was dangerous to do so. It was not that he did not laugh and drink, you understand, and was not hearty, and a good fellow, at the feasting tables. It was only that he was unwilling, it seems, to let anyone close to him again, truly close. It is possible that he may have wanted friends, and love, but that he was afraid of such things. We do not know. On the other hand, he may have been above such things, beyond them. Too, such things, clearly, ill consorted with the medallion and chain. For whatever reason, or reasons, he would keep much to himself, in the deepest sense, muchly guarding inner secrets and feelings. Few could tell what he thought. Few could claim to know him, even his women. It was dangerous, he doubtless felt, to let anyone close to him. Gathron had been close. Too, such things ill consorted with the obligations of the medallion and chain. But then, again, who knows? Perhaps he was not so weak, was not susceptible to such matters, matters such as might concern lesser men. Or perhaps such things were simply of no interest or importance to him. But rather than speculate on such matters, which is commonly fruitless, let us continue with our narrative. Our concern here, as we have said, is merely to tell what happened.

"If you did not want me to see her as a female, why did you have her bared before me?" he asked.

The judge regarded him, with fury.

"And put a necklace on her, first?" he asked.

"Be silent," said the judge.

"Was she not a person?" he asked, not quite sure what that word meant. It did not seem to mean anything, or, perhaps it meant "nothing," intentionally. He did not know.

The guards had lifted their stun sticks.

"She is a prisoner, a low woman," said the judge.

"Not a person?"

"No," said the judge. "It is all right for such as she to be looked upon with dilated pupils."

"Then what is wrong with my having done so?" he asked.

The judge reddened, angrily. She replaced the papers on the desk.

He had then looked across the court to the officer of the court, in her dark blue robe. She was young, and quite attractive. He wondered what she might look like, if she had been put in a necklace and bared before him, as had been the low woman. Probably not much different, he thought. But then he supposed that such thoughts were improper. She was of the *honestore* class, perhaps even a minor patrician, surely no more on this provincial world. But she was a woman, surely. So what difference would it make? She, looking at him at this time, gasped, and then stiffened. Then, in fury, blushing hotly, she had looked away. The judge had not noticed this exchange. It may have been one reason, of course, why the officer of the court, on the day of the games, had worn the clingabout, and come even across the sand, to appear before him, and have him bound. Perhaps she had wanted, thusly, to taunt him, and then to show him her power, that men would obey her.

"The court," had said the judge, which, under the circumstances, was herself, "is prepared to be merciful."

He had been offered the choice between life, or life of a sort, and death. Certainly his crime had been heinous, theft of a *darin* and a silver bracelet, and, in the course of its commission, the cold-blooded, unprovoked murder of two upright citizens, one a respectable local businessman. There had been nine witnesses for the prosecution, five close associates of the businessman, who had witnessed the murders, and four policemen, who had apprehended the thief with the bracelet and *darin* in his possession. The defendant had not deigned to respond to the charges. Similarly, he had not chosen to explain how the *darin* and bracelet had come into his possession. It had been established, from the records of the customs search, that he had not had them with him at the time of his disembarkation.

"You have been found guilty," announced the judge. "Do you wish to beg the court for mercy?"

"No," he had said.

That response had not pleased the judge.

But then the field quotas were to be filled.

"The court, nonetheless," had then said the judge, not pleasantly, "in her generosity, and mercy, despite the gravity of these crimes, and the seemingly unregenerate resoluteness of their perpetrator, is inclined to be lenient. After all, the moral welfare, the reformation, of a culprit, even one so undeserving of consideration, is a gratuitous but legitimate object of a justice with vision. Though a lifetime of penitence and labor is surely no sufficient compensation for the wrongs heretofore wrought, that some repayment to society is better than naught is a consideration which need not be neglected."

The peasant understood very little of this.

"There is a way," she said, "to reduce the energy, the power, the unacceptable aggressiveness, of your nature."

He did not understand.

"Too, you understand, of course, that genes such as yours,

so antisocial, so dangerous, are not to be propagated,'' she continued.

He did not know what genes were.

It was soon made clear to him however that he had two choices, one was to be smoothed, and then remanded for an indefinite time to the public fields, and the other was to be remanded to the arena. The judge, who hated and feared men such as he, in her pettiness and vanity, had thought it amusing to give him this choice, in order that it might be he, himself, who would choose his own unmanning. He would thus do her will, humiliating and demeaning himself, by his own will.

But he had said, ''No.''

There had been gasps, whispers, consternation in the small court.

The judge herself had been for the moment struck speechless.

''You leave me no choice,'' she had then said, in inexplicable fury. He was remanded to the arena, into the keeping of its master.

''Take him away,'' she had said.

Then the officer of the court, her daughter, in her dark blue robe, had stepped forth, with the guards, and he had been conducted from the courtroom.

There was a cry from the crowd as the *barang*, gripped in both hands by one of the large, soft men, after some vicious, tentative feints, held back at the last moment, at last struck loose the first head, it flying from the body. One of the waddling dwarfs, comically exaggerating his gait, to the amusement of the crowd, rushed after it, having apparently missed catching it in his basket. He seemed much chagrined. He leaped up and down, as though in frustration. He hurried to the head, putting his basket down beside it. He picked up the head by the hair and wagged his finger at it, as though scolding it. He pointed to the basket. Then he put it in his basket. The body had remained kneeling, as they will, for a time, if the blow is swift enough, and clean enough. The arterial blood, stimulated by the terror of the victim, a terror artifically increased by the feints, spurts to an unusual height. If you have seen this, you will understand what I mean, what it is like. It is ugly to watch. It is a little like a fountain. It spatters about. If one is near, it is easy to be soiled. Dwarfs, with their measuring boards, marked heights on the boards. Other dwarfs, with their hooks, the body then fallen heavily into the sand, rushed forward, striking into the body with the hooks, then drawing it across the sand, in a bloody furrow, toward the dead gate.

Another head then flew away, even farther than the first.

A cheer rang out.

There was betting here and there in the stands, on the height the blood would reach on the boards, on the distance to which the heads might fly, on whether or nor a head would be caught. To be sure, the large, soft men, it was rumored, could control such things, at least the distance and direction of the projectile, by varying the angle of the blow, by turning the blade a little, just at the last instant. It was rumored there was collusion sometimes, between them and gamblers, in the stands.

The hymn to Floon, as thin, as frail, as pathetic as it might seem, was audible in the arena.

There were, of course, far worse ways to die, at least with respect to torture, to pain, and such. There was the rack, and the pincers, the tongs, the knives, the pegs, the skewers, the knotted cords, the stake, the burning irons, such things, such devices, and many others, which would only later, much later, be brought to scrupulous perfection by the adherents of Floon himself, usually for application to other adherents of Floon, heretics, schizmatics and such. Indeed, such devices, on the whole, were seldom employed by the empire, which commonly tended to exercise a certain restraint, or taste, in such matters, given pause, seemingly, by scruples which would seldom deter the later adherents of Floon, but then the adherents of Floon would always possess, it would seem to the peasant, a certain petty, low-class vindictiveness, that of the little person into whose hands suddenly comes power. The most common device of the empire was the rack. It might even appear in courtrooms, where it was commonly employed in the extraction of testimony from slaves. Indeed, a slave was normally fastened on the rack before his testimony was taken, it being assumed that the veridicality of his testimony might be best assured by such a device. But there were the beasts, however. The empire was fond of them. Doubtless because of the spectacle they could provide. These beasts, ravenous, tortured by hunger, released into the arena, driven wild by the scent of blood and flesh, would lose little time in attacking, and feeding.

No, decapitation was presumably, as such things went, a merciful death. It was quick. The head presumably did not think for very long, if at all, after it was cut off, and in the sand, or a basket. The stroke of the barang *was doubtless superior to certain other deaths, such as those of the lingering, wasting diseases, or the cannibalistic diseases, in which parts of one's body seemed to devour other parts.*

Another head flew from a body. There was another cheer.

Most of the adherents of Floon in the arena were citizens of the empire, at least nominally. That was quite possibly why the barang *was being used. It was thought to constitute an honorable death, one acceptable for citizens. Too, of course, beasts were expensive, and had to be kept fed between shows. Some entrepreneurs transported them from world to world, in menageries, for various games, various spectacles. Sometimes they escaped on shipboard. But such rentals did not come cheap. Floon had not been a citizen of the empire. He had died in an electric chair, or in what we have spoken of as an electric chair, in order to use a term which seems sufficiently apropriate. The actual device is a sort of burning rack. The crime, if one may think of it along those lines, of the adherents of Floon in the arena, was the refusal to place a sprig of laurel on the altar of the* genius *of the empire, on the porch of the town hall. This small ceremony was usually performed by civic officials, on behalf of the town. It would commonly take place on the birthday of the current emperor, and on certain holidays, the day set aside, for example, to commemorate the acceptance into the empire of the federation of the thousand suns. Once a year each citizen was expected to come to the altar and place his sprig of laurel, or a pinch of incense, or a flower, even one plucked from the wayside, on the altar. This ceremony, as innocent as it seemed to most, at least those who were not adherents of Floon, was repudiated, at that time, by many of the adherents of Floon. The townships tended to ignore this matter, but it was of some concern to the empire. Sporadically an edict would emanate from the Telnarian worlds pertaining to the enforcement of this ceremony, it normally being construed as a touchstone for allegiance to the empire. When the empire felt most threatened it seemed it took such things most seriously. It feared, you see, as absurd as these fears might be, given the solidity and eternality of the empire, internal dissension, and even sedition. There may have been troubles at these times, too, troubles not clearly understood by most in the empire, about the borders, and their security. Sometimes one even heard absurd rumors to the effect that they might have been breached, that there might actually be barbarians, dangerous barbarians, within the territory of the empire itself. It was not always too clear just what might be occurring, so much might take place, so far away. Information, you see, was not always available, or reliable. Things then, you see, were not really so different from now. When it became clear that imperial officials were quite serious about this matter, most townships would collect a small number of the adherents of Floon, and request that they perform the ceremony. Many of them, sensibly enough, or so it seemed to the civic authorities, would do so, but some, of course, would not. This placed the civic authorities in the unpleasant situation of either enforcing or ignoring imperial edicts. Accordingly, from time to time, on many of the worlds, a number of the adherents of Floon, usually a small number, were fined, or placed in prison, or even consigned to the arena. The great majority, who tended to be quiet, law-abiding, productive citizens, were usually left unmolested, and might even be left free to visit their fellow adherents in prison.*

There was another swift stroke of a *barang*, and another head was lifted from its body, and this time one of the dwarfs caught it in his basket.

There was a cheer from the crowd.

Money exchanged hands in the crowd.

"You need not have been here," she had said, earlier, having come across the sand, before the crowds, to point to him, to order him bound. "The choice was yours," she had said. It was true. He had chosen death to castration. The judge had not understood that, or, perhaps, given her fury, she had understood it only too well. He wondered if her daughter understood. He thought perhaps she did. He thought, perhaps, within her, there was a woman.

One of the dwarfs, giggling, leaped up and down in the sand before him, waving his hook. It was an iron object, much like a poker, or grating tool, for stirring fires. It was an iron staff, with a point at one end, the hook some five inches below the point. It could thus stab as well as insert itself in objects, flesh, or canvas, to drag them about. He jabbed the object at the peasant, who drew his head back, angrily. This was doubtless to increase his heartbeat, to increase the circulation. The peasant suspected he might be saved for late in the sport.

He saw one of the large, soft men drag the head of one of the adherents of Floon up by the hair, placing it so. For the best effect the target must be kneeling upright, its head up, this directing the arterial flow upward. Otherwise it is less impressive. It is then also, of course, difficult to measure.

He looked up to the stands. The daughter of the judge was reading. Her mother, the judge, and the mayor were conversing. This portion of the sport, he gathered, was not of great interest to them. Perhaps they even found it, the slaughter of the simple, innocent, inoffensive adherents of Floon, sheeplike, tasteless, or boring, perhaps even oppressive. But he suspected that they might later return their attention to the sand. Perhaps even the officer of the court might at that time put aside her book, to watch. He wondered if they would bet on various matters.

One of the large, soft men suddenly ran at him with the *barang* raised and then ran past him.

The crowd laughed.

He saw the dwarfs, by means of the hooks, dragging bodies toward the dead gate.

One was kicking and rolling a head across the sand. Another bent down, seized up the head, and ran. The first pursued him, crying out angrily.

It was amusing.

But there were to be better things later, a beast fight, for a beast had been rented, and a gladiatorial combat, such things.

One of the adherents of Floon seemingly found his legs and leaped up, running about the arena.

There was booing.

"No, brother," cried out his fellows to him. "Come, kneel with us! The *koos* cannot die! Do not betray Karch! Karch will protect you! Trust in Floon!"

The fugitive ran to the wall of the arena. He tried to climb it, in one place, and then another, but there was no place to gain purchase. There was no need even for the poles and nets jutting from the height of the barrier above, to prevent certain agile beasts from leaping into the stands. Sometimes that had happened, on various worlds, and dozens of men and women had been clawed, several of whom died afterwards, sooner or later, of wounds and infection. The dwarfs, with their hooks, now swarmed about the distraught fugitive. He tried to defend himself, fending the blows, but, in the end, surrounded, struck again and again, he fell to the sand. Then he was dragged still living through the sand by several hooks, back before the privileged seats. He was thrust up, dying, and held in place by the points of the dwarfs' tools. Other dwarfs scolded him. A blow of a *barang* flung the head a dozen yards across the sand.

"Courage, brothers!" called out one of the adherents of Floon to his fellows.

Then they began again to sing, the hymn to Floon. The strains now seemed plaintive, desperate.

One of the large, soft men approached him. He swung the *barang* toward him, but stopped it, only inches from his throat, and then turned away, and laughed.

The heart of the peasant pounded.

"Hold your head up," squealed a dwarf.

One of the adherents of Floon turned to him. "Declare for Floon!"

The peasant, wrapped in his bonds, regarded him, angrily.

"Declare for Floon!" said the man.

But then his head was lopped away.

Others continued to sing.

The peasant did not care to die in this fashion.

Another of the large, soft men rushed at him, and, again, the blow was not struck.

He then turned away, as had the other, laughing, lifting his *barang* to the stands.

He did not see the peasant rise to his feet.

Perhaps not many did, for two dwarfs were rolling about in the sand, fighting for the last head which had fallen, each wanting to put it in his own basket. First one would take it, and then another, putting it in one basket or the other, then the other stealing it, when the back of the other was turned. Such skits had been rehearsed. Even the mayor, the judge, the officer of the court, looked on, with amusement.

"Kneel, kneel!" squealed a dwarf, running up to him, brandishing his hook.

Then the dwarf was dead, its neck broken by the kick.

Still, few, if any, took much notice of this.

The peasant then put his strength against the ropes which bound him.

The dwarf's hook lay in the sand.

The peasant regarded it.

It lay in the sand, half-covered.

It had two points, the end point, which might be used for jabbing, and the point on the hook. It had no blade.

A point might have been used, if there was time, to wedge into a rope. That might divide the rope but it was not likely, in a short time, that it would serve to break or cut it. If there had been a great deal of time, if he had been bound in a cell, left there, not observed, the hook might have been useful. A man of lesser strength, or a woman, might have been able to use it so, if there were time.

Again the peasant pressed outward against the ropes. Again he tried to pull his wrists apart. Skin was torn from his wrists.

He put his strength against the ropes.

He looked upon the hook, in fury, in frustration.

He was bound. He could not well manipulate it. It had no blade. There was little time.

Again he bent against the ropes. He was, as I have indicated, unusually strong. All the sources agree on that point. Too, it seems to be borne out by what occurred. The ropes, to him, to a man of such strength, might have been more in the nature of tenuous cords to a lesser man. We do not know. The guards, the officer of the court, however, I believe, may be excused for not having understood this. After all, how, before the fact, could one have been expected to know such a thing?

And would the ropes not have held a garn pig, a sacrificial bull? Then why not a mere man? But the peasant was not a mere man, or, perhaps better, he was not an ordinary man.

But perhaps the ropes would hold him. After all, they had doubtless been chosen with care, and were supposedly such as might easily hold any man, even one of unusual strength, even one who was enormous, one who was extraordinarily powerful.

Again the peasant strained against the ropes.

Yes, the ropes would hold him.

A dwarf came up to him, and watched him, curiously. Only that dwarf, at that time, seemed aware of the struggle which was taking place quite publicly, but yet unnoticed, at that point on the arena sand. The crowd, you understand, and the other dwarfs, and even the large, soft men, were more attentive to the antics of the performers before the privileged seats, those two with the baskets. The dwarf did not approach him closely. He was well aware of his fellow, lying in the sand, his eyes bulged, the head clearly wrong.

The peasant again, half bent over, strained against the ropes.

Wet now were the ropes with blood.

A strand, stressed beyond the weight it had been woven to withstand, broke.

Their mistake may have been to bind the peasant, as I have suggested. He might have held himself, perhaps being strong enough to do so, in the bonds of his own will, for the stroke of the *barang*. But, you see, the matter had not been left up to him. Presumably it had been taken out of his hands. The peasant had not cared for that. Decisions in such matters he would have preferred to make for himself. They did not trust him. The officer of the court had made that clear. And why should they have trusted him? They did not know him. In any event, we will never know what might have happened, had they not seen fit to bind him.

And so he stood, struggling, in the sand, not much noticed in those first moments.

The ropes might have held a garn pig, even one who smelled blood, and saw the ax; it is hard to say; the ropes might have held a sacrificial bull, a white bull, one fully grown, with gilded horns, hung with beads, perhaps even one who had suddenly sensed the meaning of the blade, and the large golden bowl. That is possible. We do not know.

The peasant strained against the ropes.

He felt, rising within him, the rage, the rage that one can sense coming.

He felt the ropes cut into his arms.

Blood ran beneath the ropes.

Those ropes might, perhaps, have held a garn pig, or a sacrificial bull. Again, one does not know.

Another strand broke.

The dwarf, watching, its short, squat body spattered with blood, from the business of the day, was not aware of this. To be sure, it would not have been easy to notice.

On the forehead of the peasant veins stood forth, like tortured ropes.

His eyes seemed more those of a beast than a man.

This was a consequence of the rage, you see. Even armies would come to fear his moods.

The dwarf, who was an intelligent creature, knew itself safe. It knew it, at least, in some intellectual sense. After all, the peasant was bound. The dwarf, nonetheless, was uneasy, even alarmed. He stepped back a few feet.

Another strand broke.

Then another.

Then the dwarf, even though he was farther away, detected a tiny brush of fiber, like a whisper of hair, standing out from the body of the rope, not bound in with it, not smooth with it. The dwarf was not certain if this were an imperfection in the rope, or if it were something which had occurred just recently, given the efforts of the peasant, standing ankle-deep in the white sand, it discolored here and there, from his struggles, with blood.

It was not easy to hear strands break, not with the singing of the adherents of Floon.

There was applause from the stands as the two dwarfs finished their skit, and bowed, and withdrew, carrying one basket between them, each with a grasp on one of the handles.

It was at that moment that the dwarf who had been watching the peasant had cried out and fled toward the stands, pointing backward. The crowd rose to its feet. The large, soft men turned about.

The peasant stood on the white sand, bloody, destroyed ropes at his feet.

· · · CHAPTER 8 · · ·

The large, soft men had scarcely time to raise their *barangs* for the peasant, the hook seized up from the sand, that which had been dropped by the dwarf, he with the bulged eyes and awry head, who had felt the peasant's heel on the side of his neck, rushed upon them, like one of the large, maddened cats, the hook slashing. There were screams, some shrill, from the large, soft men, for the nature of their voice, its timber and such, had much do to with the age at which they had been smoothed. Such a hook, gouging, flashing toward the neck, can tear open the neck, under the ear; it can rip out the jugular vein, pouring its dull, ruby flow down the chest, not bright like arterial blood; it can strike into the optical cavity, as through a fruit, then breaking the front of the skull free from the skin; it can tear through the mouth, and the side of the face, dragging out the lower jaw and tongue. The large, soft men fled back, huddling together. The hook struck at them again and again. Vertebrae were pulled out, drawn back through the skin. Ribs like curved white sticks suddenly burst into view. There were many screams in the crowd. Dwarfs flung away their measuring boards, their baskets, some even their hooks, which might have been well to retain. Such objects were scattered about, mostly in the sand before the privileged seats. One of the large, soft men, turned about, white-faced, he who had first rushed at the peasant, and then passed by him laughing, grunted, the point above the hook piercing his belly. Another, he who had secondly threatened the peasant, feinting at him, then drawing away laughing, uncertainly, quaveringly, raised his *barang* over his head, it held with two hands. "Go away," he shrilled to the peasant. He did strike down at the peasant, but the blow was blocked with the hook. There was a ring of metal. Before he could draw back for another blow the hook had lashed out, catching him in the side. The peasant held him in place with his foot, the man turned sideways, looking wildly to the side, to free the hook. He then tore the hook free, shattering ribs, drawing it forth, with it lung and tissue. The tool then with which such havoc had been wrought left the peasant's hand. Like a knife it flew through the air. Another large, soft fellow cried out, he who had made the first killing in the arena, and looked down, disbelievingly, at the handle of the tool, coming somehow out of his belly. "He is disarmed!" cried the leader of the large, soft men, he who had led them forth into the arena. But he was not disarmed for he now held a *barang* in each hand. The large, soft men screamed and pushed back against the wall of the arena, below the privileged seats. Again the *barang* struck, and again. "He is mad!" cried men in the stands, who did not understand the nature of the peasant, that there could be such a man, or the nature of the rage. "Run, run!" cried the leader of the large, soft men, and they fled. The attendants, those who had been inconspicuously by the dead gate, with their rakes, had, shortly after seeing the peasant free, withdrawn through the dead gate, and locked it behind them. They were taking no chances that he might take advantage of that aperture as a route of escape. Some of the dwarfs had fled through it, too, with them. Others had not managed to reach it in time, and were still in the arena. One of the large, soft men pulled at the handle of the gate leading up the stairs to the throne box. But it had been locked behind the officer of the court, of course, when she and the guards had reentered it. Two of the large, soft men were cut down there, reaching through it, trying to pull loose the chains which secured it. Another man ran to the place where the adherent of Floon had run earlier, who had been caught on the hooks of the dwarfs and returned, dragged back alive on the hooks, to the area of the privileged seats. He leaped up, his *barang* discarded, tearing, scratching, at the wall. Then he turned about, and sank down there, his eyes bulging with terror, and it was there that the peasant, who had slowly, implacably pursued him, treading through the sand, slew him. The peasant looked about. Somewhere in the arena, surely, was he who had cried out when he thought the peasant disarmed, he who had cried out, too, for the large, soft men to run, even though many still retained their *barangs*, he who had led them into the arena, who had first lifted his *barang* to the mayor and those in the throne box. Aware suddenly of a tiny sound in the sand behind him the peasant spun about, his barang flashing. A dwarf then fell, as he drove the *barang*, lifted over his head, to the sand, the two parts one to each side of the blade. He then saw the leader of the large, soft men, rather toward the center of the arena. The large, soft man backed away from him. It seemed he could hardly hold his *barang*. The peasant trod toward him, wading through the sand. But then, rather behind him, he heard a terrible growl, and turned about. Entering the arena, released into it, coming through the beast gate, was a tawny *vi-cat*, not a large one, such as might have graced arenas in larger towns or on more affluent worlds, but an animal nonetheless dangerous, quite dangerous. To be sure, its pelt was shabby, and in places hairless and scabrous. Its ribs were prominent. Its head moved from side to side. "Kill, kill," cried the crowd. There are many forms of "beast fight." Commonly beasts fight each other, natural enemies placed together, dogs and vi-cats, serpents and *ras* apes, prairie cats and horned *yamas*, such things, or else territorial males of the same species, the eight-footed *teino*, hoofed *sorits*, *arn* bears and such; but sometimes the fight is between a beast and rational creatures;

in such a case, it is sometimes called a hunt. But there were no hunters in the arena now. It was only the beast. Its head lifted, and moved, and its nostrils distended, seeing the air. Perhaps some incense hung still in the air, and that might have puzzled it. The peasant, however, could no longer smell the incense. The beast had green eyes. The pupils were now like tiny black points. The peasant stood very still. Men were not the natural prey of the prairie cat, as he knew from the village, and that was doubtless true of the vi-cat, as well. Such creatures, unless alarmed, angered or approached too closely, would seldom attack outside their familiar prey range, that which they had learned in their youth, unless they were old or weak, or sick. To be sure, this animal may have been trained. But probably not. The hunters might not, under such circumstances, have cared to enter the arena with it. In the wild the vi-cat might have turned away, particularly if it thought itself undetected, if eye contact had not been made, but here, in the confines of this tiny arena, it was already dangerously close. The peasant was reasonably certain that he was within the critical charging distance. The beast took a quick step forward. The peasant put one of the *barangs* in the sand. He gripped the handle of the other with both hands. He would need the strength of two hands, of his whole body, and that might not be enough. If the beast were with its hunters they could distract it, as was the technique, teasing it to one side or the other, weakening it with their darts, probably poisoned, then tangling it in their nets, and, when it was fallen, bled, sickened, scarcely able to move, finishing it with spears. No, the peasant was sure the beast was not trained. Indeed, it was doubtless a cheap beast, as such animals go, one only purchased for the slaughter. Still it was seven or eight feet in length, and might weigh some four to five hundred pounds. It seemed alert and agile. It had certainly not yet been drugged, as reputedly was often the case before such matches, when professional hunters were involved, those who had bought the animal in the first place, or had been hired by the owner, and not individuals condemned to the arena, criminals, and such. For what may have seemed a long time to those in the stands, but was perhaps no more than a few seconds, the beast and the peasant regarded one another. Then suddenly the beast charged and there was a cry of astonishment, and a thrill of horror, from the stands, for the peasant stood over the animal, and its skull had been split by the *barang*, back to the neck. Once before, when he was only fourteen, the peasant had slain a prairie cat in that fashion, though then he had had an ax. The men of the village had been hunting it for it had been taking cattle, and he, because of his youth, in spite of his size and strength, even at such an age, had been ordered to hang back, that he might be safe in the rear, but the beast had circled about. The men, hearing the noise, and rushing back, fearing the worst, had been amazed. Muchly had he been congratulated, and clapped about the shoulders. How proud and happy he had been, that night. He had given the skin to Gathron when he returned to the village, for Gathron was his best friend.

The peasant spun about, and the large, soft man, he who had first led such into the arena, who had been approaching him surreptitiously from the rear, lowered his *barang* and fled back.

A cry from the stands alerted the peasant to the entry of two hunters into the arena. They were dressed in the spotted pelts of the *hanis* leopard, indigenous to the savannahs of Lysis, sixth world of the massive star, Safa Major, or Greater Safa. Each carried a net in the left hand, a spear in the right. In their belts were the bleeding, weakening darts, like tiny, finned javelins. They spread out, one to each side of the peasant. They shook the nets, they cried out at him. Did they think he was a vi-cat, to be so distracted? He was a man, not some confused beast. He turned suddenly and charged the man to his right. One blow of the *barang* snapped his spear, the second took his arm off at the shoulder; the peasant spun about to cut the flung net in twain. With his left hand he caught the thrust spear and jerked the hunter toward him, he too tardy to release the weapon, onto the point of the *barang*. Behind him the other hunter, thrusting his shoulder into the sand, to stanch the blood, was screaming. He withdrew the *barang* from the body of the hunter who had been to his left. The man was still alive. The peasant then threw the severed cape of his own net over him, and, reaching through the toils of the net, withdrew five of the tiny javelinlike darts from his belt. He saw the tips were coated, as he had supposed. He then, one after the other, thrust them into his body. He then went to stand by the carcass of the vi-cat. He looked up to the stands.

But there was silence only for a moment, and then it was broken by a blast of trumpets, and from the gate of fighters strode forth two gladiators, those who would have been matched against one another later in the afternoon. These men were matched, trained fighters. It was not likely that one would die, for it was a small town, and an unimportant arena. It is expensive to train and maintain a gladiator. Most matches would not be to the death. The crowd, on the whole, wanted only a good fight. A defeated gladiator, lifting his hand for mercy to the crowd, was commonly spared. The crowd would have its favorites. Some gladiators were famed on a dozen worlds. Some matches, extensively advertised, lavishly promoted, were anticipated for months. Some gladiators were rich men, with villas on various worlds. It was rumored there were tricks, too, the pellet which, bitten, could leak a scarlet fluid from the mouth, the animal bladder filled with pig blood, concealed under the tunic, such things. The discovery of such scandals commonly provoked exclamations of moral outrage among the aficionados of the sport. There had been changes in the rules on various worlds. On many worlds it was now required by law to drag dead bodies, and supposedly dead bodies, from the arena with hooks, such as were carried by the dwarfs. Such regulations, and their enforcements by dedicated officialdoms, had tended to restore integrity to the sport. But, all things considered, the sport was undeniably a terrible and dangerous one, in which many men died. One did not rise to the top by victories without kills. Most gladiators were associated with various schools, in which they were trained, and which, in effect, they usually represented. Gladiators were commonly condemned criminals or slaves, seizing on the opportunity to fight for freedom and wealth, but it was not at all unknown for free men, particularly of the *humiliori*, to enter the profession, which constituted one of the few opportunities for fame and affluence open to them. In later times many soil workers would see in the arena a way to escape the bindings. Others, perhaps for similar reasons, would enter the clergy, it offering freedom from the bindings and a possible route, if one were sufficiently ambitious and clever, to a wealth and prestige, a power, that might rival that of princes. Too, of course, there were occasional scions of the *honestori* themselves, jaded youth, destitute prodigals, and such, who would see in the arena an opportunity for thrills and fame, and even recouped fortunes. There are many forms of arena fighters, or gladiators, with different varieties of weapons, and different techniques, but such matters are not now germane to our account. The two who had just entered the arena were not of the *superbii*, the gladiatorial elite, nor were they exotics. They were, on the other hand, efficient, trained men, quite competent in their craft. Each had had more than a dozen kills. Interestingly, too, and I mention it because it is relevant to our account, they were both of the same school. This was unusual, for usually individuals, and teams, from different schools were matched against one another. Rivalries existed, of course, among the various schools, and some rivalries were famous ones. These two gladiators, from the same school, or house, in such an arena, at such a time, were expected to deliver little more than an exhibition of arms.

Music began to play.

The two gladiators, entered now into the arena, as had been the vi-cat, and the hunters, marched slowly about the small circuit of the arena. They were brawny men, in bootlike sandals. They wore helmets. They paused now and then, to lift their arms to the crowd, the sheathed left arm with its buckler, the right with the small, wicked blade. Some of the dwarfs, still in the arena, leaped up and down, cheering, as they passed.

Applause came from the stands.

"Kill him, kill him!" screamed the crowd.

One of the gladiators turned to look at him, the one to his right, along the circuit of the wall.

"Kill him," chanted the crowd.

But there was no immediate concern about such matters on the part of the gladiators.

They made the circuit, they kept the formalities, the tradition.

The large, soft men had been despicable, better for little more than putting terrorized, sheeplike criminals, such as the adherents of Floon, to the sword. The vi-cat had not been a prime specimen.

It may have been diseased. The hunters were poor stuff, and better for little more than torturing and murdering a confused animal.

They, on the other hand, were of a different breed altogether. They were men of the sword, trained arena fighters, gladiators, in their way, steady, practical, experienced, competent professional killers.

No longer need the crude, dangerous peasant be feared.

The situation was now in hand.

The two gladiators, we may suppose, were inordinately pleased at being relieved of the obligation to confront one another, even in what would presumably be little more than an exhibition. The crowd, even a provincial one, expects a show. And it is hard to control the blade, given the smoothness of the metal, the speed of the exchanges, the deflections of the parrying.

The killing of a young, untrained peasant, a stranger, one raised in some primitive village, one from some half-barbarous world somewhere, would be no more than a moment's recreation for them, unless they chose to draw out the matter, lest the crowd be displeased, the sport too soon concluded. We may suppose that both had resolved to give the death stroke cleanly, however, as one might in butchering an animal, not torturing some hated foe, at whose hands one might have received an insult.

They did not bear him ill will, no more than the butcher bears the pig or calf ill will.

The two gladiators now made their way, one from each side, along the circuit of the wall, toward the privileged seats, within which was the throne box.

The match, if there were to have been one, would commonly follow the salute.

But there was to be no match, unless one might speak so of what was projected, a judicial butchery.

"Wait!" called the peasant.

The gladiators, before the throne box, turned to face him. It was hard to see their faces, because of the helmets.

"Look!" cried a woman in the stands.

Then there was applause.

"He has come to join in the salute!" called another woman.

The peasant solemnly made his way forward.

"He wishes to show his respect to the empire, before he dies," called another woman from the stands.

There was applause.

Such a gesture, its nobleness, its magnanimity, in one who might expect in a moment to die, had not been expected by the crowd, not in such a rude youth.

There was more applause.

Tears were in the eyes of more than one woman in the stands.

As he came forward, *barang* in hand, he noted the throne box, and, within it, the mayor, the judge, and the officer of the court, the daughter of the judge. All were on their feet.

"Do not salute the empire!" cried one of the kneeling adherents of Floon.

"Repudiate the empire!" called another.

"The empire is evil!" cried another.

"Down with the empire!" called another.

"Be silent!" cried men and women in the crowd.

"It is only the *koos* which is important, and Floon!" cried another.

"Repent!" cried another.

"Declare for Floon!" begged another. "The forgiveness of Floon is available to all who request it."

"Be good!" called another. "Kneel to die. Floon will protect you!"

"Kneel, and commend your *koos* to the keeping of Floon!" wept another.

"Silence, silence!" chided the crowd.

But then the peasant had strode through the kneeling adherents of Floon, of which there were some fifteen to twenty left, not seeming to hear them.

"Hail!" called the two gladiators, facing the throne box, their swords lifted, "hail to the emperor, to the empire, to all governors and prefects, to all who serve her!"

The mayor, in her civic capacity, on behalf of the power of galaxies, lifted her small gloved hand, acknowledging the salute.

The second portion of the salute was an ancient one, one which dated back to the early days of the empire, indeed, shortly after the dissolution of the republic, a consequence of the third civil war, and its replacement with the imperial dignity, and the efficiency of the imperial administration. I shall use a familiar salute, in order to achieve familiarity, for which I have striven in many cases in this narrative, but it is one which will convey, in my view quite adequately, the drift of the salute actually given in that small arena on Terennia, which was, indeed, the same salute which would have been given on a Telnarian world itself.

"We who are about to die salute you."

Such sentiments, you see, in such circumstances, tend to appear.

A cry of horror rose from the crowd for the peasant, instead of joining in this salute, had smote away the head, and part of the upper body, of the gladiator to his left, these things tumbling, the head in the helmet, to the wall. There had been two reasons for selecting the gladiator on the left for the stroke. First, the peasant was right-handed and thus could bring his blade into play most quickly from that position, and, secondly, and doubtless more important, the gladiator to his right was right-handed, which meant that his sword hand was on the side away from the peasant. By the time the gladiator on his right had turned about, then, the peasant had returned to what, within his limitations, might be characterized as a defensive position. At this point the peasant began to back toward the center of the arena.

He had few doubts about the likely talents of a professional arena fighter, and did not care to meet him there, blade to blade, before the privileged seats.

The gladiator who had been to the peasant's right had spun about instantly, his buckler forward, his blade back. This was a matter of honed reflexes. He had reacted before he understood what had happened. It was almost like the movement away from a suddenly appearing snake, the sudden drawing of the hand away from fire, reacting, not thinking, only thinking later.

The second gladiator did not immediately pursue him. He stood there now, breathing heavily.

It was only then that he began to understand what had happened. It was only then that he was stunned.

The blow, in itself, as it had taken part of the upper body

away, and not merely the head, might have given anyone pause. It was a prodigious one, something that might have been done not by a man, but by the lateral stroke of some motorized killing blade, the sort functioning as appendages on gas chariots, used to keep order on certain of the farther worlds.

Too, quite possibly, he was dismayed.

He looked at the parts of the body, and the head, still muchly in the helmet.

"Cortus!" he suddenly wept. "Cortus!"

He knelt in the sand.

It seemed he was shaken with disbelief.

The two, you see, were of the same school, or house, and therein shared the same table. Often they had fought, on one world or another, side by side, sometimes back to back. There is often a bond, a sort of brotherhood of the blade, you see, among the men of the schools, or houses, though, to be sure, it is occasionally expected that they will, if matched, kill one another.

"Kill him, kill him!" cried the crowd.

The gladiator rose slowly to his feet. He regarded the peasant. The peasant, now, had retreated to the vicinity of the slain vi-cat, where it lay, and the hunters.

"Kill him!" screamed the crowd.

How outraged it was.

The mayor, the judge and the officer of the court, the judge's daughter, were on their feet, as was the crowd.

The judge's daughter seemed to waver. She had her right hand at her breast.

"Wait for me," said the gladiator, his voice carrying across the sand. "Do not make me chase you about the arena."

The peasant stood still, as though ready, bravely, to comply with the fighter's request. Or perhaps he was too afraid to run. But, as now seems certain, he was where he was, and stayed where he was, because it was in accord with his plan.

"Kill him!" screamed the crowd.

The gladiator approached him slowly, treading the sand with care, each step a sure one.

"Stand where you are," he called. "I will make it quick."

"Kneel to die!" cried one of the adherents of Floon.

"Do not resist!" counseled another.

"Floon will protect you," said another.

"You have done enough!" said another.

"Declare now for Floon, while there is still time," called another.

Then the gladiator, half-stripped, his loins bound in heavy black leather, in the black, metal-crested helmet, with the darkly sheathed arm, and the black buckler, and the short blade, double-edged, was through the kneeling adherents of Floon, past them, and the strewn bodies about them.

The leader of the large, soft men was to one side. He had now come away somewhat from the wall. He held his *barang*. Some dwarfs were near the dead gate. It was still bolted shut, from the inside.

"Stand where you are," said the gladiator, the face muchly in shadow, beneath the jutting brim of the helmet.

The peasant suddenly reached down and seized up the one net, that which was still whole, which had been brought into the arena by the first hunter, he on whom he had first rushed, he whose spear had been snapped by the *barang*, he whose arm had been smote away by the *barang*'s second stroke.

The net, like a swirling dark cloud, spun out, over, enveloping the gladiator. It was large enough, and strong enough to contain a vi-cat. Like a shadow of cords it had descended and the gladiator cursed and struck at it. The peasant, the *barang* thrust into the sand when he had reached for the net, darted to the net and slung it more about the struggling foe, and then, by means of it, pulled him from his feet, and dragged him back to the *barang*. The gladiator, cursing, was slashing at the cords. The blade thrust up, through the toils. Cords sprang from the blade. The gladiator twisted in the net, thrusting at him. The peasant leaped back, drawing his hand back from the *barang*. Nearby lay the vi-cat, and the two hunters, the one with the splintered spear near him. The gladiator struggled to his feet. He was between the peasant and the *barang*, the hilt of which, and some third of the blade, was visible. The gladiator was trying to lift the toils from about himself. He slipped, he went to one knee, then he raised himself again to his feet. More cords leapt from the blade. The peasant tried to reach for the *barang*. The small blade thrust out, cutting flesh, and the peasant felt blood hot on his arm. He looked about to see the large, soft man hurrying toward him, his *barang* raised. The crowd was screaming. The peasant eluded a second thrust. He seized the toils of the net and flung the encumbered foe again from his feet. He seized up the butt end of the splintered, snapped spear and raised it over his head. He thrust it down, driving it through the body of the gladiator, and even a foot into the sand, such being the power of this man. He then reached down and drew the *barang* from the sand. The large, soft man stopped short, lowering his *barang*. The large, soft man was shaking his head. Then he threw his *barang* down, and fled. The peasant followed him, of course. The large, soft man could no longer run when his right foot had been cut off, at the ankle. The peasant then, blood running down his own arm, thrust him, tottering and screaming before him, toward the center of the arena, where the vi-cat lay, and the two hunters, and the second gladiator, in the shreds of a net, dead, nailed in place, pinned to the sand by the shaft of a broken spear. The tracks of the large, soft man were unusual, the furrowed, dragging tracks of the left foot, and, to the right, the bright spots in the sand where the stump of the right leg had poked down, like a bloody post. The large, soft man, standing unsteadily, partly bent over, in the center of the arena, amidst the carnage there, lifted his hand piteously to the crowd. But the peasant brought the *barang* up smoothly between his legs, and he sank then to his knees. Glistening, smooth gut spilled from the body to the sand. The large, soft man reached down, trying to hold it in his body. Then the peasant positioned the large, soft man's head, dragging it up, by the hair. Then he smote it away. He then went to the head and carried it back, by the hair, to the vicinity of the body. He then lifted it up, holding it over his head. His own arm was bloody, and the blood of the severed head, too, ran down his arm. He turned about, slowly, the head lifted, exhibiting it to the stands. He then faced the privileged seats, the head held up. He then threw the head down, into the sand.

The stands were silent.

The peasant stood there, bloody. He was then aware of how hot the sun seemed. In such small arenas, on provincial worlds, you see, they could seldom afford the huge, silken canopies, billowing in the breeze like sails, flown on their poles and ropes over the sand. He also became aware, more than before, of the blood on his arm. He put his finger in it, and tasted it. He looked down at the body of the large, soft man, at his feet. It had been spattered with blood before, like that of the other large, soft men, and that of the dwarfs, from the adherents of Floon. Now, of course, it had its own blood on it, and about it, as well. The peasant looked to the body of the gladiator, some two feet of the shaft of the broken spear rising from his chest, the rest through his body, and in the sand. He, and his fellow, had been trained, and experienced. He himself was only an ignorant peasant youth, though one who was very large, and very strong, and one with an unusually active mind. He had little doubt that the man, the gladiator, and his fellow, as well, could have killed him, either one of them, in a different sort of fight. The adherents of Floon, those still living, some fifteen to twenty perhaps, were still kneeling in the sand. There were many bodies about. Some of the dwarfs, those who had escaped with the attendants through the dead gate, could now be seen in the stands. Others were still, some with their hooks, near the dead gate itself. He supposed it could be opened now. He looked to one side where the hunter lay whose spear he had snapped, whose arm had been smote away. The shoulder, without its arm, had been thrust in the sand, and it had been there when the man had died. The sand about it was drenched, and would require much raking. The body, about the shoulder, and the sand near it, were crawling with ants. He could see them, here and there, some making their way across the sand, toward that body, others returning, doubtless to a nest, bearing tiny burdens. It was then that the peasant realized how it was that such creatures were in such a place, as there would have seemed little promise in such an environment otherwise. But then who knew what tiny particles, of one nature or another, might lie in the sand, and under its surface, after it had been raked, between the tiny grains. Doubtless there were tunnels, and passages there, little communities, tiny civilizations, unsuspected perhaps even by the attendants. The other hunter, he whom he had drawn onto the *barang*, had been alive when he had removed the tiny, javelinlike darts from his belt, the bleeding, weakening darts, which were to have been used on the vi-cat, and thrust five of them, one after another, into his body. But he was not alive now. The skin was bloated, and run with purple streaks. The darts had been poisoned, as the peasant had suspected, from the coating at the tips. That poison was obvious in the relatively hairless body of the hunter, but it would have been concealed beneath the pelt of the vi-cat. To be sure, its presence might have been suspected from certain alterations in the beast's responsiveness. Too, it could be detected, after a few minutes, in the eyes. But this was hard to see from the stands and the eyes were usually closed by the hunters, after they had lifted their spears. In this way respect was shown for the beast.

The sun seemed unusually hot.

He was aware that the throne gate had opened, and several guards were emerging through that opening. There were perhaps ten of them. Each, drawn, carried a stun stick.

The peasant looked once more at the vi-cat.

It was a poor beast, but it seemed then to the peasant to be very beautiful.

The men were approaching across the sand.

They stopped, some yards away, taking care to remain well outside his reach.

He regarded them.

He thrust the *barang* down into the sand.

He saw them level their weapons.

He wiped his forehead with his right forearm.

He spit into the sand.

He then lifted his head and faced them.

The emitted, charged fields, invisible, but suddenly disturbing the air, like waves of heat, distorting perception, enveloped him. He felt ringed with shock, gripped in the fist of some paralyzing current. He was unable to move. His body would not obey him. He sank down, into the sand.

In a moment or two he heard someone ask, ''Is he still alive?''

Another person, crouching over him, put his hand to the side of his throat. "Yes," said that person, the one by him.

He opened his eyes.

He saw another stun stick leveled at him, but a hand pressed it down.

"No," said someone.

Then the peasant, though he could scarcely move, became aware that it was not guards, the police only, who were about him. There were others, too, and even more than the guards, or police, indeed, several more. These others seemed rude, brawny men, and they wore a different livery.

"Put him in a blanket," said a voice. "Bring him to the house."

· · · CHAPTER 9 · · ·

"Thank you, my dear," said Pulendius, the delicate, shallow, transparent bowl cupped in the palm of his right hand.

He watched the fluid, ruby *kana*, in its narrow stream, no wider than a nail, descend to the bottom of the bowl, puddle there, and then rise up, smoothly, slowly, ascending the side of the bowl.

"Enough," he said.

Not raising her head she ceased pouring and backed away.

"The captain is putting her up," said Pulendius to the table.

" 'Putting her up'?" said a young man, somewhat askance, across from Pulendius, somewhat down the table.

"Tomorrow evening," said Pulendius.

"Of course," said the young man, in some confusion.

"I think it is generous of him," said Pulendius. He lifted his glass to the captain, who sat at the head of the table, who acknowledged this salute with a dismissive smile.

"The line is," said a man.

"We are paying enough for the voyage," grumbled a fellow a few seats to the left of Pulendius.

"I do not understand," said a young, dark-haired woman, sitting almost directly across from Pulendius.

"As the prize, for the winner in the contest tomorrow evening," said Pulendius.

"She is a human being," said the young woman, angrily.

"They make the best prizes," said Pulendius.

"Where humans are involved," qualified a man.

"Of course," said Pulendius, graciously accepting this qualification.

Behind Pulendius, who was an extremely rich man, and a lord of estates on Terennia, there stood two bodyguards, both huge men, half-naked, clad in leather, their arms folded across their chests. Their eyes roved about, to the door of the lounge, to other tables, to the table before them. These two men, his bodyguards, were both from his own school, on Terennia. They were gladiators, you see. This was not unusual. It was common, in spite of occasional prohibitions to the contrary, for rich men to retain such. Pulendius had originally been of the *humiliori*, and of the family of a shoemaker, but, an intelligent and ambitious man, he had managed to become rich, in the beginning in a variety of trading ventures, mostly having to do with the import and sale of *sorbian* leather. Putatively in recognition of numerous philanthropies, the repair of walls and aqueducts, the construction of bridges at dangerous crossings, and such, and in virtue of various donations and services, lavished on various towns in which he held important franchises from the governor, he had been raised to the *honestore* class. It was rumored that this was in particular a consequence of his friendship with the civil governor of Terennia, with whom he frequently exchanged invitations. It was hinted, too, that certain gifts, or antecedent renumerations, one might say, had preceded the honor of being raised to the *honestori*, not that he was not universally recognized as being fully deserving of that honor. Soon Pulendius had begun to accumulate land. His lands now constituted, in effect, a small state on the planet. Some four thousand *coloni* tilled his fields.

He had a private army, as had many rich men in the empire, his consisting of some five hundred men. It was his men, of course, who had intervened in the arena, at the time with which the reader has hitherto been acquainted, when the peasant had fallen to the sand, stunned by the weapons of the guards, or police. It should be mentioned that the men of Pulendius, even those with him at that time and at that place, several times outnumbered the entire local police force. Such men had things much their own way with local communities and local administrations. They had little to fear except from imperial troops. One might think of such men, I suppose, if the analogies are not too misleading, as local "strong men," or "bosses," perhaps something along those lines. There were, throughout the empire, thousands of such. Indeed, some imperial officials feared them, and thought they were becoming too powerful. More than once there had been confrontations between such private forces and imperial troops themselves. To be sure, Pulendius tended to be a quite law-abiding individual, but then, one supposes, most are who can pretty much have the laws arranged, drafted, interpreted, and applied or not applied, at one's convenience. It might be mentioned that the tax farmers did not "farm" the estates of Pulendius, which may, indeed, be one reason that many *coloni* flocked to his lands. The reasons for this seeming oversight on the part of the tax farmers may not be altogether clear, but, whatever they were, they were not unique with Pulendius. The estates of such men, for whatever reason, were often exempt from such attentions. Indeed, it would be a bold collector, one supposes, who would attempt, without an army behind him, to enforce a collection on such a man. More than one, on more than one world, had disappeared. It was not clear what had become of them. Some, it was rumored, had been used as training objects in the various schools. Others, it seems, had been simply hung or thrown into eel ponds. It might also be mentioned, in this brief biographical account, that Pulendius, from his earliest youth, had been a zealot of the arena. He maintained one of the finest gladiatorial schools on Terennia. His men had fought on many worlds, sometimes even on the Telnarian worlds themselves.

"Disgusting," said the young, dark-haired woman.

One of the two bodyguards behind Pulendius, his arms folded, looked upon the young, dark-haired woman. She was well sheathed in a sleek, off-the-shoulder gown of white *lim*, quite other than would have been appropriate on Terennia, but then they were not now on Terennia. She was quite fairly complexioned. Her bosom, which was very white, was not without its suggestions of delights. Indeed, her figure, though one must hazard something of an estimate at this juncture, gave the suggestion that it would prove of interest, perhaps considerably so. To be sure, she was perhaps somewhat slender for the tastes of some, but there was, on the whole, little doubt that almost any man, even one of quite moderate virility, and she had known few of even that level, would have have found it both stimulating and inviting. She had dared to wear both a closely fitting golden necklace, and clipped-on golden earrings. A golden bracelet on her left wrist completed this ensemble. The entire effect, of course, was elegant, and tasteful, or so I would think, but, on her own world, which was that of Terennia, it would have counted as being outrageously scandalous. How many men on her own world, looking upon her, as she was, even fully clothed, not even stripped to the hips, or ankles, could have looked upon her with normal pupils. Surely only the "truest of men," as her world defined such feeble creatures, could have looked upon her without dilated pupils. How cruel of her to torment men so, how insensitive, and unfeeling of her, to subject them to such temptation. How difficult it would be for any male to be a "true man" in the presence of such a creature, even tastefully and fully clothed as she was. Her hair, as I have mentioned was dark, even quite dark, and one might, had it not been bound so closely behind her head, had it been loosened, undone, have remarked its gloss and length. It might also be remarked that this woman was extremely intelligent, as this feature, in the view of some, adds considerably to the appeal of a woman. She was also, incidentally, of high birth, or reasonably high birth, and of secure social station. Had she not been, she might not have had the courage to appear at the table so scandalously attired, not that her attire was much different from that of other human females at the table. It was only that she was from Terennia. It was, however, substantially a cruise ship, a pleasure ship, and so a certain latitude in such matters seemed acceptable. The ship, the *Alaria*, which occasionally served on imperial business, the transport of ambassadors, and such, was registered on Tranos. She was now far out of the normal pleasure and commercial lanes. There was a reason for that. The bodyguard behind, and to the right, of Pulendius continued to regard the young, dark-haired woman. She was not entirely unaware of this, one supposes. More than once she had glanced toward him, and then, angrily, away. Even though such men were bodyguards, it seemed they might at least have worn pleasure robes, like the other men. But then, perhaps, those would have impeded motion had some emergency arisen. But was it necessary for them to be there, she wondered, such large, brutish fellows, half-naked, girded in leather? She glanced again at the one guard, to Pulendius's right. Then she looked down, flushing. When she looked up his eyes were elsewhere, looking about the room. Perhaps he had been regarding her, merely as he had others. But she did not think so. Perhaps she had been mistaken about his attention. But she did not think so. What an arrogant, bold fellow. Perhaps she should call his audacity to the attention of his employer. But what if it were her imagination? Would it not then be suggested that it had been she, and not he, who had been looking, who had been concerned with such matters? Would that not be embarrassing? Would she not then seem the fool? An additional note might be offered here. There was a tiny bit of trim, purple trim, on the off-the-shoulder gown, it bordering the sheath, both at the bosom and the ankles, and, also, down the left side. From one point of view this bit of trim, like a small, folded ribbon, was quite inconspicuous, though it doubtless had some subtle role to play in accenting the gown. From another point of view, however, for those who could read such things, it indicated that she was, however far removed, of the blood itself. That color, you see, was legally worn only by those who were not merely of the *honestori* but of the patricians. She was, you see, a minor patrician. Indeed, her nobility, as tenuous, as small, as remote as it was, had much to do with her presence on the ship. Had she not been of that class, she would not have been where she was. She glanced again at the bodyguard to the right of Pulendius. Yes! He was looking at her! She looked to the captain of the ship, who glanced at her, not understanding her agitation. Then she dabbed at the dessert on her plate. She was frustrated on her own world. In her, like tides, like movements of the earth itself, there was a very strong sexuality, muchly starved, of course, given the world on which she lived. And so she sat at the table, uncomfortably, looking down at her plate. The bodyguard looked once more upon her. She flushed, seemingly aware of his glance. Was this, we wonder, from the unease, the heat or discomfort, of her own thoughts, or was it because she suspected that she might once more be the subject of his regard? Perhaps it was both. This minor patrician, who so subtly with the tiny purple stripe, that little bit of trim, called attention to her claims and her birth, far above, always, that of a lout like Pulendius, who could buy his way into the *honestori*, was, as we have suggested, white-skinned, dark-haired and well figured. She was young, beautiful and intelligent. She was, all in all, the sort of woman who, on many worlds, would have brought an excellent price. Too, on many worlds, the bit of trim on the gown, the purple, would not have saved her. On barbarian worlds, it would doubt- less have improved her price, and perhaps so, too, in certain other markets, sometimes secret markets, on many of the allied and imperial worlds. Such women were prized, as they made excellent slaves.

"What do you think of her?" asked Pulendius.

The bodyguard, he on the right of Pulendius, to whom the question was apparently addressed, seemed startled.

Pulendius nodded toward the girl who had been serving the table, she who had, but a moment ago, poured *kana* into the delicate, transparent, shallow bowl.

The bodyguard turned his attention to the servant, as we shall, for the moment, think of her.

She did not lift her eyes, or turn about, to look at him.

Rather she was attentively, even as though she might not know herself now the center of the group's attention, pouring *kana* for a ship's officer, he to the captain's left.

She was brownish-skinned, and exceedingly exquisite.

The darkness of her skin was set off by the sleeveless, sparkling white serving gown.

She was shorter than the young dark-haired woman from Terennia, whose height was closer to the average for a human female, she of patrician blood, however far removed, but both would have been tiny compared to, say, the bodyguard, he behind Pulendius, and to his right, he who had been addressed.

"Of course," said Pulendius, "you will see her differently when she is on her knees, in a *keb*, cuffed, and chained to the stake."

"Yes, milord," said the guard.

"I do not understand," said the young woman from Terennia, irritably.

Pulendius smiled, and looked to the captain.

The young woman serving *kana* went to the next officer, who declined the refilling of the delicate bowl.

She then went to the next, and, receiving permission, granted by an almost imperceptible movement of the head, accompanied by the proffering of the bowl, head down, poured.

A comment or two may be in order with respect to the appearance of the current subject of the group's attention. The white gown was her single garment. Too, surprisingly, she was barefoot, her tiny feet almost lost in the luxurious nap of the carpeting of the lounge. On her left ankle, ringing it closely, was a golden band, an anklet of sorts, it would seem. One might take this, it would seem, as her single piece of jewelry.

"Perhaps I may be permitted to explain," said the captain, a bit apologetically, responding to the encouragement of Pulendius, addressing himself to the young dark-haired woman a few seats down the table, to his left.

"Please, do," she said, icily.

"Do you truly not understand?" asked one of the ship's officers.

The young dark-haired woman did not take her eyes from the captain.

There were several differences between the two women with whom we are now concerned, in background, in education, in appearance, and such. But one difference, one which is of importance here, is that the pourer of *kana* had learned to obey men, instantly, and unquestioningly, which the young dark-haired woman, she from Terennia, had not yet learned to do.

"This is not Terennia," began the captain.

"Yes?" said the young woman, coolly.

"The line," said the captain, "here and there, acquires such, on certain worlds, for various purposes."

" 'Acquires'?" said the young dark-haired woman.

" 'Buys,' " suggested Pulendius.

She looked at him, with horror.

"On Terennia," said the captain, "it is my understanding that certain forms of relationship have been declared illegal."

"Forms of relationship?" she asked.

"Yes," said the captain.

"Matters having to do with property, certain forms of ownership," volunteered Pulendius, helpfully.

"Certain things on Terennia may be owned, but not others," said the captain.

"Land, articles of clothing, such things may be owned, yes," said the young woman.

"One thinks nothing of the ownership of animals on Terennia," said Pulendius.

"Certainly," said the young woman. "One has a full and perfect right to own such."

"But only certain sorts of animals," said the captain.

"No," she said. "One can own any sort of animal."

"Any sort of animal?" asked the captain, smiling.

"Yes," she said.

"Are you sure of that?" asked Pulendius.

"Certainly," she said.

"Are we not all animals?" asked the captain.

"No," she said.

"Biology, as I understand it, begs to differ with you," said Pulendius.

"Very well," she said. "Certain forms of animals may be owned. Certain other forms of animals may not be owned."

"Surely you recognize the arbitrariness, if not the literal inconsistency, of that view," said one of the ship's officers.

She looked at him, with fury.

"You must know," said the captain, "that slavery is quite legal in the empire."

"Yes," she said.

"And on many of the barbarous worlds, as well?"

"Yes," she said.

"And on many of the most civilized, as well," he said.

"Yes," she said, reddening.

"On many worlds there is a body of property law, of considerable complexity and antiquity, pertinent to the matter," said the captain.

"You are aware of the social utility of the institution, surely," said one of the ship's officers, "with respect to such matters as social stability, conservation of resources, population control, and such."

"On Terennia," she said, icily, "slavery is illegal."

"That is true," said the captain. "On Terennia slavery is illegal."

"On Terennia," said a young officer in the imperial navy, one on leave, it seemed, who had not spoken before, some seats down, near Pulendius, to the captain's right, "it is the men who are slaves."

"None are slaves on Terennia," she said, angrily.

Then she flushed, aware, perhaps, of the gaze of the bodyguard upon her, he behind Pulendius, to his right.

"Let us not spoil the evening by dispute on such matters," said the captain.

"You know the law, of course," said Pulendius, "that if one should bring his property to another world within the empire, it does not cease to remain his property."

"Of course I am familiar with the law," she said, angrily. "The principle is a simple one, familiar from basic jurisprudence."

"Let us suppose," said Pulendius, "to take a purely hypothetical example, that you yourself were to become a slave, and were then to be brought to Terennia."

"Yes?" she said, her body stiffening.

"You would then still be a slave, would you not?" he asked.

"Yes," she said.

" 'Yes'?" he asked.

"Yes," she said, rigid on her chair, "I would still be a slave."

"Within the full rights of your master?" he asked.

"Yes," she said, angrily.

"And are you so sure," he asked, "that there are no slaves on Terennia?"

"Certainly," she said.

"Are you so sure?" he asked.

"Perhaps in the wilderness," she said, "in rural areas, away from the cities."

"And perhaps in the schools?" he asked.

"Perhaps," she said, reddening. She looked at the body-guards, particularly at he who was behind Pulendius, to his right, and then looked away, quickly. Such men, she suspected, though she was only from Terennia, might not only relish and desire women, but might actually need them, even crave them, desperately, like food and drink, quite otherwise than the "true men" with whom she was, to her boredom, more than familiar.

"Who knows?" said Pulendius, pleasantly, wiping his mouth with his napkin.

"Are you telling me that this girl is a slave?" asked the young, dark-haired woman, indicating the pourer of *kana*.

"We have not said that," said the captain.

"*Kana*, milady?" asked the pourer of *kana*, pausing at the side of the young, dark-haired woman.

"No!" exclaimed the young, dark-haired woman, drawing back.

At a gesture from Pulendius the pourer of *kana* returned to her usual serving station, somewhat behind the captain, and to his left.

"Who owns her?" demanded the young woman.

"The line," said the captain, "at least until tomorrow evening."

"After the contest," said Pulendius.

"I do not believe she is a slave," said the young, dark-haired woman.

"Surely such matters need not be made obvious," said the captain.

"She is not a slave," said the young, dark-haired woman.

"This is not a barbarian ship," said the captain.

"Are you skeptical because she is not slave clad, and not collared?" asked Pulendius.

The young, dark-haired woman tossed her head, angrily.

"The collar is a lovely adornment, and it has its purposes, identificatory, mnemonic, and such," said Pulendius, "but it is bondage which makes the slave, not the collar. Too, how do you know she is not slave clad?"

The young, dark-haired woman looked down, in consternation. "Is she slave clad?" she asked.

The young dark-haired woman seemed agitated, enflamed.

"Yes," said Pulendius.

There was silence at the table.

"She is not a slave," whispered the young, dark-haired woman, desperately.

"*Kana*," said the captain, irritably, holding forth his delicate glass.

"Yes, milord," said the pourer, hurrying forward to replenish the beverage.

"Speak clearly," said the captain.

"Yes, Master," she said.

Then she raised her eyes to the young, dark-haired woman, and in that glance there was more than a hint of anger, of defiance, but then, swiftly, as though frightened, she put down her head and returned to her station.

Such women, you see, are not free, but owned. They may not always do what they please. They are subject to authority, to punishment.

Pulendius regarded the young, dark-haired woman, she from Terennia, she who was the minor patrician, considering her, and then his eyes rested, as though amused, on the golden necklace, about a half of an inch in height, with which she had so closely encircled her throat. Self-consciously she raised her fingers to her throat, and then, hastily, returned them to the glistening cloth of the table. The necklace reminded him of a slave collar, of the interwoven-chain variety. To be sure, it was not as sturdy, and it did not have a lock.

"Shall I send her away?" asked the captain, concerned. As the captain of a cruise ship he had not only the care of his vessel to consider, but his obligations to look after the comfort and pleasures of his passengers.

The young, dark-haired woman did not answer.

"More *kana*," said the young naval officer, he of the imperial navy, he of one of the imperial fleets, he on leave, it seemed. And so the pourer of *kana* remained present.

Pulendius, nursing his *kana*, moving it about in the delicate, shallow bowl, looked upon the young, dark-haired woman. Pulendius was still a strong man, but he had, in these past years, grown somewhat corpulent, doubtless from the rich food, the softness of his life, the luxuries. He looked at the young, dark-haired woman. She seemed to him a fine, vital, healthy young animal. He wondered what sort of slave she would make. The bodyguard, too, one of the gladiators, he who was behind and to the right of Pulendius, also regarded her. He, too, wondered what sort of slave she would make.

A junior officer approached the table. Shortly thereafter, the captain rose and, wiping his lips, and making excuses, took his leave from the table.

Pulendius, and the bodyguards, watched him leave. So, too, did the ship's first officer. The naval officer, too, he on leave, as it seemed, seemed to note the captain's departure.

"There seems an anklet of some sort on her ankle, a band of some sort," said the young, dark-haired woman, offhandedly.

"Why, yes," said Pulendius. "So there does."

"That is enough!" suddenly cried the young, dark-haired woman flinging down her napkin, and rising to her feet. The entire table regarded her.

She pointed to the bodyguard, he whose presence, if not regard, seems to have made her uneasy throughout the evening.

"He keeps looking at me!" she said, angrily.

"Ah, my dear, but who would not?" said Pulendius, sooth-ingly. "Or," he added, tactfully, "at our other charming com-panions, as well?"

This addition clearly met with the approval of the other women at the table, who, to be sure, for the most part were not at all unlikely recipients of just such attentions.

Reddening, the young, dark-haired woman once more took her seat.

"It is not as though you were in a *haik*, my dear," said one of the women. This remark was greeted with laughter. The young, dark-haired woman again reddened, and looked down. The *haik* was a dark, cumbrous garment which would cover a woman from head to toe. Through a narrow aperture in the garment, that aperture itself covered with black lace, or black gauze, a woman might peer out. It was sometimes worn by the women of certain desert worlds, who would kneel behind their men, who spoke with other men of the things of men. One did not always know if the wearers of the *haik* were free women, fully clad within the *haik*, or collared, naked slave girls, waiting for the guests to leave. How embarrassed the young, dark-haired woman was. How like a fool she felt!

"*Kana*, all about!" called Pulendius.

The pourer of *kana* hastened to fill the transparent, shallow bowls.

Even that of the young, dark-haired woman was filled. The pourer of *kana* did not meet her eyes, but then she did not meet the eyes of the other guests, either.

"What is the nature of the contest of the morrow's evening?" inquired one of the men at the table of Pulendius.

Pulendius grinned at the first officer, still at the table. "It is something of a surprise," he said.

"Has it to do with the prisoner, who was brought on board at Tinos?" asked the young naval officer, sitting somewhat to the left of Pulendius.

He himself, it might be mentioned, came aboard from the shuttle, from Tinos station. Tinos, as the reader may have sus-pected, given an earlier remark, was far outside the normal lanes of imperial shipping, let alone those of a cruise ship. It may be of interest to note, for what it is worth, if anything, that communication with Tinos station had been lost some four days ago. Such disruptions, however, were not unprecedented. Indeed, communication between certain remote, diverse parts of the empire had tended, in the last few years, to become uncertain, even precarious. Certain imperial outposts had not been in contact for more than a dozen years.

"You must wait and see," chuckled Pulendius.

The young, dark-haired woman was looking at the gladiator, the bodyguard, to whom she had but shortly before, later to her embarrassment, called attention. He stood there, his mighty arms folded across his chest, at his station. He returned her gaze. He did so quite openly. There was nothing furtive, or even subtle, in it, as one might have expected, given her earlier outburst. Perhaps he felt himself secure in the favor of his lord, Pulendius. Or, perhaps it was merely that he did not fear the displeasure of any man. That is possible. That is sometimes the case with those who have lived at the edge of life, where it is coldest and brightest, where it is most close to death. And so he returned her gaze. But it seemed to her now that he did so not with the simple, candid forthrightness of his earlier regard, with its rather straightforward expression of keen interest, even of a strong man's lustful appraisiveness, but now with a subtle, almost imperceptible contempt. The mad thought crossed her mind that it would now be appropriate for her to be punished. Of course, as she understood now, she should not have risen up, and spoken out as she had. That had been a mistake. She had embarrassed herself. She felt a fool about that. But surely she had not been mistaken, not about his gaze, about its possible meaning, insofar as she could understand such things, or dared to understand them. And how he was looking on her now! Surely only a woman in a slave market should be looked upon in that fashion! And how dare he regard her, too, with that subtle contempt? Did he not know she was of the blood, of the original high families of Telnaria itself, that she was of the senatorial class, of the patricians, however far removed, that class from which the senate was to be taken, the senate, which must still, even after these eons of time, if only as a token of tradition, confirm the emperor?

But what could such a lout, he, or Pulendius, that parvenu, that upstart, or the other guard, know of such things? But he saw her only as a woman, and perhaps, worse, as a certain sort of woman, and one for which he now seemed to feel contempt. The thought crossed her mind of a woman, not herself, surely, who, stripped at his feet, in the shadow of his whip, would hasten to do whatever he might want. Indeed, what choice would such a woman, not herself, of course, have? The mad thought crossed her mind, instantly rejected, with confusion, that she would envy such a woman. She looked up, again, at him. How he looked at her! How angry she was! "I am not naked, on a chain, turning before you in a slave market," she thought. And then she thought how she might, in an obscure part of her, in the deepest and most secret part of her, beg to be such a woman, thrill to be such a woman. She looked down at her plate. She felt feelings she had never felt before, at least not in this fashion, not to this extremity, not to this degree. She felt warm, uncomfortably so, confused, vulnerable, weak, suddenly, embarrassingly, extremely feminine. She decided she hated him. Then she saw that Pulendius, amused, was regarding her.

It was at this point, to her relief, that the captain returned.

"Is anything wrong?" inquired the naval officer of the captain.

"No," said the captain. "It was nothing."

"You are just in time, Captain," said Pulendius, lifting his bowl. "I am preparing to offer a toast."

"Splendid," smiled the captain. He tapped the table once, next to the shallow bowl there, which had not been filled when the others had been filled, he then being absent, and the pourer of *kana* hurried forward, returning forthwith, almost unnoticed, so suitably unobstrusive she was, to her station.

"I offer this toast to our lovely fellow passenger," said Pulendius, lifting his bowl a little toward the young, dark-haired woman, who seemed startled.

"Certain charming, revealing anomalies in your behavior this evening, my dear," he said, "have not gone unnoticed by your friends and fellow passengers."

There was laughter about the table.

"What shall we say," he asked, "a certain nervousness, or

distractedness, an occasional jitteriness, perhaps even an outburst, perhaps even an occasional uncharacteristic tartness, quite
out of order?''

She flushed, angrily.

''And yes,'' he said, triumphantly, ''just such surprising, delightful, quite broadcast, changes in complexion.''

The portions of her body not covered by clothing, her face,
her throat, her arms, her shoulders, all such, suddenly blushed
red.

''Yes!'' he said.

There was laughter.

''With your permission,'' he said, ''I shall clarify matters for
those at the table who may not be aware of the cause of these
occasional, delightful manifestations.''

She regarded him, angrily.

''You do not mind?'' he asked.

''No,'' she said.

''It is no secret, I trust?''

''No,'' she said. ''Of course not!''

''Our lovely fellow passenger,'' said Pulendius, rising to his
feet, lifting his bowl, ''is betrothed, and, even now, on the
Alaria, an eager bride-to-be, she hastens to the arms of her
groom!''

''Yes, yes!'' said those about the table.

''No wonder then,'' said Pulendius, ''under such circumstances, that our charming fellow passenger, though an officer
of a Terennian court, seems sometimes as nervous, as frightened,
as confused, as a lass from a rural village, being led to the rope
ring.''

There was laughter.

The bodyguard found this a somewhat unlikely figure of
speech. He was himself, you see, from a rural village, a *festung*
village on another world, and he did not think many a rural lass
would be particularly nervous or frightened, or confused, being
led to the rope ring. Many would be the time they had tossed
in the hay or in the rushes, by the lake, before getting to the
rope ring. To be sure, he thought that certain urban daughters
might be nervous, or frightened, at such times, not that rope

rings were used in the urban communities, for such girls often knew little, particularly the middle-class girls, about sex, that by the intent of their parents, and the community. Some of them, on the bridal night itself, made discoveres which, for them, were quite startling. For those it might interest, as I have mentioned it, the ceremony of the rope ring was a rude form of marriage, in which the couple made their pledges, exchanging their oaths, within the circle of a rope, spread on the ground. At the end of the ceremony the lad would fasten one end of the rope about the lass's neck and then lead her thusly, publicly on his tether, about the village, and thence to his hut. It was understood in the village then that the lass was his. The ceremony was not regarded as completed until he had thrust her before him, the rope on her neck, he holding it, into the hut. The point of the display, leading her publicly about the village, is to give any who might object to the union a last opportunity to voice their protest. Various rude peoples in the empire had such ceremonies. This choice of a figure of speech may be excused on the part of Pulendius, I think, who was from an urban area, and on the whole, accordingly, unfamiliar with the ways of small, isolated rural communities. On the other hand, the figure of speech, with due respect for Pulendius, who was a highly intelligent man, may not have been as unlikely as the bodyguard surmised. It is, after all, one thing to roll with a fellow in the hay, or near the lake, and another to be thrust into his hut, before him, a rope on your neck, knowing that you are then his, and that the entire village accepts this and will enforce it. It is natural that a bride should be apprehensive. After all, who is the man, truly, to whom she is married? It is a bit like a slave, who has been purchased. She does not yet know the nature of her master, only that she is wholly his, in all ways.

"For what world are you bound?" asked Pulendius.

"Miton," she said. "It is within the first provincial quadrant," she added.

Miton was not one of the original Telnarian worlds.

The young woman, who was, of course, the officer of the court, she whom we have already met, had not been eager to volunteer the name of the world.

It was not one of the original Telnarian worlds, you see.

"And who is the lucky man?" asked Pulendius.

"Tuvo Ausonius," she said. She looked about. "Tuvo Ausonius," she repeated.

"Of course," said Pulendius.

"He is an executive in the finance division of the first provincial quadrant," she said.

"Wonderful," said Pulendius.

"He is of the blood," she said, suddenly, irritably.

"Wonderful," said Pulendius. To be sure, the young, dark-haired woman was, to the knowledge of most at the table, the only person there of such birth. We may make an exception, however, given our privileges in these matters, for the young naval officer. He, too, was of the blood, and, if it must be known, literally of the ancient senatorial class itself, and by direct line. To be sure, none knew this at the time. We might mention two points about this officer. First, it was quite unusual that one of his high birth, which was quite as high as that of the emperor himself, in these days, would have undertaken the arduous and often unrewarding tasks of military service. Second, although he was putatively on leave, he had boarded the *Alaria* when she was in orbit at Tinos, and Tinos, in its remoteness, might seem, if one paused to give the matter thought, an unlikely venue for an officer's leave. To be sure, perhaps he was returning from leave, and his home was on Tinos. It is not likely that he was stationed on Tinos because on Tinos there was no naval base, or large-scale base, only a small outpost.

"And can we hope," asked Pulendius, "that his blood is as high and noble as yours?"

"It is higher," she said.

This information was greeted with polite enthusiasm by the table.

That Tuvo Ausonius was of the blood was not at all a matter of indifference or accident, incidentally, to the projected union. Indeed, it was the essence of the entire matter.

If it must be known, many in the empire, particularly urbanites, often viewed with coolness, if not resentment, certain distinctions which seemed to them unnecessary, if not arbitrary,

*not significant distinctions, of course, like that between the hu-
miliori and the honestori, or that between the citizen and the
noncitizen, both of which were quite important for many reasons,
or even, really, that between themselves and the high aristocracy, which was still regarded with a certain awe, partly as a
matter of tradition, and partly, doubtless, because of its ancient,
historic contributions to the republic, and then the empire, but
between themselves and the minor aristocracy, the minor patricians, the members of local senatorial classes, and such, which
they often resented as being officious, pretentious and of dubious
value to anyone, including themselves. Such distinctions, as we
have suggested, were not like those between the humiliori and
the honestori, or, one supposes, even more importantly, between
the citizen and the noncitizen.*

"In any event," said Pulendius, chuckling, tactfully shifting
the group's attention to less sensitive matters, "now becomes
clear the meaning of many of your delightful manifestations this
evening, your unease, your unsettledness, your agitation, your
confusion, your charming changes of hue, all such are merely
consequences of your trepidation, yet eagerness, to fly to the
arms of your beloved."

There was laughter about the table.

The young, dark-haired woman looked down, angrily.

She had never seen Tuvo Ausonius, incidentally, nor he her,
except in transmitted pictorials. The union had been arranged
by the judge, her mother, in consultation with the mayor, also
a minor patrician, she of the Terennian town in which the small
arena was located, that in which certain events, hitherto recounted, as the reader may recall, had earlier taken place, the
name of which town we shall learn later, when it will be more
germane to our account. Although it is difficult to establish such
matters with exactness it was thought that Tuvo Ausonius was
related in the 103rd degree to the original Ausonii. The officer
of the court, the young, dark-haired woman, was related, it was
thought, to a comparable family, but only in the 105th degree.
The projected union, thusly, was much to the woman's advantage, though obviously less so to that of Tuvo Ausonius. In this
respect we can see that she was indeed fortunate, and that the

heart of her mother and that of the mayor had every right to rejoice over the success of their arrangements. Who knew, perhaps the mother, and even her friend, the mayor, were she not left behind, not repudiated, might as a consequence of this union eventually rise to heights on other worlds, heights higher than might be afforded on humble Terennia. If the officer of the court did not seem sufficiently appreciative of the efforts put forth on her behalf by her mother and the mayor, we may perhaps attribute that, at least in part, to a certain skepticism on her part as to the selflessness of their motivations. We might note, too, that she seemed insufficiently grateful to Tuvo Ausonius for the honor which he had seen fit to bestow upon her, in spite of the deficiency of her rank. Indeed, perhaps that was close to the nub of matters. In spite of her protestation, at the table, under that duress, she speaking almost without thinking, that the blood of her intended was higher than hers, which was doubless correct, in the genealogies, she was not truly prepared to admit that. Who was to say that the 105th degree, of her own family, was not superior to that of the 103rd, of the Ausonii? Too, for whatever defects, or waywardness, in her nature, she had hoped, first, for a higher match, regarding herself as quite worthy of it, and, secondly, to make matters far worse, had not been at all that enthralled with the pictorials of Tuvo Ausonius, who seemed to her to be a callow mediocrity. Too, she was decidedly not pleased, as she should doubtless have been, that his credentials, his test results, and such, had allayed any apprehensions on the part of her mother and the mayor that he might not be a "true man," as defined on Terennia. How furious she had been. How she had struggled to control her misery, her disappointment! Still were her deepest needs, her most hidden cravings, to be refused recognition? Already she held Tuvo Ausonius in an unreasoning, frustrated contempt. Already she despised him. Already she planned to make his life miserable, to dominate him, mercilessly. Who would wish to be the wife of such a one, spending her life as the spoiled, bored wife of a minor bureaucrat on a provincial world, spending, shopping, entertaining, one scarcely superior to Terennia, save that it was far closer to the Telnarian worlds? Oh, she would make him pay, subjecting him to her whims and demands, however exorbitant or unreasoning they might be, lavishly expending his resources, of whatever extent they might be, bringing him to the brink of ruin, and, if she wished, beyond it, demeaning him in public, ranting at him in private! Oh, yes, she would make him pay!

"And so," said Pulendius, "a toast to our charming fellow passenger! All happiness and delight to her! May she soon be joined in joy with her betrothed!"

The toast was then drunk.

The officer of the court blushed once more, angrily.

"Drink, drink!" called the men.

She lifted the delicate, shallow, transparent bowl to her lips, and took a sip. She looked at Pulendius, over the rim of the bowl.

"A joyous union," said the captain, lifting his glass.

"And a fecund one," said the naval officer, lifting his.

She looked at him, angrily.

"How excited you must be," said one of the women at the table.

"How eager you must be for his kisses," said another.

"Joy to you," said another.

"Happiness!" said another.

"May you leap in his arms like a slave," said another.

"Yes, yes," said several of the men.

She blushed, hotly.

How different these people were, how different from those of her home world, how different from those of Terennia!

"See her!" laughed Pulendius, once more taking his seat.

"Please," she protested.

Pulendius threw back his head, draining his bowl of *kana*. He had had perhaps too much to drink.

"We bring a virgin to Miton!" said Pulendius, who was a vulgar fellow.

He turned his bowl upside down on the tablecloth and seized up a napkin.

"But soon!" he cried.

To be sure, she, a member of a high class, even a minor patrician, was indeed, at that time, a virgin.

She looked up, embarrassed, at the gladiator, the bodyguard, he still at his post behind, and to the right, of Pulendius.

Yes, he was regarding her, and as though she might be in a slaver's house, and with that same subtle contempt as before.

How she hated him!

And then she was afraid, and a mad thought, meaningless, and absurd, coursed through her mind. "I do not want to be whipped," she thought. Then, swiftly, confusedly, she dismissed this thought, so mad, so absurd.

Many women of Terennia were virgins, or "superiors," as the phrase was on Terennia, particularly those of the educated, upper classes, sexuality being regarded as demeaning to women. Too, of course, marriage, and childbearing, and such things, were also frowned upon on that world, at least, again, among the women of the upper classes. What rational creature would wish to burden itself with such matters? The union between the officer of the court and the official, Tuvo Ausonius, we might note, had, accordingly, been arranged without a great deal of publicity, indeed, one might even say it had been arranged somewhat surreptitiously. But there could be a point in such things, you see, as embarrassing or regrettable as they might be, if they resulted in one's, or someone's, social, economic or professional advancement.

"But then!" had cried Pulendius.

And then he brought down his fist, wrapped in the napkin, heavily on the delicate, brittle, transparent bowl, shattering it into a thousand pieces.

The officer of the court shuddered, and blushed, and, doubtless heated by the *kana*, her senses reeling, almost swooned. This reaction may seem regrettably feminine, but one must consider the entirety of the circumstances, the power of Pulendius, the might of the men behind him, the laughter of those at the table, the heating of the *kana*, the fearful uneasiness in her own body, the sudden awareness, not for the first time, of its smallness and slightness, its softness and vulnerability, its great difference from that of men, and then the force of that massive fist striking down, shattering the bowl. In that moment much was conveyed to her on both a physical and a symbolic level. But I do not think we need to think of this reaction on her part, that she was then almost overcome, that she was then so shaken, that she almost swooned, as being *regrettably* feminine. That would be, after all, to adopt the values of Terennia, or of certain of its classes, and we wish to retain a neutrality in such matters, merely recounting what occurred, allowing the reader, should he feel the desire to do so, and should he feel entitled to do so, to form his own judgments on such matters. So we shall merely think of her reaction as being feminine, simply feminine, which it was, deeply, genuinely, authentically. Its explanation, moreover, most simply, was that she was a woman, and thus, for better or for worse, subject to such feelings and reactions. For such as she they were quite natural. Indeed, it would have been their denial, hitherto insisted upon in her culture, or in her class, which would have been unnatural, 'unnatural' in no pejorative sense, necessarily, but merely, even, in the quite neutral sense of being simply contrary to nature, for better or for worse. Among women, many of whom were less feminine than she, she had often felt an outcast, distrusting and fearing certain feelings in herself. She had never had the courage to be herself, what she truly was, a woman, something marvelous, and quite different from a man. She had always tried to deny and hide her womanhood, but it was there, and profoundly so, always. Certain changes would occur in her life which would have a considerable effect on such matters, which would, indeed, reverse, for better or for worse, these postures or policies. She would find herself eventually in situations, and in a condition, in which her womanhood could be, and, indeed, would have to be, fully expressed, a condition in which it was not only totally liberated, but in which it must be honestly and openly, and, indeed, fully, expressed, totally expressed, in which it was literally forbidden to her to deny it, in the least or most trivial fashion. Indeed, to her dismay, and joy, she would eventually find herself in situations, and in a condition, in which she must be herself, even choicelessly so, totally, whatever might be the consequences, for better or for worse.

"It is growing late," said the captain.

Those about the table then rose up, bidding one another the joys of the evening.

"Is there *kana* left?" called Pulendius to the bearer of the *kana* flask.

"Yes, milord," she responded.

He snapped his fingers, and she hurried to his place.

The officer of the court trembled, thrilled to see the woman obeying.

"Are you all right?" asked the young naval officer.

"Yes," she said.

Pulendius took the flask from the pourer of *kana* and offered it to the guard on his left.

No, milord," said the guard.

Pulendius then offered the flask to the guard on his right.

"Thank you, milord. No, milord," said that guard.

"Perhaps tomorrow night, after the contest?" said Pulendius.

"Yes, perhaps, milord," said the guard.

"Your hounds are well trained," said a man.

Pulendius himself then drank from the flask, and then put it down, a bit unsteadily, on the table.

Two or three of the women came about the table to where the officer of the court had risen and gently kissed her, wishing her much happiness. The officer of the court responded in kind, but stiffly, formally, self-consciously. She was, after all, from Terennia.

The bodyguard to Pulendius's right, looking upon her, decided that she was not worth a collar.

Another woman wished her well.

How stiff she was, how self-conscious.

On Terennia, you see, physical contact, the touching of one human being by another, was frowned upon, at least by members of her class.

How stiff she was, indeed, how self-conscious.

Yet, as he continued to regard her, he sensed in her, or thought he sensed in her, a significant latent sexuality, a powerful sexuality now almost entirely suppressed, one straining against cruel, grievous constraints, one such that, if it were ever released, could never again be subject to management, one which, if released, she would find uncontrollable, one at the mercy of which she would then find herself, its prisoner and victim.

Another of the women gave the officer of the court a gentle kiss.

Yes, he thought, she might not prove to be entirely without interest.

But then he dismissed such thoughts, for she was of the *honestori*, and even a minor patrician.

One did not think of such in a collar, at least not on any world with which he was familiar.

Still, he thought he had a score to settle with her, and she might look well in one.

"Good night, my dear," said Pulendius.

"Sir," she said.

Pulendius then left, a little unsteadily. She watched him exit the lounge, at one point supported by the guard at his right. She was familiar with Pulendius, of course. Who would not be, in her sector of Terennia?

He was fabulously rich, of course, with his enterprises, his lands, tilled by some four thousand *coloni*. He had much power. He must have many enemies. Guards were almost always with him, large, alert, agile men, skilled, ruthless men, gladiators, it was said.

She looked back, down at the tablecloth, at crumbs there, at crumpled napkins, at rings of *kana* there. She saw the napkin which had covered Pulendius's fist when he had struck down, shattering the delicate bowl.

How vulgar he had been!

Pulendius had his weaknesses, of course. *Kana* was one, obviously. His zeal for the arena and its sports was doubtless another. She knew he maintained a school for gladiators, a school in which men were trained in the use of weapons, both common and exotic.

The men of Pulendius, as well as Pulendius himself, seemed quite different from most of the men she had known.

How uneasy she felt in their presence. And how disturbing had been certain sensations.

She recalled the guard, he who had been behind Pulendius, and to his right.

Her fingers went uneasily to the golden necklace so closely encircling her throat. The tips of her fingers just touched it, barely, timidly.

She thought again of the guard.

Suddenly, angrily, she snatched up her small white purse and, with both hands, held it closely, tightly, against her.

How the guard had looked upon her!

She had never been looked upon in that fashion before!

How she despised him, how she hated him, that calm, half-naked giant who had dared to look upon her in that fashion.

And he had viewed her with contempt!

"I do not want to be whipped," she thought, and then again, startled at such a mad thought, she sought to hurry it out of her consciousness.

How dared he to have looked upon her so?

What right had he to do so, he, only an ignorant, illiterate lout, only a beast trained for the arena?

She was of high birth, of the patricians!

"But perhaps he would not regard me as being worthy of being whipped," she thought, and this thought disturbed her, and frightened her, and then again, such a mad thought, she rejected it, confusedly.

She saw the pourer of *kana* sorting plates on the table, preparing it for clearing.

"You," she said.

The pourer of *kana* looked up, startled.

"Come here," she said.

The pourer of *kana* came to where she stood.

"What is your name?" said the officer of the court.

"Janina, milady," was the response.

"Speak clearly," snapped the officer of the court.

"Janina, Mistress," said the girl.

"Are you accustomed to standing in the presence of free persons?" asked the officer of the court.

"Forgive me, Mistress," said the girl, and swiftly knelt before her.

"Is such a lapse not cause for discipline?" inquired the officer of the court.

"It is the will of the masters, Mistress," she said. "In deference to the feelings of certain passengers, little attention is to be drawn to my true condition in public."

"So you pretend to be a servant?"

"I serve, Mistress. But I do not pretend to be a servant. I would not dare to pretend to be so high."

"I have seen your behavior in the lounge," said the officer of the court.

"Yes, Mistress," said the girl.

"In public."

"Yes, Mistress."

"It is different in private, I take it," said the officer of the court.

"Yes, Mistress. In private, the fullness of my slavery is revealed."

"And what does that mean?"

"That I am a slave, Mistress," said the girl, trembling.

"And what does a slave do?"

"She strives to please, and obeys," she said.

"And you can be bought and sold," said the officer of the court.

"Yes, Mistress."

"You are the sort of *animal* that can be bought and sold," said the officer of the court.

"Yes, Mistress," said the girl.

"You are a pretty *animal*," said the officer of the court.

"Thank you, Mistress," said the girl.

The officer of the court turned about, angrily. Then she turned about, again, to face the pourer of *kana*. She looked down upon her, angrily.

"You are an exquisite, extraordinarily attractive slave, Janina," said the officer of the court.

"Thank you, Mistress," said the girl.

"Such as you," said the officer of the court, "are suitable for slaves."

"Yes, Mistress," said the girl.

The officer of the court then, clutching her small, white purse close to her, went to the exit of the lounge.

She turned back at the portal.

The pourer of *kana* was still on her knees, beside the table.

"You may rise," said the officer of the court. "Return to your work."

"Yes, Mistress. Thank you, Mistress," said the girl.

In returning from the lounge to her cabin, unescorted, of course, for she was of Terennia, the officer of the court paused before a giant oval port in the corridor, which looked out on the vastness of the mysterious night, a night in which galaxies drifted, like glowing fragments in a dark sea.

She felt very small and alone in such a night, even with the lit corridor behind her, even with the comfortable, enclosing steel of the ship.

She regarded her image, reflected in the portal.

She moved her hand, brushing back her hair. She was not displeased with what she saw. She did not think she was unattractive. She thought that she would be wasted on Tuvo Ausonius. Yes, she would be wasted on him. But she would make him pay for that. He would suffer. She looked herself over, carefully. Perhaps it had been a mistake to have worn the white, off-the-shoulder sheath, the earrings, the necklace. She had purchased it in a ship's shop, daringly. On Terennia they did not have such things, or, at least, she had not seen them. There, even a white, belted clingabout was thought to be scandalous. Her mother had been much against that, annoyingly, even fiercely, vociferously so, but she had worn it anyway. She was not accustomed to doing what others wanted. She was accustomed, rather, to doing precisely what she wanted, whatever she wanted, and when she wanted. She regarded her image steadily. Perhaps it had been a mistake to have worn this ensemble this evening. But then she thought not. Had one seen how that oaf, that ignorant, illiterate oaf, that guard, had looked at her? She could not recall ever having been looked at like that by a man before, saving of course by the same fellow, when he, a peasant, had stood in the dock in her mother's court. She was then well satisfied with her appearance, and the garment. She thought of the poor little creature in the lounge, what was her name, Janina, or some such. She would wear only what men decided, or approved of. The officer of the court continued to regard herself in the mirror of the portal, the stars visible beyond. "How would I be dressed by men," she wondered, "if I were a slave—or would I be permitted clothing?"

Then, suddenly, she started, gasping, for, behind her, clearly visible in the reflection of the port, was the large form of the guard, he who had been behind Pulendius, and to his right. She spun about and backed against the railing before the port.

The other guard, the other gladiator, was somewhat in the background.

"Forgive us, milady," said the guard, he so close to her. "We did not mean to startle you. We have been relieved. We are off duty now, and are returning to our quarters."

The other guard continued on his way, and the guard closest to her, he whose sudden appearance had so startled her, turned to follow him.

"Linger," she said, suddenly.

"Yes, milady," said he, turning.

"I had not seen you, until the lounge," said she, "since the arena."

"No, milady," said he, "not since you had me bound."

"You were spoken for by Pulendius, who was much impressed with your deeds in the arena."

"Yes, milady," said he.

"In deference to Pulendius, your sentence was commuted, remanding you into his custody."

"Into the custody of a keeper of a gladiatorial school," said he, "in which men are trained to kill."

She tried to step back, but the railing was behind her.

"I am now a free man," he said. "I received my freedom after my tenth victory."

She looked up at him.

"My seventh kill," he said.

"I see," she said.

"I am now as free as you," he said.

"I—I see," she said.

Need he stand so close to her? Was he still such a rude, ignorant peasant, with no understanding of civilities? Did he think himself still in some primitive, dirty village, with animals running about between the huts? Was he so ignorant of the proprieties, of the distances, on Terennia, suitable to one of her class? She seemed confused, she looked about, she felt enflamed. Not a hand's breadth separated her from that mighty chest, the shining leather stretched across it.

"Pulendius has high hopes for you," she said, unsteadily, looking to the side.

The gladiator shrugged.

How dare you stand so close? she thought.

Pulendius had some twenty fighters with him on the ship. He also had a complement of support personnel, trainers, a physician, an accountant, secretaries and such. He was bound for Iris, which, like Miton, was in the first provincial quadrant.

"I am low in the matches," said the gladiator, looking down at her.

Please don't stand so closely to me, she thought. Cannot you see I am uncomfortable?

"But even fighters like Archon and Mir San were once low in the matches," he said.

These two were known throughout galaxies. They normally performed on the Telnarian worlds themselves, even in the imperial arena.

"You—you enjoy the arena?" she said.

"Yes," he said, thoughtfully. "The light, the crowds, the music, the contest. One is very much alive there. I can understand why men seek it out. But I do not feel the arena is my destiny."

"You are free," she said. "You can leave Pulendius."

"He saved my life. I serve him," he said.

"Doubtless he pays well," she said.

"Yes," he said.

"You are of the *humiliori*," she said. "You do not have a destiny."

"Even less than *humiliori* have slaves a destiny," said he, looking down at her.

"What do you mean by that?" she cried.

"Why, nothing, milady," he said.

She felt weak, giddy. What could be the meaning of such feelings?

She feared they might be those of a slave girl before her master.

"Why did you look at me, as you did this evening?" she asked, angrily.

"Surely it was milady's imagination," he suggested.

"Perhaps," she said icily.

"Methought," said he, "that milady did have her eyes once or twice upon me."

"Never!" she said.

"How then would she know if I might have glanced upon her?"

"You are an insolent beast!" she cried and raised her small hand to strike him. But the blow did not fall and she winced for her small wrist was trapped as though in a vise of steel, helpless in the grip of his great fist.

Once before he recalled, when he had first recovered from his wound in the barrack of the school of Pulendius and had been on his feet, that Pulendius had come to see him. Pulendius, unexpectedly, had struck at him and his wrist, too, had been so caught. "If I were wearing a wrist knife," had said Pulendius to him, "you would have lost fingers."

"But, milord," had said the peasant, "you were not wearing a wrist knife."

"Excellent," had said Pulendius. "Release me, now. Your training begins in the morning."

"Please let me go," she said. "You're hurting me." He released her, instantly. She drew back her hand, rubbing the wrist. She had never guessed before what it might be like, to be the captive, so helplessly, of so mighty a grip.

"Why would I have wasted my time," he asked, "looking upon one who was a mere slave?"

"I was not the slave!" she said. "There was a slave there, she who cared for the flask of *kana*!"

"You are both slaves," he said.

"I am not a slave!" she cried. "I am of the patricians!"

"You are a slave," he said.

"No," she cried.

"I have learned in the school," he said, "how to look upon a woman, and tell if she is a slave or not."

"And I am one such, a slave?" she said, angrily.

"Yes," he said.

"Begone!" she wept.

He stepped back, and bowed. "Yes, milady," said he.

"What is the contest tomorrow evening?" she demanded.

"Its nature, until the moment," said he, "is to remain confidential."

"Are you to be involved?" she asked.

"That is my understanding, if it is necessary," he said.

"I see," she said.

"Is it milady's intention to attend?" he asked.

"Certainly not," she said.

"Good night, milady," said he, bowing, and withdrawing.

It was shortly thereafter that the captain chanced by, in the very corridor in which was the large observation port, that before which the last recounted events took place. The officer of the court stood by the port, grasping the railing with one hand, with the other holding her small purse tightly against herself. She was looking out, on the silent, lateral, unsounded depths of the night, on the tiny, clustered fires, some suns, some universes themselves. She may have seemed shaken. In any event the captain paused, solicitously.

"I am all right," she assured the captain.

"I passed in the corridor," said he, "on my way, one of Pulendius's brutes. I trust you were not accosted."

"No," she said. "No!"

How could she have been accosted? One does not accost slaves. One commands them.

"I think it a mistake that such brutes should be allowed to roam freely," he said.

"Doubtless," she laughed.

"They should be kept in cages," he smiled.

"Perhaps," she laughed.

"Are you all right?" he asked.

"Yes," she said.

She had heard that female slaves were sometimes kept in cages, sometimes quite small cages.

"I bid you a joyous evening," said the captain.

"Captain!" she said.

"Yes?"

"There is to be some sort of entertainment tomorrow evening?"

"Entertainment?"

"Games," she said, "a contest?"

"Yes," he said.

"A contest?"

"Yes," he said.

"At what time and place may I inquire?"

"It is nothing in which you would be interested, milady," he said.

"It is in the lower portions of the ship," he said.

"In the hold," said he, "Section Nineteen, an hour after supper."

"I will see how I feel tomorrow evening," she said. "If I am bored, I might look in."

"You should not wish to see it," he said.

"Oh?" she asked.

"I am not sure you would find it appropriate," he said.

"Other women will attend, I trust?" she asked.

"Doubtless," he said.

"I have every right to attend, do I not?" she asked.

"Of course," said he.

"This is a pleasure ship, a cruise ship," she said. "Entertainments are afforded. I have paid my passage."

"You are entirely welcome, of course," said the captain.

"Is anything wrong?"

"No," he said. "It is only that you are of Terennia."

"And what has that to do with it?" she asked.

"Nothing," he said.

"We shall see how I feel tomorrow evening," she said.

The captain's offer to escort her to her cabin was declined. She was, after all, of Terennia. Yet, to recount matters accurately we must mention that after his departure, for whatever reason, she began to tremble. She looked out, again, onto the night, and the stars, the worlds, and was afraid. She felt very small, and helpless. The ship itself, with its light, its warmth, its steel, its numerous life-support systems, did little to allay her apprehension. It would not have hurt, she thought, even though she was of Terennia, and who would know, to have had the company of the captain to her cabin. It was a long way there, through several passages, and she was clad in such a way that it was made quite clear, in spite of the teachings of Terennia, that she was not really a "same." She looked at herself in the mirror of the portal. No, she was clearly other than a "same." She was something else, quite different from a "same." She then hurried to her cabin, looking about her, even stopping to peer down adjoining passages, before crossing other corridors, and then, in a little while, frightened, and breathless, for she had at times even run a little, in short, hurrying steps, the most permitted to her by the garment in which she fled, she arrived at her door. In a moment she was within, and stood on the inside of the cabin, her back against the door, the door double-locked. She was frightened, and was breathing heavily. Then she moaned, and turned about, and sank to her knees behind the door, and put her hands out, touching it, touching the steel.

She was not a slave!

She was safe.

· · · CHAPTER 10 · · ·

"What a dreadful outfit!" laughed one of the women on the tiers.

The officer of the court did not deign to respond.

"Do not be angry!" called the woman. "Come, sit here beside me!" She patted a place on the tier.

The officer of the court smiled, and climbed to sit beside her.

"Have I missed much?" asked the officer of the court, lightly.

"Not at all, you are quite early," the woman assured her.

The performers, if one may speak of them in that fashion, had not yet entered the wooden-rimmed circle of sand which was ringed by the tiers. The room in the hold, Section 19, was a high one. One could see, above, the lofty girders, and steelwork, which the shipwrights had not been concerned to conceal in this area. In this section, one of a hundred such sections, one might have stored several tons of cargo. There was little in it now but the tiers, and, about the edges, some boxes, some escape capsules, or lifeboats, one might say, and such. Light in the section was from powerful overhead bulbs. They flooded the small ringed area with bright light. They were animated by switches near the door. Elsewhere the area was much in shadow. Presumably the performers were somewhere in the darkness, or, perhaps, in some adjoining area, waiting to enter this section. If there was to be an entertainment, it did not seem to be professionally, carefully staged, like the other entertainments, the shows, the concerts.

"What is to be the nature of the contest?" asked the officer of the court.

Yes, she was early. There were only a few now present.

"I do not know," the woman assured her. She was one of those who had been at the table with her, the captain's table, the evening before. She was one of those who had wished her happiness, and kissed her after the supper.

"I didn't mean to offend you, my dear," said the woman to the officer of the court. "I am sure that your ensemble is quite appropriate for Terennia."

"It is the customary garb of my class," said the officer of the court.

"For both men and women?"

"Yes," she was informed.

"I see," said the woman, it being clear she really didn't.

"We are 'sames,' " she was informed.

"The men and women?" she was asked.

"Yes," said the officer of the court.

"Don't you find that silly?" asked the woman.

The officer of the court did not choose to respond to this inquiry.

"I'm sorry," said the woman.

"That is all right," the officer of the court assured her.

The woman who had invited the officer of the court to join her on the tiers was now dressed not in the gown of the preceding evening, fit for the honor of the captain's table, but in something more appropriate for attendance at a contest, in a well-tailored pantsuit.

"It is very different," said the woman, "from the way you were dressed last night."

That was true. A world of difference separated the sleek, white, off-the-shoulder sheath, purchased in a ship's shop, which the officer of the court had dared to wear yesterday, from the version of Terennian "same garb," which she wore this evening. "Same garb" was designed to conceal sexual differences. There were many ways in which to attempt this, none of which was entirely successful. The officer of the court now wore, however, a fairly common form of "same garb," an intentionally bulky, formless, sacklike one-piece garment. It covered her completely from the neck to the ankles. It had legs. It was a sort of gray overall. In addition, she wore the "frame-and-curtain." From a projecting rectangular extension, the frame, put about the neck, there dangled, to the sides, and in front and back, an opaque, cloaklike attachment, the "curtain." The intention of this device was to conceal the delightful curves and smallness of her shoulders, and the revelatory, indicative excitements of her figure, both anterior and posterior. Uniformity was highly valued on Terennia, of thought, behavior and sexuality.

"Pulendius will doubtless be here," said the officer of the court, offhandedly.

"And the handsome brutes with him," said the woman with her.

The officer of the court stiffened. She had, of course, not been herself particularly interested in Pulendius. Irritatedly, she realized, too, that the woman beside her had understood her, only too well. She was embarrassed.

It might be mentioned at this point that although the officer of the court wore "same garb," she also wore, beneath it, now, as of today, certain other garments, purchased in one of the ship's shops, which were quite uncharacteristic of Terennia, but of such things, more anon.

These new undergarments were, of course, her carefully guarded secret. She felt she might die of mortification, if such things were known.

"Did you see how the one fellow, he on the right of Pulendius, looked at you?" asked the woman.

"You saw?" asked the officer of the court, pleased. It had not then been her imagination. Of course, she had known it had not been. Still, it was pleasant to have this confirmation. Too, she was pleased, though she was not eager to admit it, that another woman had noticed her being the object of such regard. That flattered her vanity, for she, like other women, was not without her vanity. It had been *she* on whom he had been looking.

"Of course," said the woman.

"Oh?" asked the officer of the court, who, we must confess, was eager to hear more.

The woman with whom she was in converse was now only too well aware of her interest.

"And how he looked upon you!" she whispered.

"How was that?" asked the officer of the court, pressing her.

How warm she suddenly felt in those new undergarments, hidden under her "same garb."

"Do not even ask, my dear," said the woman in the pantsuit, pretending to abandon the conversation.

"No, please speak," said the officer of the court. "I want to know."

"You are sure?"

"Yes."

"I know you are of the blood, my dear," said the woman, "and we all look up to you and admire you for it, but he looked upon you as though you might be, in reality, properly understood, no more than a common slave."

"I see," said the officer of the court.

"No offense," said the woman.

"Of course not," said the officer of the court.

"I wish that he had looked upon me in that way," laughed the woman in the pantsuit.

"I am not a slave," said the officer of the court, angrily.

"We are all, at the bottom, slaves," said the woman.

"No," said the officer of the court.

"Surely you have sometimes wondered about your value as a woman, what price you would bring?"

The officer of the court was angry, silent. It was true that she had sometimes, in her loneliness, and misery, and frustration, and need, wondered if she had any real value, and what men, under no duress, would be willing to pay for her, if anything. Many times, in her imagination, she had turned upon the illuminated slave block, the faces of the men much hidden in the darkness, and heard the cries of the auctioneer, selling her.

"He is like a barbarian god," she said.

"He is a large fellow, and of reasonably symmetrical features," she said.

"Was he not the sort of man before whom a woman would quake, and hasten to obey?"

"Not a true woman," said the officer of the court.

"Those whom you call 'true women,' " she said, "are merely women who have not yet met their master."

"Nonsense," said the officer of the court.

But she knew that it was true.

"Cannot you imagine what it might be to belong to him, really?" asked the woman.

"Not at all," said the officer of the court.

"I suspect you can," said the other woman, squeezing her hand.

"No," said the officer of the court, firmly.

"I think you would obey him," she said.

"No," said the officer of the court.

"I think a taste of the whip would soon change your mind," said the woman, smiling.

The officer of the court swallowed hard, and looked down. She had, you see, little doubt but what she would do her best to obey, and be fully pleasing, and that the whip, really, would not be in the least needed. That it was there, and that she knew it would be used, if he were not pleased, if she needed any additional incentive, would be quite enough, indeed, more than enough.

The tiers were now muchly filled. The entertainment was soon to begin.

"And what do you think you would bring?" asked the officer of the court, angrily.

"I do not know, my dear," said the woman. "I hope a good price."

"I see," said the officer of the court.

"It would not be so high as that which you would fetch, however, my dear," she said, "for you are very beautiful."

The officer of the court looked at the other woman, who was perhaps in her forties. She was clearly educated. She had striking features and was well figured. The officer of the court wondered if that woman might not bring a higher price than she. That woman, in any event, was not from Terennia. That might make a difference in the prices they would bring. Women from Terennia, the officer of the court speculated, might be thought to be poor stuff, little more than jokes in the slave markets. On the other hand, she was not prepared to admit this. Surely women of Terennia, if so unfortunate as to fall slave, if that horrifying fate were to befall them, might be taught, as well as others. Might they not, in time, with diligence, come to take their place in the markets, even among the most precious of slaves?

"Look," said the companion of the officer of the court.

The captain and his first officer, with some other officers, had just entered.

"May I join you?" asked one of the minor officers, looking up from the floor.

"Please do," said the companion of the officer of the court.

Seats were scarce. Some had been reserved below, of course, at the side of the ring, in this case, opposite the door to the section. The captain and the first officer, and certain other officers, were seated there, and some of these seats, too, had been left empty, apparently to be filled later. It might be mentioned that the officer of the court and her friend were not far from

these privileged seats. They had come rather early to the entertainment, it may be recalled. They thus had much their pick of
seating arrangements.

The officer took his seat to the right of the companion of the
officer of the court, thus away from the officer of the court. He
did this, rather than sit between the ladies, as might otherwise
have been expected, for one of them was of Terennia, and the
women of Terennia, being "sames," or supposedly so, tend to
be uncomfortable in the presence of males, and, accordingly,
tend to shun their proximity.

Shortly thereafter the lights began to dim.

"It is beginning!" said the companion of the officer of the
court.

· · · CHAPTER 11 · · ·

The lights had continued to dim until the section of the hold
was in total darkness, and then, after a moment, they came on
again, suddenly.

In the ring now, on the sand, to one side, rather toward the
door, there knelt a large, bearded man. His long hair, which
behind him fell to his waist, was bound back with a fillet of
leather. He wore a tunic of roughly sewn skins. He was heavily
chained, hand and foot.

The women in the crowd, at the first sight of him, gasped,
drawing back.

"He is clad as a barbarian," said the woman who had invited
the officer of the court to sit with her, to the minor officer.

"He is a barbarian," said the officer. "He was taken on
Tinos."

On either side of the kneeling figure, standing, were two
guards, armed not with stun sticks but fire pistols. *There are
several varieties of such weapons. They are commonly a sidearm*

of imperial officers. A common form of fire pistol, and that which the guards carried, held ten reduced, controlled charges, each emitting a narrow, bright, quarter-second beam. In this fashion the beam, in the moment of its activation, might breach materials such as wood or flesh, but could do little more than scorch and disfigure metal. This was important within a carefully regulated environment, that, say, of a ship in space. Weapons in the empire, as I have earlier indicated, were carefully controlled, and this policy was one of the reasons, doubtless, for the general security of its authority. Within the empire the manufacture of such weapons was an imperial monopoly. Indeed, even within the empire primitive weapons, clubs, staffs, pointed, edged weapons, and such, were far more common than technologically sophisticated weapons. Indeed, many in the empire knew only such weapons. Some imperial troops, as a matter of fact, had been, for most practical purposes, reduced to the use of such weapons, they being supplemented, of course, to some extent by more powerful devices. Certain forms of energy within the empire were, statistically, quite rare, many sources having been exhausted centuries ago. This was the case on literally thousands of worlds. These facts, however, must not obscure the fact that the empire still had at its disposal weapons capable of dislodging planets from orbits, even of pulverizing them into miniscule, radiating debris.

"The skins he wears," said the minor officer, to her in the pantsuit, "are from animals which he himself has killed."

"Interesting," she said.

But her interest, we may suspect, was taken less by those savage skins than by something else, by the savage himself, he so muscular, so mighty within them, he whom they so primitively bedecked.

The officer of the court swayed a little.

Her heart, like that of many of the other women in the tiers, was beating rapidly, fearfully.

Out there, somewhere, in the galaxy, there were men such as these!

What could be the fate of women in the hands of such men?
Did she not know?

The borders must hold!

"Are you all right?" asked the minor officer.

"Yes," she said.

The women in the tiers, who were educated, civilized women, looked upon the barbarian, even though he was chained, with some apprehension. How different he was from the men with whom they were personally acquainted!

The officer of the court, seeing such a man, became suddenly quite conscious of the shocking undergarments she had dared to place beneath her "same garb."

How frightening were such men. Their attitudes, their values, would doubtless be quite different from those of civilized men, gentlemen. Who knew how they might look upon a woman, or in what terms they might see her?

"Are you alarmed?" asked the minor officer, looking over to the officer of the court.

"Certainly not," she said.

"He is now quite helpless," said the minor officer.

"Are their women dressed similarly?" asked the officer of the court, as though idly.

"The women commonly wear cloth, some, the finest, obtained in trade, some, particularly in remoter areas, which they themselves have spun and loomed. The most common garment of free women is a long dress, which muchly covers them, that their men may not be driven mad with desire."

"Not all their women are free?"

"No."

"They then keep slaves."

"They are barbarians, of course," he said.

"And what is the most common garment of slaves?" she asked.

"Usually the long dress," said he, "as with free women."

"But not always?" asked the officer of the court.

"No," said the minor officer.

"And how then would they be dressed?" asked the officer of the court.

"As slaves," said the minor officer.

"If dressed?"

"Of course," said he.

"How many women do such men have?" asked the officer of the court.

"Some have several," he said.

"Both wives and slaves?"

"Sometimes," said the officer.

Despite the ponderous chains on the barbarian, and the presence of the vigilant, armed guards, many of the women continued to be apprehensive, regarding the kneeling figure.

They knew themselves to be civilized women, of course, and thus no more than prey to such men.

Such men, they understood in their bellies, would see them as women, and put them to the uses of women.

How dreadful!

At this moment the main door to the section opened and the young naval officer, he who was putatively on leave, entered.

The officer of the court gasped.

Yesterday evening she had seen him only in a lounging robe, a leisure, or pleasure, garment, one suitable for the captain's table, but he was now in what must be a dress uniform. It was white with gold braid. Too, she was startled to note, at the left shoulder, three purple cords.

As he entered, in uniform, the captain himself, and his officers, had risen, in salute. The two guards in whose custody knelt the prisoner, too, came to attention.

"Hail to the empire!" called the captain.

"Hail to the empire!" called the other officers, and the guards, as well. Even the minor officer who sat near the women in the tiers, the women with whom we are now familiar, had come to attention when the young officer had entered, as had some other minor officers here and there on the tiers. They, too, had joined in the greeting.

"Hail to the emperor! Hail to the empire!" said the young officer.

This cry was repeated by the officers, and by others, too, in the stands.

"See the cords," said the woman in the pantsuit.

"Of course I see them," said the officer of the court. She had been struck speechless when the young officer had first entered. She, of all, who was herself of the blood, would understand such insignia. But she had not realized that one of a rank far beyond hers, compared to which hers, and even that of Tuvo Ausonius, was as nothing, was aboard the vessel.

The young officer then turned to regard the prisoner, kneeling in the sand, now at his feet.

The prisoner had been made to wait, kneeling, for the arrival of the young officer.

And thus was made clear to the prisoner, and to all in the tiers, the superiority of the empire.

The naval rank of the officer was not high. We might say, to suggest something familiar, that he was an ensign. On the other hand, the cords made it clear that this was no ordinary ensign, but one of the noblest of bloods.

"The three cords," said the woman in the pantsuit.

"Yes," said the officer of the court, irritably. The three cords, of that color, indicated the highest of ranks. The blood of this young officer was doubtless as high as that of the imperial house itself.

How incredible it was that one such as he would be aboard this vessel.

Tears formed in the eyes of several of the men in the tiers.

With a gesture the young officer put the company at ease.

The young officer then, as would be in accord with the protocols of the service, saluted the captain, who smartly returned this greeting.

He then took his seat, beside the captain.

At this point Pulendius emerged from behind the tiers, opposite the main door, followed by four pairs of gladiators. These were powerful men, clad in brief leather, with their hair fastened back, their bodies oiled.

"There is to be an exhibition," said the minor officer.

The gladiators, two pairs armed with blunt spears, two pairs with wooden swords, began to exercise and stretch in the tiny arena.

Some of the women inadvertently gasped, seeing the rippling of such muscles, the movements of the mighty thighs. Doubtless most had seen fighters before, but it is not likely they had seen them at this proximity.

The officer of the court looked about for a particular gladiator, he who had been the bodyguard of Pulendius, he who had been behind him and to the right.

He was nowhere in view.

Then, after a moment he, with his fellow, appeared, both at the opening in the tiers, through which Pulendius and the others had but recently emerged.

They, as was the business of such fellows, surveyed the crowd. She sat very straight, in "same garb," with the "frame-and-curtain," making certain that she did not look at him, or, at least, not obviously. Her interest, he must clearly understand, was on the ring. See her as a common slave, would he? Let him see her now, as she really was, a high creature, one far above him, one immeasurably above him, a woman of Terennia, one even of the blood itself!

But, of course, she looked back to see if he might be looking at her, and, as one might expect, what should happen to be the case but that, to her embarrassment, their eyes met. Swiftly then, blushing, she looked away.

At least she was in "same garb," and in the "frame-and-curtain"! But she knew, too, that she had been before him not simply, in "same garb," and in the "frame-and-curtain," but in those other garments, too, those to which we earlier alluded. She could now feel them, in all their filmy, sensuous softness, on her body. She was wearing them before him. Of course, he could not see them, but she knew they were there, and that she had them on, before a man. The nature of these garments was doubtless quite innocent, but scarcely so from the point of view of a woman from Terennia. For a woman of Terennia, of her class, the garments which she now wore went well beyond the merely daring, and doubtless beyond even the perimeters of the scandalous. They were soft and sensuous, and provocative. They were the sort of thing which only a woman who should be a slave would wear. They were emphatically indecent. She could feel her breasts straining against the soft, filmy silken bonds which constrained them, she was scarcely aware of the so-brief tiny thing which enclosed her lower body, with its sweet nether intimacies, so light it was. These two garments, the brassiere and the panties, as we may think of them, not inaccurately, had both been, of course, purchased at the ship's shop. It had required great courage for her to buy them. Had the salesgirl not looked at her askance, or had she imagined it? None, of course, would know that she had purchased them, only herself. Did the salesgirl wear such things? Had there been anything strange, or disapproving, in her expressions, in her tone of voice? Did the salesgirl, herself, wear such things, she wondered. They would be her secret, of course, her secret from all the world. She would never dare to show them to Tuvo Ausonius. He would be unwilling to let such a woman in his bed. Such a woman is rather such that she is to be chained at the foot of a bed.

He could not know, of course, that she wore such garments under the "same garb," under the "frame and curtain."

But she knew.

Hotly she regretted wearing such things.

Oh, she had put them on and off a dozen times in the privacy of her cabin, sometimes even daring to look at herself in the mirror. But surely the image could not be hers. Surely she could not be that lithe, graceful, curvaceous creature in the mirror. She had decided at last not to wear such things to the entertainment, but, when she had tried them on again, just for the last time, as she told herself, she realized suddenly, to her consternation, the time, and that, if she were to assure herself of a seat, she must best be on her way. Having no choice then she had put on the "same garb," and the "frame-and-curtain," over them, and hurried out.

How handsome was the bodyguard, how strong he seemed, how small she seemed, compared to him.

Then she sat straight on the tier. She was now pleased to have worn the intimate garments. No one could see them. And they were comfortable. That was a good reason to wear them. And no one could see them. Thus no one could ever guess what sort of woman she was, secretly.

The bodyguard was not far from her, over to her left, where

one opening was in the tiers, that opposite the other, nearer the door.

Again their eyes met.

"Where is your collar?" he asked.

She stiffened, and pretended not to hear. He was referring, doubtless, to the necklace she had worn the night before. It would not go with the "same garb" and the "frame-and-curtain," of course. Too, it was a necklace. It was not a collar. Collars were for slaves. He must know that.

The minor officer glared at the gladiator, but the gladiator met his gaze squarely, and not pleasantly, and the minor officer looked away.

The woman in the pantsuit leaned over to the officer of the court, and nodded her head, subtly, indicatively, toward the gladiator. "He finds you attractive," she whispered confidingly, delightedly.

" 'Attractive'?" asked the officer of the court.

"Yes," said her companion.

"I am of Terennia," said the officer of the court. "I do not even understand such matters."

"Very attractive," whispered her companion.

"I am not in the least interested," said the officer of the court.

"Why are you blushing?" asked her companion.

"I am not," insisted the officer of the court, her skin aflame.

"He wants you," whispered her companion.

"He is an illiterate brute," said the officer of the court.

"He looks at you as though you were a common slave," said her companion.

"Perhaps he will buy me," said the officer of the court, acidly.

"And what man would not, if he could afford you?" said the woman.

The officer of the court did not deign to respond to this remark. The very thought of it, she, for sale!

"But perhaps he would merely bind and gag you, and carry you off," she said.

"Perhaps," said the officer of the court.

"He wants you," she said.

"Let him want me then, in vain," said the officer of the court.

"You might not speak so proudly," she said, "if you were on your knees before him, naked, your hands tied behind your back."

"Please," protested the officer of the court.

"And you would be made his slave," she said.

The officer of the court trembled.

"And you would serve him well," she said.

"Please," said the officer of the court.

"He would see to it," she said.

At this point the young naval officer was looking about the stands, and, to her pleasure, their eyes met. This gave her the much-desired opportunity to escape the humiliating embarrassments of her conversation with her companion on the tiers. The young officer would surely remember her from the captain's table, the preceding evening. He would recall, too, the bit of purple accenting her sheath, which, so subtly, but nonetheless clearly, proclaimed her own nobility. She, too, was of the blood! This, too, would give her a way of putting her companion in her place, who was of the *honestori*, but not of noble blood. This would make it clear to her that she must not speak in such a way to her, so frankly, so intimately, as though they might be of the same station, as though they might be equals, even as though they might both be no more than women huddled naked at the foot of a slave block, each waiting, in her turn, to be dragged to its surface, to be exhibited and sold. He was only a few feet from her, in his place on the first tier, in the place of honor, between the captain and the first officer, at the edge of the circle.

"Hail to the emperor!" she said. "Hail to the empire!"

He looked away, returning his attention to the activities of the gladiators, they preparing for their exhibition.

The companion of the officer of the court, the woman in the pantsuit, tactfully took no official notice of this episode.

The officer of the court stiffened in humiliation. Tears ran down her cheeks, which she swiftly wiped away.

She, too, said nothing of the episode.

Could the naval officer, he of the blood, have somehow suspected, or guessed, that she wore soft garments beneath her "same garb"? Was that why he had not deigned to recognize her, to return her greeting, even to indicate that he had noticed it?

She looked to the gladiator, by the opening of the tiers. He regarded her. On his lips there was, playing there, ever so subtly, a smile. It was a smile of amusement, of contempt. Quickly the officer of the court jerked her head away, angrily, looking to the sand, as though something of great interest might be occurring there.

She had never been so embarrassed, so humiliated, in her life.

There were, in the empire, you see, matters of distance, of rank and hierarchy.

Such were not to be lightly violated.

She had done so.

"Ladies and gentlemen," called Pulendius, "welcome, all, to the festivities of the evening."

All attention was upon him.

"And let us welcome, too, our special guest, one honoring us with his presence this evening," he called, pointing to the fellow kneeling to one side, in skins, laden with chains, "Ortog, a prince of the Drisriaks, king of the secessionist house of Ortog."

There was laughter, and polite applause.

The fists of the barbarian, in close proximity to one another, his wrists well confined in weighty manacles, clenched in futile rage.

This, too, caused amusement in the crowd.

Even had he no acquaintance with some patois interactive with Telnarian there could be little doubt, given Pulendius's exaggerated, pompous references, clearly directed at him, and the amusement of the crowd, that he was the object of ridicule.

It will be helpful to the reader to follow certain later events if I make clear certain relationships, certain lineages, involved here. Ortog was a prince of the Drisriaks, which was one of the eleven traditional tribes of the Alemanni nation. His house, how-

*ever, was secessionist, and thusly he was a prince of one house,
of the Drisriaks, and the king, or pretender to kingship, in
another, his own, that of the Ortungen.*

"He dared to raise arms against the empire!" said Pulendius.
"Now he kneels before us, humbled, in chains, as helpless as
a slave!"

There were cries of delight from the audience.

"We shall now see him bow to the empire!" said Pulendius.

But the back of the kneeling, scowling figure remained
straight, quite straight.

Pulendious regarded the prisoner.

But the prisoner remained motionless

Pulendius, for a moment, seemed nonplussed, but, at a nod
from the captain, he gestured to the two guards.

They seized the prisoner and, with great difficulty, forced his
head down, into the sand.

But when they released him, he straightened his body, sand
clinging about his beard and face.

In his eyes there was a terrible fire, that of a cunning, and a
covetousness, and a hatred almost inconceivable to the educated,
sophisticated, civilized passengers of the *Alaria*, a hatred which
burned, like watch fires, outside the walls of the empire.

"Had we your weapons!" he cried.

"Such men have their possibilities," said the naval officer to
the captain.

"They make fearless, but dangerous, auxiliaries," said the
captain.

"Fortunately they are apt to spend more time dealing out death
and destruction to one another than to the empire," said the first
officer.

"The emperor is under pressure from many quarters to ponder
an edict of universal citizenship," said the young naval officer.

"That would be a military mistake of capital importance,"
said the captain.

"Assuredly," said the young officer.

*As these allusions might not be clear I shall mention that
citizenship within the empire was a prized possession. And more
was involved, considerably more, than matters of prestige or*

social standing. Without it, for example, one could be denied the right to hold land, denied the right to bring legal actions, denied the right to legal representation in court, denied the right to make wills, to bequeath property, and such. Careers, too, and advancement within them, often depended on citizenship. Employment in the vast bureaucracy of the civil service, for example, required citizenship. Without citizenship one was, in certain respects, even if free, little more than an animal. It was not merely that certain offices, certain forms of political power, were closed to one, but that one was, in a sense, not being a citizen, not really a member of the community. One was, in effect, without standing before the law. It was only gradually, and over a period of centuries, even thousands of years, that citizenship had become more widely available. In the beginning it extended only to a given class on the first Telnarian world; it spread later to other classes on that world, and then to the population of that world, and then, in turn, similarly, gradually, to the other Telnarian worlds; then, of course, later, it began to spread to certain classes on the provincial worlds, and so on. The apprehension of the young officer and the captain had to do with the military as a route to citizenship. The enlistment for both the regular military and for the auxiliaries was for twenty years, followed by a pension. Sons commonly followed the craft of their fathers. On worlds where the bindings had taken place this was required, the sons of soldiers being required to be soldiers, and so on. A fellow who enlisted in the regular military, the regular forces, received citizenship after his first year of service; a fellow who enlisted in the auxiliaries received it at the end of nine years. The value of citizenship was such that noncitizens with energy and ambition often seized upon the military as a route to the prize of citizenship, which, of course, descended to their children. This policy provided the regular military, and, to a lesser extent, the auxiliaries, with a large pool of capable, eager recruits on which they could draw. Two further observations are in order. Men normally understand the value of, and respect, what has cost them much time and labor. One who has literally been forced to earn his citizenship has learned its value, and never thereafter takes it lightly. Similarly, *such men tend to remain loyal to the empire. They make good citizens. The fear of the young officer and the captain is now clear: If citizenship were universally extended throughout the empire, this would remove one of the major enticements for men of quality to enter military service. Too, of course, obviously the universal extension of citizenship throughout the empire would cheapen it, and, in effect trivialize it. Those who do not care to earn their citizenship, of course, are muchly in favor of receiving it as free gift, like bread and entertainment in the cities. The agitation, and the riotous nature, of such elements constituted a force which could be exploited, of course, in a variety of ways by those politically adept at such matters. "Power to the people," so to speak, is always a popular slogan with those who have plans for putting the people to their own purposes. We can begin to understand, then, something of the factionalisms involved in such matters, and certain of the pressures to which the emperor and senate were sure to be subject.*

The barbarian, Ortog, growling with rage, more like a beast than a man, attempted to struggle to his feet, but was forced down again, on his knees. His eyes roved the tiers balefully. Women shrank back.

"Fear not, gentle ladies," said Pulendius, "for you are safe from such monsters."

The barbarian looked down, and fought the chains.

A ripple of uneasiness coursed among women in the tiers.

"Do not fear such brutes, beautiful, gentle ladies," said Pulendius. "The empire will protect you."

The barbarian suddenly, unexpectedly, cried out with rage, and, half rising, tore at the chains.

Some women in the stands cried out in fear.

The guards forced the barbarian once more to his knees.

"Do not be alarmed, beautiful, gentle ladies," said Pulendius. "The empire, invincible and eternal, stands between you and such beasts."

But there remained fear in the eyes of more than one. And here and there small, delicate hands fluttered at trembling breasts.

"He is quite helpless," said Pulendius. "He is well chained, as is appropriate for such brutes."

Again the barbarian cried out with rage, and attempted once more to rise to his feet.

A woman, startled, screamed.

Then the barbarian, sullen, his wrists bleeding, forced once more to his knees, ceased to tear at the chains.

"You see he is quite helpless," said Pulendius. "And he knows himself such."

A sound of relief escaped several in the stands.

"Behold him, on his knees, as such should be, before the empire."

There was laughter in the stands.

Suddenly again, in fury, the barbarian strove to rise to his feet.

At a sign from the captain the two guards, with blows, brought the barbarian again to his knees.

Blood streamed about his head.

"An admirably dangerous man," said the young naval officer, musingly.

"Yes, milord," said the captain.

Again the barbarian tried to rise. This time, with the nod of the captain observed, Pulendius gestured for two of the gladiators, one of the pairs with blunted spears, to rush forward. They did so, and struck the kneeling, chained figure several times, brutally, with the shafts of their implements. He was then bent over, on his knees, in the bloody sand.

When the barbarian straightened his body he, bloodied head up, sand clinging to his face and beard, regarded the captain and the young officer. In his eyes there was smoldering hatred. The young officer, he with the cords of the blood at his left shoulder, met the gaze calmly. The barbarian then looked about the tiers. Suddenly, his gaze stopped. He regarded the gladiator near the opening of the tiers, to his left, as he knelt, with a glance that was both keen, and, to some extent, of awe. This puzzled the gladiator, for he had never seen the barbarian before. After all, he was a fighter, and, before that, a mere peasant from a *festung* village, that of Sim Giadini, far away. The fascination of the prisoner with the features of the gladiator was noted by the young officer, who, himself, turned and regarded the gladiator. He saw nothing unusual in his features, nothing to warrant the scrutiny, apparently a fascinated, almost an unbelieving regard, of the barbarian. Then the young officer, curious, turned, again, to the gladiator. "Do you know him?" he asked.

"No, milord," said the gladiator.

"You have not met before?"

"Not to my knowledge," said the gladiator.

"Let the exhibition begin!" cried Pulendius, and called forth the first pair of gladiators, one of the two pairs with wooden swords. In the exhibition some rudiments of swordsmanship were demonstrated, and, in a few minutes, Pulendius himself adjudicated a mock match, one in which blows were drawn. The second pair demonstrated certain techniques of the spear, and then, as had the first, engaged in a mock match, which Pulendius again adjudicated, and expertly. The third match was again between a pair with wooden swords, only the swords were this time not the surrogates of the common wicked, short blade of the arena, but rather of the long sword, wielded with two hands, a weapon favored by certain barbarian peoples. The last exhibition was between the last pair of gladiators, also armed with spears, these formed however to resemble the long, double-headed spears of Kiros, a world in the Lidanian system. Both ends of the shaft were painted red, indicating a scoring surface. It was with these implements that the barbarian had been beaten. Pulendius, in his expert commentary, mentioned various facts about diverse weapons, their strengths and weaknesses, the diverse techniques of their employment, and such. There is, of course, a lore and history of weaponry, and weapons of diverse types, like musical instruments, tend to be the result of a long period of refinement and development. And the profession of arms, like other professions, has its complexity, and its masters. Those who do not understand, or appreciate, the expertise, the effort, the long hours of practice, the days and nights of thought involved, are naive, and in an area where naiveté can be dangerous. The sport of arms is an intricate and demanding one. Too, it is a quite serious one. Its games are not such as may be lightly lost.

From time to time the glance of the young naval officer passed musingly, thoughtfully, from the barbarian to the gladiator who crouched, intent on the exercises, near the entrance to the tiers.

The ensign pondered, curiously, what he had earlier noted, the reaction of the barbarian upon seeing the gladiator. But the gladiator was only a paid minion of Pulendius, a common sort. Too, it was extremely unlikely their paths had crossed.

The barbarian did not note the interest of the young officer, nor did the gladiator. The barbarian, bloodied, chained, doubtless sick from his beating, continued to regard the gladiator, whom he viewed, the officer noted, with a sort of wonder, of hostility, even of apprehension. The gladiator, on the other hand, was intent on the matches, perhaps noting how one man feinted, how another moved, how another communicated his intentions by pressing the ball of his foot into the sand, firmly, just before a thrust.

"Score!" called Pulendius, slapping one of the last fighters on the back. That fighter stood over the prostrate form of the other, the blunt, red-painted end of the mock spear but an inch from his throat. Then the victor stepped back, and, sweating, grinning, lifted his spear, turning, before the crowd. The other fellow scrambled up from the sand, retrieved his broken weapon, and exited.

There was applause.

"And now," called Pulendius, "for the climax of the evening's entertainment!"

The small crowd on the tiers leaned forward.

Pulendius turned dramatically toward the barbarian. "Stand," said Pulendius.

The barbarian, with some difficulty, rose to his feet. He then stood there, a little unsteadily, in the sand.

"Release him!" said Pulendius, pointing dramatically to the barbarian.

The barbarian himself did not seem surprised at this development.

"No!" cried a woman from the stands, frightened.

"Keep him chained!" cried another.

But, to the apprehension of many in the stands, and, we suspect, not merely of the women, one of the guards bent down, and undid the locks on the shackles which fettered the ankles of the barbarian.

"You see this pistol, and you know what it can do?" said one of the guards, brandishing it before the barbarian.

The barbarian did not deign to respond. But doubtless he was only too familiar with such devices, or devices of that sort.

"Undo the manacles," said Pulendius.

"No!" cried a woman.

But the guard who had attended to the shackles, and doubtless understood what was expected of him, and the projected course of events, unlocked the manacles. The barbarian then stood there, free, but within the scope of the fire pistols, indeed, at point-blank range.

"We shall see what stuff these fellows are made of," said Pulendius.

"He is not to reach Miton," said the minor officer to the woman in the pantsuit.

The woman in the pantsuit looked at the minor officer reproachfully.

"He will, of course," said the minor officer, "have his chance for life."

"Who will you fight?" asked Pulendius.

The barbarian turned toward the young naval officer, and pointed to him. "He," he said.

"Alas, no!" cried Pulendius, in dismay.

"They will put the barbarian against trained men, professional killers, gladiators?" said the woman in the pantsuit angrily to the minor officer.

"He could always be nailed to a public gate on Miton, or starved to death in a cage, thence to be thrown into a garbage pit," said the officer.

"Is this how the empire deals with its foes?" she asked.

"We deal with barbarians," said the officer, "as they deal with us, and with one another."

"I see," she said.

"You do not know the nature of these creatures," said the officer. "They must be dealt with mercilessly."

"You speak as though we might be at war," said the woman.

"We are always at war," said the officer.

The woman looked at him, incredulously.

"We have exterminated worlds of such creatures," said the officer. "But energies become precious, and it seems there are always more."

" 'War'?" asked the woman.

"War," said the officer.

"I did not know," she said.

"Such things occur mostly at the borders," he said.

"Is the empire not expanding?" asked the woman.

"The empire has contracted its borders, for defensive purposes," said the officer.

There might then have seemed a glimmer of fear in the woman's eyes.

"It is a strategically sound move," said the officer. "Do not fear. There is no danger. After a respite the empire will expand once more."

"Excellent!" she said.

"Let us enjoy the show," he said.

"Yes," she said.

"What weapons will you choose?" inquired Pulendius of the barbarian.

"Doubtless you have some in mind," said the barbarian, looking about himself.

Pulendius then mentioned some exotic weapons, that only fighters in exotic weaponry would be practiced with, the knife buckler of Ambos, the Kurasian darts, the Loranian torch, such things.

"Perhaps, then," said Pulendius, "the net and trident, the short sword and buckler?"

"I do not know them," said Ortog, prince of the Drisriaks, king of the Ortungen.

He seemed for a moment, then, suddenly, in spite of his rather proud mien, his folded arms, and such, to sway a little. He caught his balance.

"He seems weak," said the woman sitting beside the minor officer.

"He has not been overly fed," said the minor officer.

"You have starved him, to weaken him?" she said.

"The line would not wish to have to compensate Pulendius for the loss of a man," said the officer.

"I have chosen my weapons," said the barbarian.

"And what are they?" asked Pulendius.

"These," said the barbarian, lifting his hands.

Pulendius laughed.

But then he looked to the young naval officer, who lifted a hand, acceding to the barbarian's choice.

"Hinak!" called Pulendius.

One of the two fellows who had given the exhibition with the two-headed spears of Kiros, or the semblance of such, stepped forward. It was he who had been defeated in the mock match.

"Now, you have an opportunity to redeem yourself, Hinak," said Pulendius.

But Hinak did not seem amused.

Rather he was measuring the barbarian.

"And now, captain," said Pulendius, "may we not add some spice to the contest?"

The captain signaled to two of his men, who had been standing rather back in the shadows, between the tiers.

They retreated behind the tiers and then, after a moment, came out again. They carried what was, in effect, a sturdy metal pipe, about five feet in length, about four inches in thickness. Fixed on it were two rings, rather toward one end, one above the other, each about four inches in diameter. One of the sailors, then, with his foot, brushed sand away from a metal cap. He then removed this cap and put it to one side, outside the perimeter of the small arena. Revealed then, hitherto concealed by the sand and cap, was a cylindrical aperture. They set the postlike stake into this aperture, or socket, which was just within the wooden ring of the tiny arena, and to the left of the captain's party. It sank about two feet into the socket. From the sound the bottom of the socket was metal. The two rings fastened to the object clinked against its side. They secured this object in place with a bolt and lock, and put the sand back about its shaft.

The two men then went back again, behind the tiers.

Those in the tiers looked upon the pipe, with its rings, locked in place, in the sand.

One of the men in the audience slapped his knee.

The heart of the officer of the court began to pound madly.

In a moment she gasped, both in horror and protest, for the girl, Janina, by a chain and collar, she whose exquisiteness she had so envied the night before, was half led, half dragged into the tiny arena. From her right wrist, which was inclosed in a metal cuff, there dangled, on a short chain, another cuff, but one which was open. She was put down kneeling, behind the stake. The sailor who had not led her in took the free cuff through the lower of the two rings on the pipe, placed it about her left wrist and snapped it shut. She was then handcuffed to the pipe. Almost at the same time the other sailor locked the free end of the collar and chain about the higher ring on the stake. Janina was then fastened to the stake in two fashions, by the handcuffs and by the chain on her neck. Keys, tied together on a small cord, presumably to these devices, were laid on the surface of the wooden ring circling the sand, before the young naval officer.

"See how she is dressed!" exclaimed the woman in the pant-suit.

"That is called a *keb*," said the minor officer.

The officer of the court felt weak.

"You would think," said the woman in the pantsuit, "that she would at least have been permitted some form of slave tunic."

"But she is at the stake," said the minor officer.

There are many varieties of slave tunics. They are commonly light, sleeveless, quite short, one-piece garments, open from the hem to the waist on both sides, thus scarcely a tunic, no more, really, than a scandalously brief, revealing rag.

But the girl was not in such a garment, one so comparatively modest.

She was in a different form of garment, that called the *keb*.

The garment, before it is worn, resembles a long, narrow sash. The material of this *keb* was a loosely woven gray *corton*. It is put on the slave by first haltering her breasts, snugly, the knot behind her back. The long, dangling end is then taken down, behind her back, and up, snugly, between her legs. There it is held at the waist with one hand while the other takes the continuing free end about the body. When the free end has circled her body, it is passed about the portion which was being held, holding it in place, and is then tied.

"How dreadful a garment," said the woman in the pantsuit, approvingly.

"Yes," whispered the officer of the court.

Yet the garment was not, really, too different from the intimacies which she herself wore beneath her "same garb," only there, down there on the sand, of course, the woman was publicly so revealed.

The *keb*, of course, can be fastened on a slave in a variety of manners. For example, it need not be used to conceal the beauties of her breasts. It may simply be wrapped about the hips, and tucked in. An advantage of the *keb*, too, of course, is that it may serve a variety of purposes when not on the slave, such as hooding her, blindfolding her, gagging her, binding her, and such. Too, it might be remarked that it may be used as a sling for the carrying of burdens.

"You understand, of course," said the minor officer, addressing the woman in the pantsuit, "that she would not be in even the *keb* at the stake, if this were not a civilized pleasure cruise."

"Ah!" said the woman in the pantsuit, delightedly.

"Doubtless you are concerned for her," said the minor officer, smiling.

"No," said the woman in the pantsuit. "She is only a slave."

The officer of the court, trembling, looked down to the sand.

Janina, who seemed frightened, and perhaps had never been at the stake before, clung to the metal of the pipe, pressing herself fearfully against it, the palms of her small hands, too, up, against the metal.

"Any ladies who care to do so may now leave," suggested Pulendius, considerately.

But not a woman stirred in the tiers.

Pulendius smiled.

The officer of the court felt weak.

Pulendious turned to the barbarian, and, with his hand, indicated the girl at the pipe. "What do you think of her?"

"She is merely another slave," said the barbarian.

Janina moved a little, her chains making a tiny sound against the pipe.

"I do not understand," said Pulendius.

"Like these others," said Ortog, prince of the Drisriaks, king of the Ortungen, waving his hand toward the tiers.

Women shrank back. Many cried out in rage, in protest. Even men cried out, in anger.

"You let your slaves out of their collars," said the barbarian.

"Those are free women!" cried Pulendius, as though offended.

"At best, slaves," said Ortog, his arms folded across his chest.

"Absurd!" cried Pulendius.

Ortog then turned toward the young naval officer, he with the three purple cords at his left shoulder.

"Let them kneel before true men, and learn to be women," said Ortog.

The young naval officer met his gaze dispassionately.

The officer of the court put her hand to her breast. How conscious was she then of the intimate garments she had concealed beneath her "same garb," beneath the "frame-and-curtain."

"Hinak!" called Pulendius, angrily.

Hinak came forth, half bent, his hands ready, toward the center of the sand.

The barbarian assumed a similar position.

They began to circle one another.

"Wait! Separate!" said Pulendius.

The contestants backed away from one another.

The door had opened, you see, that main door leading into the hold, and a minor officer had entered. He hurried about the ring, before the tiers, and spoke quickly, seemingly urgently, certainly confidentially, to the captain. The young naval officer watched, curiously.

The barbarian, too, interestingly, observed this intrusion.

In a moment the captain rose, and turned to the crowd. "Forgive me," he said, smiling. "It is nothing. There is a small matter to attend to." He then left, followed by the first officer and the minor officer, he who had just entered that section of the hold.

"Please continue," said the second officer, he now of highest rank in the room.

"Begin!" said Pulendius to the contestants in the ring.

In a moment all attention was returned to the contest.

Madly was beating the heart of the officer of the court. She had never understood anything could be so real, so meaningful. Here, on the sand, knelt a girl, scarcely clad, a helpless prize, chained to a pipe, the stake. There, on the sand, men prowled about, eyeing one another, in a combat that might well issue in death for one of them.

A strange, wild, primitive dimension of possible existences opened up then before the startled, expanded imagination of the officer of the court, vistas of terrifying battles and rude kingdoms, with savage ways, vistas of huts and shelters, of halls and tents, of pavilions and palaces, of fortresses and castles, within which men were men and women, women, totally so, and other vistas, too, vistas of green leaves, and rocks, and the feel of wet earth beneath bare feet, vistas of dark forests, of the weaving of coarse cloths, of the cooking by open fires, of waiting anxiously, hopefully, for the hunters to return, vistas of truth and reality she had suspected, but had scarcely admitted could exist. How far away then seemed the dusty tomes of the law, the tedium of litigation, the procedures of the courts, the endless, meaningless trivialities of protocol, civility and discourse, which things seemed then but the remote semblance of a reality, a reality always somewhere else. There was reality here, the reality of the growth of crops, rising out of the moist earth, of rainfall, and storms, of the truths of animals, and of men and women. She had never realized the nature of reality before, that it was not documents and legalities, and banal conversation, and pretense, and hypocrisy, but that it was different, that it was as hard, and perfect, and as natural, and as simple, and as uncompromising, as wood, and stone, and iron and steel. The true world, the unsheltered world, was as real, she suspected, as a coiled rope or a diaphanous, clinging sheet of silk, as real as a weighty golden coin or the leather of a whip.

"Stop!" cried Pulendius, in alarm.

One of the guards rushed to the barbarian, holding his fire pistol to his temple.

The barbarian held Hinak from behind, his arms under Hinak's, his hands clasped behind the back of Hinak's neck, pressing slowly forward, and down.

With a grunt the barbarian released his hold, and Hinak went forward, on his knees, in the sand.

In another moment surely his neck would have been snapped.

Hinak rose up, and hurried away. Grateful he was to leave the sand alive.

"The barbarian has defeated a professional fighter," said the woman in the pantsuit, wonderingly.

"By some trick of wrestling, not with weapons," said the minor officer to her right.

At that moment there was a soft cry of surprise from many in the tiers. The officer of the court, as well, felt her body move backward, swaying back, just a little, on the tier.

"The ship is accelerating," said the minor officer.

"Am I not victorious?" asked Ortog.

Janina looked up at Ortog. Her small hands were pressed against the pipe to which she was chained.

"Oh, the contest is not yet done," Pulendius assured him.

The officer of the court noted how closely the steel encircled Janina's small wrists. They were small cuffs. The officer of the court realized, suddenly, they had been made for women. They would fit her as well as Janina. The collar was about Janina's throat. Had she been in such a collar she could have slipped it no more than the slave.

Ortog threw back his head and laughed knowingly.

"Why did you not kill him?" asked the young naval officer.

"I choose whom I kill," said Ortog.

The question of the young officer had made it clear to those who might be perceptive in the tiers that the barbarian was not intended to survive the evening. Perhaps he might then have availed himself of the satisfaction of destroying one enemy, perhaps in the same moment that the trigger on the fire pistol could have been pulled.

"Ambos!" called Pulendius, irritably. This fighter was from the world, Ambos, and was known professionally by that name. This was not uncommon in the arena, naming the fighters for worlds, or cities, or animals, or appearance. He was the fellow who had been successful in the last mock match, that with what were intended to represent the two-headed spears of Kiros. We do not know his real name. One account gives it as 'Elbar.' More importantly, for our purposes, he had once wrestled professionally on Ambos, before applying to the arena masters.

Ambos came forth.

"Kill him," said Pulendius, indicating the barbarian. He then stepped back. There was to be no mock adjudication of holds, of breaks, and such, in this match.

Ambos, of course, had watched the previous match, and had noted the fate of Hinak. The barbarian was clearly not a trained wrestler, but he was unusually strong, and that made him dangerous. Ambos had no intention of taking him lightly.

"Close! Finish him!" said Pulendius.

But the two men, together in the center of the ring, only thrusted, feinted, and reached for holds.

"Finish him!" said Pulendius.

Suddenly the two men grappled, locked together, swaying back and forth.

"Finish him!" cried Pulendius.

But to the horror of Pulendius and those in the tiers the barbarian, slowly, by sheer strength, drew Ambos from his feet, and then slowly turned him, and placed his back over his knee, his hands pressing down, the knee as the fulcrum, the spine a doomed lever, subjected to terrible force at each termination, surely in a moment to snap, surely incapable of withstanding such pressure.

But then the barbarian let Ambos, gasping, wild-eyed, slip to the sand.

The barbarian rose to his feet.

"Am I not victorious?" he asked.

"You did not kill him," observed the young naval officer.

"I did not choose to do so," said the barbarian.

Ambos was helped from the sand by two of Pulendius's men.

"And whom would you choose to kill?" asked the young naval officer.

"One worthy," said the barbarian, his arms folded.

"Me?" asked the young naval officer, quietly, amused.

The barbarian turned about and lifted his arm. He pointed at the gladiator with whom we have been hitherto acquainted, he who had been raised in a small *festung* village, that of Sim Giadini, he who had been behind Pulendius, and to his right, on the evening of the captain's table, he who had looked upon the officer of the court, who was even of the blood, as though she might be naught but a common slave, one such that she might be purchased in any market, and thence put to the common purposes of slaves.

"He!" said the barbarian.

"Why?" asked the young officer, puzzled.

The barbarian was silent.

"Who is he? Who do you think he is?" asked the young officer, leaning forward, keenly interested.

Again the barbarian refused to respond.

"Where are you from, fighter?" asked the young officer of the gladiator.

"From the *festung* village of Sim Giadini, milord," said the gladiator. He also identified the world, but we think it best, again, at this point, in order not to anticipate, to withhold its name. It was, however, we recall, one of the claimed worlds within the imperial system.

"No," said the barbarian. "No."

"It will be with weapons!" said Pulendius, angrily.

"Let him live," called a man.

"He has been victorious!" called another. "Free him!"

Pulendius looked angrily toward the source of such cries.

"Kill him!" cried a woman.

"Kill him!" cried the woman in the pantsuit.

"Kill him!" cried another woman, a young woman. The officer of the court saw that it was the salesgirl, she from the ship's

shop, from whom, earlier that day, she had made certain purchases. She had not noticed her in the tiers before. She was
terribly embarrassed, now, to see her there. After all, she knew
the nature of those purchases. Had the salesgirl seen her here,
had she looked at her? Would she have wondered if she, from
Terennia, had such things on, beneath the "same garb," beneath
the "frame-and-curtain." But of course she did. But would the
salesgirl suspect that? How embarrassing! Too, what right had
the salesgirl to be here, such a person, a mere employee of the
line, at an entertainment for passengers! How embarrassing, the
whole business!

"Let him live!" cried a man.

"Kill him!" cried the woman in the pantsuit.

"Kill him!" cried the salesgirl.

"It will be with weapons, and we shall choose!" said Pulendius.

"The barbarian is finished now," said the minor officer to the
woman in the pantsuit.

"The short sword, without buckler," said Pulendius.

"Excellent," said the minor officer.

Suddenly, again, there was an unsteadiness on the tiers, and
some soft cries of surprise. One of the guards went down to one
knee, his balance briefly lost, and then, again, stood.

"A change in course," explained the minor officer to the
woman in the pantsuit.

To be sure, the change in course was one rather abrupt for
such a ship.

"We have a dog to set on you," said Pulendius.

There was laughter from some of his men.

"Dog!" summoned Pulendius.

The gladiator, he with whom we have been hitherto acquainted, stepped forward, over the wooden ring, onto the sand.

Women gasped, for the figure was a mighty one, that of he
who had now come onto the sand, well into the light.

"I am Ortog," said Ortog, announcing himself to the gladiator, as he had not to the others, "prince of the Drisriaks, king
of the Ortungs."

"Do you know the short sword?" asked the gladiator.

"No," said Ortog.

"Choose some other weapon," advised the gladiator.

"The small blade will be satisfactory," said Ortog.

"Some regard me as reasonably skilled with the weapon," said the gladiator.

There was laughter from the men of Pulendius.

The gladiator, you see, was, of all the school of Pulendius, he who was most skilled with that blade. It had served him well on four worlds, and in ten arenas. Pulendius had even hopes that his skills might carry him to the imperial arenas of the Telnarian worlds themselves. Often Pulendius had wondered at his almost incomprehensible aptitude with such weapons. The naturalness, the quickness, the ease, with which he handled such weapons was not to be expected in one who was a peasant. One might expect that gigantic strength to be sometimes found in a peasant but seldom, if ever, such speed, such subtlety and finesse. It was almost as if the use of such things was as natural to him as that of teeth to the vi-cat, of talons to the hawk. It was almost as though the use of such things were somehow bred in him, were somehow in the blood itself.

"I choose the short sword," said Ortog.

"It is my assumption then," said the gladiator, "that you are familiar with the weapon."

Two such weapons, wrapped in scarlet silk, were brought.

The gladiator tested each, and then indicated that Ortog might have his choice of blades.

Ortog took one and backed to the opposite side of the circle.

"Is it that you wish to die?" asked the young officer of the barbarian.

"If I am to die," said Ortog, "it is not unfitting that it be at the hands of such."

"A common gladiator?"

"You think him such?" asked Ortog.

The young officer shrugged.

Ortog laughed, and hefted the blade. It seemed he liked its balance.

"It is much like a knife," he said.

It did have something of the advantages of a double-edged

knife, the capacity to slash on both the forestroke and the back-
stroke, the capacity to shift direction quickly, the capacity to
thrust, at close quarters. On the other hand it had some of the
advantages of the sword. It was long enough to keep a knife at
bay, to outreach a knife, and to make fencing, parrying and
disengaging, and such, practical.

"He is indeed a dog," said Ortog, viewing the gladiator. "But
that is not his name."

"His name is 'Dog,' " said Pulendius.

"What is your name?" asked Ortog of the gladiator.

"I am called 'Dog,' milord," he said.

"Do you think I do not know your house?" asked Ortog.

"I am Dog, of the school of Pulendius," said the gladiator.

"Do not kill him immediately," whispered Pulendius to the
gladiator. "Carry him for a bit, for the crowd."

This remark was overheard by Ortog, and his eyes glistened
wildly, just for an instant.

He looked about himself, at the enclosing steel walls of the
ship.

At that moment the ship swerved and people on the tiers cried
out, surprised. More than one lost his balance, and fell against
others. Those standing on the sand, Pulendius, and the gladiator,
and Ortog, almost lost their balance. The girl, Janina, she in the
keb, chained at the pipe, was thrown to her left, and only kept
from falling further by the handcuffs, the chain of which, fastened in place through the ring, pulled against the pipe. Then,
again, the ship steadied itself.

The second officer rose briefly to his feet. "It is all right,"
he said. "These are adjustments in our course. There is no reason
to be alarmed."

The crowd then, somewhat uneasily, returned its attention to
the sand.

"Our peoples," said Ortog to the gladiator, "have been hereditary enemies for ten thousand years."

"I am Dog, of the *festung* village of Sim Giadini," said the
gladiator.

After the first moment of crossing steel, no more than four or five touches, sensitive, exploratory, the gladiator stepped back. "Choose another weapon," he said.

"I am Ortog, prince of the Drisriaks, king of the Ortungs, of the Alemanni."

"Choose another weapon," advised the gladiator.

"Die, dog of an Otung!" cried the Ortung, and hurled himself at the gladiator, who stepped to one side and did not slip his blade into the side of the barbarian, who went past him.

The barbarian fell to his knees in the sand.

He turned about, on his knees, in fury. "You dare to humiliate one who is a prince and king?" he cried.

"Forgive me, milord," said the gladiator.

The barbarian again charged the gladiator, who, again, evaded the charge. Such a charge might have been comprehensible with the mighty long sword, two-handled, like a weighty bolt of edged lightning, sweeping aside all before it, but it was not practical with the shorter blade.

The gladiator looked to Pulendius.

The disgust of Pulendius was evident.

"Kill him," said Pulendius.

The barbarian once again engaged, but his every thrust was parried away harmlessly. He might have been trying to pierce a fence of steel.

"Kill him," said Pulendius.

The barbarian thrust again, but the gladiator had drawn the thrust, by seeming to provide his opponent an opening, and Ortog extended his thrust, overextending it, the gladiator fading back. It was a mistake one more practiced with such a weapon would not have made. The gladiator's blade, behind his guard, was against the side of his neck.

Both men stood very still.

"Kill him," said Pulendius.

The gladiator then stepped away from the barbarian.

The barbarian then again, this time in mindless fury, rushed toward the gladiator and then, suddenly, was sprawled in the sand, on his back. The heel of the gladiator's bootlike sandal crushed down on his wrist, and the sword left his hand, lost to the side, half buried in the sand, and then he lay there, sweating, gasping, in the sand, on his back, at the gladiator's feet. The gladiator's sword was at his heart.

"You are an Otung of Otungs," said the barbarian, looking up at the gladiator, in awe.

"I am Dog, of the *festung* village of Sim Giadini," said the gladiator.

"Strike," said the barbarian.

"Kill him," said Pulendius.

The gladiator looked up to the tiers.

"Let him live!" called a man in the tiers.

"Kill him," cried many of the women.

"Kill him!" cried the woman in the pantsuit.

"Kill him!" called the salesgirl.

"Strike!" commanded the barbarian.

But the gladiator stepped away from the figure in the sand, and lowered his weapon.

"Kill him!" said Pulendius.

"No," said the gladiator.

"Why not?" asked Pulendius.

"He was much beaten," said the gladiator, "he is weak, he does not know the weapon."

"Do not let one of lesser blood kill me!" said the barbarian.

The gladiator did not understand this remark.

"Fellow," said the young naval officer.

"Milord?" said the gladiator.

"I am surprised you did not kill him," said the officer.

"Surely, milord," said the gladiator, "only a king may kill a king."

"He is a barbarian," said the officer.

"But a king," said the gladiator.

The young naval officer picked up the keys which lay on the surface of the wooden rim circling the sand, and tossed them, on their cord, to the gladiator.

"You are victorious," he said.

"My thanks, milord," said the gladiator.

He looked down at the slave, who, kneeling in the *keb*, it twisted about her body, was looking up at him, excitedly.

"Look at her," said the woman in the pantsuit. "She is like a pretty little animal."

"In heat," said the minor officer beside her.

"Yes," said the woman in the pantsuit.

The officer of the court trembled within the "same garb," within the "frame-and-curtain."

A woman in heat, one with sexual needs, how fearful seemed such a thought!

"Please unchain me, Master," said the slave to the gladiator, "that I may render my obeisance!"

The gladiator threw the keys, on their cord, to one of the sailors, who then bent to undo the locks, that on the collar, those on the cuffs, that the slave might be loosed from the pipe.

The barbarian rose unsteadily to his feet, near the center of the sand. He did not pick up his sword, which still lay in the sand, half buried.

Freed of her restraints, the cuffs, the collar and chain, the slave crawled to the feet of the gladiator, and then, kneeling before him, looked up at him. She then put down her head and began to lick and kiss his feet.

"Who would permit a woman to do such a thing to him?" asked a woman.

"Such as he!" said another.

"And might command it!" said another.

"One who is a master!" said another, thrilled.

The gladiator did not seem surprised at the action of the slave.

The officer of the court conjectured, to her chagrin, that this might not be the first time a woman had been thusly at his feet. She suspected then that slaves might be kept, secretly, in the schools.

"Look at her," said a woman nearby. "It is true. She is in heat."

"She had better be," said a man.

The officer of the court felt faint.

"See her!" said another woman.

"Such are born to lick the feet of men," said another.

"So are you all," said a man.

"Please!" protested the woman.

The officer of the court blushed, hotly, muchly then again sensitive to the garments beneath her drab, bulky "same garb," beneath the "frame-and-curtain."

The officer of the court trembled.

"What would it be like to be a slave," she wondered, "to be owned by a man, to be subject to punishment, even to death, if he pleased, having no choice but to obey him, immediately, perfectly, unquestioningly?"

"She had better be in heat," had suggested the man, some vulgar fellow.

"If she were a slave," she thought, "would she not, too, at least at times, have to be in heat? Would the master not require it?"

"Too," she thought, shuddering, "if I were owned, truly owned, I do not think I could help being in heat, at least sometimes, whether I wanted it or not."

The gladiator stepped back from the slave.

Then he, and Pulendius, turned to face the barbarian. The barbarian, arms folded, stood near the center of the ring. The sword lay near his feet, unretrieved.

The barbarian seemed to be listening, though it was not clear what he might be hearing, or thought he heard. Perhaps it was feet running in the passageway outside.

"Kill him," said Pulendius.

"No," said the gladiator. "Forgive me, milord."

Pulendius looked at him.

"I am a free man, milord," said the gladiator.

Pulendius turned to the young naval officer.

"It is quite all right," said the young officer, rising. "Give me your pistol," he said to one of the guards.

The weapon was instantly surrendered to him.

"Kill him!" cried the woman in the pantsuit, pointing to the barbarian.

"Kill him!" cried the salesgirl.

"Kill him!" cried others.

"You are, at most, slaves!" said the barbarian to the women.

"Kill him!" cried yet more of the women.

The young naval officer leveled the pistol at the heart of the barbarian.

At that very moment there was a deafening, crashing sound and a screaming of metal. Tiers collapsed and sand, like a storm, swirled into the air. Everyone was thrown from his feet. There were screams and curses. The lights failed, and then came on again. Doubtless many were injured. The officer of the court, and others, were now on the steel floor of the hold, splintered planking about them. The young officer, on his knees, pistol in hand, looked wildly about. He could not see the barbarian. It was not clearly understood at the time, but in that first hit, one of the upper decks of the vessel had been opened, and tons of debris were blasted loose into space.

The ship began to spin sickeningly.

The second officer, followed by others, was staggering toward the door.

· · · CHAPTER 12 · · ·

The Alaria, as we may recall, was far from the customary lanes of commerce and traffic. We may speculate that her earlier orbiting at Tinos had something to do with taking aboard the young naval officer, who had had business on that world, it perhaps having to do with negotiations of a sort, that world serving sometimes as a neutral ground, a meeting place, between various barbarian nations in that area and the empire. Similarly, there were, here and there, trading worlds, or ports thereon, where commercial transactions, and various forms of intercourse and communication, between diverse, perhaps mutually suspicious worlds, could take place. The use of such points and worlds was to reduce the possibilities of espionage, terrorism, sabotage, contagion, and such. Too, it was at Tinos that the barbarian,

Ortog, a prisoner, had been brought aboard. It is possible that he was given into the custody of the empire as some token of good faith, as a pledge of some sort. Later, however, as we may recall, contact had been lost with Tinos, or, at least, Tinos station, the small imperial base on Tinos. What had occurred was that the barbarian fleet, that of the Ortungs, or Ortungen, those ships loyal to Ortog, hearing of his capture, and his conveyance to Tinos, had set out in pursuit. It had been learned at Tinos station, from several imperial officials, subjected to lengthy tortures, best left undescribed, that Ortog had been taken aboard the Alaria. The officials had also, at last, under severe duress, provided the Ortungen with access to the charting codes which enabled them to establish the itinerary, and probable course, of the Alaria.

We shall briefly sketch the events of the next four days.

The Alaria, which was not purely a pleasure ship, as you may have suspected, gave a rather good account of herself, considering her speed, maneuverability and armament. One of the seven pursuing ships was destroyed, and another seriously damaged. Still, after the first moments, after the closing, which took place at a distance of some twenty-five hundred miles, the issue could not be seriously in doubt. The Alaria, twisted, scorched, portions of the upper decking lost, the hull opened, lighting dimmed, life-support systems out in many sections, spun slowly in space, powerless.

In four places hollow "moles," the boarding tubes, drilled into the hull, and then, just as the plating, in its gigantic burned circle, better than ten feet in diameter, was snapped free, torrents of fire burst inward, shearing away any possible resistance, melting even the lighter steel of the opposing walls, those lining corridors opposite the mole. Through these apertures then, hurrying through, rushing over the steaming steel, through that large glowing opening from which molten globules still descended, blasting left and right, poured armored warriors, Ortungen.

There was resistance, of course, within the ship, but it was scattered, pathetic and doomed.

On the first day the Ortungen established control of the middle

*decks, this dividing the defenders. On the second day they seized
the commissaries, and the arsenal, which, in any event, had
been available only to a small number of defenders. There was
some fighting with crew members, from cabin to cabin, and
corridor to corridor, but the passengers were, on the whole, in
accord with imperial policies, not armed. Little quarter was
given. Crew members were, on the whole, killed. Many prisoners
were taken. These were stripped, and sorted through. Most were
killed. The strongest, healthiest men tended to be spared, and
the most attractive of the women. The male prisoners were then
separated from the female prisoners and both were conducted
through the moles to the barbarian ships, where they were placed
in separate steel holds. They would be kept for slaves. There
were many uses, heavy labor, work in the fields, and such, to
which male slaves might be put, and there were, of course, many
uses to which female slaves might be put, as well. On the third
day the Ortungen secured access to central engineering, which
gave them selective control, among other things, of all lighting,
heating and life-support systems which were not self-contained,
and designed for functioning on a temporary, emergency basis.
Soon, one by one, overcome by darkness and cold, coughing,
gasping for breath, the tiny pockets of resistance succumbed.
They then emerged, as commanded, the men standing, their
hands clasped on their heads, the women crawling, to be taken
into custody. Again, the fates of these were decided, as had been
that of their predecessors.*

*Not all the passengers, and such, of course, fell to the bar-
barians.*

*There were, naturally, many escape capsules, or lifeboats,
on the* Alaria. *Some, we might recall, had been stored even in
Section 19, of the hold.*

After the initial hit on the *Alaria*, one of several, the officer
of the court, buffeted, and squirming, fighting with other passengers, had fled from Section 19, thinking of nothing else, in
her terror, as many of the others, but of reaching her own cabin,
as though there might be some safety there. She did reach it,
through a bedlam of cries, of tearing metal, of warning klaxons
and such, and locked herself within. After a few hours the light

went out in the cabin, some cables doubtless cut somewhere. A little later she tried the lever in the washbasin, and found there was no water.

Huddling inside the cabin, behind the steel door, she occasionally heard cries outside, and running feet. More than once she heard the hiss of a weapon.

On the second day she heard pounding on cabin doors farther down the corridor, and harsh voices, ordering occupants to come forth, men standing, their hands clasped on their head, women on all fours.

She heard a scream from outside, a woman's scream. She also heard a blow, perhaps a kick, and a cry of pain.

"Strip her," she heard.

"A pretty one," said a man's voice, after a moment.

The officer of the court, incidentally, at this point, no longer wore the bulky "frame-and-curtain," and she herself had unclasped it, fearfully, almost of necessity, in the press, in the rush and buffeting to escape from the hold, lest she be turned about by it, or even strangled in its confinement, and, in a moment, it had been torn away from her, lost and trampled somewhere below. She did, however, continue to wear the cumbersome, drab "same garb," and, beneath it, of course, certain other garments, those of a sort which she would never have dared to show to one such as Tuvo Ausonius. He would never accept such garments on a free woman, only, if at all, on a slave. Indeed, he might command them of a slave.

"They will keep her," said the first man.

The officer of the court wondered if she herself, under such circumstances, would be kept, if she would be found pleasing enough to be kept. She hoped so, desperately.

"Crawl, to the end of the corridor, hurry!" commanded the second man.

She heard weeping.

"Hurry!" she heard, and another cry of pain.

"Would they keep me?" wondered the officer of the court. "Would I be pleasing enough to be kept? Oh, I hope so. I hope so!"

Then, in a moment, she heard pounding on her own door,

ordering that it be opened, and that men were to come forth in one fashion, and women in another.

She drew back from the door, terrified.

The door was tried.

"Bring the spike," she heard.

She heard something being put against the door, pressed against it. Then there was a sudden whirring sound, as of metal being shaved away. She then heard something drawn back, out of the door. She then heard another sound, as of something forced into an aperture. Faint, frightened, crouching by the door in the darkness, she reached out and felt it, something like a small conical nozzle. Then, in an instant, she heard a hiss of gas. She fled back into the cabin and behind the bed, and knelt there, terrified, distraught, hearing the gas entering the cabin. Then, knowing nothing else to do, terrified, she pressed herself beneath the bed, concealing herself there. There was very little room there, no more than in some devices for the confinement of slaves, some even, barred, beneath the master's bed, in which a slave might be kept, until she was wanted for serving. More importantly the space was small enough not to seem to afford an obvious hiding place. The officer of the court, moreover, as we remember, was a slender young woman, and such might be kept in spaces even smaller. For example, magicians have used such women for certain "vanishing tricks," in which the woman occupies a very small space, one so small that it occurs to few that that space, perhaps at the bottom of a trunk, could afford a concealment.

She fought to retain consciousness.

She heard the door break in.

A light flashed about, in the room.

"It is empty," said a voice.

"Look about," said a voice. "Look in the closets, in the lavatory."

The officer of the court, naturally, had no mask. She could feel the harsh nap of the rug against her left cheek as she lay, her head toward the door. She saw the boots of a man, or the borders of them, illuminated for a moment, in the light.

"Look under the bed," said a man.

Her fingers, in misery, cut at the rug.

"There is no room there," said a man.

"Look," said the other.

She saw the light flash, the beam illuminating the gas in the room, under the side of the bed, that farthest from where she lay, that which was nearest the cabin door.

"There is nothing there," said a voice.

It was possible he might have gone to the other side of the bed, or conducted a more thorough investigation, but, perhaps thinking it fruitless, he did not do so.

Too, just then a voice called from outside, in the corridor, and the two men exited the room.

She had then lost consciousness.

She had awakened a few hours later, sick, thirsting, and terribly hungry.

She crawled to the basin and again tried the lever, but, again there was no water. She then went to the lavatory bowl, willing to avail herself of even this source, as might have a thirsting slave, but found to her dismay that it was dry. It had been drained, and, of course, could not be replenished. Men, or slaves, had come later to the cabins, checking them, to make certain that even such sources would not be available to the defenders. The doors, too, had been set awry on their hinges so they could not be locked, or even closed. That had presumably been done by men, with tools.

She returned to her place beneath the bed but, in a few hours, miserably, weakly, crawled out.

She went to the dark corridor.

She could still smell a slight fragrance of the gas in the room, behind her, and in the corridor.

There might be some food in the lounge, she thought. Perhaps something in the adjoining serving area, or kitchen, perhaps even scraps, crumbs, on the floor, beneath the table and the chairs. Too, here and there, in the corridors, there were litter vessels, and who knew what might have been cast aside, thoughtlessly, into one, what precious things, perhaps a bit of a roll, or the core of a fruit.

She kept on all fours in the corridor.

Thusly, if light should suddenly be cast upon her, perhaps the strangers, the boarders, might not instantly fire. Was this not the fashion in which they wished civilized women, at least initially, to be before them?

Once away from her cabin area there was a dim lighting in the corridors.

This frightened her, but the corridors seemed empty, empty and very long.

She rose to her feet, but kept close to the walls of the corridors.

At points she noted certain passages, of which she would have liked to avail herself, were sealed, and the pressure gauges indicated a near vacuum behind them. The elevators were doubtless inoperable, and in any case, were to be avoided. But she would not have needed them, in any event, or stairs, to reach the lounge from her cabin, the main floor of the lounge.

She cried out.

There was a body bolted to a bulkhead, to her right. It was in uniform. It was that of the minor officer, he who had sat near her on the evening of the entertainment, he who had conversed with the woman in the pantsuit, the same evening the *Alaria* had come under attack. The front of his uniform had been drenched with blood, now long dried. He had served as the target, it seemed, in some primitive contest.

In a moment she had come to the large viewing port in the hall, not far from the lounge.

She had looked through this before. It was here that the gladiator had come up behind her, and here that the captain had offered to escort her to her cabin.

Outside she could see, from this vantage point, the outlines of four barbarian ships. The *Alaria* was illuminated in their search beams. Here and there, there were pieces of debris, floating in space, seemingly suspended there in a calm steadiness and stillness. And then she saw, too, the shattered wrecks, blasted apart, of certain escape capsules, of lifeboats. Such, clearly, had been fired upon. Others had perhaps been blown open but propelled outward into space, then as lifeless as small asteroids. The strangers, the boarders, doubtless had guns ready, set to track and fire on such vessels. A number must have fled the *Alaria* in the first hours of the attack. She wondered how many might have been successful in their escape, what the crowding would have been. She remembered the press at the door of Section 19, in the hold. She knew nothing of the mechanisms of the lifeboats. Too, she would be terrified to trust herself to such things, so tiny, such frail barks in such vast seas, like lonely motes of steel in the enormous night, so far from commercial lanes, in an area of space scarcely charted.

Perhaps it would be too open, too bold, she thought, to proceed directly to the lounge.

And might they not have it guarded, lest others, like herself, think to find food or drink there?

Perhaps she could approach it, she thought, by means of the upper balcony of the general entertainment hall, which gave access, through a passage, to the lounge's upper balcony. Then she could look down into the lounge, the main floor, and see if it were safe.

At this point she heard, from the hallway behind her, feminine laughter.

She cast about, wildly, looking for a place to hide.

But there seemed none.

Then, as the voices seemed almost upon her, she crouched down, back, between the lower rim of the port and the railing, to the right, as one would face the port. If one were searching for her there one would doubtless have discovered her, but if one were not looking for her, it was not unlikely that her presence in this simple ensconcement might be overlooked.

"Move!" said a female voice, sharply.

"Yes, Mistress," said another female voice, frightened.

"It is heavy, Mistress," said another female voice.

"Hurry," said another female voice, this one, too, with uncompromising sharpness.

"Yes, Mistress!" said the female voice which had complained of the weight of something.

The officer of the court heard, too, the sounds of chains.

She pressed herself back into her nook.

Two women, stripped, passed her. Between them they bore a bulging silken sheet filled with a miscellany of precious items, doubtless loot taken from cabins. They could scarcely manage their burden. The officer of the court noted, to her horror, that their ankles were shackled. These were the chains she had heard. But even more startling to the officer of the court was the nature of the two women who followed the laden pair, two who stood to them obviously in some strict supervisory capacity, this made clear by their mien, and, too, by the whips they carried. It was the laughter of this second pair which had reached her ears but moments before. These two women following the shackled pair were among the most sensuous women she had ever seen. They were garbed, if one may so speak of it, in brief tunics, incredibly brief, and muchly open. On the wrists of these women, and on their arms, and slung about their throats, was much jewelry, things doubtless from the loot, with which they had bedecked themselves. On the wrist of one was a bracelet of diamonds that might have been the ransom of a city. Suddenly, startled, the office of the court noted, about the throat of the other was a golden necklace which she had little doubt was her own, that which she had worn at the captain's table. But beneath the neck-laces, and strings of jewels, and such, which these women had flung about their necks in lavish prodigality she could detect, clearly, closely encircling each's neck, a different device, a chain. This was locked shut, behind the back of the neck. Although the officer of the court could not see this from her vantage point, there depended from this chain, in front, a disk. On this disk appeared the name of the barbarian ship to which each was assigned, and a designation of the quarters upon it which each must serve and clean. These two women were vital, and held themselves beautifully. Muchly did their appearance contrast with that of the wretched, shackled creatures they supervised, creatures which they obviously held in the greatest contempt. One of these women held in her hand a piece of roasted fowl.

"Please, Mistress, let us pause, but for a moment!" begged one of the bearers of loot. Indeed, it is not unlikely that precious objects once her own lay mixed somewhere within that weighty heap which so tested the strength of herself and her miserable companion. Indeed, perhaps she could see them.

"Very well," said one of the muchly bejeweled women. They were ship slaves. Barbarians do not like to be without their slaves.

The burden of the two shackled women was lowered to the floor, gratefully.

The officer of the court, fearfully, shrank back further in her nook.

"Kneel," said one of the supervisors, "hands on your thighs, where we can see them."

Instantly the two shackled women obeyed.

"You need not open your knees," said the other supervisor. "You are not now before men."

One of the shackled women moaned.

The supervisors laughed.

The supervisor with the bit of roast fowl tore off a bit of it in her teeth, and chewed on it.

"Please, Mistress," said one of the kneeling women, "may we not be fed?"

"Do not dare to look upon us," said one of the supervisors. "Keep your head down."

"Yes, Mistress," said the woman, hurriedly lowering her head.

"You have not yet finished your work," she was told.

"Yes, Mistress," said the woman.

Suddenly the other supervisor, laughing, cracked her whip.

The two shackled women cried out in misery.

"Up," said the supervisor, "resume your burden!"

"But Mistress!" protested one of the women, for they had knelt but a moment before.

Then she cried out as the lash fell upon her.

"Please, no, Mistress!" she wept.

"Instant obedience is required of slaves," she was informed.

"Yes Mistress!" she wept, and she and her companion hastily rose to their feet, and each, again, seized up two corners of the sheet and, with difficulty swung it up, free of the floor.

"Turn about, move, slaves!" said the angry supervisor.

Then the two shackled women bore again, between them, their heavy burden.

The one supervisor cast aside the bit of roast fowl, having had what she wanted of it.

She wiped her hand on her thigh.

The officer of the court heard the lash fall twice more.

"Hurry, slaves!" she heard.

"Yes, Mistress," she heard. "Yes, Mistress!"

When the women had disappeared down the corridor the officer of the court crept forth from her hiding place and seized up the bit of roast fowl, eagerly biting away what particles of it clung still to the light, hollow bone. Then she licked and sucked the bone, and her fingers, for the least bit of grease. But such minums of provender could do little more than mock the rage of her hunger. Bitterly she knelt on the floor, before the window, recalling food she had refused, dishes she had rejected, returning them to kitchens with her sharp words for cooks. Now she would have eagerly addressed herself to such largesse, such gifts, even head down, feeding from a plate set on the floor, beside a master's chair. And her throat was parched. Never had she been so hungry and so thirsty.

Were there passengers and crew members still free on the ship? She did not know.

Could the ship be regained?

It did not seem likely. She recalled the openness, the indifference, the assurance with which the two women, supervising the bearers of loot, those bearers, too, doubtless loot as much as any they bore, had walked the corridor.

She recalled the two women with the whips. They had been among the best-postured, best-figured and most sensuous women she had ever seen. She had not doubt but that they were dieted, exercised and trained. Such, you see, is permissible with animals, and slaves.

What was she to do?

She was afraid to surrender.

She did not even know if she would be permitted to do so. She might not even receive an opportunity to do so. She might be fired upon, a moving object, instantly, at first sight, cut in two in some corridor by a blast of fire.

Perhaps she might surrender to ship slaves.

But she was afraid of them, and their strictness, and the contempt in which she knew they would hold her.

She thought of herself naked, in shackles.

And she knew they would not hesitate to use their whips.

But would men not protect her, if she made it clear to them that she would strive to please them, and desperately and eagerly, in any way they might desire, literally in *any way* they might desire?

Might they not find her body of interest, and the beauties of her face, so sensitive and expressive, and her softness, and her dispositions, to love and serve?

But how could she even think such thoughts, she, an officer of a court?

Surely they were the thoughts of a slave!

Was she naught, in her heart, but a slave?

But she had gathered that not all prisoners were assured of being kept.

She had gathered that from a remark of one of the strangers, one of the boarders, almost outside her very door.

Would they regard her as suitable to be kept, to serve them, or to be exhibited on a slave block?

She did not know.

She was afraid.

But she must have food. She must have drink.

She was frightened.

Perhaps she could continue to hide.

Then she cried out with misery, for, from where she knelt, she could see out the port, and now, outside, against the glassine substance of the port itself, adrift in space, on its back, she saw the body of the captain.

Then she fled from that place, one so open, to an emergency stairwell, one reached through a heavy steel door, in which there was a small panel with wire-reinforced glass, one from which she could reach the balcony of the theater, and thence, the upper level of the main lounge.

She stayed for a time in a narrow corridor, reached from the stairwell. She crouched there, frightened, as might have an animal in its burrow. Then she heard a sound to her right, and hurried away from it, arriving in a moment at an entrance to the balcony of the theater.

She was afraid to open the door, but heard steps behind her. She opened the door a tiny crack and crawled through, onto the carpeting of the balcony of the theater and then hid between tiers of seats. The steps passed by, outside the door. She found a piece of candy, on the carpeting beneath a seat. She seized it up and pressed it into her mouth, devouring it. She looked about for more, but found none. She heard voices below. She crawled to the front of the balcony, to look down, toward the stage. On the stage and in the area immediately below it and before it there was set up a sort of headquarters or communication center. There were several tables there and men monitored various devices. Behind one of the tables at the center of the stage, considering a chart, surrounded by men, was Ortog, prince of the Drisriaks, king of the Ortungs. How different he seemed now, no longer a haggard, demeaned, starved prisoner, but now, armed and mighty, a vital, commanding, merciless, fearful, terrible giant of a man. Seeing such a man she trembled, and muchly then did know herself a woman. Other men came and went, delivering reports, receiving orders, utilizing the lower entrances. Suspended by the wrists, at the left of the stage, and several feet above it, there hung, lifeless, two men. They had no feet. Their feet had been cut off and then they had apparently been drawn aloft, where they had bled to death. Their bodies suggested that they had undergone interrogation before being disposed of. These were the first and second officer of the ship. On the floor of the stage, to the right, chained closely, hand and foot, and by the neck, there knelt three naked, blond women. When a man glanced at them they shrank down, cowering. The officer of the court saw that they had been taught fear.

"We shall have engineering shortly," a man was informing Ortog. "Then it will be but a matter of hours."

Ortog nodded.

The officer of the court heard this with horror. She was neither a scientist nor a technician but she knew enough, surely, to surmise that somewhere within the intricate labyrinth of engineering sections would be found the control devices for the central life-support systems of the ship.

Another man brought news of major loot, imperial bullion, five imperial ingots, any one of which might purchase a ship, such serving usefully as bribes, among other things, to barbarian kings, to encourage them to keep the peace with the empire, to attack enemies of the empire, to intervene in sensitive areas on the empire's behalf, and so on; another brought news of coined metals, gold and silver, tons thereof, taken in taxes, from four provincial worlds; and another of a bottle of wine, one of seven known to exist, from the vinyards of Kalan, on Cita, a world destroyed in the civil wars a thousand years earlier.

"It will be our victory wine!" said Ortog, of the last item in this accounting of significant loot.

There was enthusiastic assent to this.

In many sections there were self-contained support units, but these were designed to function only on a temporary, emergency basis.

It was with misery that the officer of the court crept back, again, between the seats, and began to make her way between them toward a door which led to the passageway giving access to the upper level of the main lounge.

She felt faint with hunger. She could hardly move, for her thirst.

She thought of the chained women on the stage. They were doubtless educated, civilized women, even citizens of the empire, but she did not think that that would make much difference to the barbarians, except, perhaps, to cause them to be regarded with a certain contempt, as weaklings and decadents, fit at best for the collar, in which at last they might be put to some use, in which at last they might find some justification for their existence. That they had once been citizens of the empire, prior to their embondment, might, of course, the officer of the court supposed, lend a certain flavor or pleasure to their use. But they had doubtless been chosen for their beauty. Certainly they were beautiful. Barbarians, she had heard, long ago, to her horror, enjoy exhibiting women at their courts. But how dare the barbarians exhibit these, female citizens of the empire, as though they might be no more than chained slave girls? "But is that not all they now are," she asked herself, trembling, "chained slave girls?" "Yes," she thought to herself, "that is now all they are, chained slave girls." She recalled how they had cowered at the glance of a man. That frightened her. She wondered if they had been fed.

She crept along the passage toward the upper level of the lounge. The doors to the lounge were of plate glass, also on the upper level. Arriving at one of these upper doors, she edged to it and peered through it. She opened it a small bit, enough to admit herself, and then held it, easing it back, that its return be silent, and with as little motion as possible. There were the upper tables around this area, with their chairs and white cloths. She crept among them, and peered down into the main lounge. She felt sick with misery, for, below, the lounge was muchly occupied. Ship slaves, and their helpless, naked charges, came and went, entering with the charges, attractive female passengers, struggling under burdens of loot, then returning to cleared decks and cabins, to fetch more. She now noted, for the first time, the metal disks fastened to the neck chains of the ship slaves. She had no doubt but what they were meaningful. She could smell cooking. The smells made her faint. She wanted to cry out. But she dared not do so. The ship slaves were armed only with their whips, but these were quite sufficient, not only because they were frightening and terrible in themselves, and she muchly feared them, but because they were in their way symbols, symbols that behind the ship slaves, somewhere, lay the power of men. Some of the ship slaves were eating, at one table or another, or standing about, eating. In the center of the lounge, where tables had been moved to one side, there was a great heap of loot, with a diameter of several yards, a height, in the center, of better than a yard. This great heap included an incredible miscellany of items, not just necklaces, and bracelets, armlets, anklets, rings, pins, brooches, and such, but chronometers of diverse sizes and types, vessels of various sorts, craters, vases and amphoras, showers of silverware, heaped phials of perfumes, disks of cosmetics, rolled tapestries, and small rugs. Clothing, too, and footwear, was cast into that pile. She saw a shackled prisoner, one who had been surely one of the lovelier of the passengers she had seen earlier on the voyage, stagger in, bent under a bulging sack. The sack had been formed from a satin sheet. She was prodded forward by the whip of her supervising ship slave, and then, the whip held before her, was stopped. Gratefully the shackled prisoner lowered her burden and knelt wearily on the carpeting, her head down. The ship slave then emptied the sheet at the margin of that vast disorderly melange. The officer of the court noted that the clothing had been taken from her own cabin, and was the wardrobe she had brought with her, including what would have been her trousseau, anticipating her projected nuptials with the executive, Tuvo Ausonius. In the first looting of the cabin it had apparently been her jewelry, her papers, her money, her watch, such things, that had been taken. In the second looting less valuable items had been gathered. The ship slave drew forth from the garments the white sheath and held it up before another ship slave who, regarding it, laughed and made some remark. The first ship slave then held the garment against the kneeling prisoner, she who had brought in the garments, and then jerked it away from her. The two ship slaves laughed. The kneeling prisoner kept her head down and her hands on her thighs. The first ship slave then threw the garment to the pile. Also, among other items, she drew forth a pair of black high-heeled pumps. She tied these together and flung them onto the pile where there was an assemblage of footwear. The officer of the court had worn these pumps with the white sheath at the captain's table. The shackled prisoners were barefoot. So, too, were the ship slaves. The officer of the court wore the mannish boots which were a portion of her "same garb," and, within these boots, drawn up closely about her small, shapely feet and lovely legs, high black stockings, those of a sort common with women of her class on Terennia. The officer of the court had sewn some purple thread at the top of these stockings, to indicate that she was of the blood.

The ship slave who had emptied out the satin sheet spoke to the kneeling prisoner and the prisoner went immediately forward, unquestioningly, to her hands and knees, and then, within the constraints permitted her by her shackles, made her way, head down, on all fours, about the pile of loot to a place, rather back, toward the double doors leading into the lounge from the kitchen, where knelt, in a group, several of the shackled prisoners. She joined them, kneeling with them.

In her circuit of the store of loot, she passed between it and other objects, tables and chairs, at which sat some resting, feeding ship slaves. She also passed one table on which, above her head, as she crawled, on the sparkling linen table cloth, there lay, on her back, spread-eagled, a secured prisoner, not shackled, but bound, hands and feet, separated, tied to the table legs. Some ship slaves fed on the same table, using the hair of the secured prisoner as a towel, wiping the grease from their hands on her body. "Please feed me," begged the prisoner. "You have learned to be good, haven't you?" inquired one of the ship slaves, holding a bit of roast fowl toward the lips of the prisoner. "Yes, Mistress! Yes, Mistress!" said the prisoner, straining to reach the tiny piece of meat. The ship slave put the meat close and then pulled it back, once, twice, and the prisoner tried futilely each time to reach it. Then the ship slave put the tidbit into her own mouth and chewed it, ostentatiously savoring it. "It is good," she said, and then swallowed it. The prisoner put her head back, turned it to the side, and moaned. The crawling prisoner passed, too, another prisoner, similarly secured, but one she might have looked down upon had she dared to turn her head and do so, for this one was fastened, on her back, spread-eagled, to an inverted table. But the crawling prisoner did not cast her eyes upon this other prisoner. She kept her head and eyes down, and her head straight. The ship slaves had apparently made it quite clear to their high-class charges that they were expected to attend to their duties, and that careless, roving glances were not encouraged, such rendering them liable to discipline.

"We are hungry, please feed us!" called one of the prisoners kneeling by the double doors. "Yes! Yes!" begged others.

"Silence, slaves," said one of the ship slaves, and cracked her whip.

These upper-class prisoners, or perhaps more fittingly now, these slaves, shrank back.

"Perhaps there is more work for you to do first," said the ship slave.

The women groaned.

"Do not fear," said the ship slave. "Your slops will be ready soon."

The women regarded one another, apprehensively.

On what was it that they would be fed?

But the officer of the court, from the anguished looks of them, did not think they would be particular.

"Lie down!" said the ship slave.

Immediately, obediently, in their shackles, crowded together, they lay on the carpeting.

"Man!" suddenly cried one of the ship slaves, and, to the astonishment of the officer of the court, all the ship slaves, losing no time in the matter, fell to their knees.

Gone then was the illusion of their superiority, which obtained only with the prisoners.

Into the lounge there strode, armored and helmeted, a barbaric figure, a Telnarian rifle strapped to his back, a fire pistol in his holster.

The ship slaves had assumed a common position of obeisance, their heads down, touching the carpeting, the palms of their hands, too, on the carpeting, as well.

The officer of the court saw women before men.

The barbaric figure, who seemed garbed as some sort of high officer, looked about the lounge.

He paused to regard the prisoners, who lay cowering on the carpet, hardly daring to look up. He seemed to regard them with contempt. But what did he expect of them? Did he think they should behave in some different fashion? Surely he was not kind. Surely he did not understand them. Could he not be compassionate? Could he not understand what was now so different about them, that which made all the difference in the world with them, that they were now owned by men?

But, too, now, it seemed, he looked upon them with care. The women, terrified, lowered themselves still more, pressing downward, their softness against the carpeting. Surely he could see that they were lying down, as they had been told! Surely he would not have them beaten! He made his way into the group. The women shuddered, and shrank away from him, drawing back their bodies, pulling their legs up, tightly, terrified that such a figure, even his boot, might brush against them. Many covered their heads with their hands. He went to one figure, and seized her by the hair, pulling her head up and turning it to face him. Then, after scrutinizing her features, he flung her back down, with her sister slaves. Her hair coloring, the officer of the court noted, was not unlike her own.

Then, in a moment, the helmeted, armored figure withdrew from the group. He went to the double doors leading to the kitchen, swung them apart, and peered in. When he had opened the doors she had heard the cry of "Man!" from within. And when the doors were open, he holding them widely apart, she had seen, on the tiles of the kitchen, within, one of the ship slaves, in a position of obeisance, doubtless hastily assumed. He looked about, standing in the doorway, mighty there, between those widely separated doors. Then, with a mere gesture of his head he indicated that those in the kitchen should rise and be about their duties. There were only ship slaves, she gathered, in the kitchen. Presumably the shackled prisoners would not now be allowed in such a place, lest they be tempted to steal food, and must then be beaten or slain. They could always be taught cooking and domestic duties later. Then he turned about and left the lounge, exiting through the main doors, those through which he had entered. When he had departed the ship slaves in the main lounge resumed their feet.

Shortly thereafter two ship slaves, carrying buckets, emerged from the kitchen.

They stood before the enforcedly recumbent slaves.

"Kneel," said a ship slave.

The prisoners rose up, to kneel.

"Your dinner, miladies, has been prepared," said the ship slave.

Eager looks coursed among the prisoners.

"But first, you must learn to perform obeisance," said the ship slave. "None of you properly assumed the position, though in the presence of a master."

Then the prisoners were instructed in the proper way in which to perform various obeisances in the presence of men, or, indeed, free persons. Such obeisances, they also learned, might be required of them even in the presence of slaves, if the slaves stood to them in some position of authority.

The officer of the court watched, horrified, fascinated, as various positions were adjusted, as various instructions were issued. Upper-class women, down in the main lounge, before her very eyes, to her horror, were being instructed in matters of courtesy and etiquette, of respect and deference.

"Excellent, miladies," said the ship slave who was managing these matters. "You learn quickly." The officer of the court thought that she, herself, might do as well, that she, too, might learn as quickly, but then she dismissed such a thought, frightened.

"You have been complimented, miladies," said the ship slave reproachfully.

The prisoners looked at her.

The officer of the court wondered what it might be, to render obeisance to a man.

She shuddered, thrilled.

"Have you no manners?" inquired the ship slave.

"Thank you, Mistress," they said.

"Now," said the ship slave to the two ship slaves who held the buckets, "throw the slaves their slops."

Then, in handfuls, the two slaves with the buckets cast bits of food, some of which was doubtless garbage, discarded residues from their own meals, or those of others, among the slaves, who scrambled, and even fought, most eagerly for them.

How mixed were the feelings of the officer of the court seeing this spectacle.

She was horrified, of course, to see how the women fought for the food.

"Please, more!" cried a woman.

"Me! Me!" begged another, putting out her hands.

But, too, she was acutely aware of her own hunger and thirst. She feared she might die.

Could she have secured some of those scraps if she were

below? Would she be quick enough, agile enough? Would the slaves with the buckets take pity on her and throw her something? Could she keep it? Would larger, stronger women take it away from her? Could she pull away, and thrust it in her mouth and swallow it before another could deprive her of it?

She did not know.

She looked down at the women, scrambling for what scraps might be cast to them.

At least they were being fed, as she was not. They had, at least, the chance, down there, on the carpeting, to snatch up some bit of food.

The ship slaves, she was sure, did not fight in such a way for their food.

Presumably this form of feeding was a lesson, that the prisoners must now depend on the will of others, for even their food.

How cruel seemed the ship slaves to the prisoners. She did not think that masters would be so cruel. Indeed, might not masters even grow fond of their slaves, being careful, of course, not to relax the discipline in which they were held.

Let the prisoners then hope that they might soon escape the supervision of the ship slaves, that they might soon, by gift or sale, come into the ownership of men, whose interest and affection they might strive to win by their heat and beauty, and devotion and selfless service.

"You feed eagerly," said one of the ship slaves. "Obviously you know it is better than you would receive in the steel bins."

The officer of the court shuddered.

But this suggested there must be other prisoners, or slaves, doubtless kept on the barbarian ships.

There had been a passenger list of over two thousand.

The officer of the court did not think the ship could be recovered. Moreover, she had heard, in the theatre, that engineering was soon expected to fall into the hands of the barbarians. That would surely mean the end of resistance. Too, in the early moments of the fighting, if not earlier, distress signals had doubtless been sent out. The barbarians would not risk their vessels, presumably, against imperial cruisers. Ortog had been studying a chart. Perhaps on it, hour by hour, were being marked the advances of an imperial force. She remembered the men monitoring various devices. But this was a remote sector of space, at the fringe of the empire. The arrival of an imperial force was surely not imminent. It was not likely that one could arrive for several days, if one were on its way at all. Certainly the barbarians seemed in no hurry to abandon the vessel. It seemed they wished to obtain all the loot possible, human and otherwise, from the *Alaria*. The thought struck her, frightening her, that she herself was, from the point of view of the barbarians, booty, as much as a golden coin or those black high-heeled pumps, tied together, which the ship slave had cast onto the pile of loot. What hope was there for her? Was she not, already, in effect, a woman owned by men, like the women below, only that she was not now naked, and her ankles were not shackled, assuming that they might find her of sufficient interest to keep her? Too, she had little doubt that when it came time for the barbarians to leave the *Alaria*, perhaps to slip away from an imperial force, they would not be likely to simply leave her behind, even as a silent, lifeless wreck, dead in space. She would be destroyed, to eliminate any witnesses who might somehow have survived, eluding discovery and capture, and to eliminate any evidence that might prove relevant to the identity of her attackers. The officer did not know it, of course, but her conjectures were quite sound. Tending to confirm them would have been the information that the small base on Tinos had been destroyed. What hope was there for her? To hide, and then to be blown to pieces in space, with the shattered *Alaria*, or to hide and then, in some tiny obscure confine, die of thirst or hunger? "No," she thought to herself, "I must surrender." "Am I not already, in effect," she thought to herself, the thought strangely unnerving her, and thrilling her, "a woman like those below, one owned by men?"

She then stood up, behind the railing on the upper level of the lounge, between the white tables, her mind made up. She placed her hands, clasped, on the top of her head, as she understood the barbarians wished men to surrender, for she was, of course, of Terennia. Too, they could not have seen her otherwise, where she was, for the railing. She stepped toward the railing. For a moment she was in full view, up, behind the railing on the higher level of the lounge. Any who had glanced up at that moment would have immediately seen her. But none at that moment happened to have had their attention directed in that unlikely direction. Had they done so they would have noted not only the officer of the court, but also the large, armored figure who had come up behind her.

Suddenly a large, gloved hand had closed, from behind, over the mouth of the officer of the court, holding her head back. She was helpless. Her right upper arm, too, was clasped in a mighty grip. She was drawn back.

A voice whispered in her ear. "Do not struggle, stupid little slave."

Both were now no longer visible from the main floor of the lounge.

The officer of the court felt giddy, being held with such strength.

As if her struggles might have been availing against it!

But she obediently ceased even to squirm.

Too, she was frightened that she might, somehow, for who knew what strange sorts of things men were, excite it, with who knew what fearful consequences, if she struggled.

She was then drawn backwards through a side door from the lounge, and down a long, dim corridor. She did not understand this. She had not expected to be taken into custody in this fashion. He had not even given her a chance, yet, she, a citizen of the empire, of the *honestori*, even of the blood, to formally surrender to him.

Then she was drawn into a small, dark, steel room, something like a utility room, it seemed.

The door shut with a heavy sound.

She could feel air in the room.

He removed his gloved hand from her mouth and she sank down, weakly, to the steel floor, she sensed at his feet.

She put out her hands and touched the heavy boots. She knelt before him and put her head down to those boots. "I am a slave," she said. "I confess myself such, honestly and openly. Please do not kill me."

Then she pressed her head down upon the boots, and then,

drawing back a little, she kissed them, clearly, firmly, that he might well understand, even in the dark, that it was done. She then licked them, on the tops and the sides, making certain, too, that her cheeks rubbed down, now and again, firmly, against them, that there be no mistaking the matter, even in the darkness.

"Yes, you are a slave," said a voice, which she feared she might recognize, and then the light in the room snapped on.

She looked up from the boots and saw herself surely before the large, armored figure who had, but moments before, been on the main floor of the lounge. The armor, the weapons, the accouterments, the insignia, were the same. The helmet, muchly concealing his features, and its markings, too, were the same.

Startling her, to one side, to her right, on the steel flooring, there lay a woman. She had long, blond hair, which was plaited in two thick braids, which, had she been standing, would have fallen to the soft flesh at the back of her knees. She was naked, and gagged, and bound, hand and foot.

She looked over, in consternation, and rage, at the officer of the court.

The huge figure removed his helmet.

"You!" cried the officer of the court, for it was the gladiator.

"She is poor stuff, Master," said a voice. "Why do you bother with her?"

The officer of the court, turning, saw the slave girl, Janina.

The officer of the court, in fury, sprang to her feet.

"Kneel!" said the officer of the court to Janina, in fury.

"Be silent, slave girl," said Janina.

The officer of the court looked immediately to the gladiator, for redress, that he would cruelly punish the errant slave, but he made no motion to do so.

The gladiator grinned.

Would he not adjudicate the matter? Surely he did not think she was merely, too, a slave?

She turned to Janina, angrily.

But Janina stood her ground against her, insolently, it seemed.

The officer of the court turned, then, lightly, to the gladiator.

"Where did you obtain your present garb, and accouterments?" she asked.

"From one who loaned them to me," he said. "I do not think his neck is broken, but he is likely to remain unconscious for several hours."

The gladiator crouched beside the blond captive. He loosened her gag, pulling it down about her neck. "You understand what you are to do?" he asked.

"Yes," she said, angrily.

Doubtless her mouth had a foul taste.

The officer of the court looked again at Janina.

Janina was now clad not in the *keb*, but in garments of barbaric splendor, muchly bedecked with primitive ornaments. This garb, the officer of the court suspected, had once been that of the bound captive, to her right. The captive, for example, did not have locked about her neck, closely encircling it, the chain and disk of a ship slave. That suggested that she was a free woman and, given the raiment on Janina, perhaps one of considerable importance.

"Yes, what?" inquired the gladiator.

"Yes, milord," said the blond woman, bitterly.

"That word costs you much, does it not?" asked the gladiator.

"Yes," she said, angrily.

He looked at her.

"Yes, *milord*," she said.

"Who is she?" asked the officer of the court, looking down on the blond captive.

The gladiator rose to his feet.

"I have been remiss," he said. "May I introduce Gerune, a princess of the Drisriaks, and one who chose to join the secessionist house of Ortog."

"A princess!" exclaimed the officer of the court.

"To be sure," said the gladiator, "she is now indistinguishable from a comely slave."

The captive squirmed.

"Are you not pleased, milady," said the gladiator, "that your face and figure might fetch a goodly price in a slave market?"

"Wretch!" hissed the captive.

"May I introduce our new guest?" the gladiator asked the captive, indicating the officer of the court.

"I do not greet commoners," she said.

"I am of the blood!" said the officer of the court.

"You are only a Telnarian bitch, fit, at best, for the collar," said the blond woman.

"Barbarian!" said the officer of the court.

"Slave!" said the blond captive.

" 'Slave'!" exclaimed the officer of the court.

"Yes, *slave*," said the captive. "Did you not, a moment before, bespeak yourself such?"

The officer of the court felt faint.

"Do you think such words can be unspoken?" asked the captive. "Once uttered, it is done. You are then powerless to alter or qualify them in any way."

"Surely you jest," said the officer of the court.

"It is the law," laughed Janina, "slave."

"And, too," said the blond captive, "it was not I who in the darkness, it seems, licked and kissed at a man's boots!"

"I thought him of the strangers, of the boarders!" said the officer of the court.

"And what does that matter, slave?" asked Janina.

"I am not a slave!" said the officer of the court to the gladiator.

"My plan," said he, "is as follows. We shall descend to the hold, and seek out Section 19, for there, I think unbeknownst to our friends outside, there are stored several escape capsules. You may recall them, from the evening of the contest. Some of these, by Pulendius and others, were, two days ago, taken on their tracks to the elevators, and conveyed upward to space locks."

"I saw damaged capsules, useless, outside, by the ships," said the officer of the court.

"It is my hope that some escaped," said the gladiator. "I know that many did not."

"Why did you not try to escape then?" asked the officer of the court.

"Can you not guess?" asked Janina, angrily.

"No," said the officer of the court. Then she said, frightened, "Surely it has nothing to do with me."

Janina laughed, bitterly.

Then the officer of the court said, "Oh!" for a rope was being knotted about her neck.

"Kneel," said the gladiator.

The officer of the court knelt. She looked up at the gladiator.

"I do not understand," she said.

She saw the end of the rope on her neck tossed to Janina.

"I do not think it is so hard to understand," he said.

"Please," she said.

"Surely we have much to discuss," he said.

"Please!"

"Janina will wear the royal robes of a princess of the Dris-riaks," said the gladiator.

"What are you going to do with me?" asked the officer of the court.

"We think," said the gladiator, "that with her robes about her face, Janina may pass for the princess. My garb, I trust, will serve as my disguise. The princess, gagged, on a neck rope, her hands bound behind her, will be marched before us, to be taken for a captured passenger. If she should attempt to struggle or flee, or give any sign of her distress or identity, I will gun her down immediately with the fire pistol. You understand, princess?"

"Yes, milord," she said.

"If she is recognized, she will prove a valuable hostage," said the gladiator.

"You will accompany us as another captured prisoner, one not yet even stripped, on all fours, on your leash, held by Janina. Perhaps it will be assumed she may have selected you for a serving slave. Perhaps you have the makings of a useful serving slave. One does not know. I have the fire pistol, and a Telnarian rifle, as extra insurance."

"I am to be marched before you, as I am?" asked the blond captive.

"Yes, milady," said the gladiator.

"I am the sister of Ortog, king of the Ortungen!" she said.

"Let him then understand you in a new light," said the glad-iator, "a light in which brothers seldom understand their sisters, that other men might find them of great interest as slaves."

"Wretch!" cried the princess.

"And I am somehow not overly fond of Ortog," said the, gladiator.

"And so you would march his sister thusly?"

"Certainly."

"You are a barbarian!" said the officer of the court, aghast.

"I do not know who I am," said the gladiator.

The officer of the court recalled that Ortog had identified the gladiator, obviously mistakenly, as of the blood of the Otungen, whoever they might be. Indeed, the names, to her civilized ear, though clearly distinguishable, sounded too much alike. The Ortungen was a secessionist house of the Drisriaks, a tribe of the Alemanni. She had no notion of who, or what, the Otungen might be. Nor, it seems, had the gladiator.

I despise you!" said the princess.

"But it will be you who will be naked, on the rope," said the gladiator.

"How dare you treat me so?" asked the princess.

"Do not peoples such as yours often march the women of the enemy, even women of the royal houses, through the forests naked, on ropes?"

"How dare you do such a thing!" she exclaimed.

"It is in accord with my plan," he said.

"You are a man of no name, of no people!" said the blond captive.

"I have heard," said Janina, "that it is not uncommon for barbarians to march the captured women of defeated royal houses on the ropes of common soldiers, men of no repute, that they may understand their lowliness as compared to the victors, that they, compared to the victors, are no more than slaves."

The blonde squirmed angrily in her bonds.

"I would beware, milady," said Janina, solicitously, "lest you excite the master."

Instantly the blond captive ceased struggling.

Janina laughed.

The blonde looked up at her, in fury.

The officer of the court put her hands on the rope on her neck.

The blond captive, seated, ankles crossed and bound, wrists

crossed and bound, behind her, the gag down about her neck, looked up at the gladiator.

"Who are you, truly?" she asked.

"I am Dog, of the *festung* village of Sim Giadini," he said. He added, as well, the name of the world but that name we, again, choose to omit at this point.

"You are no peasant," said the blond captive.

"It does not matter," said the gladiator.

"I see," said the princess.

"It only matters," said the gladiator, "that I am he in whose power you now are, totally. Do you understand?"

"Yes, milord," she said.

"We shall go publicly through the corridors," said the gladiator. "That, I think, will be safer than attempting to have recourse to ventilator shafts, crawl spaces, and such, which, as they are obviously surreptitious passages and hiding places, will presumably be guarded. We shall, with luck, reach Section 19, in the hold, and then, while I move one of the escape capsules to the elevator, Janina will supervise you two. Once we enter the capsule into the lock, we can set the timing device for opening the hatch, and can then launch."

"It is a mad plan," said Janina.

"One may always hope that our departure will pass unnoticed, that, after all this time, the gunners will not be alert, that the crews of pursuit launches will be tardily dispatched, such things."

"What of me?" asked the officer of the court, kneeling at the feet of the gladiator, the rope on her neck, its free end grasped by Janina.

"Does the little slave feel neglected?" asked Janina.

"What of me?" asked the officer of the court, ignoring Janina.

"You do not think I have ever forgotten you, do you, my dear?" asked the gladiator.

"What are you going to do with me?" asked the officer of the court.

"I am going to take you with me," he said.

"I do not understand," said the officer of the court.

"She is stupid," said Janina.

"What could you possibly want with me?" asked the officer of the court.

"Can you not guess?" asked Janina.

"No! Oh, please, no!" whispered the officer of the court.

The gladiator regarded her, a tiny smile playing about the corners of his lips.

"No!" whispered the officer of the court.

"Yes," he said, softly.

The officer of the court slumped to the floor of the small room.

She awakened, lifted to a sitting position, she did not know how much later, to find the spout of a canteen at her lips. She reached for it, and clutching it tightly, drank.

"Enough," said the gladiator, after too short a moment.

He handed the canteen to Janina.

The officer of the court trembled.

"Eat this," said the gladiator, kindly, pressing a roll into her small hands.

Madly, like a starving animal, she crammed the bit of food into her mouth.

"See, Janina," said the gladiator, "how a lady eats, with such daintiness. You might take a lesson from this."

The officer of the court chewed eagerly, swallowing entire pieces at a time, almost as though afraid what was not yet swallowed might be pulled from her mouth.

"Methinks, Master," said Janina, "it is rather the way a starving slave feeds."

"Perhaps," said the gladiator.

"And surely it is fitting for the starving slave," said Janina.

The gladiator smiled.

"Food will well control her," said Janina.

"Doubtless," said the gladiator.

"And the whip," said Janina.

"Perhaps," said the gladiator.

The officer of the court trembled. She had no doubt but what she would obey the whip, and well. But they spoke of her, or at least the slave girl did, as though she herself might be no more than a slave.

She looked to the gladiator.

But she was given no more food.

The officer of the court saw that the feet of the blond captive were now unbound. Too, there was now a rope on her neck, running to a stanchion. To the same stanchion ran another rope, that which was on her own neck. The princess's gag, the officer of the court noted, had not yet been resecured. It was still loose, down, about her neck.

"We will leave now," said the gladiator.

The two ropes were freed from the stanchion.

"Up," said the gladiator to the princess. She rose to her feet. He held her rope.

"To all fours, slave," said Janina. The officer of the court went to all fours. Her rope was held by Janina.

"Face the door," said the gladiator to the princess.

She did so.

He then looped her rope about his wrist and went behind her, to adjust her gag.

He put his hands on it.

"Wait," she said.

He paused.

"You are going through with this?" she asked.

"Yes," he said.

"Take me with you," she said.

The officer of the court gasped.

"How can I face my people after this?" asked the princess. "What good can I be?"

"Do not tempt me, luscious female," said the gladiator.

"Do not make me do this," she begged.

"It will be an excellent experience for you," he said. "It will help you to become more aware of your womanhood."

Her small hands pulled a little, weakly, at the bonds that held them secured behind her back.

"Do you understand?" he asked.

"Yes, milord," she said.

Then she said, "Oh!" for her gag was lifted, drawn back and fixed in place.

She would not now speak, nor could she, until relieved of its constraint.

"Should this one, too, not be gagged, Master?" inquired Janina, indicating the officer of the court.

"Will it be necessary to gag you?" asked the gladiator of the officer of the court.

"No," said the officer of the court.

"I have your word, as one of the *honestori*, as a citizen of the empire, as one even of the blood, that you will be silent?" he asked.

"Yes," she said.

"Beware," said Janina to the officer of the court. "Slaves may be slain for a lie!"

"Let us go," said the gladiator, facing the door.

Then he said, "Stand straight, Gerune. Put your shoulders back. Be sensational. Remember that you are not a free woman now but a slave."

Gerune, princess of the Drisriaks, sister of Ortog, king of the Ortungen, straightened her body and threw her shoulders back. How proudly then she stood.

"How beautiful she is!" exclaimed Janina.

"Ah," breathed the gladiator.

Even the officer of the court was struck with awe, seeing how beautiful a woman could be.

The gladiator boldly threw open the door.

"March," he said.

The group then exited the small room.

Janina, who was the last to leave, snapped off the light.

· · · CHAPTER 13 · · ·

"Some are still here!" said Janina, delightedly.

The officer of the court, still on her hands and knees, was on the sand, it covering her wrists, her knees, too, partly sunk in it. She could feel sand on her knees, which were sore, as were her hands. She could feel it, too, in its hundreds of tiny grains, slipped within the "same garb" where it had opened at the knees, roughened and parted by the slow procession through the corridors. Happily, elevators had been functional to this level. She could see, before her, the princess, her bared feet in the sand, it up almost to the ankles. The rope was still on her neck, and Janina held it. The princess's rope was in the keeping of the gladiator.

Many were the ironic salutes and lustful, demeaning catcalls which had greeted the princess as she had been paraded through the corridors. She counted, the officer of the court, gathered, as a prize catch, one which would doubtless bring an excellent price in a slave market.

The officer of the court wondered if she, too, might possess such value.

To be sure, it was hard to tell, encumbered as she was with "same garb."

"There are two left," said Janina, peering ahead, the way illuminated by an electric torch, which implement had been numbered among the several accouterments appropriated by the gladiator.

Originally there had been several escape capsules in the hold. Several, however, had been used by passengers, and perhaps crew members, trying to escape the vessel.

These were on tracks which led to the lifts, from which, on further tracks, they could be taken to locks.

"They do not know of these, Master," said Janina.

"I do not think so," said the gladiator.

There was no sign, as far as they had been able to determine, that Section 19 of the hold had been entered by the barbarians. It was, at that time, among putatively less important portions of the ship, portions which might well be left for later consideration. It had not figured in the fighting.

The gladiator flashed the light of the torch about the dark hold, over the wreckage of the fallen tiers.

He flashed it, too, upward, toward the girderwork about the ceiling.

Section 19, illuminated here and there by the darting beam,

seemed very different from when it had been well lit, and muchly occupied, as on the night of the entertainment.

The officer of the court found it frightening, and eerie. She wondered if they were truly alone in the place.

"Kneel them," said the gladiator, handing the princess's rope to Janina.

"Kneel, milady," said Janina to the princess, who knelt in the sand.

"Kneel, slave," said Janina to the officer of the court, "here, behind the princess, and to her left."

The officer of the court, angrily, knelt where she had been told.

"Hands on your thighs," said Janina to her charges. "You may keep your knees closed, milady. But you, slave, will keep yours open."

The officer of the court was angry, but she knelt as she had been instructed. Kneeling thusly, even in the "same garb," she could not help experiencing strange, disturbing sensations. Was it not thus that slave girls must kneel, or slave girls of a certain sort?

"It is as I feared," said the gladiator, who was now a few feet away. "The lifts to the locks are not operational."

It would be difficult to move the escape capsules on the tracks, not that they were large, but they were weighty, but it could be done. Two men could manage it, or one, with unusual strength.

"Oh, Master!" moaned Janina.

How then could they be brought to the level of the locks?

"The cables seem intact," said the gladiator, with satisfaction. "There are counterweights, of course."

The officer of the court thought she heard a small sound somewhere to her left, back, among the tiers.

Neither Janina nor the gladiator, who was concerned elsewhere, flashing the torch into the shaft, noticed it.

"I will move the capsule into the lift," said the gladiator. "Then, perhaps, I can draw it upward."

"It would take several men to hoist the lift, Master," said Janina, fearfully.

But already, the iron wheels grinding on the track, the gladiator, by main strength, was moving one of the capsules into the lift.

He returned, briefly, to Janina. He handed her the fire pistol and the electric torch.

"Put them to their bellies where they are, in the sand," said the gladiator. "If either should prove troublesome, or recalcitrant, you may burn them where they lie."

"Yes, Master," said Janina. Then she said to the princess, "Please assume a prone position, milady, with your legs widely spread." The princess complied. Doubtless Janina herself had often been put, in one situation or another, in this same position. It makes it harder to rise. Then she said to the officer of the court, "To your belly, slave, and get your legs apart, as widely as you can!"

The officer of the court complied. She did not doubt but what Janina might well blast through her back, perhaps even boiling and melting the sand beneath her. The fire pistol in her grasp was not one of reduced charges, as had been those of the crew members, a safety precaution for use on the vessel. It was much more powerful, and might, if its charge was sustained, cut through metal. To be sure, it was less powerful than the Telnarian rifle which the gladiator retained.

She heard, foot by foot, the lift being raised by hand. She could scarcely believe the strength required for this. Such a man, she knew, might snap her neck with one hand.

Then she thought she heard, again, a tiny sound, again back, and to her left.

It did not seem that Janina noticed this sound, if it were indeed a sound. Her interest, it seemed, was focused on the gladiator's struggle with the weights in the lift shaft.

The gladiator then ascended the shaft by means of a ladder within it.

In a few moments he returned. "The capsule is in the lock, positioned," he said.

"Master!" breathed Janina, delightedly.

"I have heard strangers about," he said, "but they seem to be in another corridor."

"What are we to do," asked Janina, frightened.

"We must move quickly," he said.

He took the fire pistol from Janina and replaced it in its holster.
He extinguished the torch and put it on his belt.

"Up, Gerune," he said. As soon as she was on her feet, he
scooped her up and, to her consternation, threw her lightly over
his shoulder. "Come last, Janina," he said.

"Yes, Master," she said. Then she said to the officer of the
court, "Get up, slave, follow your master."

"I am not a slave," said the officer of the court. "He is not
my master."

But she rose promptly to her feet.

The gladiator had already begun to ascend the ladder, Gerune
on his shoulder.

"Climb the ladder, slave," said Janina, "up, behind your
master."

The officer of the court did not bother responding to Janina.
Let her think that she was a slave, and that the great lout was
her master. What difference did it make? It wasn't true, was it?

She ascended the ladder.

The rope, held by Janina, was still on her neck.

In a moment she and Janina had reached the level of an outer
corridor. The door to the lock, a few feet to the right of the
elevator, as one would emerge from it, was open.

The gladiator, in his armor, was in the hallway, just outside
the port, setting the timer.

Gerune was at his feet, kneeling. The rope was still about her
neck, but now its free end had been looped about her ankles,
which had been crossed, and tied there, rendering her bound,
hand and foot.

"Kneel," said Janina, looking about nervously.

The officer of the court knelt.

Her own heart was beating rapidly, seeming to pound madly
within her.

She heard voices, those of barbarians, from a nearby corridor.

"The timer is set," said the gladiator.

The officer of the court saw the hatch on the escape capsule
opened.

She knew that she and Janina were then to hurry to the hatch and climb through, it doubtless then to be closed behind them by the gladiator, he the last to enter.

The officer of the court was terrified.

She realized she had knelt before this man in the darkness and proclaimed herself slave. She knew herself then, almost giddy with fear, to be subject to claimancy. Indeed, Janina seemed to think that she was already claimed, and thus, having been subject to claimancy, was now owned, indeed, that she was the gladiator's slave!

But see the princess!

The princess was looking wildly up at the gladiator. Tears ran from her eyes, down her cheeks, against the gag. Then, to the amazement of the officer of the court, the princess put her head down to the boots of the gladiator.

She heard the sounds of voices coming nearer.

She cast a glance at exquisite Janina, now muchly bedecked in the barbaric robes of the princess.

Janina was a slave, not she!

Too, she saw the princess, her beauty brazenly bared, as it had been decided by the will of the gladiator, her head to his boots.

She felt a rush of anguish, and rage, and jealousy!

How could she compete with two such women?

"I am not a slave!" she suddenly cried, aloud. And she sprang to her feet. "Help! Help!" she cried.

The gladiator looked up, startled. His astonishment was evident.

"Help!" she screamed. "Help!"

But then the gladiator, looking past her, lifted his hands, suddenly.

The officer of the court looked back and saw, just emerged from the shaft of the lift, having climbed the ladder, the young naval officer, he of the purple cords, of the blood, whom she had not seen since the evening of the entertainment. He held a fire pistol leveled at the gladiator.

Behind the young naval officer, emerging now from the shaft of the lift, completing the ascent of the ladder, one by one, were other figures.

She was not sure how many there were.

She realized then that these must have been hiding in the hold, in Section 19.

At this moment, apparently rushing to investigate the cries of the officer of the court, several barbarian warriors, helmeted, armored, appeared in the corridor.

"Hold your fire!" cried one of them. "The princess!"

They mistook Janina in her regal garb for Gerune.

"Surrender!" cried one of the barbarians to the young naval officer.

"Be careful," cried one of the barbarians to his fellows. "A commander, too, is in the line of fire!"

They took no thought for the real princess, who, naked, bound hand and foot, and gagged, they took naturally for a prisoner or slave.

The naval officer snapped off a charge and one of the barbarians spun about, the armor on his chest blackened.

Janina screamed.

The officer of the court, too, cried out in misery. Clearly the shot must have passed her.

"What shall we do, Commander?" called one of the men down the hall.

"Hold your fire," said the gladiator.

Gerune, in her bonds, shrank down, small, in misery. She had been seen naked, at the feet of a man. What would be the consequences of that, when her identity might be established? Too, she had been paraded as a slave girl through the corridors, an object of lust and ridicule to hundreds of men.

"Move aside!" said the naval officer.

The gladiator stepped to the side, keeping his hands raised.

"The timer has been activated!" said the young officer. Then he cried to those with him, "Into the capsule!"

"Alert the gunners," said a man down the hall.

One of their number lifted a communication device and began to speak rapidly into it.

The young naval officer then, carefully, fired four shots down the hall. Three of these shots struck targets. One fellow staggered back, his armor blackened and scarred; another lost part of his

armor, it blasted away from him; he scrambled away; a third
shot struck the helmet of a man at the side, half tearing his head
from his body. The other shot, the barbarians having broken for
cover, passed harmlessly down the corridor, until it subsided,
and left a line of fire on the carpeting more than a hundred yards
away.

"It seems we owe our lives to your presence, Princess," said
the young naval officer.

Janina began to tremble.

The young naval officer then, his suspicions aroused, jerked
away her hood. "You are not a princess," he said. "I know
you! You are a slave!"

He then looked down at Gerune. "Your hair," he said,
"shows you to be barbarian, and you are not ankleted, or brace-
leted, or collared, no mark of bondage is upon you, not even,
it seems, a brand, so you must be free. Perhaps it is you who
are the princess! Well, it does not matter. Many women, once
barbarian princesses, are now slave girls in the empire. It is
where such as you belong, at the feet of gentlemen."

"My thanks to you, whoever you may be," said the young
naval officer to the gladiator. "We were not capable of bringing
the escape capsule to the lock, the lift being inoperative. You
have been of great help."

He glanced at the timer.

"We must be leaving now," he said.

Then he looked at the officer of the court, who was backed
against the corridor wall, near the lock, on its left, as one would
enter it.

He regarded her with contempt.

"I am a citizen," she said. "I am of the blood!"

"You are a stupid, loud-mouthed bitch," he said. "Your
cries could have gotten us all killed. And why did you cry
out? Are you so eager to be killed, or cast into the chains of a
slave?"

"Sir!" she protested.

"Get in the capsule, bitch," he said.

She cast one wild glance at the gladiator and then, hurriedly,
entered the capsule.

The timing needle was now close to the point at which the automatic launching sequence would be activated.

"How are we to escape?" asked the gladiator.

"Who are you?" asked the officer.

"He who defeated Ortog in the contest," said the gladiator.

"The Otung?" said the officer.

"I know not the meaning of that word," said the gladiator.

"You are the one Pulendius calls 'Dog'?"

"Yes," said the gladiator.

"You may be an Otung," said the officer. "Surely you are not of the empire."

"I have brought the capsule to the lock," said the gladiator.

"My thanks," said the officer.

"How are we to escape?"

The officer threw a quick glance at the needle.

"I have no time to trust you, or disarm you," he said. He then, twice, pulled the trigger on the fire pistol, and the gladiator staggered backwards, the armor black with heat. He then, spinning about, fell to the side of the shaft, near the ladder. Another shot blasted him back into the open area of the shaft, by the ladder.

Janina screamed.

"I am sorry," said the officer.

He regarded both the distraught Janina and the princess, who had scrambled back as she could, bound, and was now to the left of the lift entrance, as one might enter it from the corridor. She jerked madly at the bonds, but, of course, was held, perfectly.

"You will remain here, slaves," said the officer to Janina and the princess.

Then he hastily leaped through the lock port a moment before it shut. He slid through the hatch on the capsule and secured it. A moment later the outer portal opened, and, an instant after that, the capsule burst free of the *Alaria*.

· · · **CHAPTER 14** · · ·

The gladiator lay at the bottom of the lift shaft.

Janina fled to the ladder and climbed down, to crouch beside him.

He half sat up, then fell to the side.

"Master! Master!" she wept.

There was the sound of racing feet, approaching. The gladiator crawled from the bottom of the shaft, across the tracks on which the escape capsule had been moved, to the flooring of the hold.

Faces appeared at the opening to the lift shaft, above.

"Princess!" called a man. "Are you all right? Commander! Answer me!"

The gladiator sat up, awkwardly. The chest plate of the armor had taken three charges, two at almost point-blank range. It was loose on the left, half-unhinged. The gladiator tried to rise, but fell back.

"She lied," he said. "She gave her word. But she lied."

"Master!" whispered Janina, frenziedly.

"Princess? Commander?" called the voice again.

"She lied," said the gladiator.

The gladiator slipped loose the fire pistol from its holster.

"We are lost!" wept Janina.

"Courage, Princess!" called the voice. "We are coming down immediately!"

"Stay where you are!" screamed Janina.

"That is not the voice of the princess!" said a man, from somewhere above.

"Commander! Commander!" called another voice.

"My helmet, remove my helmet," said the gladiator, weakly.

Janina struggled to lift the helmet, and then put it to the side.

Within the collar of the armor, where it had been pressed back, under the helmet, there was blood.

The blaze of electric torches, from above, darted about the shaft.

The gladiator lifted the fire pistol weakly.

Then he put it down, beside him.

"She lied," he said.

"Oh, Master, Master," moaned Janina.

"Who are you, woman?" called a voice from above.

"Commander!" called a man, from above.

"It may not be a commander," said another.

"Who is the captain of the *Gelstane*?" called down a man.

"Who is the subcaptain of the *Borsa*?" called another.

"Can you speak, Commander?" asked a man.

"Answer our questions, female," demanded a voice.

"Here," said another, "ungag this slave and beat her. She will speak!"

"Hurry!" said a voice, with authority.

The men drew away from the opening above.

"She is a beauty," said a man.

"A not unattractive slut," said another.

"I saw her earlier, in the corridors," said another.

"I, too!" said another.

"She walked well on her leash," said another.

"That she did!" laughed a man.

"Kneel her here, before me. Strike her," said a voice.

There was in a moment the sound of a blow and a soft cry of muffled pain.

"Do you wish to be struck again, slut?" asked a man.

There was a muffled whimper of protest, of denial.

"When you are ungagged," said a man, "you will speak instantly, clearly and truthfully."

"Get the gag out of her mouth," said the authoritative voice.

"Master, what are we to do?" whispered Janina.

The gloved hand of the gladiator reached out, groping, for the fire pistol, and then he had it, again, in his hand.

"I am Gerune, princess of the Drisriaks, sister of Ortog!" cried the princess above, in misery, and pain.

"Hear the slave!" laughed a man.

"The commander of the *Gelstane* is Surogastes, the subcaptain of the *Borsa* is Tethgutha, the commander of the *Vorgaard* is Bradow, son of Astarax! Bring me clothing, now!"

"Bring sheets," said a man.

"Cover her," said another voice, startled.

"Hurry the princess away," said a man, frightened.

"Fools, fools, fools!" wept the princess.

"Sever her bonds! Carry her from this place!" said the authoritative voice.

The gladiator had now crawled to the foot of the shaft, and lifted the fire pistol. With one bolt he melted the ladder from the top of the shaft.

"Who are these others?" asked a man.

One of the men above leaped to the foot of the shaft, but there, for a moment, lost his footing, and then took the charge of the gladiator full in the chest of the armor, which blasted him back against the side of the shaft, and he sank down there, unconscious. Another man followed, but the gladiator, shaking his head, steadying the fire pistol with both hands, struck him full in the belly. A shot ripped above his own head. The gladiator pulled the trigger again. The fellow spun about and then, drunkenly, seized the ladder and began to climb, but, in a moment, he had come to the melted termination of the ladder, feet from the top, and could go no further. He clung to the ladder, and then, struck by a third charge from the pistol, was thrust from it, and then, in a moment, fell sideways, and then down, clattering to the bottom of the shaft.

"Bring gas," said a voice from above.

"We are lost, Master," said Janina. "There is no escape!"

The gladiator stood unsteadily, parts of his armor dangling, and drew a bead with the pistol on the door, across the way, that giving the main entry to Section 19. He fired once into the side of the door, sealing it to the steel portal.

Running feet could now be heard again, above, more men approaching.

There was blood running down the side of the gladiator's leg, on the plating, from beneath the armoring of his torso.

He slipped down on one knee.

"She lied," he said.

Across the way he could see, through the observation panel, the faces of men. He heard the door being tried.

"Get in the escape capsule," said the gladiator, from one knee, to Janina.

But she fled to him. She put her arms about him. "Master is mad!" she wept. "He is mad with confusion and pain!"

He struggled to raise his head.

"There is no lock here, Master!" she said.

"Go," he said.

"Let Janina rather die in his arms!"

Then his head was raised, and he looked upon the slave, and his visage was fierce and terrible.

"Janina hastens to obey!" cried the girl with fear and she fled to the inactivated capsule, the second of the two which had been in the hold.

She struggled only for a moment with the hatch, as it had been opened before, by the fugitives. They had been sustaining themselves on the supplies in the capsules.

Across the way the butt of fire pistols smote at the wire-reinforced glass, and then the muzzle of a pistol, poking through the wire, bits of glass, clinging to it, intruded into the hold. It fired over the escape capsule, rippling the wall of the hold.

"Masks!" called a man, from above.

The gladiator fired a shot toward the observation panel and glass and wire spattered backwards, into the corridor outside.

Gas began to hiss downward into the hold, through the lift shaft.

It could be seen now, like fog, creeping from the shaft.

Across the way the door was being struck with charges like hammers. The door began to glow.

The gladiator rose unsteadily to his feet.

The door now seemed lost in a blaze of sparks and charges.

The gladiator staggered toward the escape capsule.

He climbed the two iron steps, leading to the hatch of the capsule, and then leaned against the capsule, weakly, over it.

"She lied!" he cried, suddenly, and wept, and struck down on the capsule with an armored fist. "She lied!" he cried.

"Master!" cried Janina, from within the capsule. "Master!"

Gas was now billowing from the lift shaft into the hold.

The gladiator unslung the Telnarian rifle from his back.

Across the way the door suddenly burst loose from the steel portal.

He slipped into the opened hatch, but stood in it, his body half out of the capsule.

Janina, within, crouched on the steel plating.

Men, masked, weapons raised, emerged through the portal across the way.

The gladiator heard two men leaping to the floor of the lift shaft.

He aimed the Telnarian rifle at the side of the hold.

He pulled the trigger four times, placing four charges in the form of a square.

Some of the gas began to move suddenly, hissing, toward the wall. The gladiator laid the rifle on the surface of the capsule before him, and then, with the pistol, with its last charges, each set on the narrow sustaining beam, linked the four points of impact of the rifle.

The gas was now whipping toward the wall. The atmosphere in the hold was rushing past him, tearing at his hair.

"No!" cried someone behind him.

Then men were fleeing.

The gladiator lifted, once more, the Telnarian rifle.

He fired the last charge in the rifle at the center of the pattern.

Suddenly the side of the hull seemed to leap away from him and, the capsule tumbling on its side toward the hole, he slid within it, turned the wheel, and secured the hatch.

In a moment the capsule was tumbling through space, leaving the *Alaria*, and the Ortung fleet behind, like specks in the night.

CHAPTER 15

"What are those sounds?" asked Janina, frightened.

"They are horns, hunting horns," said the gladiator.

"This world, then, is not uninhabited," said Janina.

"It would seem not," said the gladiator.

He kicked dirt over the small fire they had built on the bank.

"My clothes are not yet dry!" protested Janina.

"Put them on wet, or carry them," said the gladiator.

"I am exhausted," she said. "We almost died. I cannot move."

She looked up at him, pathetically. She knelt on leaves. Her hair had been loosened, that it might be dried near the fire.

"Then I shall rope you to a tree and leave you behind," he said.

She rose to her feet and hastily began to gather her clothes from the cord stretched between two trees.

"Forgive your slave," she said.

The gladiator stood very still, listening.

"What world is this?" she asked, rolling the garments of Princess Gerune into a small bundle.

"I do not know," he said, softly.

"Forgive me, Master," she said, realizing she might have disturbed him.

The gladiator looked up at the sky. The descent of the capsule, last night, might have been visible, particularly in the upper atmosphere. It might have been mistaken for a meteor at first, a falling star, perhaps even later, when the fearful rush in the atmosphere, like a hurricane over the trees, was audible. But, too, there may have been a visual contact, when the descent slowed and the capsule began to skim the trees, the sensors searching for level surfaces, where the adjusting thrusters would be activated for a landing. But then, too, perhaps not. How could one know?

Again the horns sounded.

The gladiator threw the last bits of the armor into the river. These, with certain other supplies, he had salvaged from the capsule.

"Master, I cannot swim!" had cried Janina, last night, first waist deep in the current, trying to help bring the capsule to the shore, then her footing lost, falling, her hands slipping from the wet metallic surface, being swept downstream.

The capsule, when it had left the Alaria, sped by the brunt of the decompression, had tumbled uncontrolled from the rupture in the hull, and only moments later had the gladiator, within the darkened, stifling cabin, been able to locate the launch release, the engagement of which had two primary effects, the first being to activate the clearance thruster, used for distancing the capsule from the mother ship, to protect it in the event of explosions or radiation, and the second being to activate, after the clearance burn, various systems internal to the vehicle, which supplied heat, light and oxygen. This delay in activating the clearance thruster kept the capsule cold when the first tracking shots left the Ortungen fleet. Two missiles, which tracked from the ships themselves, by means of monitors, not heat, had followed the capsule for over fifteen hundred miles. Then it had disappeared from the monitors. The gladiator had, of course, manually, disengaged the locating beacon, and turned off internal and external lighting as soon as these devices could be located. He had also reduced the noise level in the vehicle as much as possible, levering down even the life support systems to minimum settings. The ship was then like a silent, dark mote in a silent, dark sea, a mote which seemed to be nowhere, but might be anywhere. A pursuit craft had been sent out, but it was soon recalled to the mother ship. It paused only long enough to collect the two missiles, which had then been disarmed by signals from the mother ship. It was not clear to the gladiator why the pursuit had been so soon terminated. The capsule had suffered damage in its emergence from the Alaria. This damage rendered accessible navigational equipment inoperative and impaired the utility of manual devices for controlling the vernier thrusters, used for course adjustments. In effect the ship was, manually, blind and rudderless. This injury was not, under the circumstances, however, a serious one. The escape capsules, you see, were not designed for skilled, practiced operators. Their functioning was largely a matter of automatic sequences. Once the launch sequence had been activated, the capsule was designed to clear the mother vessel, initiate life support and transmit a tracking signal. One purpose of the verniers, of course, was to make it possible to remain in the vicinity of the initial launch, in case rescue might be imminent. To be sure, that would not have been wise under the circumstances which then prevailed. I think there is little doubt that the gladiator was fortunate to have escaped from the vicinity of the Ortungen fleet. For example, his capsule being largely uncontrollable he could not have used a launch trajectory which might have made use of an Ortungen ship as a shield, so that it would be exposed only to the guns of the shield ship, have engaged in complex evasive activity, engaged and disengaged engines in such a way as to leave a scattered, confusing track of dissipating heat behind it, made use of distant stars and bodies, and occasional debris, and such, to mask its position, and so on. To be sure several escape capsules, over the past few days, had managed to successfully elude the Ortungen fleet, most often when they burst forth together, using the schooling effect to disconcert the predator. Although it is not immediately germane to our narrative, it is of interest to note that Pulendius was among those who had managed to flee the Alaria successfully. Some days later he and his party were picked up by one of ten imperial cruisers. The presence of these cruisers in the vicinity was no accident. They had come in response to the distress call of the Alaria. This was the reason, incidentally, that the pursuit of the gladiator's ship, and, indeed, of another, as well, had been so soon terminated. Most escape capsules, however, as you may have gathered, were not successful in eluding the Ortungen fleet. Indeed, only a handful was successful; most were destroyed. Indeed, an escape capsule which had left the Alaria only moments before that of the gladiator had, several hours later, as a result of the explosion of a pursuing missile, been severely damaged, and cast adrift thereafter amongst the gravitational geodesics of that portion of space. The clearance thruster had been detached, the explosive bolts being fired, shortly before the projected strike of the missile. The missile had struck the trailing thruster and not the escape capsule. The capsule itself, however, given the proximities involved, and the quantity and speed of the debris, both of the thruster and the missile, had been severely damaged. If one detaches the thruster, or such a device, prematurely, it is unlikely to be useful as either a decoy or a shield. It is unlikely to be useful as a decoy because, at least within practicable detection distances, it can be distinguished from the target. As a shield it must appear suddenly enough and close enough to the missile's target that it is not possible for the missile, closing on the target, to avoid it. It must, accordingly, be interposed at almost the last moment, and the attendant risks accepted. Had the escape capsules been war vessels, of course, they would have been equipped with more sophisticated defensive devices. As it was, they were not even armed with handguns. Weaponry, as we now well know, tended to be carefully controlled by the empire. And, indeed, the escape capsules which had been stored in Section 19 were supernumerary capsules, and not a part of the regular escape complement, which complement consisted of capsules readied in the locks. Accordingly, they were not even equipped with charts, not that these would have been of great use to most civilian occupants. They were equipped, however, happily, with the usual complements of stores. In the case of the last two escape capsules, those with which we have been recently concerned, these stores had been to some extent depleted by the fugitives, those who had been hiding in the hold. On the other hand, this matter was not serious, as a very limited number of passengers was involved in both cases.

"The horns, Master!" said Janina.

"Yes," he said.

The horns had again sounded.

The gladiator had lost consciousness a few hours after the

launching of the escape capsule. He had awakened later, it was not clear how long he had been unconscious, to feel a dampened rag being pressed in the darkness to his brow.

"Master?" had asked Janina.

His armor had been removed.

They knew not where they were.

He had then again lapsed into unconsciousness, weakened from the loss of blood, bruised, shaken, from the impact of the armor blasted back against his body.

After two days they had illuminated the cabin.

The gladiator had lain on one elbow, and looked at the slave.

She cast her eyes downward, shyly.

"Remove your clothing," he said.

"Yes, Master," she said.

He then took her in his arms and turned her beneath him, onto the steel plating of the escape capsule flooring.

"Master is strong!" she whispered.

"Be silent," he told her.

"Yes, Master," she had said.

When a slave is told to be silent, you see, she may not speak.

But, in a few moments, she gasped, and cried out, and then, later, clung to him, his, subdued.

The capsule had drifted in space for weeks, lonely and rudderless, tugged this way and that by forces so subtle they could not have detected them, but then, eventually, as the consequence of the invisible geography of gravity, they began, slowly at first, and then more rapidly, to spiral toward a world. The testing sequence was initiated, and it soon became clear to the capsule's occupants that, for one reason or another, whether from a lack of necessity or because of inoperability consequent upon damage, the secondary clearance system was not going to fire. The implementation of the landing program had begun, of course, immediately after the processing of the results of the testing sequence.

There had been several tiny ports in the escape capsule, of only some four inches in diameter. It was difficult to see through them. The monitoring cameras, fore and aft, were not functioning.

They could feel heat, even within the capsule, as the atmosphere was penetrated.

In the descent something must have gone wrong, for a disk at the bow began to flash redly.

A whining, sirenlike sound filled the cabin for a brief moment, and then stopped. The disk stopped flashing.

They could see trees below.

They were moving laterally. Behind them, but visible through one of the ports, was a rope of fluid, aflame.

"There is no place to land," had screamed Janina.

The terrain below was, indeed, rugged, and forested.

There was a frightening sound as the speeding capsule lashed through branches and then, suddenly, climbed, again, upward. Then it spun about, and hovered, and seemed to slip in the air, down a dozen feet, and then another dozen feet. It righted itself. It began to descend again, and then, again, abruptly, in the light of what obstacle the occupants knew not, rose up again.

Two needles, though this was not noted by the occupants of the vehicle, now verged, suddenly, as though broken, at the bottom of their gauges.

"We are falling!" said Janina.

The gladiator crawled to the wheel which controlled the fins of the craft, usable in an atmosphere. Their use had been clear from experimentation in space, though they had been ineffective in that medium.

He drew back on the wheel and the craft soared upward.

"There is no power!" said Janina.

He leveled the wheel, and sought to peer out the bow port. Then he swung the wheel to the right, and then back, somewhat, to the left, and then pressed it forward.

He tried to follow the course of the river.

He sped between the trees, over the water, and then pressed the wheel forward again, and the escape capsule hit the surface of the water like a stone, and, splashing, flew into the air, and then descended, and did this again and then again, and was then rushing through the water, it flying to both sides, and then the capsule was on gravel, scraping, and then water, it rushing beneath, and then gravel again, and then, at last, half on the bank of the river, and half in the water, stopped.

They had lost no time in leaving the capsule and withdrawing into the forest, shielding themselves behind trees and rock.

When it became clear that the capsule was inert, they returned to it.

It was deeply scarred, and a far different vehicle, now space-worn, and scorched, and pitted and gashed, from the one which had tumbled free of the *Alaria* so long ago. There were streaks of vegetable matter on it where it had flashed through branches. It was tipped. Two of its wheels, for the tracks, were broken away. "We are alive," said Janina.

"We will use the vehicle for a shelter," he said.

"No, please, Master!" she said. "We have been within it so long! Let us sleep in the open!"

"There may be danger here," he said.

"Animals?" she said, frightened.

"Or worse," he said.

She looked at him.

"They might like you on a rope," he said.

"I belong on a rope," she laughed.

"And so does every woman," he said.

"Yes, Master!" she said.

"But we must leave the vehicle soon," he said. "We must learn this world."

"Do you think it populated, Master?" she asked.

"I do not know," he said.

"Perhaps we should build a shelter somewhere else," she said, looking about herself, frightened.

"It is late," he said.

Before they retired for the evening, he thrust the vehicle higher on the bank. He also put some branches about it, to conceal its outline.

Early that afternoon, miles upriver, over an area of several square miles in extent, there were heavy rains. This was not understood by either the gladiator or the exquisite young slave, Janina, she whom he had won, a lovely prize in a contest. Doubtless they had been exhausted by their ordeal, the escape from the *Alaria*, the long weeks in space, the terrors of the landing, the awesomeness of finding themselves on an unfamiliar world, a new, seemingly primitive, surely beautiful, perhaps uncharted, world. In any event, the waters from upriver, flowing from innumerable rivulets, from dozens of streams, from several tributaries, like veins in the surface of the earth, draining an area more than a hundred square miles, began to move downstream, slowly at first, and then with gathering force. These swelling waters, borne by the now swift current, crept up the banks at many points, even higher than most of the diverse levels already recorded in the clay, indeed, until, here and there, they almost touched the grass, and, at shallower places, were plentifully overflowing the banks. The capsule, even thrust higher as it had been, was lifted from the bank, and the gladiator awakened suddenly, the capsule lifting, then rocking, then beginning to turn, beginning to wash downward toward the current. He had aroused the slave instantly and together, as it seemed clear the capsule might be lost, they had flung certain supplies, a medical kit, blankets, the rifle and the pistol, though these were now without ammunition, and such, out the hatch, high onto the bank, above where the water now reached. This they did in the darkness, and in a driving rain, and in the midst of thunder and lightning, for their area, too, was now much affected by storms, quite possibly a portion of the same weather system which had been active upstream earlier.

The gladiator emerged from the capsule, the water to his thighs, half-blinded by the wind and rain, and pressed against it with his hands, where they slipped on the slick surface. He slipped in the water. He tried to get his back to the vehicle and turn it, to thrust it up the bank. It was rocking. It was hard to grasp. He cut his arm on the stabilizer. The vehicle spun about.

Janina, her clothing soaked with rain, stood on the bank. She had, moments before, wading, made her way ashore.

To the gladiator's right a great dark branch, its leaves beaten down by rain, swept past.

The capsule turned in the overflowing waters. The gladiator lost his hold on it, and, slipping, moved about it, to get once more between it and the main channel of the river.

Water streamed from the capsule.

It would be suddenly illuminated, eerily, whitely, in flashes of lightning.

So, too, was the slave on the bank, and the trees behind her.

"I cannot hold it!" cried the gladiator.

It was at that point that Janina had waded forth into the black, swirling waters, to lend her small strength to his.

Too, almost at the same time, no more than a moment or two later, he had, unexpectedly, managed to brace himself on some solid surface on the overflowed bank, doubtless an outjutting rock.

Janina was waist-deep in the water, about the capsule, to his right, as he was braced.

He did not even understand, at that time, where she was, or what she was doing.

"I have it!" he cried. He thrust it back a bit, toward the bank. He felt with his feet for another purchase, one six inches closer to the bank.

It was at that point that Janina had lost her footing in the rushing water. She clutched at the capsule but her hands could close on nothing. They slipped on the large, slick, oval surface. She fell to her back in the water, her hands losing contact with the capsule. It was at this point, as the current took her, and she had begun to be swept downstream, that she had cried out. "Master, I cannot swim!" she cried.

The gladiator turned to seize her but she was swept past him. For a moment or two the air trapped in her robes would hold her to the surface. He saw her hand, the robes falling from it, lifted. "Master!" she screamed. He left the side of the capsule and plunged after her, wading, but she was already yards away. He then began to swim toward a point at which he hoped to intercept her. But she was not there. So swift was the current. He saw her then, in a flash of lightning, yards downstream, clinging to a rock, the waters rushing about it. But when he reached the rock she had been swept from it. He pushed away from the rock, slipping, and hastened downstream. He turned in a minute, fighting the current. Might she not be near? Something struck his leg and he reached down, but it was a branch. "Master!

Master!'' he heard, and once more he hastened downstream, lashing the water. He saw, in another flash of lightning, her head disappear under the roiling surface of the dark waters. As he swam he tried to judge the feel of the current on his body, its turnings, its deflections, as it was shaped by the contour of the banks, the irregularities of the riverbed. At times the water rushed over his head, and he rose, shaking his head, looking wildly about. He saw the capsule moving downstream, to his right, tipped, awry in the current. A scream was before him in the darkness to the left. Again he sped toward a projected rendezvous, the location dictated by an instant's calculation of the physics of time and current. But, of course, she was not an inert object, but one which moved, and struggled, and the robes, too, clinging about her, influenced her movements. How could one judge such things, and in the darkness, the turbulence? She was, again, not at the projected point of rendezvous, or, if she was, it was in the darkness, or perhaps even momentarily beneath the surface, eluding his grasp, perhaps by inches. "Master!'' he heard, a scream half choked with water. Then he sped directly downstream, anything to be somewhere ahead of her. He crested the current and rushed before it, half borne by it, half racing it. Then he turned about in the water, fighting against the current. "Scream!'' he cried. "Cry out!'' He wondered if she were under the water, perhaps feet away, speeding toward him. He wondered if she was drowned. Then, in a flash of lightning, he saw a fold of garment, and, in another stroke of lightning, he got his hand on it. He jerked her head out of the water. Then, swept downstream, he struck against something. In the center of the stream, temporarily arrested there, caught on a rock, was the large branch, almost a tree in itself, which must have washed away from some bank, and which had passed them earlier. They were then, in the pouring rain, enmeshed in the smaller branches. He reached for branches, and they broke off. He steadied himself against the wet, black trunklike main branch. He gasped for breath. Her head was back, her eyes wild. "I have you, slave,'' he said. "Master!'' she cried, her face streaming with water. The branch then, pressed in the current, suddenly, unexpectedly, awkwardly, moved, slipping away from the rock. It was then loose in the current, and spinning downstream. Then it rolled and the smaller branches, like a barrel of spokes, forced them both under the water. The gladiator reached up, partly climbing, partly tearing through branches. His fingernails were bloodied from tearing at the bark. Then he emerged into the storm again, his left arm about the slave's neck. In a flash of lightning he saw the escape capsule, far downstream, deep in the water, listing. The river churned inches from the opened hatch. He did not doubt, from its depth in the water, that the capsule had already shipped a considerable amount of water. He was afraid to release the branch. He did not know if he could reach the shore. An uprooted tree swept past. "Look!" he cried, clinging to the branch. Downstream, in the darkness, there was a sudden bluish glow, and then the escape capsule, its entire large, oval surface, began to crackle with sparks and flame. Then again there was darkness. "Beware!" he said, and braced himself, for the trunk of a tree, like a spear, smote into the branch to which they clung, spinning it about. "Are you all right?" asked the gladiator. "Yes, Master," cried the slave. There was now, under the roar of the storm, another roar, somewhere ahead, a roar which grew progressively louder. The gladiator tried to peer through the darkness and rain. He fought for breath. The water must have reached yet another system in the escape capsule, for, far downstream, it began again to glow, but this time with an orangish color. And then, suddenly, it was dark. It was as though the glow had been suddenly snapped off, like a light. A part of a tree swept by, a catlike beast clinging to its trunk. Its fur was sleek with rain. The branch to which the gladiator and the slave clung caught for a moment on another rock. "What is the noise, not the storm?" the gladiator asked himself, confused. "Is it a thousand beasts? Is it thunder from afar?" "Too," he asked himself, "what of the capsule? How did it cease so suddenly to glow?" The roar was now becoming even louder. It competed with the wind, the storm. Suddenly he heard a wild screech of terror from ahead, which then faded suddenly. It had to be the animal which they had seen, but moments before. Now the roaring was deafening. In the darkness the gladiator, as the slave cried out in terror, in protest, thrust away from the branch, and, with one arm, as he could, fought for the shore. He was swept muchly downstream, but twice caught against rocks. Then, when the roar was unmistakable, even to one confused in the darkness, one wrought with titanic strain, one exhausted from physical effort, he got the mud and gravel of the riverbed beneath his feet, and, the slave terrified and bedraggled in his arms, made his way to the bank. In the next flash of lightning he saw, holding the slave, the edge of the falls, some yards away. Curious he went to its brink. The drop was something in the nature of a hundred feet. He saw the sopped, catlike beast slide through the water, its ears back, and scratch its way up to the shore. It was possible, he thought, that they might have survived the fall. To be sure, it is difficult to make judgments on such matters. He did not see the capsule. He did not know if it were still afloat or not. After resting for a time, he once again lifted the slave in his arms, who was trembling, and began to make his way back upstream, to where they had salvaged some of their goods. After a time the rains stopped. He had then managed to build a small fire. This was managed with leaves and brush from rain-sheltered places. The fire was lit with the lighter, from the survival kit, one of the objects removed earlier from the capsule. They had then stripped and set about drying their clothes. His had dried first, easily, as they were lighter, less voluminous, less cumbersome. Janina had been kneeling near the fire, drying her hair, when they first heard the horns.

"There are several horns now," said Janina.

"They are on this side of the river," said the gladiator. "We will cross."

"Not the river!" said Janina.

"The level is much subsided," said the gladiator.

"I fear the river!" said Janina.

"This," said the gladiator, "will prevent you from being swept away."

He knotted a rope about her neck.

"That is its only purpose, is it not, Master?" she asked.

"What do you think?" he asked.

She looked down, shyly, smiling. Janina, in the arms of strong masters, had learned her womanhood.

The remains of the armor he had cast into the river. Its utility was grievously impaired, it having been muchly damaged on the *Alaria*, and he feared, too, that on this world it would constitute little more than a clumsy, weighty encumbrance. Could one manage edged or pointed weapons, even staves or clubs, well, if one were so housed? Might one not be tripped, or caught, or be for most practical purposes helpless in such garb? Would it turn the blow of an ax, for example, or be of much service if one were caught in a noose, cast from a tree? Too, men seen in such things might be taken to be the barbarians of the ships, and he doubted that such would be likely to be popular with primitively armed rustic or sylvan populations, if they knew of them, at all. The armor, of this sort, which weighed in the vicinity of a hundred pounds, had its place, surely, in a world of fire pistols, and weapons of a similar sort, but it did not seem that it would be of great value in a primitive, natural, savage world, one where survival was more likely to be a function of speed and agility, and will, intelligence and ferocity, than an arrangement of relative impenetrabilities.

The gladiator prepared a bundle, consisting of most of the materials they had salvaged from the capsule, including some rations, and also Janina's clothing. This bundle the slave would bear. He himself slung the empty Telnarian rifle across his back. He retained the belt from the armor, and housed the empty fire pistol in its holster. He also put on the belt a sheathed knife, from the survival kit. He was, for the most part, however, unencumbered. He cut himself a staff, both as a weapon, and to assist in the transit of the river. He then, leading the slave on her rope, she bearing the bundle of supplies, and such, on her head, steadying it with her hands, waded into the river. In a few minutes they had safely crossed.

On the other side he wound the free end of Janina's rope about her neck. There were then several coils about her neck. He tucked in the free end.

"You will follow me," he said.

"Yes, Master," she said.

In this fashion she would bear the rope herself, and it would be conveniently at hand, obviously ready for a variety of employments.

Toward noon they heard the horns again.

The horns, now, were on their side of the river.

One seemed to be behind them, and another to their right. They then began to move left, through the thick, dark forest.

But, in an hour, they heard a horn before them.

They then resumed their original march, away from the river.

"They are closer, Master," said Janina, a little later.

"Yes," said the gladiator.

"Those are hunting horns, Master?" asked Janina.

"Yes," said the gladiator.

"What are they hunting, Master?" asked Janina.

"Us," he said.

· · · CHAPTER 16 · · ·

"Keep behind me," said the gladiator.

Janina, the rope on her neck, crouched down, behind him.

The gladiator stood with his back to a large rock. There was a clearing here, in the forest, and several such outcroppings.

"Abandon me, Master," Janina had begged.

But he had turned about, in anger, and cuffed her to silence. She had not even requested permission to speak.

To be sure, he had not made a practice of requiring this deference of Janina.

She had then knelt at his feet and gratefully kissed them.

He had seen shadows in the forest, about them.

Shortly thereafter he had come to the open place, and had gone to the rock, a large, high, broad rock, where he had turned about and placed himself as he now stood.

There had been more blasts of horns, some doubtless summoning blasts, others perhaps signaling that the quarry had been brought to bay, and then, in a few minutes, the shadows among the trees, darknesses among darknesses, had become numerous.

Nothing emerged from the forest.

The gladiator sat down, cross-legged, then, waiting.

He picked up pebbles, after a time, and threw them about.

Janina continued to crouch behind him, eyeing the forests.

Then, something like a quarter of an hour later, a man emerged from the forest. He had a leather headband. He was clad in skins. There was a large ax tied across his back.

He sat down, also cross-legged, back near the trees. He was some twenty yards from the gladiator.

After a time the gladiator called to him. "Can you understand my speech?"

"Yes," said the man.

After a time the man called to the gladiator. "You are Drisriak."

"No," said the gladiator.

"You have their weapons," said the man.

"I am not Drisriak," said the gladiator.

"There are too many of us for you to kill," said the man.

"I mean you no harm," said the gladiator.

"We have bowmen," said the man. "A hundred arrows, in an instant, could strike you."

"If you are marksmen, only one would be needed," said the gladiator.

There was an angry sound from the forest behind the man, and he lifted his hand, to silence it.

"You are bold, Drisriak," said the man.

"I am not Drisriak," said the gladiator.

"You have not come for the tribute?"

"No," said the gladiator.

"We keep our produce, our pelts, our women, for ourselves," said the man.

"I mean you no harm," said the gladiator. "I shall put my weapons aside."

"Only a fool disarms himself," said the man.

The gladiator very slowly, very carefully, unslung the Telnarian rifle and put it to the side. He, too, undid his belt and placed it to the side, with its holstered fire pistol, and the sheathed knife.

"You are without ammunition," said the man.

"You are discerning," said the gladiator.

"Why do you not try to threaten us," asked the man, "because you are somehow without your ship, without your armor, without usable weapons?"

"I am not Drisriak."

"What is your people?"

"I have no people," said the gladiator.

"Everyone has a people," said the man.

"No," said the gladiator. "In the empire there are millions who are alone, who have no people."

"I have heard of the empire," said the man.

"It is far away," said the gladiator.

"Who are you?" asked the man.

"I am called 'Dog,' " said the gladiator.

"That is an animal," said the man.

"Yes," said the gladiator.

"Is that your true name?"

"I do not think I have a true name."

"You are a slave?"

"No."

"What are you?" asked the man.

"I am a peasant," said the gladiator.

"No," said the man. "You are Drisriak."

"Why do you say that?"

"The woman," he said.

The gladiator was silent.

"You have her naked, with a rope on her neck," he said.

"Yes," said the gladiator.

"That is no peasant's woman," said the man. "She is beautiful. She is beautiful enough to be a tribute girl."

The gladiator was silent.

"That is a slave-block woman," said the man.

"All women are slave-block women," said the gladiator.

There was assent to this from the forest.

"That is a Drisriak's woman," said the man.

"No," said the gladiator.

"She is beautiful enough to be a Drisriak's woman," said the man.

"Then their women must be very beautiful," said the gladiator.

"They are," said the man.

"You seem not fond of the Drisriaks," said the gladiator.

"We conceal ourselves in the forest from them," said the man.

The gladiator shrugged.

"Where is your ship, the others?"

"We are alone. There is no ship."

"How came you here?"

"We fled the captured imperial vessel, the *Alaria*, in an escape capsule. It brought us here. The capsule is lost to us. It was by the river."

"Who took your vessel?"

"The fleet of Ortog, who is an Ortung."

"Ortog is a prince of the Drisriaks," said the man. He spat to the side.

"His house is secessionist," said the gladiator.

"Who, then, will come for the tributes?"

"Will any come?"

"They have."

"Who?"

"Ortog, for the Drisriaks," said the man.

"Perhaps there is an end now, to such things," said the gladiator.

"There is never an end to such things," said the man.

"But you are concealed in the forests."

"They will come," said the man.

"Then you must fight."

"They can destroy the forests," said the man.

"They have such power?"

"Yes."

They were then silent for a time.

"You are not Drisriak?" said the man, finally.

"No," said the gladiator.

"Give us the woman," said the man. "You can then go."

"No," said the gladiator.

Janina crept more closely to him.

"You would give your life for a woman?" he asked.

The gladiator did not respond.

"She is a slave, is she not?" asked the man.

"Yes," said the gladiator.

"She can be bought and sold, like a pig," said the man.

"Yes," said the gladiator.

"You would give your life for her?"

Again then was the gladiator silent.

"We can take her," said the man. "We are many. You are one."

"I gather that honor does not exist in the forests," said the gladiator.

"It is only in the secrecy of the forests, hidden away, that honor can exist in these times!" said the man, angrily, rising to his feet.

The gladiator, too, then, rose to his feet.

"We will buy her," said the man. "Two pelts of the black wolf!"

"She is not for sale."

"Three," said the man.

"No," said the gladiator.

"But you might, in honor, give her away," said the man.

"True," said the gladiator.

Janina crept even more closely to the gladiator.

"Give her to us," said the man.

"No," said the gladiator.

"Give us the pistol, the rifle," said the man.

"No," said the gladiator.

"But you claim they are without ammunition."

"That is true."

"Give them to us."

"No."

The man then removed the ax from his back. The gladiator,

not taking his eyes from him, reached down and picked up the staff he had cut.

At the same time, from the forest, emerging into the clearing, came some seventy to eighty men. Behind them, now detectable among the trees, were others.

"There are so many, Master!" said Janina.

"Yes," he said.

The men continued to emerge from the forest.

"Master," moaned Janina.

Then the gladiator and the kneeling slave were muchly enclosed, on three sides.

Altogether there may have been some three hundred to three hundred and fifty men. They carried a variety of weapons, most spears, some bows, some swords, some axes.

"Give me to them, Master!" said Janina.

"No," said the gladiator.

"Master!" protested Janina.

Angrily he lashed back with the back of his left hand, striking her from her knees, flinging her back to the rock behind them, where she turned, and then half-knelt, half lay, bleeding, a chastised property.

"Clear a place," said the man with the headband, stepping back a few feet.

Men parted.

"You would match an ax to a staff?" asked the gladiator.

"Cut a staff," said the man.

A fellow left, to go into the woods. In a few moments he returned, with a stout, trimmed branch.

"Your staff," said the man with the headband, "is too long, too thick, too unwieldy."

But he did not know the strength of the gladiator, that he could wield such a thing as a lesser man might have a stick.

His ax handed to another, the man in the headband hefted the staff just cut for him. It was springy, and green. It would have something of the resiliency of a whip, with something of the lash of such an object. It would not be likely to break, unless struck with incredible force.

A wide circle was traced in the dirt, there in the clearing. The men from the forest lined the circle. Janina, the rope unwound from her neck, it then again serving as a leash, was pulled to the edge of the circle, where she was knelt down. The leash was shortened, by looping, so that, as she knelt, the fist of her leash holder was but a foot from her neck.

The staves were crossed.

"Begin!" called a man, striking upward with the butt of his spear, with a sharp crack separating the staves.

The gladiator stood in the center of the circle, his staff not lifted, in no defensive posture.

The man with the headband moved about him, and the gladiator turned, to follow him.

The man with the headband feinted, and then again, but the gladiator made no move to counter a possible blow, nor to initiate one of his own.

Then the butt of the man's staff thrust at him.

It was a tenative, exploratory touch. But it left its mark.

"He fears to fight," said a man at the side.

The man with the headband then struck the gladiator a round blow.

Men cried out. Such a blow might have felled a lesser man.

"He is strong," marveled a man.

The man with the headband then, perhaps as astonished as the others, struck the gladiator again, this time even harder.

"Are you weak, Astubux?" jeered a man.

In fury then the man with the headband again struck the gladiator, but it was as though he might be smiting an inert, natural thing, the rock, a tree.

"Aiii," marveled a man.

Then the man with the headband, whose name was Astubux, again struck the gladiator, as hard as he might.

But, again, the gladiator did not lose his footing. He hardly flinched. But the stripes on his body, the rising of the dark welts, evidenced the authenticity of the blows.

"Fight! Fight!" screamed Astubux. "Are you a coward?" he asked.

The gladiator's eyes, for a moment, were frightening to read. In them, but scarcely detectable, there was suddenly suggested something terrible. It was like a movement in a dark forest, one perhaps of some dreadful beast, one best left unaroused.

Astubux stepped back.

The gladiator eyed him.

Then the strange thing, fleeting, terrible, in the eyes was gone. It was as though the beast had turned away.

Astubux rushed forward, striking down with the staff, but this time the blow was simply blocked, smartly, as was the next, and the next. This the gladiator had decided. Then the staves were braced against one another and the gladiator, step by step, forced Astubux toward the edge of the circle, where men, in awe, drew back. But he did not force him from the circle. He forced him three times to its perimeter, and each time let him return to the center. Astubux was now wide-eyed, and sweating. Then the gladiator pressed down on Astubux's staff and Astubux, in the center of the circle, was forced to his knees. Then the gladiator drew back the great staff and smote down, breaking the staff of Astubux. Astubux tried to move backward but was forced by the butt of the gladiator's staff to his back. Then, for a moment, the beast appeared once more in the gladiator's eyes, as he lifted his staff, like a spear. Then, again, it was gone. He drove the staff downward. It sank six inches into the soil beside Astubux's head.

"Be pleased I did not choose to fight," said the gladiator. He then turned about, and left the circle.

Astubux scrambled back out of the circle, and stood, outside it, breathing heavily.

The man at the edge of the circle who was holding the leash of Janina, it muchly looped, pulled her to her feet by it and led her to the gladiator. He placed the loops of the leash in his hand. The gladiator then wound the leash, again, as it had been before, about the neck of Janina. She then knelt beside him, the coils of rope on her neck, acknowledged his.

"What people are you?" asked the gladiator.

"We are the Wolfungs," said Astubux, "the remnants of one of the five tribes of a once mighty people, one long since scattered, as legend has it, about the worlds."

"And what people was that?" inquired the gladiator.

"The forest folk," said Astubux. *This is the same people, we might note, or so it seems from the records, which were later to appear in so many of the chronicles as little more than a legend of terror, that people known more generally as the Vandals, or Vandalii. We have already touched on certain difficulties in connection with the etiology of the name.*

"And what are the other tribes?" asked the gladiator, for he was suddenly keenly interested in this matter.

"They may no longer exist," said Astubux.

"What were they then?" asked the gladiator.

"The Darisi, the Haakons, the Basungs, and the parent tribe, the largest and fiercest of all the tribes, the Otungs."

"Ortog believed me to be an Otung," said the gladiator.

"Why?" asked Astubux.

"I do not know," said the gladiator.

"Who are you?" asked Astubux.

"I do not know who I am," said the gladiator.

"If you are an Otung," said Astubux, "then they have not perished."

"We would be of kindred peoples," said a grizzled fellow.

"I do not know who I am," said the gladiator. "I am only a peasant."

"If you are of the Otungs," said the grizzled fellow, "you are not a peasant, you are a warrior, a warrior among warriors, a warrior of a race of warriors."

"No," said the gladiator, shaking his head. "I am only a peasant."

At that moment there was a terrifying crashing, and breaking and roaring in the forest. The very earth shook. Some hundreds of yards away flames leaped upward. A moment later smoke rose from the trees.

"It is the sign of the Drisriaks!" cried a man.

"They have found us!" cried another.

"There is no escaping from them!" cried another.

"Come!" said Astubux to the gladiator. He, followed by the gladiator and several of the other men, climbed the tall rock, from the summit of which they could survey the forest, for miles about. Janina, too, followed.

"There! See!" said Astubux, pointing.

A broad stream of fire, perhaps a mile in width, as though from the stars themselves, poured down into the forest.

"It is the sign of the Drisriaks!" said Astubux.

"No!" said a man. "It is different! Look!"

The broad swath of fire was being intelligently directed. It was carving, in the forest, a sign, one which the gladiator had seen before. Indeed, it had been on the armor which he had discarded. It was on the buckle of the belt, which he had left below, with the empty fire pistol and the sheathed knife. It had been, too, on the vessels of the Ortungen fleet.

"That, I think," said the gladiator, "is the sign of Ortog, or of the Ortungs."

"It is not the sign of the Drisriaks," said a man, studying the pattern of flame and smoke.

"Ortog, as I understand it," said the gladiator, "has left the house of the Drisriaks."

"But he comes, as before, for the tribute, as he had before, for the Drisriaks," said a man.

"I think so," said the gladiator.

"Only to be gathered now for himself," said the grizzled fellow.

"It would seem so," said the gladiator.

"Their envoys will be at the village in a few days," said Astubux, glumly.

"What will you do?" asked the gladiator.

"We will pay," said Astubux. "What else is there to do?"

"Who is your chieftain?" asked the gladiator.

"We have no chieftain," said Astubux.

"How can that be?" asked the gladiator.

"The Drisriaks kill our chieftains," said Astubux.

"It is their way," said the grizzled warrior.

"Now none will be chieftain," said Astubux.

"Who would be so?" asked another.

"What are spears to the power of the Drisriaks?" asked another.

"And thus they deprive you of leadership?" asked the gladiator.

"And our manhood," said another, bitterly.

"To the loss of such one might prefer death," said the gladiator.

He recalled a courtroom, and an arena, far away.

"We have no leader," said a man.

"Astubux speaks for us," said a man.

"Yes," said another.

"It is he who deals with the envoys," said another.

"To my dishonor," said Astubux.

"You must proclaim a chieftain," said the gladiator.

"That he may die, that we then may all die?" said a man.

"It is a long time since one has been lifted on the shields," said a man.

"You are free to go," said Astubux.

They stood on the summit of that high, bare rock, and looked out upon the forest, where, in a roar of smoke and fire, in long lines, each a mile in width, burned into the forest itself, there blazed the sign of Ortog.

"See how they announce their arrival," said a man.

"See how they insult us," said another.

"I am not pleased with this," said the gladiator.

"It has nothing to do with you," said a man.

"It is our grief, not yours," said Astubux.

"It should not be your grief, but your provocation," said the gladiator.

"It is no concern of yours," said Astubux.

"If I should be somehow of Otung blood," said the gladiator, "would we not be kindred?"

"Yes," said a man.

"And would this insult not then be done to me, as well?" asked the gladiator.

"Yes," said a man.

"I do not accept it," said the gladiator.

"I do not understand," said a man.

"You are a peasant," said Astubux.

"What is a people with no chieftain?" asked the gladiator.

"It is no people," said a man.

"A wolf with no head, with no eyes, with no will," said another.

"A beast that sleeps," said a man.

"You," said the gladiator to a man standing nearby. "Go below and bring here, to the summit of this rock, the bundle of clothing with my things."

The man seemed startled for a moment, but then he turned about and went down the escarpment, and then, in a bit, reappeared on its summit, bearing the bundle of clothing.

Smoke from the fires drifted about the rock.

Animals could be seen below, fleeing, mostly frantic, bounding ungulates.

The gladiator accepted the bundle of clothing from the Wolfung warrior, and then he threw it to Janina. "Put it on," he told her.

The garments were now muchly wrinkled and soiled. Too, they were frayed, from the escape capsule, and torn, from the rocks and the branches in the river, but they still retained, even in their current state, more than a hint of their original splendor. The colors, even if faded, were still clearly discernible, and intact were the complex embroidered designs, and the insignia of station and house. Janina, too, put about herself the rich jewelry, the necklaces and bracelets, which had been accessory to them.

"Those are the colors of the Drisriaks," said a man, in awe.

"See the designs, the insignia," said another.

"The jewelry!" said another.

"Those, if I read them aright," said Astubux, "are the robes of Gerune, princess of the Drisriaks!"

"They are," said the gladiator.

"This then," cried a man, pointing excitedly to Janina, "is Gerune! You have captured her!"

"The sister of hated Ortog!" said a man.

"Kill her!" said another.

But the gladiator put his hand on the man's spear, and thrust it aside.

"No," he said, "this is not Gerune. It is a common slave."

"Surely it is Gerune!" said a man.

"Strip, and rebundle the garments," said the gladiator to Janina.

"It must be Gerune," said a man.

"She wears the royal garments," said a man.

"We can hold her for ransom," said a man.

"He has Gerune," said a man. "His rope is on her neck!"

"We can use her to bargain with the Drisriaks," said another.

"It is not Gerune," said the gladiator. He took the bundled garments from Janina, the jewelry wrapped inside. He handed this bundle to the fellow who had originally fetched it upward from below.

"Gerune wears his rope on her neck," said a man.

"It is not Gerune," insisted the gladiator.

"Surely it is," said Astubux.

"How careless then," said the gladiator, irritably, seizing Janina by the arm and turning her about, so that her left flank was to the men, "that the Drisriaks should have had their princess branded."

On Janina's left thigh, high, just under the hip, a common branding site, was the small flower, the slave rose.

"It is not Gerune," said a man.

"How came you then by the garments of Gerune?" asked a man.

"I took them from her, on the ship," said the gladiator. "She figured in my plan of escape. The garments were worn by this slave, that she might be mistaken for Gerune."

"And what of Gerune herself?" asked a man.

"I marched her before me, gagged, naked, bound, on a rope, through the corridors of the captured ship, before hundreds of warriors of Ortog."

The men cried out with pleasure.

"I think you had best kneel," said the gladiator to Janina, who hastily, belatedly, knelt.

"Hands on thighs, knees spread," said the gladiator.

Janina complied.

"Keep your head down," suggested the gladiator.

Janina put down her head.

"And what is Gerune, sister of Ortog, like?" asked a man.

"I think you would find that her body would be that of a pleasing slave," said the gladiator. "Before I left the ship her head was at my feet."

"It is the Drisriaks who take our women," said a man.

"Perhaps," said the gladiator, "it should be you who take their women, for your naked slaves."

"Glory to the Wolfungs!" said a man.

"It is a long time since we have tasted glory," said a man.

"You have no chieftain," said the gladiator.

"Of what avail are the blades of spears against fire from the stars?" asked a man.

"I have a plan," said the gladiator.

"It is time a chieftain was proclaimed," said a man.

"It would be suicide for anyone to dare to be lifted upon the shields," said a man.

"He would be killed by the Drisriaks," said a man.

"Let such matters be the concern of the chieftain," said the gladiator.

"You are not a Wolfung," said Astubux.

"Choose then one of your own," said the gladiator.

The men looked at one another.

"Astubux?" asked a man.

"No," said Astubux.

"Would you deal with the Drisriaks?" asked a man of the gladiator.

"Certainly," said the gladiator.

"And what would you offer them?" asked a man.

"Defiance," said the gladiator.

"It is a hopeless matter," said a man.

"Nobility," said the gladiator, "is most easily purchased in an impossible cause."

"What will our women say?" asked a man.

"They will obey," said the gladiator.

"It has been a long time since we have had a chieftain," said the grizzled man.

"You have a plan?" asked a man.

"Yes," said the gladiator.

"Let us return to the village," said a man.

And so the group left the summit of that high rock and assembled below. In leaving they trekked through the circle which had been scratched by the butt of the spear, that within which two men had done contest with staves. Astubux and the gladiator, with others of the leading warriors, led the group. Behind the gladiator, and to his left, in the heeling position, sometimes stumbling, came Janina, the rope wrapped still about her neck, bent under her burdens as before, including even the bundle of clothing and jewelry which had once graced the figure of Gerune, princess of the Drisriaks, sister of Ortog, king of the Ortungen. As she was a slave it was appropriate that she be laden. The others were, of course, free men. The party also crossed, at one point, a broad swath of blackened trees. The carcasses of incinerated animals lay here and there. An occasional scavenger looked up as the party passed. Birds had come to the area in hundreds, to peck out burned grubs and worms, and small animals, where the brush and leafy cover of the forest floor had been seared away. The ash was still warm to the bare feet of Janina.

Toward evening they arrived at the village.

That night, in the light of a great fire, blazing in the center of the village, amidst much shouting and the beating of weapons, a new chieftain was proclaimed, that by the Wolfungs, one of the lesser tribes of the Vandals, the gladiator being lifted upon the shields of warriors.

· · · CHAPTER 17 · · ·

"I have done more than my share of work," said the officer of the court.

"Would that you were a slave," snapped the young naval officer. "Then you would know what work is!"

"Well, I am not a slave," she said, angrily.

"Nor am I!" said the other young woman.

"Be silent, lowly *humiliora*!" said the officer of the court.

"You want to get out of all the work!" said the angry young woman who had just been addressed.

"There is much work to be done," said an older woman. "Let us help him."

"It is his fault that we are here!" said the officer of the court.

"It was you," he said, angrily, "who cried out in the *Alaria*, who alerted the barbarians, who compromised our escape."

"Do not speak to me so!" said the officer of the court. "I am a citizen, of the *honestori*, of the blood!"

"What do such things matter here?" inquired the other young woman. "What does anything matter here?"

"Be silent, shopgirl!" said the officer of the court.

"Do not quarrel," advised the older woman.

This group, as you have doubtless conjectured, was that which had escaped the *Alaria* shortly before the somewhat improvised departure of the gladiator and the slave, Janina, in the second of the two escape capsules which had been stored in the hold. It consisted of the young naval officer and three women. One of these women was the officer of the court. She had been on her hands and knees, in her "same garb," a rope on her neck, in the grasp of Janina, in the corridor near the lock where the gladiator was preparing the first capsule for launch. When the young naval officer had made his appearance in the corridor and appropriated the waiting vehicle, she had joined his party. Earlier the young naval officer had participated in the defense of the ship, which gradually, obviously, had become more and more hopeless. When a group with whom he had been fighting had surrendered, thence to meet diverse fates, he had fled, and later, seeing no prospect of recovering the vessel, had determined to seek out one of the escape capsules in the hold, hoping to make use of it to depart the vessel. It had been a great disappointment to him to discover that the lift mechanism had been inoperative, and he had been unable to get the vehicle to a lock. In the hold, he had encountered two women, who had fled there to hide, and were living on the supplies in the capsules. In a sense, we have heard of both these women, though they were strange companions, considering the hierarchies in the empire. One was the striking woman in the pantsuit, who had been in attendance at the contest, and who had invited the officer of the court to sit with her. The other was the salesgirl, or shopgirl, from whom the officer of the court had, earlier that same day, purchased certain surprising and uncharacteristic garments. The officer of the court, as we may remember, had been scandalized that an individual of that class and station, and merely a lowly employee of the line, should have been admitted to the entertainments.

"Fetch water," said the young naval officer to the officer of the court.

"No," she said.

" 'No'?" he asked.

"I am of the blood," she said. "Such as I do not draw water."

"Then you fetch it," said the officer to the other young woman.

"Not if she does not," she said.

"I will fetch it," said the older woman.

She left, to go to the small stream nearby.

The capsule which had been appropriated, or comandeered, by the young naval officer, had been, as we recall, severely damaged in the incident of the pursuing missile, that which had been prematurely exploded against the jettisoned clearance thruster. As a result the capsule had been left much at the mercy of its momentum and position, lost in the winds of space, so to speak, subject to the numerous subtle forces, primarily gravitational, obtaining in that area at that time. It had eventually drifted into a scarcely tangible current, if one may so speak, and, some days later, had found itself, like a speck in an invisible whirlpool, caught in a rapidly degrading orbit, at the focus of which was a remote world, one on which they had managed, two days ago, to effect a successful landing, thanks largely to the skill of the young naval officer, the viability of certain viewing and measuring instrumentation, and the proper functioning of a manually responsive landing system.

"We will need firewood," said the young naval officer to the officer of the court.

"Have you repaired the radio?" asked the officer of the court.

She knew, of course, that it had been damaged beyond repair, various components shattered in the injury to the capsule, others literally melted and fused as a consequence of the short-circuiting attendant on the impact. That had been determined within an hour after the impact.

"It cannot be repaired," said the young naval officer.

The officer of the court tossed her pretty head. Why then should he expect her to gather wood? Too, had he not insulted her, by responding as though her question might have been an honest, civil one, pretending to ignore the hint that he was somehow to blame for its damage? To be sure, it was he who had interposed, almost at the last moment, the clearance thruster. Might he not have jettisoned it earlier, perhaps a hundred miles earlier?

"You go, then," said the naval officer to the shopgirl.

"I might crack my nails," she said, looking at the officer of the court.

"If you do not work," said the young naval officer to the two young women, "you will not be fed."

"Do not amuse us," said the officer of the court.

The young naval officer clenched his fists.

"You must feed us," said the officer of the court. "We are citizens of the empire."

"Yes," said the shopgirl.

"It is our right to be fed," said the officer of the court.

"Yes!" said the shopgirl.

"Better you had both been left on the *Alaria*," said the young naval officer, "at the mercy of the Ortungen."

"Do not speak so!" chided the officer of the court.

"Perhaps they could have gotten some good out of you," he said.

"Beware your speech!" said the officer of the court.

"But they probably would not have found either of you of sufficient interest to be kept," he said, "even as naked slaves."

The shopgirl gasped, putting her hand before her mouth.

The officer of the court was furious, and, for a moment, speechless. Then she said, "Arrange for our rescue!"

The young naval officer glared at her.

"Put out a signal, or something!" she said.

"Do you think you are on a beach, on some civilized world, with transports overhead every hour?" he asked.

"Light a beacon," said the officer of the court.

"And who would see it?" he asked.

"Surely there is someone on this world," she said.

"That is possible," he said.

"Surely someone!" she said.

"But who?" he asked, meaningfully.

The officer of the court, and the shopgirl, were silent.

The young naval officer withdrew.

The shopgirl stood up, and looked about herself. "This is a beautiful world," she said.

The officer of the court sniffed.

"It is primeval," said the girl, "untouched, unspoiled."

"I am glad you like it," said the officer of the court. "You may spend the rest of your life here."

"What did he mean," asked the shopgirl, "that he did not know who might see a beacon?"

"I do not know," said the officer of the court. "I am sure we are alone on this world."

"I am not so sure," said the shopgirl.

"Why do you say that?" asked the officer of the court.

"I thought I saw something, yesterday," she said.

"What?" asked the officer of the court, apprehensively.

"I do not know," she said.

"Perhaps it was a beast," said the officer of the court, uneasily. Surely, last night, when they were locked in the capsule, they had heard things outside, prowling about. Too, there had been howling, roars, in the forest.

"Perhaps," said the shopgirl.

"He took the pistol, of course!" said the officer of the court, angrily.

"It has only a charge or two left, surely," said the shopgirl.

"What will protect us, if something comes?" said the officer of the court, looking about herself.

"We can run to the capsule," said the shopgirl.

"Where is he?" asked the officer of the court.

"Doubtless he has gone for firewood," she said.

"I'm hungry," said the officer of the court.

"I wonder if there are men here, on this world," said the shopgirl, looking at the darkness of the trees.

"I would not know," said the officer of the court.

"It there were, they would almost certainly be barbarians," she said.

"Undoubtedly," said the officer of the court.

"I wonder how they would view us," she said.

"As persons, as ladies," said the officer of the court.

"But if they were truly barbarians—" said the shopgirl.

"I wonder where Oona is," said the officer of the court. This was the name of the woman in the pantsuit, it now frayed and dirty, who had gone to fetch water.

It seemed she should have returned by now.

There was some cause, incidentally, for the guarded reply of the young naval officer, that having to do with his response to who might see a signal, or beacon, if one were set. He had, you see, seen earlier some signs of human habitation, footprints by a stream, and a broken spearblade. Too, yesterday they had smelled smoke, from afar. He had climbed a tree and discerned the fire, but it seemed no ordinary fire, centered in a locale, then spreading, much at the mercy of wind. Rather, though he had not called this to the attention of his companions, it had been a fire of unusual pattern, one seemingly in defiance of nature, surely nothing one would expect to result from a simple blast of lightning, and, too, from where would have come such a blast, out of a clear sky?

"I am hungry," said the officer of the court, and began to sort through the rations, put outside the capsule, to be sorted and divided. This was in connection with an inventory intended by the young naval officer. It was now miserably close in the capsule, the life-support systems shut down.

"Do not touch the rations!" said the shopgirl.

"Do not speak so to me, *humiliora*!" snapped the officer of the court.

"You are fat enough!" said the shopgirl.

"I am not fat!" said the officer of the court. "It is the modesty of my garmenture!"

"You look like a balloon and you smell!" said the shopgirl.

"My garb is designed with a purpose in mind, one which you are incapable of appreciating, in your pretty little slacks and jacket!" said the officer of the court. "And you smell, too!" she added.

The officer of the court and the salesgirl refrained from making further untactful allusions to certain odors, as this was a sensitive issue, and one in terms of which they were both clearly vulnerable. The young naval officer and the woman in the pantsuit had, yesterday, gratefully, after weeks in space, at respectfully separate intervals, washed in the nearby stream. The waters, however, had been much too cold for the likings of the officer of the court and the salesgirl. Too, who knew who might be watching? This consideration, in particular, alarmed the officer of the court. For example, could she truly trust the young naval officer? Too, they could always bathe tomorrow. It might be warmer then.

"It is designed to conceal from others, and from yourself, that you are a woman!" said the shopgirl.

"Insolent bitch!" said the officer of the court.

"But then you are probably not a woman," said the shopgirl.

"I am a woman!" said the officer of the court, somewhat surprising herself by this declaration, one not really to be expected from a woman of Terennia.

"Fat!" said the shopgirl.

"I am not fat!" said the officer of the court.

"If you were a slave," said the shopgirl, "your figure would be trimmed until it was sexually stimulating to men!"

"Do not dare to speak to me in that fashion," cried the officer of the court. "I am an officer of a court, of the *honestori*! You are only an employee, a salesgirl, working in a shop on a cruise ship. You are only of the *humiliori*. Do not dare speak so to me, you meaningless little snip. I am of the blood itself!"

"See if you speak so proudly when your hair is pulled out!" said the shopgirl, angrily.

"Do not dare touch me!" said the officer of the court, alarmed.

Angrily the salesgirl turned away. The least that might happen to her now would be that she would lose her position with the line. The *humiliori* were expected to exhibit a proper deference toward those of the *honestori*. Too, she might then find it difficult to locate another position. On certain worlds she could be fined, or sentenced to a penal brothel, even to being close-chained to her pallet. On many other worlds she could be simply remanded to slavery. Perhaps she would be purchased by the person whom she had offended.

The officer of the court opened a box, one containing concentrated survival chocolate.

"Do not eat that," said the shopgirl.

"I do as I please," said the officer of the court.

"It is for all of us!" said the salesgirl.

"Be quiet," said the officer of the court.

"Fat!" said the shopgirl.

"I am not fat," said the officer of the court.

"Where are you going?" asked the shopgirl.

"I am going to the stream, to get a drink," said the officer of the court.

Their water, you see, had been muchly depleted in the capsule, not only over time, but in virtue of their needs, given the physical dehydration which tends to occur in such an environment. The water in the stream, too, constituted a considerable improvement over the water in the capsule's stores. The water in the stream, tested pure, was cold and fresh. It was not stale. It did not reek of the taste of containers. Indeed, it was the best water that the officer of the court had ever tasted. On Terennia, the water in certain town reservoirs, such as that in which the officer of the court had resided, tended to be heavy with the taste of various sanitizing chemicals.

Chocolate, too, of course, of which the officer of the court had taken a considerable portion, and was eating even now, on her way to the stream, tends, predictably, to make one thirsty.

"Fat!" called the salesgirl after her.

"I am not fat!" said the officer of the court, angrily.

The stream was not far from the camp, where the capsule

was. The officer of the court walked through the trees. They were tall and thick, on both sides of her. There were many shadows at any time in that place, but there were a great many more now, as it was rather toward dusk. As she made her way toward the stream she finished the chocolate. She wiped her fingers on the thighs of her ''same garb.'' Near the edge of the stream, no more than a few yards from it, she stopped. Ahead, a few feet back from the edge of the stream, fallen, she saw an object. She approached it more closely and discovered it to be the container which the woman in the pantsuit had borne toward the stream, to fill with water. Almost at the same time she heard, from her right, tiny, helpless, muffled sounds. She turned in that direction and saw, to her consternation, the figure of the woman in the pantsuit. Her back was to a large tree, and her arms were back, one on either side of the tree. Behind the tree her wrists had apparently been linked by some device, perhaps a foot of rope. The lower portion of her face seemed muffled in heavy cloths.

The officer of the court did not know what to do. She took a step, a frightened, uncertain step, toward her, but the woman shook her head, wildly. Then the officer of the court thought she saw a shadow among the trees, and then another. The tiny, muffled cries emanating from the bound woman seemed clearly enough to constitute a warning.

The officer of the court turned about and fled back toward the capsule.

She broke into the small clearing of the camp, and her distraught condition startled and alarmed the salesgirl, who leaped to her feet.

Breathless the officer of the court, her eyes wide, pointed back wildly toward the stream.

She had no sooner turned back toward the camp, gasping for breath, than she detected, emerging from the opposite side of the camp, not far from the capsule itself, the stumbling figure of the young naval officer. It seemed he had been pushed forward. But she could see no one behind him. His upper body was swathed with rope. Cords had been tightened in his mouth, pulled back tightly between the teeth.

"Run! Hide!" wept the officer of the court and she fled toward the capsule. The salesgirl, terrified by her demeanor, followed her. They hastily entered the capsule and closed the hatch, spinning the wheel which secured it.

They crouched inside, in the darkness.

"I can't breathe!" said the salesgirl.

"Go outside," said the officer of the court, angrily.

For a time there was silence about, and then the two young women cried out, suddenly, in alarm, startled by a sudden pounding of metal on the outside of the capsule.

"They can't get in," said the officer of the court.

"Who are they?" asked the salesgirl.

The officer of the court crept to one of the tiny ports, something like four inches in diameter.

"I cannot see who they are," she said.

Then she drew back, because a stone, held in a fist, struck against the port.

"They cannot get in," said the officer of the court, backing away.

There was more pounding on the exterior of the capsule. They could also hear the external hatch wheel being tried. It would not open, of course, as the hatch had been sealed from the inside. Then there was more pounding at the port. After a time the heavy material in the port was chipped away. A stick was thrust into the capsule, jutting in, then rimming flakes of glasseous substance away.

"We are safe," said the officer of the court. "They cannot enter."

The salesgirl drew a deep breath. It was less stifling now in the capsule. Air could enter through the opened port.

"Are they men?" asked the salesgirl.

"I do not know," said the officer of the court.

"Look!" said the salesgirl.

"You look!" said the officer of the court.

The salesgirl rose to her feet and timidly looked out the nearest port.

She quickly drew her head back.

"What are they?" asked the officer of the court, crouching on the floor of the capsule, anxiously.

"They are men," said the salesgirl.

"What sort of men?"

"By their garb—barbarians," said the salesgirl, crouching down.

"Be pleased," said the officer of the court, bitterly. "You will make a pretty little slave girl."

"So, too, would you!" said the salesgirl.

"I jest," said the officer of the court. "It is fortunate for us that they are barbarians. That means we have little to fear."

"How is that?" asked the salesgirl.

"As barbarians," said the officer of the court, "they will be stupid. They will have no patience. They will soon leave."

"What if they do not?" asked the salesgirl.

"They will," said the officer of the court. "They are stupid."

"I have heard that barbarians enjoy making slaves of civilized women," said the salesgirl.

"If they can get them," said the officer of the court.

"What if they wait outside?" asked the salesgirl. "We have nothing to eat or drink within."

"They do not know that," said the officer of the court.

"I am afraid," said the salesgirl.

"Do not be afraid," said the officer of the court. "They are barbarians. They are stupid. They will quickly grow weary of waiting, and depart. We will then leave the capsule, and escape. Nothing could be simpler."

"We shall outsmart them," said the salesgirl.

"Certainly," said the officer of the court. "We are far more clever than they are. We are civilized women."

"How then is it," asked the salesgirl, "that we are bought and sold, and kept as helpless slaves, on so many worlds?"

"It is quiet outside now," said the officer of the court.

"What of Oona and the ensign?" asked the salesgirl.

"We must think of ourselves," said the officer of the court. "They were stupid enough to permit themselves to be captured."

"It seems very quiet," said the salesgirl.

"Perhaps they have already left," said the officer of the court.

The salesgirl stood up and looked through a port. "They have not left," she whispered.

"Then they are not as impatient as I thought," said the officer of the court.

"No," said the salesgirl. "They are even more impatient than you thought."

"They are leaving?"

"No."

"I do not understand."

"But they are not as stupid as you thought," said the salesgirl.

"I don't understand," said the officer of the court.

"They are bringing brush, and wood," said the salesgirl, "and placing it about the capsule."

In a few moments the flames were roaring about the lower hull of the capsule.

"I cannot breathe!" wept the salesgirl.

"Ai!" cried the officer of the court, touching the side of the capsule.

The officer of the court lifted one foot, and then the other, from the heated floor.

The salesgirl wept with pain, wringing her hands.

"What are we to do?" wept the officer of the court.

"That has been decided for us, has it not!" cried the salesgirl.

"What choice have we?" wept the officer of the court.

"The only choice they have accorded us!" wept the salesgirl. "A slave's choice!"

"Ohh," wept the officer of the court, crying, gasping for breath in the heated vehicle.

Then she heard the salesgirl struggling with the hatch wheel.

"Me first! Me first!" cried the officer of the court, thrusting the salesgirl aside. The hatch wheel burned her hand. Then she thrust it up. Her hands were burned on the rungs of the hatch ladder.

The outside of the capsule had begun to glow redly.

The officer of the court burst from the hatch, crying, and gasping for air. She felt herself seized in strong hands, on each side, and flung to the dirt on her belly beside the roaring fire heating the capsule. She turned her face away from the blaze. She felt her hands pulled behind her and tied there, securely. She was aware, too, of a similar fate befalling the salesgirl, who had followed her from the capsule a moment later. She was still gasping for breath, shuddering, on her belly, trying to pull her hands apart, when she felt a rope being tied about her neck. She turned about and saw that the salesgirl was bound, too, just as she herself was, and that she, too, now, had a rope on her neck.

· · · **CHAPTER 18** · · ·

"What irons are these?" inquired Otto, chieftain of the Wolfungs.

"My chieftain knows, surely," said Astubux.

"They are slaving irons," said Otto.

"Yes."

"But surely not made by our smiths," said Otto.

"No," said Astubux. "These are irons formed on other worlds, civilized worlds. They are such as are used by the Drisriaks to mark women for sale throughout the galaxies."

"The flower," said Otto.

"Yes, Master," said his slave, Janina. Her own thigh bore a not dissimilar brand.

The chieftain considered the irons.

They would leave behind a small, tasteful mark, but one which would be clear and unmistakable.

"The slave rose," said Otto, the chieftain. This seems, incidentally, the first time, then in the village of the Wolfungs, that he was known by this name. It may be surmised that he chose it for himself before being lifted on the shields. The name, incidentally, was a common one in the Vandal nation, even at that time. Research has made that clear. It is not as though it only became so later. It is also interesting, in the light of historical studies, that he chose that particular name. It was one which had been borne generations earlier by Otung kings.

"Yes, Master," said Janina, putting her head down.

"How came they here?" asked Otto.

"They were left by the Drisriaks, to remind us of their power," said Axel, who was the older, grizzled Wolfung warrior who had been with the hunting party which had first made contact with a marooned gladiator and slave.

"When they come for tribute," said Astubux, "they pick out what goods they want, including women. Then they brand them before our very eyes."

"They should be here soon?" said the chieftain. The sign had been burned into the forest two days ago.

"I would say three or four days," said Axel.

"They wish to give us time to gather together the tribute," said Astubux.

"Twice we have fled, but they have always found us."

"We flee no more," said the chieftain.

"They are not pleased when we hide," said Axel. "They kill off men and take twice the tribute."

"We hide no more," said the chieftain.

"It was from the first vengeance that they denied us chieftains," said Astubux.

"You now have a chieftain," said Otto.

"I fear your tenure as chieftain will be brief," said Astubux.

"It is I who will face them, who will bear the brunt of their wrath," said Otto.

"Let us fly, Master," urged Janina.

"I am chieftain," said Otto.

"They need never know we were here!" said Janina.

"Do you wish to be tied at the whipping post?" asked the chieftain.

"No, Master!" said Janina.

Quickly she withdrew to one side, and knelt, and put her head down.

"You have a plan?" asked Astubux.

"Yes," said the chieftain.

"And if it fails?"

"I fear then, good Astubux," said Otto, "you will once more be without a chieftain."

"No!" said Astubux.

"Things then, good Astubux," said Otto, "will be much the same for you as they were before, no better, no worse."

"But we would have no chieftain!" said Astubux.

"As before!" laughed Otto.

"We will follow you, all of us, into the forest," said Axel. "Let us hide again."

"We have hidden long enough," said the chieftain. "One day the Wolfungs must come from their forest." Then he went to the door of the hut, and looked out, over the palisade, toward the trees beyond, and the horizon, and the sky. "Let the Wolfungs be the first," said he.

"What means my chieftain?" asked Astubux.

"Nothing," said Otto. He regarded the sky, moodily.

"Who knows," said Axel, "what strands the sisters of destiny have woven into the rope of fate."

"Last night," said Otto, "the skald sang not only of the Wolfungs, but of the Darisi, the Haakons, the Basungs, the Otungs."

"The people, the nation," said Astubux.

"You think long thoughts," said Axel.

"Has it not been demeaned, and scattered and persecuted long enough?" asked Otto.

"Yes," said Axel.

"Is it not among the fiercest of warrior nations?"

"It is the fiercest, and most terrible," said Axel.

"It once was," said Astubux.

"And has your blood grown thin and cold?" asked Otto.

"Spears," said Astubux, "are no match for fire from the stars."

"Unless we, too, can stand among stars, and grasp that fire," said Otto.

"You have long thoughts," said Axel.

"Yes," said Otto.

"Is there a way?" asked Axel.

"Yes," said Otto.

"I fear the chieftain is mad," said Astubux.

Otto turned about and lifted Astubux toward the roof of the hut, and laughed. "Yes," said he, "your chieftain is mad! Come, share his madness, and die a man!"

"Better than to live as a *filch*!" said Axel.

"I hear horns," said Otto, and he lowered Astubux good-naturedly to the floor of the rush-strewn hut. "I am not yet familiar with their signals," he said. "Tell me their meaning."

"Do not attend to the horns," said Astubux. "Rather prepare for the coming of the Drisriaks."

"What is the meaning of the horns?" asked Otto.

Axel listened for a moment.

"Prisoners," he said. "Prisoners have been taken."

"What more?" asked Otto.

"Three women, and a man," said Axel.

· · · CHAPTER 19 · · ·

Otto sat alone in his hut.

Outside, beef roasted on a spit.

Beer, in drinking horns, was being passed about.

From where he sat, Otto could hear, clearly, the blows of a smith's hammer.

The huts of the chieftain's village, within the palisade, tended to circle about a rather large open space. It was larger than was required for the huts in the chieftain's village itself, and served as a place of assembly for not only the occupants of the chieftain's village, but of the several nearby Wolfung villages as well. It was in this open place that Otto, that being the name he had taken for himself, as we have learned, had been lifted upon the shields, to the clamor and acclaim of the Wolfungs. Too, the palisade of the chieftain's village was the stoutest of any of the villages, and his village, in case of need, was intended as a bastion of defense and a refuge for the Wolfungs for miles about. There were also supplies stored in the capital village, so to speak, which might alleviate the hunger of a great many people, in case of the failure of local croppage, or in the unlikely event of a siege conducted by men armed similarly to themselves. To be sure, a single blast from a Telnarian rifle would have blown the gate away. There was, at one point within the palisade, a deep well, which, within living memory, had never gone dry, even in the late summer. The largest hut, but primitive, as well, was the chieftain's hut, which had only recently been reoccupied. Its floor was strewn with rushes, but there were rolled skins and furs there, which might also, if one wished, be spread upon the floor. The roofs were thick, and thatched. The walls of most of the huts were of daub and wattle, but the walls of the chieftain's hut were made of timbers and roughy hewn planking. The interior area of the chieftain's hut, the roof supported by several posts, gave an area with a diameter of some fifty feet. It could house then, in council, the high warriors of the Wolfungs. Others, women, retainers, and such, could wait outside. There were also, within the palisade, and within the palisades of other villages, as well, coops, stables and pens for domestic animals, which we shall call, for purposes of convenience, chickens, cattle, sheep and pigs, such terms being sufficiently appropriate for our purposes. Many of these were gathered in at night. Some cattle, in particular, milch cows, as we shall call them, were housed with families, in their own huts. There were also, here and there, cages, mostly quite small, with thick iron bars. The Wolfungs had their smiths, you see, who attended to their metalwork, in particular, the forging of weapons, spearblades, and such. There were also other devices, such as log kennels and chaining logs.

"My chieftain," said Astubux, appearing at the entrance to the chieftain's hut.

Otto then rose to his feet and went outside, to the open place.

He lifted his hand to the Wolfungs, who cried out upon seeing him, who raised drinking horns and spears in salute.

Janina, who was now clad in the long, loose garb of a Wolfung woman, hurried to kneel beside him.

"Here," said Astubux, gesturing toward the large chair, on a wooden dais, set up a few feet from the fire, where the chieftain was to have his seat. Across the back of the chair was flung the pelt of a forest lion. Skins of this beast, too, were strewn on the platform.

Otto took his seat, and indicated that Janina, his slave, should kneel beside the seat, on its left.

She hurried to do so.

The officer of the court, the salesgirl and Oona, the woman in the pantsuit, knelt near a post in a hut, not far from the gate. It was dark in the hut but, clearly, outside, there were festivities. They could see, through the chinks in the daub-and-wattle siding of the hut, the flickering of a fire, the light of torches being carried about, such things. They could see bodies, too, like shadows, passing back and forth, the men in rough tunics of pelts, the women in their long dresses, of some plain cloth. There was an excellent reason why the three women knelt near the post. They had been roped to it, closely, by the neck. Their hands were still bound behind their bodies. The three women and the ensign, prisoners, had arrived in the village in the late afternoon. They had been immediately separated, the women put in this hut and the ensign taken elsewhere. Although the officer of the court would scarcely have admitted this to herself, she, and we may speculate the others as well, had been dismayed at the special selection, the special treatment, exhibited in this matter, at their being totally separated from the ensign. This keeping them together, without the ensign, did much to impress upon them, and quite acutely, that they were women. It made them, somehow, feel far more helpless and vulnerable than might otherwise have been the case. They were now merely captured women.

Two large Wolfung females then entered the hut, one bearing a lamp.

The one without the lamp removed the ropes from the prisoner's necks. Then she untied their hands.

She indicated that they should precede her out of the hut. In a moment they were conducted between numerous men and women into the vicinity of a large fire, and knelt down before a rude dais, on which a chair had been set.

The officer of the court shrank down, and put her head down, for, to her consternation, her astonishment and horror, she recognized the figure in the chair.

She lifted her head a little and looked about. She and her fellow prisoners were the object of much attention, of both the men and women.

She gasped.

She saw Janina beside the great chair. She was kneeling there. How fitting for a slave! She hoped that Janina would not recognize her.

Where was the ensign, the young naval officer? He was nowhere in sight. She hoped he had not been killed.

She knew barbarians thought little of death. They lived with it. They were familiar with it. She remembered what had been done by the Ortungs on the *Alaria*, to the officer who had sat with them at the entertainment, to the captain, to his first and second officers, doubtless to many others.

But she, and the insolent, vain salesgirl, and Oona had not been killed, at least not yet.

That could have been done at the capsule.

It would have been easy enough there.

What did that mean?

Please spare me, she thought. I will do anything!

"You!" said the barbaric figure, in regal pelts, sitting on the chair, pointing.

The officer of the court thought she might die, but she realized, then, that it was not at her that he had been pointing.

"Stand," said the chieftain, "and come closer."

The salesgirl, in the slacks and jacket, these garments now foul with sweat and dirt, trembling, stood up.

She approached the dais.

"What is your name?" he asked.

"Ellen, milord," she said.

"Free women," he said, "will be killed. Slaves, if found acceptable, may be spared, at least for a time."

He regarded her.

"Do you understand?" he asked.

"Yes, milord," she said.

"What are you?" he asked.

"I am a slave—Master," she said.

"Remove your clothing," he said, "completely."

The men watched intently, and so, too, fearfully, and then in indignation, and then in envy, did the officer of the court. She gasped, seeing that garments much like those hidden beneath her "same garb" had been beneath the jacket and slacks. She is a slut! thought the officer of the court. But how beautiful she is! thought the officer of the court.

"Shall we keep her, at least for a time?" called the chieftain to the assembled Wolfungs.

"Yes, yes!" they cried. Some pounded on shields with spears.

Ellen, the salesgirl, sank to her knees to one side of the dais, trembling.

"You!" said the chieftain, pointing to the officer of the court.

She shrank back, hoping she would not be recognized.

"Stand," said the chieftain, "and come closer."

Numbly the officer of the court, on this remote world, in the presence of barbarians, rose to her feet. She approached the dais, and stood before it. She did not dare to meet his eyes. She hoped that he would not recognize her.

"Free women," he said, "will be killed. Slaves, if found acceptable, may be spared, at least for a time."

He regarded her.

"Do you understand?" he asked.

"Yes," she said.

She resolved to offer him defiance, to proclaim her freedom. Was she not in "same garb"? Was she not an officer of a court? Was she not of the *honestori*? Was she not of Terennia, where men and women were absolutely the same in all ways? Was she not of the blood itself?

"What are you?" he asked.

"I am a slave, Master," she said.

"That is known to me," he said, in contempt.

Her heart sank in misery. He knew her. He recognized her. Too, she had always known, even from the first moment his eyes had fallen upon her, seeming to see her, even though she was in the dark, voluminous robes of the court, as though she might be stripped and shackled on a slave block, that he had somehow pierced to the most profound secrets of her heart, discerning there her true self, the waiting, concealed, yearning slave.

"Remove your clothing," he said, "completely."

Almost fainting, wavering, her fingers fumbling with the closures, the officer of the court opened the drab, bulky "same garb" and then, shuddering, lowered it to her hips.

"Ah," said a man.

"Slave, slave," said a man.

"You are beautiful," whispered Oona.

The men were intent.

The officer of the court then lowered the same garb to her ankles, and stepped from it.

She heard an intake of breath.

She looked at the chieftain.

Then she sat on the ground and removed the bootlike shoes she had worn, and the long dark stockings. These stockings, as we may recall, had some purple thread sewn at their top, to show that she was of the blood. Then she had removed the brassiere and the panties.

She then stood before him, and them, a stripped slave.

"What was your name?" he asked.

"Surely you know," she said. Then she said, "Tribonius Auresius."

"That is a man's name," he said.

"It is—was—my name," she said.

"Why?" he asked.

"My mother put it on me," she said.

"Why?" he asked.

"I do not know," she said. "Perhaps that I should think of myself as a man."

"Are you a man?" he asked.

"No," she said.

"Did you try to think of yourself as a man?" he asked.

"Yes," she said.

"What are you?" he asked.

"A woman," she said.

"You are no longer permitted to think of yourself as a man," he said. "You must now think of yourself as what you are, a woman."

"Yes," she said.

"Yes, what?" he asked.

"Yes, *Master*," she said.

"This one," he said to the crowd, "I will decide personally, whether she is to be kept or not, at least for a time."

There was assent to this.

The officer of the court then, frightened, knelt beside Ellen, both at the foot of the dais, and a bit to the chieftain's left. She did not even know if she would be kept, even for a time.

Perhaps she could please him. Perhaps that is what he would want. Certainly he had looked upon her often enough in a way which suggested that he would not be displeased to have her at his feet.

She shuddered, considering what it might be, to be at the feet of such a man.

The woman in the pantsuit was then ordered to rise, and to approach the dais.

She did so, slowly, frightened.

The two slaves at the foot of the dais muchly feared for her.

She, too, as the others, was questioned.

"But none will be interested in me!" she wept.

"Stand straight, put your shoulders back," commanded Otto.

There was a coursing through the crowd, of admiration.

"I am a slave, Master," she responded.

"Remove your clothing, completely," she was told.

"Please, no, Master," she said.

"Strip," she was ordered, "utterly."

She began to remove her garments.

"And you will be whipped," he said, "for having dallied in response to an order."

"No one will want me!" she wept.

"Stand straight," he said.

A man clapped his hands with pleasure.

"Ah!" cried Axel.

Oona had a striking figure.

She seemed surprised, even startled, at the response of the men. It had not even occurred to her that she might be of interest.

"Shall we keep her, at least for a time?" inquired Otto, laughing.

"Yes, yes!" called men.

Axel stepped forward, towering over Oona. "Are you a good slave?" he asked.

"She does not smell, like the others!" called a man.

"I will try to be the best slave I can, Master," said Oona, frightened.

"I want her!" announced Axel.

"Are there any objections?" asked Otto.

There were none from the Wolfungs.

"Kneel there, my slave," said Axel, indicating a place near the other slaves.

"Yes, my master," said Oona, looking at him with awe, and stirred by feelings she had thought she might never again feel, save in her thoughts, and in her dreams.

"Bring the other!" said Otto.

In a few moments the ensign was brought, moving with short steps, before the dais. His ankles were shackled. It was the sound of the smith's hammer shaping these devices to his ankles to which the chieftain had listened, before emerging from the hut. A cloth, simple and brief, had been twisted about the loins of the ensign. It was not such that it might conceal a weapon. He stood before the dais, his arms folded.

"These are slaves," said Otto, indicating the women kneeling to the left of the dais, as one would look outward from the chieftain's chair.

"At least two are," said the ensign.

"All are," said Axel.

"Is it true?" asked the ensign of the women.

"Yes, Master," said the former salesgirl.

"Yes, Master," said the former officer of a court.

"Yes, Master," said the other woman, the slave who had been put under claim by Axel, a counselor of the chieftain.

"Are you a slave?" asked the chieftain of the ensign.

"No," said the ensign.

"That is known to me," said the chieftain.

"What do you want of us?" asked the ensign.

"The utility of female slaves is evident," said Otto.

"And what of me?" asked the ensign.

"You will work in the fields," said the chieftain.

The ensign regarded him.

"I think," said the chieftain, "that, in time, you may be worth a ship."

"I am worth a thousand ships," said the ensign.

Men whistled in awe.

"Who is this?" asked Astubux.

"Your name," said the chieftain.

"I am Julian, of the Aurelianii," said the ensign. The men and women about looked at one another. This name meant little to them. It was, however, much like the names one tended to associate with the remote, mysterious empire.

"Know, slaves and prisoner," said Otto to the four before the dais, the kneeling women, and the standing male, "that the forests about us are dangerous. They teem with beasts. Your safety, particularly in the night, depends on your being within the palisade. Too, there is nowhere to go, nowhere to run. There are no friendly forces, no imperial outposts, no escape for you, on this world. Do you understand?"

"I understand," said Julian, of the Aurelianii.

"I understand, Master," said the slaves, each, as his eyes fell upon them.

"We will talk later," said Otto to Julian, of the Aurelianii.

Julian nodded.

"This prisoner," said Otto to men near him, "is to be kept in a log kennel at night. During the day he is to be used in the fields. See that he is worked long and hard."

"We will do so, our chieftain," responded a man.

"Take him away," said Otto.

The ensign was then turned about and conducted from the presence of the assembled Wolfungs.

"Let these two stinking slaves be washed," said the chieftain, indicating the former salesgirl and the former officer of the court. "Then let them all be tied at posts, to await the heating of the irons."

"Yes, my chieftain!" said a man.

"Now," said Otto, rising from the chair, and standing on the dais, "let the feasting begin!"

"Please, no!" cried the former officer of the court, as she was forced down by two brawny Wolfung women into the wooden tub of cold water.

She shrieked with misery, chilled, but was held in place. Sometimes she was bent double, her head forced under water, to make certain that the dirt in her hair might be soaked free. She rose sputtering from the water, shuddering and shivering. She moaned and protested, but was silenced with a blow, as heavy brushes were applied to her body, and not with gentleness by the free women, for she was a slave, and little love is lost between free women and slaves. In a nearby tub the former salesgirl, shivering, and whimpering and crying out, underwent a similarly abusive, rude scouring.

The two slaves were then drawn from the tubs and dragged by their impatient attendants to short posts. There they were knelt down with their backs to the posts. Their ankles were tied together, behind the post, and their hands were taken up, and behind the posts, where their wrists were tied together, and fastened there, behind the post, to a ring.

"I am cold!" wept the former officer of the court, but the women had left. Looking to her right she saw the former salesgirl at another post, similarly secured. Looking to the left she saw the woman who had been put under claim by Axel. She, too, was similarly secured. She had been there earlier, as she had not been subjected to a bath, it not having been deemed that she needed one.

The former officer of the court looked up.

"Master!" she said.

Before her there stood, looking down upon her, a drinking horn in his hand, Otto, the chieftain of the Wolfungs.

"They bathed me!" she said, appealing to him.

"You do not expect us to brand a filthy body, do you?" he asked.

"Surely I am not to be branded!" she said.

"Look," said he, indicating, nearby, a brazier, glowing with heat. From the brazier there protruded the handles of three irons. Two men crouched near the brazier, tending it.

"Please, no, Master," she said.

"The word 'Master' fits well on your lips, very naturally," he observed.

"You have known it would, have you not?" she asked.

"Yes," he said.

"How long have you known I was a slave?" she asked.

"From the first moment I saw you," he said.

"How?" she asked.

"From your body," he said, "and from its movements, and from your least expressions."

"What is the brand?" she asked, fearfully.

"It is one common in the galaxies," he said, "the slave flower."

"Do not mark me with that," she wept, "or I shall always be a slave. It is known everywhere!"

"But you are a slave," he said. "It is fitting that your body be marked with the flower of bondage. No longer is your inner truth to be hidden from the world. It is rather, now, to be proclaimed, to be made public, to all, by that mark."

"Will you keep me?" she asked.

"Axel," said he, "will tie his disk on her neck." He pointed to the woman who was under Axel's claimancy.

"What of me?" she asked.

"She," said the chieftain, indicating the former salesgirl, "I will, at least for the time, take."

The salesgirl looked wildly over at him, from her post.

"But what of me, Master?" asked the former officer of the court.

"Yes, what of you?" he asked.

"Keep me!" she begged.

"Why?" he asked.

"I would be your slave!" she wept.

"It is my intention," he said, "to put my disk on your neck, at least for a time."

She tried to move toward him a little, but could not do so.He looked down upon her.

"Do I have a name?" she asked.

"No," he said.

"Master!" she wept, but he had turned away.

There were the sounds of much feasting.

She watched the brazier, glowing in the shadows, as though it might be filled with jewels of fire.

Astubux sat on the dais, a drinking horn in hand, and the chieftain had returned to his place there.

"My chieftain," said Astubux.

"Yes," said Otto.

"What of the prisoner?"

"His taking has muchly pleased me," said Otto, moodily.

"You can add him to your plans?" asked Astubux.

"His presence here considerably increases their probability of success," said Otto.

"Which, I gather, is slight at best," said Astubux, glumly.

"Drink, feast," encouraged Otto.

"And the slaves?"

"I am thinking that two of them may figure in my plans, but only in a small way, as is fitting, as they are females, and slaves."

"Axel has the one who was called 'Oona,' " said Astubux.

"Does it concern you that we have given her to Axel, who is one my advisors."

"Am I not, too, a counselor of my chieftain?" asked Astubux.

"You looked closely upon the blonde, whose name was 'Ellen,' " said Otto.

"What man would not?"

"Would you like her, to tend your hut?" asked Otto.

"Yes!" said Astubux, turning about.

"She would probably know little about tending a hut," said Otto.

"I could teach her quickly enough with the knout," said Astubux.

"I am thinking of giving her to you in a few days," said Otto.

"My chieftain!" said Astubux.

"You would like her?" asked Otto, smiling.

"Yes!" said Astubux.

"She is only a slave," said Otto.

"No matter!" said Astubux.

"Your disk will be on her neck," said Otto. "But wait some days."

"Yes, my chieftain," said Astubux.

"More drink," called Otto.

"What of the other one, the young brunette," asked Astubux.

"I will, for the time, put my own disk on her neck," said Otto.

"And what then?" asked Astubux.

"I do not know what I will do with her," said Otto.

"You seem angry, my chieftain," said Astubux.

"She is a worthless slave," said Otto.

"But surely a pretty one."

"Yes," said Otto, angrily.

"She would fetch a good price," said Astubux.

"Perhaps I will sell her," said Otto.

Then Otto, chieftain of the Wolfungs, put back his head and drank, and so, too, did Astubux, one of his counselors.

Shortly thereafter there was a cry of pain. A few minutes later there was a second cry, much like the first. Then, a few minutes after that, there was a third cry, it quite like the first two.

"The slaves have been marked," said Astubux.

"Yes," said Otto, chieftain of the Wolfungs.

A nameless brunette, a slave in a primitive village on a remote world, was thrust into her master's hut, before him. She fell to the rush-strewn floor before his seat. It was a large hut, with posts here and there supporting the roof. There was a fire in the firepit.

He sat then in the chair, and she looked up at him, from the floor.

"Put more wood on the fire," he said.

She found wood at the side of the hut.

"Enough," he said.

"Kneel here," he said, indicating a place before his chair.

She complied.

She put her hands on her thighs, but kept her knees closely together.

He looked down upon her, moodily, angrily.

She pressed her knees even more closely together.

He did not speak.

"I have been marked!" she said, suddenly.

"Put your knees apart," he said.

The slave did so, feeling strange sensations.

On her neck, tied there, on a leather string, there was a leather disk.

A similar disk was on the neck of the blonde, but she had been put in a cage.

A disk, too, had been tied on the neck of the woman put under claim by Axel. She had understood that that was Axel's disk, marking her as his. He had then tied her hands together, with a leather strap, before her body, and then, with one strand of the strap, extending from her wrists, had led her to his hut. She had followed timidly, but had not held back.

"Are you not frightened to belong to such a man?" the brunette had asked her, when the women, after their marking, had been crouching together.

"Better to be owned for an hour by such a man," she had said, "than to live a lifetime with a weakling."

Then she had been pulled to her feet, and Axel had put his disk on her neck. Then he had bound her hands before her.

"Do not forget," had said the chieftain, "that she was tardy, earlier, in responding to a command."

"I shall not, my chieftain," had grinned Axel.

The brunette had then shuddered, for she recalled that the woman was to be punished for her laxity. She doubted that the woman would fail to profit from the lesson. Indeed, from even the thought of this lesson she and the blonde had already profited, having learned that these were not men such as they had hitherto known, that these were not men to be trifled with.

Axel had then led the woman to his hut.

Shortly thereafter they had heard the lash. Axel was sharp with her, but short. Axel, she gathered, was fond of the woman. He had wanted to do little more than let her know what the lash was like, and that it would be used upon her if she were not pleasing. Axel would be kind to the woman, but not lenient. She would not forget that she was a slave. She would be kept under perfect discipline.

The chieftain had then had the two young women stand, and, from behind, he had tied the string about their necks, and each, then, was tagged with his disk.

She wore it now, before him, but dared not touch it.

She had been elated when the chieftain had had Janina conduct the blonde to a cage, and lock her therein. But then she had been terrified, when he had taken her by the arm, and thrust her toward his hut. She was within it now. They were alone. Janina was not present. She had been told to go to a certain hut. It was the hut where the three slaves had been kept, before being brought forth at the feast. Janina had not been pleased to go there. The brunette had smiled. She would have cause to regret that later. But, to be sure, the brunette was also apprehensive. She had never been alone with a man before, certainly not like this, not a slave with her master.

"You are a long way from the court now," said Otto.

She looked up.

"And from the arena," he said.

"Yes, Master," she said.

Somewhere outside, beyond the palisade, there was a frightful roar, as of some great carnivorous beast.

She trembled.

"It is a forest lion," he said.

"You treated me with insolence and cruelty," he said. "In the arena you had me bound. On the ship you attempted to embroil me in difficulties with Pulendius."

Once again there was the roar from outside the palisade.

"Do you wish to be put outside?" he asked.

"No, Master!" she said.

"One such as you," he said, "should not be fed to lions, but thrown bound to *filchen*."

The *filch* was a tiny, rodentlike creature. They were omnivorous. In certain seasons they tended to run in packs, swarming over the ground like insects.

"Please, no, Master," she said.

"You are low, and petty," he said.

"Yes, Master," she said.

"You look well where you are, kneeling naked before a man," he said.

"Yes, Master," she said.

"It is where you belong," he said.

"Yes, Master," she said.

"I hold you in utter contempt," he said.

"Master?" she asked.

"I had thought, once," said he, "you might have the makings of a worthy slave."

"I do not understand," she said.

She watched him draw forth a leather strap. "Lift your hands, wrists crossed," he said.

She watched while her wrists were bound together. A loose end of the same strap extended from her wrists, leashlike, as it had from the wrists of Axel's slave.

She was then pulled, on her knees, to one of the posts, and her wrists were tied to the post.

"Master?" she asked.

"You are frigid, aren't you?" he asked.

"I do not know, Master," she said.

"The lash," said he, "informs a woman that frigidity is not acceptable."

"I do not think I am frigid, Master!" she said.

"Oh?" he asked.

"Try me," she said, looking back, over her shoulder.

"Try you?" said the chieftain, amused.

"Yes!" she said. "I have strange feelings! I have never felt them before, not like this, not with such intensity. I do not think I am frigid! I want to be in my master's arms!"

272 • John Norman

"You," he asked, amused, "once an officer of a court, a woman of Terennia, ask to be taken in a master's arms?"

Suddenly, helplessly, astonished, squirming, she pressed herself against the post.

"Yes," she begged. "Yes!"

"Surely," said he, "you do not think I have put you at the post merely to lash the ice away from your body?"

"Am I to be whipped?" she asked. "Why?"

"You were a slave by law when you submitted to me in the darkness, on the *Alaria*," he said. "But I did not enforce your bondage. I continued to respect you, according you honors appropriate to a free woman, to one of the *honestori*, even to one of the blood, and, as such, or as though you might still have been such, I did not gag you, for I had been given your promise that you would remain silent. But you lied to me. I accepted your word, and was betrayed. You cried out. You brought guards down upon us. We might have all been killed. You were a treacherous, lying slave."

"Master!" she protested.

"You could have been slain, as a lying slave!" he said.

She looked back at him, in agony.

"I learned then," he said, "that you were worthless, that you were meaningless, the least of slaves, the most contemptible of slaves!"

"Not the whip!" she wept.

"Be punished, worthless bitch!" he cried.

But he struck her only a few times. Then he threw down the whip, in fury.

Then he untied her from the post and she slipped down, beside it.

He returned to his seat, and sat there, moodily, angrily.

She lay crumpled, her legs drawn up, near the post to which she had been fastened.

She could not believe what had been done to her.

She had never felt a blow, until the abuse of the free women, when they had scoured her in the wooden tub, that her body might be fit to be branded. Now she lay at the post, on the rushes, a whipped slave.

"I have been punished, have I not, Master?" she asked.

"Your punishment," he said, "has not even begun."

She rose to her hands and knees, and crawled to him, and then lay before him. She put his foot upon her head.

"The slave begs the forgiveness of her master," she said.

He pulled his foot back, angrily.

"I ask only the opportunity to please you," she said.

He did not respond.

"Surely my body is not without interest," she said.

She said this for she thought, the naive little fool that she was, that this would be what would be of most importance to him, a particular configuration, and not the delicious, sensitive wholeness of her, the total female and slave. She knew herself, of course, that the true depth of her bondage lay in her heart and belly, in her thoughts, in her devotion, in her heat, in her love, in her desire to serve selflessly, abandoning herself to the master, surrendering herself wholly to him, his slave, his to do with as he pleased. That her body might be beautiful, or exciting, or of interest, was a joy to her, surely, and, too, one for which she was grateful, for it helped her to express the inwardness of her bondage, of her love, for you see, from the first moment she had looked upon the titanic, fiery youth on Terennia, she had wanted him to want her, to care for her, to be attentive to her, to place her uncompromisingly in his chains, to own her, and fulfill her.

"Let me serve you," she said.

"What does a woman of Terennia know of serving a man?" he asked.

"Teach me," she begged.

"A taste of the whip, and you are ready to learn," he said, angrily.

She put her head down.

"Do you think I have brought you here to serve me?" he asked.

"Master?" she asked, raising her head.

"I brought you here only to denounce you, and chastise you," he said.

"Let me prove to you that I am truly what you think me to be," she said.

"And what is that?" he asked.

"A slave, Master," she said.

"And what sort of slave?" he asked.

"A loving slave who would serve you with every bit of herself, with her whole body, her whole heart, with all that she is, and ever hopes to be!"

"Clever slave," he sneered.

"Master?" she asked.

"Lying slave!" he cried.

He cuffed her.

She struggled to her knees, wiping her mouth with the back of her hand. She looked at him and felt, suddenly, a wave of fear, and hatred, and misery, and desire, and helplessness.

"I have strange feelings!" she wept. "I cannot help myself! Treat me then, if you wish, as a hated, despised woman. Abuse me! Are you dissatisfied with me? Have I displeased you? Make me pay! Make me pay well! Ravish me. Subdue me. Teach me I am a woman. Leave me in no doubt as to the matter. Make me beg for more. But attend to me! Do not ignore me!"

"And what are these feelings?" he asked.

"I think—I think that I am in—in heat, Master," she said.

"Yes," he sneered. "Even a woman such as you, one so vain, so petty, so meaningless, so contemptible, with a disk on her neck, will find herself in heat!"

But then once again her helplessness, her vulnerability, her love, overcame her. "I am yours, totally, Master," she said. "Please be kind to me, my master," she begged.

He rose from the chair and went to the portal of the hut. "Janina!" he called. "Janina!"

In a few moments, summoned, Janina appeared at the portal.

He indicated the brunette, now on her hands and knees, on the rushes, before the chieftain's chair.

"Get this slut from my sight!" he said. "Cage her!"

Janina rushed to a side of the hut and seized up a switch and ran to the brunette. She lashed down at her with the switch, and the brunette cried out in misery. "Get out! Get out!" said Janina.

The brunette fled from the hut, switched.

"That way!" said Janina. "There! Down on all fours!"

"Yes, Mistress!" wept the brunette.

"Get in it!" said Janina.

A stroke of the switch hastened the entry of the brunette into the heavy but tiny cage. She turned about, on her knees, within, to see the door flung shut and the two padlocks, heavy, flung on the hasps, over the staples, and snapped shut.

The brunette, kneeling, clutched the bars, looking up at Janina.

"Earlier you smiled at me, when you thought to be alone with the master," said Janina, angrily. "Now I smile at you!"

"Forgive me, Mistress!" said the brunette.

"Janina!" called the chieftain, and the slave ran to him.

In her cage the brunette lay down. It was cold. She wept.

· · · CHAPTER 20 · · ·

At the rude table in the chieftain's hut sat four men, Otto, the chieftain, his principal advisors, wily, cynical, pessimistic, Astubux and stalwart, sage Axel, and the ensign, Julian, he of the Aurelianii.

In the back of the hut a blond girl, who had once been a salesgirl on the *Alaria*, and whose name was 'Ellen,' that name now having been put upon her as a slave name, and another slave, one as yet unnamed, a brunette, knelt before their first girl, who was standing, whose name was Janina. Another slave, the only other slave in the village, was in the hut of Axel, lying naked on the furs, as she had been ordered, awaiting the return of her master. Her name was 'Oona,' that name having been put on her as a slave name.

"The meal is prepared," said Janina. "It is now time to serve it."

"We know nothing of pleasing men," said Ellen to Janina.

"Please teach us, Mistress," said the brunette.

"The main thing is to be the slaves you are," said Janina to the two young women.

"Bring food," said the chieftain.

"Yes, Master," responded Janina.

Janina was in the modest garb of the Wolfung woman, with its long sleeves, its high neck, and its long skirt, down about her ankles. Her two charges, however, the blonde and the brunette, were in improvised *kebs*, that form of garment in which Janina herself had been exhibited at the stake, during the contest on the *Alaria*.

"Put forth the trenchers," said Janina.

Her two charges rose up and, each taking two trenchers, went to the table, to begin the serving.

The brunette dared not meet the eyes of the ensign, though she sensed them upon her, idly, as a man's glance may peruse a slave, appraising her.

Astubux reached out and touched the hand of the blonde, who put the trencher before him.

She drew her hand back, frightened, but then, quickly, put it forth again, that he might touch her, if he wished, for she was slave.

Too, she trembled, a little. She was an intelligent woman and was not unaware that Astubux had several times looked upon her.

When the free men had come to the hut, Janina, head bowed, had welcomed them. The lower serving slaves, in their revealing *kebs*, had knelt, putting their heads down to the rush-strewn floor of the hut. When the ensign had entered, unaccompanied, his ankles no longer shackled, clad now in a rough cloth tunic, the brunette had looked up at him, and then, quickly, put down her head. She had blushed scarlet. It was the first time he had seen her thusly, as a slave.

"You do not have a radio?" said the ensign to the chieftain.

"No," said Otto. "But the Drisriaks, the Ortungs, will have a radio. Do you think you could use it?"

"I think so," said the ensign. "Their radios may even be stolen radios of the empire, or copies of such designs. At the very least I should be able to transmit some sort of primitive message.''

"Drink," said Otto, lifting a drinking horn.

The brunette, head down, hastened to serve him.

Otto drained the drinking horn. He put it to one side.

"Your plan seems to depend on many variables," said the ensign.

"On some, and on honor," said the chieftain.

"Honor is a frail reed on which to rest hopes," said the ensign.

"We are not dealing with those of the empire," said Otto.

"Once we knew honor," said the ensign.

"Timing is important," said Otto. "We must buy time. It is certain that the Drisriaks will not accept the secession of the Ortungs."

"Your plan is to buy such time with what you call 'the challenge'?" asked the ensign.

"Yes," said Otto.

Otto regarded the brunette. She was beautiful in the *keb*, barefoot on the rush-strewn floor of the hut. Timidly, questioningly, she lifted the vessel she carried, just a little, that from which the drinking horn might be replenished. But he looked away from her.

"Things might be much speeded up if a radio signal could be sent," said the ensign.

"Precisely," said Otto.

"What is a radio?" asked Astubux.

"It is a device," said the ensign, "which enables one to speak to those who are far away."

"It must be very loud," said Astubux.

"You understand, of course," said the ensign, "that I will attempt to contact an imperial ship."

"I am counting on it," said Otto, grinning.

"You do not fear that?"

"It is part of my plan," he said.

"But the Drisriaks will surely intercept such a signal," said the ensign.

"Yes," said Otto, "and they are likely to be much closer than any imperial ship."

"You are devious," said Julian.

"The chieftain has long thoughts," said Axel.

"Enough of that," said Otto.

"What weapons do you have?" asked the ensign.

"From the *Alaria* a rifle and a pistol," said Otto, "but both are without ammunition."

"There is the pistol taken from me in the forest," said the ensign.

"It contains only one charge," grinned Otto.

"I know," said the ensign.

"Slave!" snapped Otto.

Quickly the brunette hastened to him.

"Turn about," he said.

The slave complied.

"You do not mind?" he asked the ensign.

"No, of course not," said the ensign.

The chieftain removed the *keb*, tossing it to the side.

"Turn about," he said.

The slave turned to face him.

Otto then lifted his drinking horn. "Drink," he said.

"Yes, Master," said the slave.

"I, too, would have drink," said the ensign.

"Yes, Master," she said, and filled, too, the drinking horn of the ensign.

"She is a pretty slave," said the chieftain. "Do you not think so?"

"Yes," said the ensign.

"Would you like to have her tonight?" asked the chieftain. "I could send her crawling to your hut, with a whip in her teeth."

The girl, in consternation, in mute, frightened, helpless protest, viewed the chieftain.

She trembled.

She knew, of course, that she could be assigned to whomever, and whenever and however, her master might please.

"Perhaps, sometime," said the ensign. "But tomorrow I must be up early, for I have a long day in the fields."

"I hear you work well," said Otto.

"You have seen to it," said the ensign.

"My chieftain!" called a voice.

"Enter," said Otto.

One of the Wolfungs entered, carrying a small bird. He brought the bird to the table, where Astubux removed a tiny message, a single sign, inscribed on a bit of leather, bound to the bird's left leg.

"What is its meaning?" asked Otto.

"The Ortungs will be here tomorrow," said Astubux.

· · · CHAPTER 21 · · ·

"You have fed us well," said Hendrix, envoy of the Ortungs.

Otto nodded, accepting the compliment.

"The metal, the furs, the pelts piled here," said Gundlicht, second envoy of the Ortungs, "the grain, the vegetables heaped outside, are better than we expected to find."

"But we have brought chains, too," said Hendrix. "We would not care to return with them empty."

"How many women do you want?" asked Otto.

"Assemble your women naked within the palisade, all of them," said Hendrix, "and we will pick fifty."

" 'Fifty'!" cried Astubux.

"You hid in the forest," said Hendrix. "Too, the markets are depressed now, with the wars, many women falling to the collar. We need more, to make up the difference. Too, it is a long way to take them to a world where they will fetch a good price."

"Fifty is too many," said Astubux.

"We will leave you enough to produce more," said Hendrix.

"The Wolfungs are good breeders," said Gundlicht.

Astubux sprang to his feet.

But a pistol, suddenly produced from the holster of Gundlicht, the Ortung, was aimed at his heart.

"How is it," asked Otto, "that you speak to Astubux, and not to me?"

Astubux sat down.

Gundlicht holstered the pistol.

"He is spokesman for the Wolfungs," said Hendrix.

"I am chieftain of the Wolfungs," said Otto.

"They have no chieftain," said Gundlicht.

"I am he," said Otto.

"You have prepared, so far, excellent tribute, and you have fed us well, and your beer is good," said Hendrix. "So we are prepared to ignore the fact that you have, for a little while, pretended to be a chieftain."

"I am chieftain," said Otto.

"Give up the chieftainship," said Hendrix.

"No," said Otto.

"We do not permit the Wolfungs to have a chieftain," said Hendrix, menacingly.

"Perhaps you would care to see a sample of the women in our village?" asked Otto.

Hendrix grinned. "Why not?" he asked. The proposal seemed clearly to be a conciliatory one, a concessionary, disarming one, one offered to ease a tense moment.

What was there to be feared, then, from the Wolfungs?

"Ho!" cried Otto, to men outside.

Some men entered, and spread pelts over the rushes on the floor of the chieftain's hut.

Hendrix and Gundlicht watched with interest.

The men then remained within the hut.

"Ho!" called Otto, and then there entered the chieftain's hut a slim blond woman. She stood upon the pelts. She stood before the men. She wore a long wraparound garment fashioned from the cloth used for dresses and cloaks by the Wolfung women.

Hendrix and Gundlicht leaned forward.

She slipped the garment down to her hips, and turned away. Then she let it fall.

"Ai!" said Hendrix, softly.

"Ah!" said Gundlicht.

Then she lay on the pelts, to the left of the men, as one would face them.

"Ho!" called Otto, and a second woman, an exquisite brunette, entered, and turned before the men, and disrobed gracefully, similarly.

Then she, too, lay on the pelts, but to the right of the men, as one would face them.

"Ho!" called Otto, and the third of the women, who was Janina, entered. She came well forward and then turned away, and then, some feet from the men, slipped the garment away.

"Turn about!" cried Hendrix.

She did so, seemingly demurely, her head down and to the side, one foot toward them, the other to the right, this turning her hip out.

"Come closer!" cried Hendrix.

"Aii!" said Gundlicht.

Janina, you see, was a trained slave.

Then she lowered herself to the pelts before them, and looked first to her left, to the blonde, this being the signal for Ellen to move upon the pelts, and as a slave.

Astubux almost cried out with pleasure.

Ellen's movements had been to some extent rehearsed, and coached by Janina, of course, but she was in her own right a man's dream of pleasure, and one who, now liberated by bondage, and joyfully choiceless in the matter, was excitedly and meaningfully one with her sexuality. No longer, as a slave, need she be forced to fight her sexuality, or fear it, or suspect it, or feel anxiety about it, or guilt. She could now utilize it, revel in it, express it, joyfully, to her heart's content.

Then she lay again on the pelts, seductively, as one might have in the sawdust on a large, rounded, smoothed slave block, hearing the bids, and knowing oneself an unusually attractive object of desire.

Janina then turned her head to her right, to the brunette who lay there, and the brunette, too, casting first a glance at the chieftain, began to move on the pelts, and as a slave.

Her movements, in a sense, were directed to the chieftain,

constituting in one sense a brazen, shameless exhibition of slave charms, but perhaps in another, a secret plea for his attention. The former officer of the court, now a stripped slave, performed on the pelts before her master, writhing, twisting, turning, displaying his property to him in its manifold, luscious aspects. In one instant their eyes had met, but only for a moment, and doubtless not noted by others. "I am yours," had said her eyes. "I beg to be wanted."

"Excellent!" said Hendrix.

"Superb!" said Gundlicht.

Then the brunette lay upon the pelts, on her stomach, her head down, it turned to the side.

She was breathing heavily.

Janina then performed before the men.

"Marvelous!" breathed Hendrix.

"Aiii!" cried Gundlicht, in disbelief, in mad pleasure.

Then Janina, too, lay before the men, she on her back, breathing heavily, her left knee raised, the soft palms of her hands upward.

"Are not such women worth ten of the normal sort?" asked Astubux.

"Do not think we will take less than fifty!" said Hendrix.

"But those three will be among the fifty!" said Gundlicht.

"Certainly," said Hendrix to Gundlicht.

"And," inquired the chieftain, "does not even the normal free woman undergo a remarkable transformation when she becomes a slave?"

"Yes," said Hendrix. "They do."

Astubux clenched his fists.

"They are women," Otto reminded Astubux.

"We will take these three, and others, fifty others, of your most beautiful women," said Hendrix.

"That would be fifty-three," said Astubux.

"True," said Hendrix.

"These three," said Gundlicht, indicating the slaves on the pelts, "have already been branded, doubtless with our irons."

"One, she most before you, was already branded," said Otto. "We used your irons for the other two."

"Our thanks," said Hendrix. "You have saved us the trouble of marking them."

"Would you like the blonde, for yourself?" asked Otto of Hendrix, who was the first among the two envoys.

"Yes!" said Hendrix.

"Astubux," said Otto, "I give her to you."

"Thank you, my chieftain!" said Astubux.

Hendrix regarded the chieftain, startled.

"Hurry to your master," said Otto to Ellen.

Quickly she sprang up and ran to kneel beside Astubux. She looked up at him, frightened. She did not know what sort of master he would be. She did know she belonged to him, totally. She put down her head and kissed his feet.

"Is this some joke?" asked Hendrix.

"The other two, she most before you, and the other, the small brunette," said Otto, "are both mine. They will continue to wear my disk."

Janina looked gratefully at the chieftain. So, too, did the brunette, so small and helpless, stripped before the men, on the pelts.

"I do not understand," said Gundlicht.

"I have shown you hospitality," said Otto. "It is now time for you to return to your camp."

"But the women, the tribute," said Hendrix.

"There is no more tribute," said Otto. "We have brought these things here, the furs and such, and outside, the produce, and such, merely to give you some understanding of the wealth of the Wolfungs, to indicate to you that we might pay an excellent tribute if we were so minded, but we are no longer so minded."

"No tribute?" said Hendrix, incredulously.

"No tribute," said Otto.

"It seems," said Hendrix to Gundlicht, "that the Wolfungs have had a chieftain long enough."

"Before you pull the trigger," said Otto, regarding the pistol in Gundlicht's hand, "I suggest you look to your right and left."

Glancing about Hendrix and Gundlicht saw, to their left, a fellow with a Telnarian rifle. The Wolfungs on the other side of the hut moved well away, out of the range of fire, for a blast from the rifle would take the wall itself from the hut, in a blaze of fire. On the other side Hendrix and Gundlicht saw two men, each armed with a fire pistol.

"We can destroy your village," said Hendrix. "Your villages."

"But of course you would both be dead then," said Otto.

"Where did you get such things?" asked Hendrix.

"From our source of supply," said Otto.

"They are not with charges," said Hendrix. "They are empties, discarded weapons. They have no ammunition."

"Give me a pistol," said Otto.

He put out his hand toward one man. He knew, of course, the pistol he needed.

Otto took the pistol in hand, and held it to the head of Hendrix, who began, suddenly, to sweat.

"Shall I pull the trigger?" he asked.

"Do as you wish," said Hendrix, sweating.

The chieftain then moved the gun away from Hendrix and aimed it at the floor of the hut. He pulled the trigger, and there was a sudden torrent of fire which fell between Janina and the brunette slave, both of whom screamed and spun away. Between where they had lain there was now a deep, narrow, smoking hole. The charge had burned through the pelts there, and the rushes, and tore down, into, and through, the floor of the hut itself. Some small rocks glistened in the sides of the trench. Some others, like droplets, now cooling, lay in the bottom of the trench where, for an incandescent moment, they had been molten. There was the smell of burned hair from the pelts, strong in the hut. The charge fired, of course, had been the single remaining charge in the village, that which had remained in the ensign's pistol.

Again Otto held the pistol to the head of Hendrix.

"Shall I pull the trigger?" he asked.

"No," said Hendrix.

Otto handed the pistol to the fellow who had held it before.

"Take this message to your lord, Ortog, prince of the Drisriaks, who calls himself king of the Ortungs," said Otto. "Tell him that there is no more tribute from the Wolfungs, but if he wishes to have a reconciliation, he may send us gifts, gold, weapons, and women. We shall then consider such a reconciliation.''

"Reconciliation?" said Hendrix. "The Alemanni and the Vandals have been hereditary enemies for ten thousand years!" It may be recalled that the Drisriaks were one of the tribes of the Alemanni, of which, traditionally, there were eleven, that number not including, of course, the Ortungen. The Wolfungs were one of the five tribes normally taken to constitute the Vandal nation. The largest and fiercest tribe of the Vandals was, or was once, the Otungs, but this tribe, in wars with the empire, had been muchly decimated, and its remnants had been scattered here and there throughout the empire, sometimes as little more than castaways, sometimes as *federates*.

"As you wish," said Otto.

Hendrix and Gundlicht rose to their feet.

"Before you go," said Otto. "Leave your weapons." He indicated one of the Wolfungs, a man standing to one side.

Hendrix and Gundlicht glanced about themselves, and then, angrily, handed their belts, with the holstered pistols, to the indicated Wolfung.

"One more thing," called Otto, addressing the departing pair, when they neared the portal.

They turned, in fury, to regard him.

"Ortog, your chieftain, who calls himself king of the Ortungs, is put under challenge by Otto, chieftain of the Wolfungs."

"You are mad," said Hendrix.

"We can destroy your forests, your world," said Gundlicht.

"He is put under challenge to personal combat," said Otto.

"That is absurd," said Hendrix.

"Chieftain to chieftain, as in days of old, not forgotten," said Otto.

"Such things have not been done for a thousand years," said Gundlicht.

"The challenge is issued," said Otto.

"Chieftains do not so risk themselves," said Hendrix.

"He may, of course, choose a champion," said Otto.

"The idea is preposterous," scoffed Hendrix.

"Are not the Wolfungs an acknowledged tribe of the Vandals," asked Otto, "one whose legitimacy is unquestioned?"

"Ah," said Hendrix, softly.

"Who are the Ortungs?" asked Otto. "Do they exist?"

"In such a way, before all the Alemanni, and in the eyes of all the barbarian tribes, one might perhaps establish the legitimacy of the secession," said Gundlicht.

"Certainly," said Otto. "If the Wolfungs, of the Vandals, recognize the Ortungs as a legitimate tribe of the Alemanni, who could, with any plausibility, decline to do so?"

"You tempt us," said Hendrix.

"Convey the challenge," said Otto.

"No," said Hendrix.

"In honor, how can you refuse to convey the challenge?" asked Otto.

"In honor, we cannot convey it," said Hendrix, rather regretfully.

"How is that?" inquired Otto, chieftain of the Wolfungs.

"No provocation could be adequate to justify accepting such a challenge," said Hendrix.

"Axel," said Otto.

Axel then brought forth a bundle.

Otto took it from him, and opened it. He carefully took, in one hand, the jewelry, the necklaces and bracelets which were within it, and held them up, dangling, to view. He then, retaining the jewelry in one hand, took the garments in two hands, the one holding the jewelry, the other free, and shook them out, displaying them.

"You recognize these?" he asked.

"That is the jewelry, those are the robes, of the princess, Gerune!" exclaimed Hendrix.

"I put them upon a slave, on the *Alaria*, that slave!" said Otto, indicating Janina, who shrank back, beside the trench in the hut floor, not at all pleased with the turn events were taking.

"You dared to put such garments upon a slave!" cried Hendrix, in fury.

"Is it true, mere slave?" asked Otto of Janina.

"Yes, Master!" she cried, in misery.

"On a branded slut?" asked Hendrix.

"Yes!" said Otto. "And the princess Gerune herself I marched before me, naked and gagged, and bound, on a rope, through corridor after corridor of the *Alaria*, exhibiting her, as one might a slave, before hundreds of the warriors of Ortog!"

"No!" cried Hendrix.

"Surely," said Otto, "you have heard secret whisperings of these things in your halls, in your drinking places, in your hangars, on your ships. Surely they are whispered even by your ship slaves."

Hendrix and Gundlicht exchanged glances.

"Take these things to Ortog," said Otto, bundling them. "Let them serve as witness to the truth of what I say. Too, tell him that his sister looks better without them, as I have seen her several times, kneeling at my feet."

"Dog!" cried Hendrix.

Otto cast the bundle of jewelry and clothing, wadded, and soiled, into the arms of Hendrix.

"Convey the challenge!" said Otto.

"It will be conveyed!" cried Hendrix.

"And convey as well my greetings to the princess Gerune," said Otto. "And tell her that I did not think her body would be entirely displeasing as that of a slave, and that I may one day have her as such at my feet."

"Dog! Dog!" wept Gundlicht.

He took a step forward, but Wolfungs interposed themselves.

"Come, Gundlicht," said Hendrix. "Insults such as these are best answered in the ancient way, with steel."

They then turned on their heels, and left.

"Have you not forgotten your tribute?" called a man after them, from outside.

"It is done," said Astubux.

"Are you a dog?" smiled Axel.

"Once," said Otto, "but I am now Otto, chieftain of the Wolfungs."

"They can destroy the world," said Astubux.

"That would not avenge the insult," said Otto.

"No," said Axel. "That would be insufficient to avenge the insult."

· · · CHAPTER 22 · · ·

"The forests are quite beautiful," said Julian.

He, the chieftain, Astubux and Axel, and four slaves, who had been brought to carry food and drink, had climbed to the top of the high, wide rock whence, several days ago, the chieftain, then a mere fighter, a gladiator, and a slave, Janina, and Astubux and Axel, and certain others of the Wolfungs, had watched the sign of the Ortungs being burned into the forest. One could still see the tracks of the ravaging of the forest, where it bore, still, like a brand, the mark of the Ortungs.

Otto, the chieftain, looked up, into the blue sky, filled with clouds.

"We have heard nothing for several days," he said.

"No," said Astubux.

"I wonder if your signal was heard," said Otto to Julian.

"It was transmitted, I am certain," said Julian. "One does not know."

"It was quiet," said Astubux. "I did not hear it."

"The hearing of the imperial fleet, and of the Drisriaks, may be keener," said Julian.

Astubux shrugged.

"Leave us," said Otto.

He and Julian then remained on the summit of the rock.

"Should the imperial fleet arrive," said Otto to Julian, "you are free, of course, to go."

Julian nodded.

"The slaves, of course, will remain," said Otto.

"Of course," said Julian. "They are slaves. We know the law."

"The empire is wondrous," said Otto. "I stand in awe of it."

"It extends over galaxies," said Julian. "It is the most magnificent invention of all time."

Otto was silent.

"It must not be lost," said Julian.

"It is eternal," said Otto. "It has always been, and will always be."

"There was a time before the empire," said Julian. "My family was there, long ago, at the beginning."

"You love the empire," said Otto.

"It is threatened," said Julian.

"The empire is invincible," said Otto.

"It must be defended."

"Surely it is in no danger," said Otto.

"Men must be found, fearless men, true men," said Julian, "to defend it."

"It needs no defense," said Otto.

"Barbarians are outside, threatening her," said Julian. "The men of the empire accept her privileges, her luxuries, but decline their responsibilities, their duties."

"Men will be found to defend her," said Otto.

"There must be men capable of facing barbarians, of standing up to them," said Julian, "men as ruthless, as terrible, as implacable as the foe itself."

"Barbarians to fight barbarians?" asked Otto.

"Who will fight for the empire, not against it," said Julian.

"You would bring in wolves to protect sheep?" asked Otto.

"It is a gamble," said Julian. "I see no other way. The sheep cannot protect themselves."

"Why are you speaking to me in this fashion?" asked Otto.

"Ortog thought you an Otung, on the *Alaria*," said Julian.

"Yes," said the Chieftain.

"I am curious to know who you are," said Julian. "Surely you are curious, as well."

"Yes," said Otto.

"Otungs, of the Vandals, over a generation ago," said Julian, "were defeated, for the third time, in the eighteenth imperial war, during the reign of Halban. Most were destroyed in the war. The remnants, captured, were disarmed and scattered about galaxies. The survivors of the fiercest and most dangerous of the Otung clans, the Elbi, were settled on a remote, perilous world."

"For what purpose?"

"To raise crops for the empire," said Julian. "Is it not amusing, that the hands of warriors, hands that knew the spear and sword, would now be set to the hoe and plow, to raise food for the worlds of their conquerors?"

"No," said Otto.

"But I have reason to believe that these people, if they have survived, and certainly the other remnants, as well, have maintained an oral tradition, in which they sing their history, and the deeds of their heroes."

"They have not forgotten themselves?"

"No," said Julian.

"Interesting," said Otto.

"I wonder if we will emerge from this alive," said Julian, studying the sky.

"I do not know," said Otto.

"The Alemanni are numerous," said Julian. "The empire fears them."

"The empire need fear no one," said Otto.

"Do you know what the Alemanni are called within the empire?" asked Julian.

"No," said Otto.

"The Aatii," he said.

"I did not know that," said Otto.

"On the *Alaria*," said Julian, "you defeated Ortog, a Drisriak, of the Aatii, the Alemanni."

"He will not fight again," said Otto. "He will select a champion. The champion will choose weapons with which I am not familiar."

"But you defeated Ortog, in personal combat, with steel," said Julian. "That is the sort of thing barbarians understand, and respect. It means more to them than watching screens and fighting at distances of thousands of miles apart.''

Otto shrugged. What the citizen of the empire had observed was undoubtedly true.

"From where do you come?" asked Julian.

"From a small *festung* village, that of Sim Giadini, on the heights of Barrionuevo," said Otto.

"On what world?" asked Julian.

"Tangara," said Otto.

"That is the world," said Julian, "to which the remnants of the fiercest and most dangerous of the Otungs, the Elbi, were exiled."

"Interesting," said Otto.

"Indeed," said Julian, "it was to that world that the very king of the Otungs himself was exiled, who was of the Elbi.''

"Interesting," said Otto.

"If we should survive what is to come, I would like to go there with you," said Julian, "to learn who you are."

"Why?" asked Otto.

"The empire may have need of men such as you," said Julian.

"But what if I should be an Otung, a Vandal?" asked Otto.

"It is my hope that that is what you are."

"Brother Benjamin, of the *festung* of Sim Giadini," said Otto, slowly, "may know something of my origins."

"That is a clue," said Julian.

The two men then descended from the high rock and rejoined the others, at its base.

The men, with the exception of Julian, of the Aurelianii, the ensign, wore pelts. Julian wore a rough tunic, as before, of cloth. The three slaves all now wore long cloth dresses, much like those worn by the Wolfung women. The dresses, however, were sleeveless, that their lovely, rounded arms might be displayed. They were, after all, slaves. Each had hung about her neck, fastened there on a string, a disk, on which was inscribed the sign of her master. These disks were round, and of leather, and the string which supported them was of leather, as well. Each disk was pierced once, and in the piercing there was a tiny leather loop. It was through this loop that the string was run. In this way the disk hung evenly at the base of the throat. It was easy to lift the disk and see the sign. Their feet were wrapped in rags, to protect them from the needles of the forest, and the stones.

"You may go ahead," said Otto.

Axel and Astubux, and Julian, turned their steps toward the village. Axel was heeled by a strikingly well-figured woman, his slave, Oona, and Astubux by an exciting, slender blond slave, whose name was Ellen. These slaves heeled their masters perhaps somewhat more closely than was necessary, but they desired to be close to them. Both were burdened, each carrying on her back certain objects, supported there with an arrangement of straps, containers in which food and drink had been brought, rolled cloaks, and such, things with which the masters did not care to inconvenience themselves, their hands being left free for the use of weapons. When the men had fed they had been served by the slaves. The slaves, though serving the food, were forbidden to touch it themselves. They might, however, take it from the hands of their masters. Three of them, Oona, Ellen and Janina, were thusly fed by hand, drink, too, being held for them by their masters. One, an unnamed brunette, knelt to one side. Her master, from time to time, when it occurred to him, would toss a bit of food to the grass before her, which she must take, touching it only with her mouth. A pan of water was also set forth for her, which, too, she must not touch with her hands. "Thus does a bitch eat and drink," she was told. "Yes, Master," she had said.

Exquisite, beautiful, trained Janina went on for a little way, but then stopped, some yards away, and waited.

Otto, chieftain of the Wolfungs, looked down on one of his slaves.

"Prepare to bear your burden," he said.

"Master!" she begged.

"Perhaps you are overdressed?" he asked.

She looked up at him, in agony. Often, in the privacy of his hut, and even publicly, when she had served table, and men feasted, she had been stripped.

"I enjoy seeing you, and your brand, slave," he had sometimes said.

"Yes, Master," she had said.

How far away was Terennia!

And how great the gulf between the slave and free!

But in all the cruelty, and all the contempt, he had shown her, he had never touched her, save to administer an occasional blow, or reprimand, usually with the back of his hand.

At night she was returned to her cage, though she was now permitted a blanket.

"What is wrong?" he asked, for tears were streaming down her cheeks.

"You have not touched me," she said. "I am a slave. I am now only a helpless slave! I would be touched!"

He regarded her.

"I beg mercy, Master!" she said.

He did not speak.

"I am not what I was. Surely you must understand that!" she wept. "I am now only a slave, your slave. I beg to be taken in the arms of my master!"

He did not speak.

"Is that not a purpose to which a slave is to be put?" she asked.

He did not speak.

"I am hot, and lonely, and in need. I am on fire with the love of my master, and he will not deign to touch me, save to strike me!"

He did not speak.

"You have not even named me!"

"True," he said.

"I would be named," she said.

"You have not earned a name," he said.

"Give me an opportunity to earn a name, Master," she begged.

He turned away from her.

"Bear your burden," he said, not looking at her.

"Yes, Master," she whispered.

He went down the trail, and was followed by Janina.

The nameless slave, weeping, then fixed her burden on her back, and held it there, by the straps. Then she hurried after the party, which was already some yards down the trail.

Overhead the sky, as of now, was clear.